17.00

Jesse McMinn is a Canadian writer, gamer and student. He's been an aficionado of fantasy of all types since before he can remember, and enjoys both developing his own ideas and learning about the ideas of others. After writing as a hobby for over a decade, he produced *Loria*, his first complete work. He's currently studying computer science at Dalhousie University in Halifax, Nova Scotia.

D0922237

Book 1 of the *Tower* Series

Loria

by
Jesse McMinn

Newmarket Public Library

This is a work of fiction. The events and characters portrayed herein are imaginary and are not intended to refer to specific places, events or living persons. The opinions expressed in this manuscript are solely the opinions of the author and do not necessarily represent the opinions of the publisher.

Loria
All Rights Reserved
ISBN-13: 978-0-9923020-4-7
Copyright ©2013 Jesse McMinn/IFWG Publishing, Inc
V1.0

This book may not be reproduced, transmitted, or stored in whole or in part by any means, including graphic, electronic, or mechanical without the express written consent of the publisher except in the case of brief quotations embodied in critical articles and reviews.

IFWG Publishing, Inc.
www.ifwgpublishing.com

APR 1 1 2014

To Mom, Dad, Em, and Nicole,
Without whom this book wouldn't have been written.

The *SS Caribia* was not the prettiest cruise ship in the world. It only had room for two hundred passengers and its features did not include an indoor rock-climbing wall, but it did manage to sell tickets. It did so for two main reasons: one, because the berths were quite cheap, and two, because not everyone came specifically for luxury.

In Kyle Campbell's case, the *SS Caribia* represented an escape from his problems, which currently included unemployment and sobriety. The solution to at least one of these problems could conveniently be found on the *Caribia* itself, and so it was that during the ship's launch, Kyle could be found on deck, leaning on the rail, armed with a gin and tonic.

As the ship peeled away from the harbor, Kyle let his mind wander. He had been searching for a job for months now; all the traveling, interviews, and subsequent disappointment and drinking sessions had blurred together in his mind. He told himself that it wasn't because he hadn't been making an effort; he had tried more in the past couple of months than most people did their entire lives.

It must be something about my face, he thought, *or the way I carry myself*. His resume was flawless and his references were good, but employers just weren't interested. He had tried cutting his hair to look older and spiking it to look younger; he had worn jeans and checkered shirts to look casual and full suits to look formal. His poor beard had never been through such a rough time, being shaven and trimmed into a myriad of different styles: this one a bit more serious, that one a bit more outgoing.

Somehow, his countless interviewers must have penetrated this façade and seen Kyle and his hair and beard for what they really were. When he wasn't trying to please his prospective employers, his hair was a lank black mop that fell in front of his eyes and his beard a scraggly growth that clung to his chin like moss.

Kyle took another sip of his drink, noticing that its level was already getting alarmingly low. If he had had a job, he would have been drinking his pay. At least he had enough money from his last job to keep himself going for a while.

Kyle was aware of someone walking up beside him. Through his peripheral vision he could see a young man with ginger hair, a few years younger than him, leaning on the railing of the boat. Although Kyle was trying not to tilt his head in the man's direction, since that could indicate interest, he did notice the circular beard and glint of glasses that just screamed 'student'.

Please don't say hello to me.

"Hey," said ginger beard.

Damn.

There was nothing for it. He turned to face the man that had penetrated his bubble of silence.

"Hey," he replied, trying to inject into that one syllable as much disinterest as possible. The man seemed not to notice.

"What're you in for?" ginger continued, with a little laugh. He looked as though he was going to nudge Kyle, but must have thought better of it.

"Just taking some time off," Kyle replied, and then, on the basis that skimming through details would make the conversation go faster, added, "I've been job hunting."

"Oh." Ginger beard seemed slightly thrown off. "Me too—well, not the job part. I just graduated from University—figured I'd take some time to myself."

Kyle was tempted just to grunt, but society made him say, "Oh. Nice job. What were you studying?"

"Socio-economics," the student said proudly, clearly pleased that Kyle had shown interest.

Have fun finding a job with that, thought Kyle.

He said, "Oh, nice."

Kyle felt he would never understand the way most people worked. If *he* had seen himself leaning on the ship railing, by himself, most of the way through a stiff drink, he would have recognized his need for privacy, and avoided himself. Ginger beard didn't seem to get that not everyone was interested in his life.

He became aware that beard was saying something. He tuned back in.

"Sorry?"

"I said, 'where did you use to work?'"

"Oh. I was a database developer for a car company."

"Nice. Why did you quit?"

He assumes I quit. If his opinion of ginger beard had been higher, he might have been flattered.

"They were downsizing because of the recession. They said I could stay on, but that they'd have to cut my pay. I thought I could do better somewhere else, so I quit."

"Ah," said ginger beard.

They leaned in silence for a while, Kyle imagining himself making ginger beard's head explode using telekinesis.

"Well," the man said finally, when the silence had become awkward, "I'm sure you'll find something soon. See you later—I'm Ryan, by the way."

"Kyle," said Kyle, shaking his hand.

After Ryan had left, Kyle quickly drained the last of his drink. He waited for a while on deck before going to the bar to get it refilled, since Ryan might have gone in that direction.

The passenger demographic of the *Caribia* was the typical blend of older couples enjoying a thrifty retirement, younger couples whose love still had the ability to make up for money, and the random single people enjoying a couple weeks of freedom. Over several days, Kyle had the opportunity to refine his already advanced ability to avoid all of them. The younger couples were easy, since most had time for nothing but each other, and the older couples could often be headed off by appearing sufficiently flaky. Most of the single people on the boat were either weirdoes or lone wolves like Kyle, but the Ryan-type personalities on the cruise started to become a problem. For some strange reason, people seemed to gravitate towards him in the exact same way that jobs didn't. The most irritating part of the whole ordeal was that Kyle was probably the only person on the boat who tried as hard as he did to actively ignore people.

One night below decks, Kyle had even been accosted by one of the aforementioned young couples, a nice enough pair slightly older than him who were enjoying a subdued honeymoon. The way they talked to him standing with their arms around each other's waists and a permanent smile fixed to their faces set Kyle's teeth on edge. Even though they were only two years older than him (as he found out against his will), they talked to him as though he were a child. It was probably subconscious, as they showed every indication of taking genuine joy in Kyle's company. It didn't matter that he was jobless, spouseless, and permanently nursing a drink; to them, apparently, he was the most interesting man in the world.

Still, the days ticked on, and when he stood up on deck and looked out at the sea, he at least felt as though he was going somewhere.

It was the sixth day of the cruise. Kyle was sitting in the lounge reading a mildly interesting magazine on boating, a drink, as always, close at hand. Four arpeggio notes sounded on the speaker system.

"Hello, passengers. This is your captain speaking. There is a storm front approaching the vessel that should pass over us sometime this evening. We request that you remain below decks during the storm. Thank you."

Damn, Kyle thought. Apart from the fact that on deck at the front of the boat was Kyle's favorite place to stay, the storm meant that everyone would be packed below decks for the night, probably all clustered around the bar. He'd just have to stock up on drinks beforehand and spend the night in his room.

He read for a bit longer, ate dinner, and then went down to the bar with that aim in mind.

Kyle was already on a first-name basis with the bartender, Eddie—his aversion to people didn't extend to those that were willing to serve him drinks.

"Hullo, Eddie," he said, leaning on the counter.

"Kyle!" The man put down the glass he was rinsing and walking up to face him. "What'll it be? Another gin and tonic?"

"Could be. How much booze are you willing to sell me at once?"

"Depends. You buying for someone else?"

"As far as you're concerned, I'm having a party in my room tonight," Kyle said with a smile.

Eddie laughed loudly and began to make up a tray for Kyle to take.

Ah, low standards, Kyle thought, as he walked back up to his room, *something that money can't buy.*

The storm hit at about eight o'clock in the evening. It was a big one; lightning crashed, rain fell in buckets and the ship heaved.

Kyle sat in his room, attempting to enjoy the pitiable view as offered by his porthole window. He was having a good time. He had already taken the top layer off of all the drinks so that they wouldn't spill, and was now working his way through them one by one. It was a blessing that Kyle had a strong stomach; the ship pitched one way and another constantly.

He was also alone—which was always good—and was finding the storm outside very entertaining. Storms were one of his few interests; they seemed not to belong to 'nature', which in his mind was always associated with camping, hiking, and other things that city slickers did in order to feel connected with the outside world. Instead, they seemed to be the weather's way of asserting its dominance over humankind.

Kyle drained the last of his drinks and, for the fun of it, ate the celery stick that had been stuck in it. *It's a cruel world*, he thought, looking down at the tray. The more drinks he had, the faster he seemed to go through them. Why couldn't he be one of those people with weak stomachs, who only had to polish off a couple before they returned the favor?

He surveyed the tray in sadness, and with difficulty counted the glasses. He got six once and seven twice, and so went with seven. Either way, it just wasn't enough. How had he thought it would be?

Through the haze of alcohol, it no longer seemed like such a bad idea to go down to the bar and get some more. He imagined the dark and the press of bodies, and thought, why not. Besides, he was finally starting to feel a little sick, and if he threw up in front of the other passengers, they might finally avoid him.

After a couple of false starts, he got to his feet and left his room, the boat's rocking causing him to shoot out of the door with a series of small, scurrying steps.

Kyle lurched unsteadily down the hallway, the ship's rocking compounding with his own swagger to somehow keep him upright. As he passed a woman heading in the opposite direction, the ship gave a particularly large heave and she staggered, almost falling down. She righted herself and scuttled past him, shooting a worried glance in his direction.

Kyle laughed silently at the woman's lack of coordination, before he realized that he himself had fallen against the wall, and was sliding slowly downwards. With difficulty, he pushed himself upright and kept walking.

The rest of the trip to the bar progressed in more or less the same fashion. Kyle leaned heavily on the railings and he made his way downstairs, often completely ejected from the ground as the storm battered the ship. He passed other people heading up to their rooms, all wearing worried, rushed expressions.

They need to chill out. Tone it down. Keep it cool. It's not like the storm is hurting anyone.

Another four notes sounded on the loudspeaker.

"This is your captain speaking. The storm is stronger than anticipated, and we would like to remind you once more not to go outside under any circumstances. Those passengers with special needs should be escorted back to their rooms immediately."

Kyle ignored the message, as he was quite sure that drunkenness didn't count as a special need.

The scene inside the small bar was just as Kyle had expected. People huddled in small groups, many of them standing up as all the seats had been taken. Kyle waited on the stairs for a moment or two, enjoying the view. With every larger-than-normal rocking of the ship, the room filled with gasps and yelps as people lost their footing and spilled their drinks.

Hah. That'll teach you to be innocent and well meaning.

There was no question of reaching the bar itself with so many people, but Kyle was not in a mindset to take no for an answer. He pushed his way through the crowd, sometimes on purpose, sometimes by accident, not listening to the numerous expletives people shouted in his direction. He ducked and wove under arms and around large groups, enjoying himself immensely. He was proud of himself when he finally knocked aside the last couple and slumped onto the counter.

"Eddie!" he cried happily, waving an arm wildly.

The barman looked him up and down, an expression of mild shock on his face.

"Bloody hell, mate," Eddie said in a concerned voice, "you look awful."

Kyle's mouth opened and shut. He hadn't expected *that*. Why did Eddie sound so worried? He felt fine.

"I feel fine," he said with a small hiccup. "Whatcha talking about? How about another drink?"

But Eddie was shaking his head.

"You should go for a lie-down, mate. S'not healthy, drinking like that during a storm."

Only now was Kyle aware of the stares he was attracting. His voice must've been louder than he thought. Suddenly, as though Eddie's concern had drawn Kyle's attention to himself, he started to feel horrible. His stomach ached, and there was a nasty throbbing going on behind his eyes. His legs felt like jelly and his knees buckled, so that his head landed hard on the plastic bartop.

He vaguely heard a couple of gasps from the people around him and Eddie asking, "are you okay?" but he wasn't listening. He was staring at a piece of lint on his shirtsleeve, thinking, *this is where I've gotten. I'm on some stupid cruise ship surrounded by boring old people and a barman with a fake Australian accent. I gave up an old job that I hated for another job that I can't find, and that I'll probably hate even more. I bought a ticket for this ship…why? It's not like it's going anywhere.*

Kyle thought of when he was a child, just learning how to ride a bicycle. His mother had worried about him going too far or too fast, and so had limited his range to the small court in front of his house. He'd never be able to count how many times he must have cycled around that little court, over and over again. That was like this ship. Just one little circle around the court, and then he was back where he started.

"Hey! *Hey!* You all right, mate?"

Kyle resurfaced, and noted with bemusement the concerned faces of the people around him. Normally he would have snorted at their expressions, but right now, he just wanted to get as far away from them as possible.

He planted his hands on the bar and pulled himself up heavily, his expression glassy. He looked from face to face, expecting each of them to break out laughing and jeering at any moment.

Hearing several variations on the question 'are you all right?' passing through the crowd, Kyle said, "I'm fine. I just need…some fresh air. Excuse me."

He broke through the press of bodies once more, this time heading in the only direction he could think of—to the deck at the front of the ship, where he had spent his first day.

The scene in the bar had sharpened Kyle's mind considerably, even though his stomach and head were still aching and his legs were weak. He remembered the route to the prow of the ship off by heart, in any case.

There was no one guarding the door to the outside. It was a testament to the *Caribia's* low standards that while the door had been latched, it was not locked from the inside. Kyle fumbled with it for a brief moment and then went out.

The storm was…well, there were no words to describe it. Kyle had seen many a storm before, but none that raged quite like this one. The noise was unbelievable, but even more awe-inspiring was the sky itself. Kyle walked like a zombie towards the railing to get a better view, not even noticing the icy rain that had him drenched within seconds.

The clouds were pitch black, with white edging that sizzled with lightning. There were brighter patches between the clouds, and they were blue; but instead of the baby blue of a clear sky, they were dark blue like the bottom of the ocean.

Kyle butted up against the railing and stood, gripping it, in silence. The sky lit up constantly with flash after flash of lightning, and so the scene switched constantly from daytime to nighttime, nighttime to daytime. The lightning lined the crest of every wave and lit up the horizon, lending the scene an unearthly cast.

Out here, Kyle seemed to feel the movement of the boat twice as strongly as indoors. It groaned and creaked as it seesawed up and down; on the ascent Kyle's knees buckled with the effort of holding himself up, and on the way down he felt completely weightless, in danger of simply floating over the edge.

Strangely, Kyle felt totally calm, even in the middle of the storm's wrath. He smiled as the ship rolled, and whooped out loud with each peal of lightning.

"That's what I'm talking about!" he shouted at the sky as it roared angrily at him. This whole stupid cruise was worth it, after all! He reached into his pocket to pull out his phone and take a picture.

"Hey! You! What are you doing out here?"

Kyle spun around, his heart frantic. A large man in a sailor's uniform was making his way across the deck towards him, shouting angrily.

"Are you insane? What the hell do you think you're doing, you jackass? Get back inside!"

"I'm just enjoying the view!" Kyle called back, irritated. *Or at least I was until you butted in*, he thought sourly.

The man swore profusely as he slipped and slid his way across the deck. Kyle watched him with apprehension and annoyance.

"I'm fine out here!" Kyle shouted again, getting angrier and angrier by the second. Why couldn't people just leave him alone for once in his life? He could take care of himself, for Christssake.

The man was shouting something else, but Kyle couldn't hear him; partially because of his own anger, but mostly because the storm was actually picking up. The ship gave a sickening lurch, and Kyle was thrown to the floor, just barely managing to keep a grip on his phone. Swearing, he rose to his feet. He was going to miss the best part!

As he got up, however, he heard a deep groan coming from the ship, louder than any previously. At the same time, the entire ship tilted sideways and didn't recover. The exhilaration Kyle had felt before suddenly turned into fear. *What's going on?*

Kyle finished pulling himself up by the banister. He leaned over the edge and his mouth fell open.

The ship had been caught up in the current of a massive whirlpool. The wind whipped sideways and the clouds twisted themselves into a spiral above it. Water frothed and roared, flowing into the center of the whirlpool with a sound like the world's biggest bathtub being drained. The center seemed to pull at Kyle's very gaze, gluing his eyes to it. It was dark like nothing he had ever seen, darker than pitch, darker than the black of space.

At that moment, something heavy collided with Kyle's back. His phone flew out of his hands and into the waves below; he swore vehemently, but before he could even react to this he felt strong hands grab him. He flailed and fought back as the sailor tried to pull him away from the railing. The man was screaming at him furiously, but Kyle wasn't listening, because he himself was screaming.

"Look at that thing! Do you see it? You're going to get us killed! We're going to die—"

The ship leapt. Kyle felt the hands release him. His hip cracked as it collided with the banister, and he would have cried out, but there was no air in his lungs. He lost all sense of direction as he tumbled head over heels. The banister caught him again on the back, and then he fell over the edge.

There was a brief moment of peace as Kyle saw the ship falling away from him and heard the wind whipping around his body. He expected it to hurt when he hit the water, but all he felt was cold. His tongue tasted salt as water poured down his throat, and then he felt rapid motion as the whirlpool snared him.

His senses were a jumble of salt, bubbles, water, darkness, and pain. He flopped like a rag doll as the water pulled him this way and that. He got one last clear picture of the scene before he went under: the boat, still following the curve of the maelstrom. He saw the sky and the sea, etched in colors that couldn't be described. But mostly he saw the center of the whirlpool, as black as the center of a galaxy, lightning dancing around its rim.

Then the water pulled him under, and he remembered no more.

The first thing Kyle became aware of was the beating of his heart. He had never heard it beating so loudly—not when he was running, not when he was scared, not even during his first time with a girl. He listened to it first with relief, then with mild annoyance. Even though it was a welcome reminder of his continued existence, it still got in his way as he was trying to think.

Slowly and painfully, Kyle tried to assemble his thoughts. What was going on? There seemed to be a lot of noise between him and his body; it ached like a limb to which blood was returning, but he didn't have any control over it.

The pain was suddenly very acute and he passed out.

The next time he came to, his thoughts reassembled themselves slightly faster. The ship, of course. He had fallen off of the *SS Caribia*. He wondered briefly about what had happened to the sailor. He didn't really care. As long as the man left him alone now, it was fine with him.

The prospect made him quite concerned, and he spent the rest of this period of consciousness dreading the moment when the strong hands would grab him again, and the man would yell at him angrily. However, this moment never came, and Kyle sank once more into oblivion.

Kyle woke again. Where was he, now? Oh, that's right. He had fallen off of the *Caribia*. But then, what was going on? Was he drowning? Despite the fact that every single part of his body throbbed with pain, he felt quite comfortable. He felt dizzy and weak, and so maybe they were hauling him up to a rescue helicopter on a stretcher. If so, they certainly worked fast. He was impressed. He'd have to congratulate the rescue squad for responding so quickly…

Kyle woke up. For a moment he was confused. Hadn't he been drinking in his room on the *Caribia*? He must have fallen asleep. Strange, he usually had a very strong stomach. Oh, wait…he had run out of drinks and was going to go down to the bar for more. No, he had done that already…he remembered Eddie's concerned advice and the stares of the other passengers. And, yes, he had gone outside to get away, and the storm, and the whirlpool…

Of course. He had fallen overboard and been rescued. He had already decided that. He was certain of it, in fact; why else would he still be alive? He could move his fingers and toes now, if he focused very hard; they felt material above and below, which made him think, *bed sheets*.

This made him pause for a moment. His last memory was of a stretcher—or so he thought. Perhaps he was in a hospital already? But of course his mind would've been addled by the fall. Maybe a whole day had passed already.

In any case, the pain was still very strong, and Kyle was dimly aware that as he became more alert, it would probably get worse. His body ached like nothing he had ever felt before. If it was possible for your whole body to feel painfully hungry as the stomach did when starved, the feeling might have been comparable to what Kyle was experiencing. Maybe they would give him an anesthetic…

The next time Kyle came to, his eyes were finally somewhat working again. All he could see were giant blobs of color, but it was something, at least. He blinked, trying to get his eyes to focus. The blobs shrank somewhat, and Kyle made out the rough outline of a room. It was quite bright.

Kyle heard a noise that sounded as though it was coming from underwater and there was a disturbance in the blobs in front of him. What sounded like a voice reached Kyle's ears, although all he could make out was:

"Blurr bloop. Bleep blarp woop bloop?"

"Thanks for showing up so quickly," Kyle attempted to say. He had no idea what he actually said, though, because he couldn't hear his own voice.

"Blooh bloop?"

"When I fell off the boat," Kyle tried to explain, "you showed up quickly. Rescued me." He tried to make hand gestures, but his arms didn't want to hear any of it.

"Bleep. Bloop bloop bluh," the voice said. Kyle sensed another disturbance in front of him.

"I was just trying to be appreciative," Kyle said, irked. "Sheesh."

Soon after, he passed out again.

Pain woke him. Not the aching he had felt before, but sharp, serious pain, like a fire lit on his chest. He tried to scream and flail, but his senses were so confused he had no idea what he was actually accomplishing. Noise met his ears, but he wasn't sure whether it was his own voice or someone else's. His eyes opened wide and he saw—not perfectly, but much more than before. There was a green blob directly in front of him, and a larger yellowish blob behind it. He could vaguely make out the corners of a small room, and a darker rectangle at the foot of his bed was probably a door.

Of course, he wasn't in much of a position to digest all this. Pain was blossoming from his chest; it crept under his ribcage and lanced down his arms and legs. He could feel weight at the source of the pain; it seemed to correspond to where the green blob was sitting.

He tried to lash out at it, but had no idea how to get his arms working. He could now tell that both blobs were making noises. The pain grew, and he blacked out yet again.

Silence.

Kyle was aware of it. Silence and darkness. His brain was working much better. Funny how, when the brain wasn't working, it could be fooled into thinking that it was, but when things really were in order one realized just how wrong it had been.

He kept his eyes closed and tested his limbs. His hands and feet worked fine up to the wrists and ankles, and he could shift his weight around well enough. The pain had subsided somewhat, and now he mainly felt tired.

Okay. Go for open eyes next. One, two—

The room was better defined than ever. He could see that it was paneled in natural wood, minimalist and very small. His bed was white, on—he slid his hand to the left—what felt like a wooden frame. There was in fact a door in front of him, and a suggestion of light coming from behind made him think, window.

As he marveled at his newly returned senses, the door of his room opened. He tried to sit up, but only managed to prop his head up slightly.

A man entered the room. Kyle's perception was off, but he seemed quite large. His hair was a huge, spiky, a golden mane that fell past his elbows, and he was broad across the shoulders.

The man folded his arms. Kyle was just thinking that the long hair couldn't be very sanitary, when the man spoke.

"Well, look who's up. You feeling any better?"

Kyle was amazed at how well he could hear, and how clear his mind was.

"Yeah, quite a bit. The fire in my chest seems to have gone away."

"That was us, I'm afraid. Nee was trying to help you. It looks like it worked, but I was afraid he was going to kill you. You were screaming like hell."

Ah, so my voice had *been working.*

"What was he doing? Giving me a shot or something?"

"A shot?" The man seemed confused. "Never heard that term, but I guess I don't know a lot of that jargon. He was trying to give you a magic infusion."

"A what infusion?"

"A magic infusion. You were starved pretty bad when we picked you up. Or so Nee says. You sure looked horrible, anyway."

Kyle didn't say anything for a moment, as he was trying to form his thoughts. Because the idea of jargon had just been planted in his mind, he now assumed that 'magic' must be a slang term he hadn't heard of, maybe for adrenalin or something.

"I think," he said slowly, "that there's a lack of communication here."

"Could be," the man agreed. "You still sound pretty dopey. Just try and rest now, we can talk later."

Kyle was going to point out that the lack of communication wasn't *his* fault, but decided it wasn't worth the effort. The man had turned and walked out the door. When it had closed, Kyle suddenly realized how much effort it had taken to prop his head up. He let it fall back down on the pillow, and fell asleep almost instantly.

When he woke again, some of the pain had returned, bringing a splitting headache with it. Kyle thought that this was very unfair. Hadn't he suffered enough?

This thought made him reflect on his recent experiences. They were very strange, no matter which way you looked at it. The cruise ship had been odd enough for him, and then the storm, and the whirlpool, and now his convalescence in this room. He looked around. It didn't really look like a hospital room, now that he thought about it. Weren't they usually white?

After a while, his door began to open. He pulled himself up, gasping as the pain in his head grew massively. He managed to get into a reclining position, resting his shoulders on the pillow and his head on the headboard.

He watched the door with mild interest. It swung open, but there was no one there that Kyle could see. A scuffling sound came from ground level, and then a tiny pair of hands appeared, grabbing at the foot of Kyle's bed. They were green.

Kyle was too sick to be afraid, so he merely watched in fascination as the hands were followed by a pair of elbows, a foot, and finally a head. He sat, mouth agape, as a tiny creature, completely green, strode up his bed, between his legs, and stood on his chest.

Kyle's sight still wasn't perfect, but at this distance, it didn't need to be. The creature was two feet tall, with a relatively large head and big, brown eyes. Its skin was a pale, chalky green. It had no ears that Kyle could see, but there was a large, spirally something on either side of its head where the ears should have been, like green seashells. It was wearing a simplistic, exotic-looking black getup that reminded Kyle of a karate uniform, and a pensive expression. Its tiny arms were folded, and it was tapping its foot on Kyle's chest, a foot that ended with three clawed toes.

"Uh," Kyle said. There wasn't really anything else to say.

The creature sighed and sat on Kyle's ribcage. Its features were…sort of like a baby's, Kyle thought, with large eyes and a small nose and mouth. Of course, babies weren't usually green with seashell ears, and never had an expression of such cynic intelligence passed across such a face.

"Are you feeling alright?" the creature asked. Its voice was nasally and slightly high, though much lower than would be expected based on its size. Kyle assumed it was male, if these things could be male.

"Better." Kyle said, and then moved right into, "What are you?"

The creature blinked. "You don't get out much, do you," it said. "I'm a Call of course."

"Oh, very funny," Kyle said.

"What's funny about that?" the Call asked.

"You're a creature called a Call. Very creative."

There was a long silence after this. The Call seemed to be thinking.

"I think your mind might be addled slightly," it said matter-of-factly. "Of course, I'm not surprised. You were in the most advanced state of magical deprivation I've ever seen when we picked you up. It's a miracle you survived."

"Yeah," Kyle said, who had reached that state of sickness and fatigue that allowed him to take everything with a grain of salt, "that whirlpool was wild stuff."

"Whirlpool?" the Call asked, surprised. "Where was there a whirlpool?"

"In the ocean," Kyle said. *Duh*, he thought.

The Call tilted its head and raised an eyebrow.

"I think you need more rest. There's no point in us talking with you like this. How do you feel, anyway?"

Kyle didn't answer right away. This was going to take some thought.

"I'm really tired," he finally said, "and I've got a huge headache. And you're sitting on my chest. And you're green."

"Nothing wrong with being green," the Call said reasonably. It seemed not to have heard what Kyle had said about the chest-sitting.

"I've never met someone who was green before, and I've been drunk a lot. That's pretty weird."

The Call sighed. "You know, somehow, I feel like what you're saying and what I'm hearing aren't the same thing. How about you go to sleep for a while. We can talk later."

"But–"

"No buts. Do you think you could handle some soup?"

This transition caught Kyle completely off-guard.

"Uh?"

"Soup. You've heard of soup, right? You need to eat to get your strength back."

"Um. I guess," Kyle said, lost in a sea of soup.

"Great. I'll have Lou bring you some soon."

"Is he a Call, too?"

"Just go to sleep, why don't you," the Call said irritably.

Lou turned out to be the same golden-haired man who Kyle had seen earlier. Now that his vision was returning, Kyle could see that he wasn't very old at all, probably around the same age as Kyle himself, although taller and much more fit. He also had four ears.

Kyle stared. The man's ears were long and pointed, and stuck out and back along his head. There were two sets, one stacked on top of the other.

Kyle felt that he should point this out, but Lou didn't seem bothered by his excess aural equipment. Besides, he was bringing soup, and Kyle had grown so hungry that he could deal with any amount of ears if it meant that a meal was forthcoming.

"Here you go," Lou said, handing him a wooden bowl. "Nee says not to eat it too fast, or you'll barf. Hopefully it'll make you feel better."

Kyle accepted the soup gratefully, thinking about what Lou had said.

"Is Nee that green guy I was talking to?" he asked.

Lou laughed. "'Green guy'? That's a new one. Never say that when Nee's around or he'll give you a smack."

"Well, he *is* green. What kind of creature is a Call, anyway?"

Lou looked shocked. "What, you're telling me you've never met a Call before? Where are you from, anyway?"

"Cleveland," Kyle said.

Lou scratched his chin. "Never heard of it. Of course, I don't pretend to know everywhere in the world. Where is it?"

"In the US," Kyle said with mild apprehension. While he understood that the world was a big place, surely he hadn't ended up so far away that the people here hadn't heard of Cleveland? Oddly enough, the fact that the person he was currently talking to had four ears, and that the only other he had seen was two feet tall and green, hadn't even passed through his mind as a concern.

"The US?" Lou asked, his brow furrowing. "Is that a city or a country or what?"

"You know, the USA?" Kyle said, now almost panicking. "The United States of America?"

"The United States of *where?*"

"*America!*" Kyle almost shouted. "You know, like North America? As opposed to South America? West of Europe?"

His heart was beating madly in his chest. What was going on? How could this man not have heard of America? Surely, surely anyone who could speak English would at least *know* about it?

Lou was looking at him gravely. When he spoke, his voice was quiet.

"I can't deal with this," he said. "There's something freaky going on here. This is Nee's territory."

Kyle was speechless. His mouth kept opening and closing. "You don't know…you've never heard of…?"

Lou was shaking his head. "Have some of that soup. Rest up. Let's get you walking again first, then we can worry about where you're from."

Kyle could only sit and stare as Lou turned around and left the room. He couldn't believe what had just happened. The other things Lou and Nee had said and did finally started to register in his brain. Nee had talked about magic withdrawal, and Lou had mentioned before that Nee had tried to give him a magic infusion. Again, this could just be jargon, but…Nee…what was he, anyway? Lou's ears could at least be explained away by plastic surgery or makeup…but Kyle had no idea how something as strange as Nee could be faked. *And why would it be, anyway?*

Maybe this is some freaky experiment or a prank that's being played on me, like a weirder Truman Show. Maybe there are cameras planted around my room, watching to see how I react.

As the idea struck him, Kyle immediately started looking around his room for any signs of oddness. There wasn't much to go over: his room consisted solely of his bed and a minuscule desk to his right that served as a bedside table. There was a dagger hung up on display on the wall; apart from that, the walls and ceiling were completely bare. By twisting his head around, Kyle could see that there was a window behind him—it was small and circular with a cheap curtain hung over it.

Kyle settled back and stared into his bowl of soup. So there were no hidden cameras. That didn't rule out the idea of a prank, but who could possibly bear such a grudge against Kyle that they would go to such elaborate lengths to fool him?

Ah…but wait. A prank would rely on Kyle falling off of the *SS Caribia* in the first place, and no matter how he twisted it around, he couldn't see how that event could have been engineered.

In conclusion, he said to himself, *I'm hungry. I will now eat this soup.*

And he did. It was thick, creamy and, to Kyle at least, delicious. He felt much better after he had finished it. He felt sleepy again and the headache had started to ebb away.

It doesn't matter what's going on, he told himself. *Not yet, anyway*. He could talk to that crazy green guy when he woke up...

Night was falling when Kyle woke up, or perhaps he had slept for longer than he thought, and morning had already arrived. In any case, faint light was coming from the window behind him, and so, although his room was quite dark, he could see well.

He felt much, much better. The headache was gone completely, and his limbs actually responded when he tried to move them. He sat up easily, and, spurred on by this success, threw the blankets off and climbed out of bed.

The first second or so was a bit uncertain. Kyle stumbled slightly and had to steady himself on his bedside table. He carefully shifted his weight off the table and back onto his own feet; this time, he managed to stay upright.

Kyle looked around his room. Nothing had changed, really. He noticed his empty soup-bowl from last night and grabbed it before heading outside.

He found himself in a small hallway, paneled similarly to his room and carpeted with a dull green. Strangely enough, the floor and ceiling were both trimmed with a golden metal—brass, he assumed—and the lamps that lined the hallway were of the same material. The overall effect was that of an old-fashioned hotel.

The hallway was lined with doors in both directions; to his right, it ended with another doorway. To his left, it looked like it opened up into a room. He could hear voices coming from that direction, so he struck off towards them.

And entered...the bridge of a ship? Kyle was no expert, but even he could see that this wasn't a room you would find in a house. It was shaped somewhat like a prow, round at the front and flat at the back. Kyle had emerged from the left side of the back wall. There was a massive window at the front of the room, through which could be seen the blue and gold of a pre-dawn sky. A curved control panel matched the contour of the window, and at its center was mounted a ship's wheel. Standing on a tall wooden stool in front of the wheel, tiny hands holding it steady, was Nee. His back was to Kyle and he seemed not to have noticed him.

"Well, look who's up!"

Kyle jumped, almost dropping his bowl. Lou had been standing up working at a desk along the far wall—he had just turned around and noticed Kyle in the room.

Nee turned to see what was going on, hands still on the wheel.

Lou put down his papers and strode over. "Welcome back to the world of the living, friend," he said, winking. "You had us scared for a moment there."

"A couple moments, I should say," Nee interjected in his nasally voice. He adjusted the wheel slightly and twiddled some levers on the control panel. He then jumped down from his stool and walked over, leaving the wheel turning gently on its own.

"Well, sorry to worry you," Kyle said, unfazed. He was feeling quite light-headed.

Lou laughed, and then reached out his hand for Kyle's soup bowl. "Here, let me get that for you."

Kyle handed it to him, and Lou walked over to the left wall of the room, along which a small sink and cooking range had been set up, like a mini-kitchen at a hotel.

Kyle looked down at Nee, who in turn was looking up at him with an appraising expression on his face.

"Hi," he said brightly, "you're Nee the Call, right?"

Nee winced. "You're pronouncing it wrong," he said. "It's *coll* with an 'o'. K–O–L, Kol."

"'Kole'?" asked Kyle, taken aback.

"Close. *Kol.*"

"Kol?"

"Good enough," Nee sighed.

Kyle thought for a moment. "How do you spell 'Nee'?" he asked.

Nee shot him an irritated look. "N - I - H - S."

Kyle said the word to himself in his mind. "What's the 'h' doing in there?" he asked.

By this time, Lou had come back from the kitchen, and was laughing silently to himself. Nihs looked scandalized, but Lou just held out his hand for Kyle to shake.

"I don't think we were properly introduced. I'm Lou, spelled L - U - G - H."

"Pleasure to meet you," said Kyle, grinning light-headedly. "I'm Kyle, spelled K - Y - L - E. Kyle Campbell."

Lugh raised an eyebrow. "Campbell? That's a strange name."

"Not as strange as Nihs—or Lugh."

Lugh's grin faded. "They're common names, both of them," he said slowly.

"I've never heard them before," Kyle said.

Nihs and Lugh looked at each other. They did it so fluidly that Kyle received the impression that they had done it many times before.

"Yeah...about that," Lugh said a bit awkwardly. "I was telling Nihs about what you said earlier..."

"About you coming from a city named Cleveland in a country called the USA," Nihs cut in. His tone of voice was slightly accusatory, and Kyle felt a twinge of fear.

"Yeah...What about it?"

"I asked on the overhead," Nihs continued, "and there's no such place."

"But—" Kyle started, but Nihs held up a hand.

"Just listen. Now, Lugh and I are of a certain social caste that is very understanding towards people who, for some reason, don't want their past catching up with them. But these are our rules: if you want us to help you, you have to come clean. We won't judge you, not if you're a decent sort. Where are you from...really?"

Kyle looked from face to face, one green and several feet below him, the other peach and a foot above him. Both were serious.

Okay. I have to handle this really carefully.

"Look," he said slowly, "I don't know what's going on here. I don't know where I am or what happened to me. I don't know if this is a joke, or a trip, or what. But I'm telling the truth. I *am* from a city called Cleveland, and it *is* in a country called the USA. I can't come clean any more than that."

Both Nihs and Lugh studied him intently. Lugh didn't seem to know what to think; Kyle could tell, however, that Nihs was thinking furiously.

"This USA you mentioned," he said suddenly, "what continent did you say it was on?"

"North America," Kyle said.

Lugh opened his mouth to speak, but Nihs cut in front of him.

"What's the name of the planet you live on?"

Kyle's mouth fell open. "What?" he asked.

"It seems like a pretty simple question to me," Nihs said.

"The Earth," Kyle said, now quite beyond caring.

Nihs looked pensive, but Lugh snorted with laughter.

Kyle was about to say something rude to Lugh for laughing, but Nihs, possibly sensing this, said quickly, "We refer to our world as 'the Earth' as well," he explained. "Is there another name for your world—perhaps an older or scientific one?"

Kyle thought about it for a moment.

"I guess…Terra," he said slowly. "That's 'Earth' in Greek. Or maybe Latin. I can't remember."

Nihs nodded, satisfied. "I thought so. You see, the scientific name of our world is Loria, a Kollic word meaning 'of great age'."

There was an awkward pause.

"Huh," said Kyle. His brain, perhaps in self-defense, was refusing to process the information his senses were sending him. It was a strange feeling, to be able to look at Nihs and Lugh and hear the strange things they said without realizing what it meant.

"So…what are you saying?" Lugh asked Nihs. "That he's from a different world?"

"I'm not *saying* that," Nihs snapped. "The situation just…suggests it."

"That's impossible," Kyle said, feeling the need to assert himself. "There's no such thing as fantasy universes. I'm probably just tripping out." Even as he said it, he became more and more convinced that this was the truth.

"They probably just picked me up and gave me some drug to keep me alive," he said to himself. "Makes total sense." A strange thought then hit him. "Or maybe I've died, and this is someone's messed up idea of heaven."

Nihs and Lugh, quite understandably, were looking at him as though he were crazy.

Which at the moment, I probably am.

Nihs shook his head. "I only understood about half of that," he said, "but I know this: I'm not some figment of your imagination. *My* life was progressing quite well before I met you, thank you very much."

"Well, what would you rather believe?" Kyle snapped. "That I fell through some kind of portal and ended up in an alternate dimension? That's ridiculous."

"You're telling *me*," Nihs retorted. "All science and philosophy strictly denies the existence of alternate worlds. It's nonsense."

"Maybe someone messed with Kyle's brain?" Lugh suggested. "They could have wiped his memory and created some weird alternate past."

"That's certainly possible," Nihs said, tapping his chin. "I suppose his memory could also have been warped by his magic deprivation. I've never studied the effects of a case as serious as his. Perhaps it could have even driven him insane."

"I'm *not* insane!" Kyle said. *Probably.*

"He doesn't *act* like a crazy person," Lugh agreed.

Nihs stuck his tongue in his cheek and regarded Kyle, as though considering him in terms of possible lunacy. Kyle tried to smile encouragingly. Lugh looked back and forth between them, and then shrugged.

"I'm getting a drink," he said, and walked over to the small kitchen.

Nihs and Kyle ignored him.

"What we need to do," Nihs said, "is to think of all the possibilities, and eliminate them one by one. Why could Kyle be under the impression that he's from a different world?"

"I *am* from a different world," Kyle said. Then he caught himself. "Wait. That's not right, either. I'm *not in* another world. This has to be just some elaborate prank, or a dream, or—"

"Listen," Nihs said irritably. "I don't understand what's going on here, but you can stop trying to convince yourself that this isn't reality. Even if *you're* not convinced, the billions of other people living in this world sure are."

"*You* were the one who was suggesting that my memories are just messed up," Kyle retorted, "which means that the world I'm from doesn't exist. How is that any different?"

"He's got a point," Lugh called over from the kitchen. He had taken three glasses from a cupboard above the sink and was pouring a clear, bright blue-white liquid from a jug into them.

"I was actually going to get to that, if you two would stop interrupting," Nihs snapped in Lugh's direction. He huffed and turned back to Kyle.

"I was *going* to say, an illusion so powerful that it could rewrite your entire past perfectly is a magical impossibility. Such a grand illusion would be bound to be very feeble in places. Does your entire past seem consistent? Which is to say, are there any memories that don't seem to fit, or are missing, or that just give you a weird feeling?"

"I don't really know what you're asking," Kyle said honestly. "But my memory seems fine. I can remember my entire life pretty well."

Nihs thought about this. "I should check, just in case," he said. "One moment," he added, as he ran to the wheel to grab the stool he had been standing on.

"What?" said Kyle.

"Don't worry about it," Lugh said, returning with the drinks and placing Kyle's on a nearby table. "He's just going to check your memory for any funkiness. I don't really know how it works, but from what I understand, if an illusionist creates a fake memory for you, he has to sort of stitch it together with your other memories—make them all fit, sort of thing. If you're good at magic, you can tell if a memory doesn't belong in someone's head."

The word 'magic' had now come up several times in their conversation. Kyle wanted to ask about it, but at that moment, Nihs returned with his stool. He set it down in front of Kyle and scurried up it. Even with the added height, he had to reach above his head to put his hands on either side of Kyle's forehead.

"Just sit still," he instructed Kyle, who was making faces to show his confusion. "This just takes a second."

Kyle stood there and looked at Nihs, not having anything else to do.

The Kol's hands felt dry, like the skin of a lizard. Nihs closed his eyes and concentrated. All of a sudden, the seashell shapes on his head, which Kyle had thought to be solid, unraveled themselves and became two tentacles, about a foot long each, starting thick and tapering towards the end. They stuck out horizontally from Nihs' head, undulating slightly as though caught in a light current.

Before Kyle could react, he felt a sudden force that snapped his eyes shut. They started zooming around under his eyelids like in REM sleep; vague images and shapes flickered in Kyle's mind. He could tell that they were scenes from his own memory, but they passed by too quickly to be identified. The overall effect was strangely hypnotizing, and Kyle felt he could almost drift off into sleep until—

The pain started in his forehead, where Nihs' hands were touching him. It burned as though the Kol's hands were made of fire. He cried out, loudly, and instinctively thrashed his arms to break Nihs' contact with him.

He felt the hands pull away and his eyes opened again. It took him a moment to take in the scene. Nihs had fallen backwards off of the stool, which had toppled over, and Lugh was standing between him and Kyle in a slight crouch, one arm held out in the direction of each.

Kyle lifted his hands to his forehead. The pain was ebbing away, but it was still quite acute.

"What the hell was that?" he demanded.

"Chill out, okay?" Lugh said quickly. "He wasn't trying to hurt you. The same thing happened when he tried to give you a magic infusion."

"What does that even mean?" Kyle snarled.

Nihs picked himself up off the floor. He was massaging his hands with a frown on his face, and it was obvious that he had been hurt by the contact, as well.

"When we found you," he said, "you were in an extremely advanced state of *reursis*…magical deprivation. I tried to infuse you with magic to save your life. It worked, but you woke up and screamed while I was doing it. It hurt me, too," he added, holding up his hands.

Several questions occurred to Kyle, but he wanted to cover the most important first.

"You keep saying magic," he said. "There's such thing as magic in this world, then?"

Both Nihs and Lugh's jaws dropped.

"Such thing as magic?" Nihs spluttered. "Of *course* there's such thing as magic! How else could it be?"

"There's no such thing as magic in my world."

Nihs gave him an incredulous look. "What kind of crazy world do you live in?"

"I thought it was a pretty normal one. How does magic work, then? It doesn't make any sense."

"*Sense?*" Nihs sounded scandalized. "Magic forms the basis of the entire universe! If you break down anything—a solid object, a soul, a thought—you get magic! Kollic scholars have spent thousands of years testing and perfecting theories as to how magic behaves! And you're telling me that a universe based around magic doesn't make any *sense*? How can a universe *without* magic exist?"

"Steady, there," Lugh said quietly. Nihs didn't seem to hear him. "If there's no magic in your world, how is there matter?" he questioned.

"I don't know," Kyle said, rubbing his forehead. He felt in desperate need of a drink. "I'm not a scientist. Matter is made out of atoms. That's basically all I know."

"Atoms?" Nihs asked curiously.

"Yeah, they're these little bundles of particles with other particles orbiting around them—"

"And how are they held together?" Nihs' angry tone had suddenly dropped, and he now sounded strangely fascinated. "What force drives them, if not magic?"

"I'm not sure," Kyle said, trying to dredge up knowledge gained from high school science class. "Wait…I think there's four forces. Yeah…there's the strong force and the weak force…and…electromagnetism…and gravity. Something like that."

Nihs seemed dissatisfied with this explanation. "Strong force and weak force? What does that mean?"

"They're nuclear forces," Kyle said wearily. "I don't know what they do. I said I wasn't a scientist."

"What was that word?" Nihs asked eagerly.

"What? Nuclear?"

"Nuclear." Nihs rolled the word around in his mouth as though it were a piece of chocolate. He turned to Lugh.

"Nuclear force and magical force," he said, looking happier than Kyle had ever seen him. "Two different fundamental forces for two different universes. Isn't that something?"

"I guess," Lugh said, shrugging, "if you're into that kind of thing."

"So you're admitting that I'm from a different world now?" Kyle pointed out.

Nihs' eyes narrowed. "You do seem to be telling the truth. No one in the world is that good an actor. But just because *you* think you're telling the truth doesn't mean you *are*."

"Well, what did his memories look like when you checked them out?" Lugh asked. "Did you manage to get a good look at them?"

"They seemed to be in order," Nihs said grudgingly, as though it had been a great disappointment to find nothing wrong with Kyle's mind.

"Well, there you have it!" Lugh said happily, clapping his hands together. He recovered Kyle's drink and handed it to him, then grabbed Nihs' glass, which was barely bigger than a shot glass, and passed it down.

"Here's to the freak from another planet!" he said, raising his own glass.

Nihs rolled his eyes. "We haven't decided that yet," he said snippily, but Lugh ignored him.

"Is this stuff alcoholic?" Kyle asked, raising the blue liquid to eye level. *Please let it be.*

"Sadly, no," said Lugh. "What with one thing and another, we usually need our wits about us when we're travelling. The people in our profession who get drunk on the road rarely stay drunk for long, if you know what I mean."

Kyle shrugged, and took an exploratory sip. The drink was sweet and cool, with a strange zing to it that made him feel as though his throat was being iced over.

"What is this stuff?" he asked, holding up the glass again.

"Freezer," said Lugh. "Sweetened liquid ice. Like it?"

"Yeah," he replied, finding that he did, despite the fact that it didn't contain alcohol. Something, however, nagged at him.

"Liquid ice?" he asked. "Isn't that just water?"

"If there's no such thing as magic in your world," Nihs said, "you wouldn't be familiar with the process of sedonisation. It basically means you artificially change the state of an object without changing its properties—such as making ice a liquid even below freezing temperature. It happens to be unhealthy to ingest sedonised particles," he added, shooting a reproving look at Lugh.

"Oh, come off it," Lugh said, waving his glass. "If we avoided everything that was unhealthy in this world, we'd die of starvation."

Apart from this brief tiff between Nihs and Lugh, the drinks actually proved to be quite effective for calming the situation. They earned the three ten seconds of silence as they all drank and thought.

Nihs was the first to speak. "What's the last thing you remember before you fell into this world?" he asked Kyle, "You said something before about a whirlpool."

"There was a whirlpool," Kyle confirmed. "I was on a cruise ship. Do you know what that is?"

"Yes. I assume it was over water?"

"Yeah. Well, one night, there was a storm. They told us to stay inside the ship, but I was…sort of drunk at the time. I went outside to watch the storm, and there was this huge whirlpool that the ship got caught up in. One of the crew members tried to grab me to take me back inside, and I fell off the ship while we were fighting."

"Hmm," said Nihs, "very strange."

"Why? How did you guys find me in this world?"

"You fell out of the sky," Lugh said at once.

"*What!*"

"It's true. We thought you were a comet or something. You had a tail and everything. Ask Nihs."

"He's serious," Nihs said, nodding. "We were just flying around, and then the sky flashed and this thing with a blue tail came flying down from the sky and landed in front of our ship. We flew over to see what it was and found a little crater with you inside."

"And I said, 'congratulations, Nihs, it's a boy'."

"You're a scream. Anyway, at first, we thought you were dead—I mean, people don't routinely fall out of the sky and live to tell the tale—but when we picked you up we found you were still alive, although with barely a scrap of magic in you. I thought you had come out second best from a magic duel or something."

"How could I have survived falling like that?" Kyle asked incredulously.

"Don't ask me," Nihs said, shrugging. He paused, staring into space, and his eyes suddenly opened wide. "I just thought of something!" he said excitedly.

"What?" Kyle and Lugh asked at the same time.

"Your magic deprivation…the reason why my infusion hurt you…it makes sense now!"

"Mind telling us why?" Lugh asked.

"If Kyle is from a world that contains no magic," Nihs explained, "then he must not have a soul, right?"

"Thanks," Kyle said sourly.

"No, I mean…look, in Loria, a living being is made of three components, all right? One physical, one electric, and one magical: body, mind, and soul. If there's no magic in your world, then your being wouldn't have a magical component."

"Makes sense."

"That wouldn't be a problem in your world, because obviously creatures there suit their environment. But over *here*, you had the symptoms of someone deprived of magic. And my infusion and reading of your memories hurt us…probably because magic particles and nuclear particles react to each other."

"But didn't you say that everything here was made of magic?" Kyle asked. "Wouldn't that mean that I'd be hurting all the time?"

Nihs tapped his chin. "It must just react with charged particles," he mused. "Particles that are used in magic have much more power than the mundane; they have to, in order to get them to do what you want. Atmospheric particles must not have enough energy in them to react noticeably."

They thought about this for a moment.

"So does that mean that every time someone uses magic on me, it's going to burn like that?" Kyle asked.

"I suppose so." Nihs sighed. "I wish I could sense auras; I want to see how magic acts around you."

"You're just one big failure, Nihs," Lugh said, shaking his head.

"Oh, shut up."

Kyle had been thinking of something else that Nihs had said. "You said you were in a ship," he said, "but also that you were flying. You have flying ships in this world?"

"Oh, yeah!" Lugh said enthusiastically. "You're in one—mine, in fact. The airship *Ayger*. One of the best ships in the world," he added with a distinct note of pride. "Here, come check out the view—the sun should be coming up soon."

Without waiting to see if Kyle was following, he strode back in the direction of the wheel, heading down a staircase on its left that Kyle hadn't noticed before. He followed, and found that the staircase led to an observation balcony set below and in front of the control panel. It was obviously designed purely for looking out of the front picture window; it even featured a white-cushioned bench set against the wall and a couple of telescopes set into the railing. It curved slightly with the shape of the ship, and Kyle could see another staircase at the end of the balcony mirroring the one he had come down.

Kyle's jaw dropped. The view offered by the window was—there was no other word for it—beautiful. They were flying—he could see that now—a thousand feet up from the ground, over a hilly, forested terrain. Just ahead and to the right glimmered a lake of the brightest blue. The countryside was temperate, as the trees were deciduous and extremely numerous. The pre-dawn light glinted off of the leaves of the trees and the surface of the lake, making it seem as though the whole Earth was swaying and shifting slightly. Although the shapes of the trees, hills, lake and clouds were all familiar, something in the way they were colored and illuminated made the scene seem alien. Kyle was reminded instantly of the strange storm that had apparently brought him here.

Despite the strange feeling Kyle received when observing the land— or perhaps because of it—the scene was so perfect he couldn't tear his eyes off of it. When he leaned on the railing and looked directly down, he could see the ground passing smoothly by beneath them. Now that he was listening, he could hear a low booming coming from outside the ship as the wind blew past.

He stared out of the window in silence until the *Ayger* had drawn up beside the lake. When he finally forced himself to look away, he saw that Lugh was watching him with a smile on his face.

"Quite something, isn't it?" he said. "I've owned this ship for three years and I still haven't gotten sick of it."

"It's pretty sweet," Kyle admitted, awed into uncharacteristic complete honesty. But then his brow furrowed. "Wait a minute. Nihs left the wheel. Who's steering this thing?"

"It's on autopilot," Nihs called from the control panel. "The ship's not as fast, but it saves a lot of effort."

"Why isn't it as fast?" Kyle asked.

"The Buorish police imposed a speed restriction on ships in autopilot mode," Nihs explained. "It's built into all of them now. It's to stop ships from crashing into things during storms—their sensors don't work so well when the weather is poor."

"Oh!" Lugh said suddenly, smacking his palm against his forehead, "speaking of things crashing into things, we never told Rogan that Kyle was up!"

"Who's Rogan?" Kyle asked curiously.

"Our mechanic," Lugh said, "slash repairman slash deckhand slash all-around useful guy. He generally lurks in the engine room when there's nothing interesting going on. He's a Minotaur," he added, as an afterthought. He started to make his way back up the stairs.

"A Minotaur?" Kyle said, with slight apprehension, following him.

"What, you've never heard of them before, either?"

"I've heard of them, but they don't exist in my world. They're just a myth."

"*What's* a myth?" Nihs asked once they had gotten back upstairs.

"Minotaurs."

The Kol shot him an incredulous look. "So there are none where you come from? What *do* you have in your world? Are there any Kol? Any Selks?"

"That's me," Lugh said helpfully.

"No, just humans."

The look Nihs gave him as he said this was penetrating, and almost accusatory. The Kol looked about to say something, but Lugh talked over him.

"Let's give Rogan a call," he said, "and why don't we land the ship while we're at it. He was complaining before that we wanted time to do some repairs, so it might as well be now."

"Sure," replied Nihs, and he started to drag his stool back over to the wheel.

Lugh had put his finger on a small device to the left of the wheel. It looked like a blue crystal set in a small circular depression, over which was strung a small dome of wiring. As he pressed down on it, the depression sunk slightly into the control panel; the crystal lit up, and emitted a slight whining sound, like an old TV.

"Rogan? Rooo-gan," Lugh called into the crystal.

There was a slight pause, and then a voice, distorted and crackly, sounded from the strange speaker. It could have been the bad sound quality, but Kyle thought the voice sounded low and gravely.

"Yeah. What is it?"

"That guy we picked up has woken up. He's very anxious to meet you," Lugh said, smiling.

"Well, he'll just have to wait. Do you know how much converter six is acting up? If I leave the engine room now, we'll all be eating dirt before I can reach the helm."

"We were thinking of just landing the ship for a while," said Lugh.

"So that I can repair the converter or visit your shooting star?"

"He means you," Lugh said to Kyle.

"Yeah, thanks, I got that," Kyle said.

Lugh grinned, turning back to the speaker. "Both, if you think you can handle it."

"Pah. Fine. Just say the word. Try to land it somewhere flat, this countryside is bumpier than a bull's behind."

"Yes, thank you, Rogan," Nihs sniffed from the wheel. "I *do* know what I'm doing, you know."

"I'll believe it when we've landed."

"Bye, Rogan!" Lugh called cheerfully.

"Yeah, yeah, I'll see you in a few."

Lugh took his hand off the crystal, and its glow faded.

"I'm going to put it down near the lake," said Nihs, neck craning to see over the wheel. "Looks like it's pretty flat down there."

"Great," Lugh said gloomily, "I wanted to spend my afternoon picking bugs out of my teeth."

Because Kyle was standing in the helm, he couldn't see much of what was going on as the *Ayger* landed. He could feel himself getting slightly lighter as the trees seen through the picture window got closer. Kyle noticed a whining sound that got lower in pitch as they began to land—he assumed this was the ship's engine, as it sounded somewhat like a plane from the inside.

Nihs' eyes twitched back and forth between the numerous objects on the control panel and the window. He had one tiny hand on the wheel, and another on a lever on his left, which Kyle assumed, was the throttle. He was adjusting each constantly and minutely. Kyle caught the signs of the obsessive perfectionist.

Finally, when a couple of trees had passed very close by to the ship's front, Nihs heaved on the controls and the engine fired up greatly, then he quickly let off the controls and there was a gentle crunching sound and feeling that announced their landing.

"Smooth," Rogan's voice sounded on the speaker. "I'll be up in a minute or two."

Nihs pulled a small object from a slot on the control panel and pocketed it, and jumped down from his stool.

"All right," he said, clapping his hands together, "now what?"

Lugh shrugged. "I should probably pour Rogan one of these," he said, wielding his half-empty freezer. "It pays to keep him in a good mood," he added, winking at Kyle.

Kyle felt slightly apprehensive. The only Minotaur he knew of was a mythical creature that had lived in a maze and killed people. Judging from his voice over the speaker, Rogan didn't seem the sort to disembowel you, but that only slightly helped to curb Kyle's fear.

A moment later Kyle heard the creaking of the ship as something heavy moved behind him, and he turned around just as Rogan shouldered his way into the room.

It's a good thing Lugh had told me Rogan's a Minotaur, Kyle thought. Even being somewhat prepared for the sight, he almost jumped with fear.

Rogan was huge, taller even than Lugh; he must have been close to seven feet. His shoulders were extremely broad, and his arms were like sacksful of basketballs. His waist and legs were relatively small, but they were still muscled, and his feet were two hooves the size of dinner plates. A pair of red eyes glinted out from under a brow shaped like a brick and a fringe of brown hair. Two curved yellow horns, each eight inches long, framed Rogan's face. He moved with surprising grace for such a large creature, and his footfalls were almost silent on the carpeted floor. His brown fur was matted with sweat, and he carried with him an odor that Kyle liked to call 'auto shop in summer'.

Rogan looked from one face to the other. "Please, please," he rumbled, "there's no need to get up."

"Oh, very funny," snipped Nihs, dragging his stool back into a suitable position for conversation. Lugh waltzed over and handed him a drink.

"Thanks," he said, raising his glass. He took a large gulp, and then shook his head. "You're working that engine to death, Lughenor," he said to Lugh. "It's not just number six. All the converters are burnt out. It gets so hot down there these days that you could fry an egg on my chest."

"We're adventurers," Lugh sniffed, buffing his nails, "travel is what we *do*. That's what ships are *for*."

"Well, it's your ship," said Rogan, shrugging massively. "I'll be able to keep it running, but you're killing its lifespan by pushing it so hard." Apparently finished with that angle, Rogan's eyes alighted on Kyle.

"Hello there," he said.

"Hey," Kyle replied, fighting to keep his voice calm. He was still feeling overwhelmed and lightheaded from his sickness, and the appearance of Rogan hadn't helped.

"You look better than when we brought you in," the Minotaur said. "You seem in pretty good shape, considering the fact that you fell out of the sky."

"That's what they tell me," Kyle said diffidently.

"So what happened to you? I've seen some strange things in my life, but I'll admit that I've never seen a human comet."

"Uh," Kyle said, not sure how to approach the issue. "We're trying to decide on that. I think I fell here from another world."

Rogan blinked, and then turned to Nihs. "Isn't that supposed to be impossible?" Kyle was struck by how quickly Rogan had accepted the idea.

"Well, yes," Nihs said irritably, "but we're running out of other explanations and Kyle's story seems to check out. The only thing I can think of is that his mind was warped by his *reursis*—his magical deprivation."

"It was pretty bad," Rogan agreed, although he added, "but can *reursis* do that?"

"I was going to ask on the overhead," Nihs said.

"While you're at it, why don't you ask if people can fall here from other worlds?"

"If Kyle turns out to be a legitimate…world-jumping…thing, I don't really want the entire world to know. It could cause trouble for us—and everyone else."

"Good point," said Rogan.

"I'm going to ask right now," Nihs said, clambering down from his stool. "Try to hold the fort down without me."

Nihs walked over to the far side of the room, where he sat with his back against a small shelf of books. He crossed his legs and lightly rested his hands on them, as though he were meditating. Seconds later, his eyes shut and the strange tentacles on his head had unfolded themselves, weaving this way and that. A small circle of blue-white light started shimmering on the ground around him, accompanied by a soft sound like a finger sliding around the edge of a wine glass.

"What's he doing?" Kyle asked quietly.

"The Kol can all talk to each other from far away," Lugh explained. "They call it 'the overhead'. Nihs tried to explain it to me, but we can't really know what it's like, right? As far as I understand it, they can all sort of see each other and see how far away they are and in what direction. They can hear each other's thoughts, too."

"Wow," said Kyle, watching Nihs and imagining what it would be like to be able to talk with anyone whenever you wanted—and then he realized that people in his world *could* do that. He toyed briefly with the idea of trying to explain the idea of the Internet to Lugh, but decided against it. He didn't even know if they had computers here—or electricity, for that matter. Judging from what Nihs had said this ship probably ran on magic or something.

"What are those tentacles on his head?" he asked instead.

"His ears," Lugh said, surprised.

"Really?"

"Yeah. They use them for magic and talking on the overhead and stuff. Apparently the Kol evolved them specifically to make them more receptive to magic."

"Oh." Kyle said. He didn't want to keep asking questions, but his curiosity was too strong.

"Why do you—" he started.

"—Have four ears?" Lugh finished for him, laughing.

"Yeah."

"One set to hear the land, one set to hear the sea," he recited, looking out through the picture window. "That's what they say, anyway. See, the Selks are water folk, meant to live next to the ocean. According to legend, we grew this second set of ears so that we could always find our way back to it if we lost it."

"So you can hear the ocean from a long way away?"

"Any water, as long as its strong flowing," Lugh said, shrugging, "but it doesn't work so well while we're flying the *Ayger*, and it's not exactly useful these days anyway. It's not like we ever get lost—even if the *Ayger's* map system stopped working, Nihs can always just ask the overhead where we are."

"Right," said Kyle.

They stood in silence for a while, watching Nihs communicate silently with the rest of his race. As both Kyle and Lugh had finished their freezers a while ago, Lugh went and poured them some more. With a crash that shook the floor, Rogan sat down; even like this, he was still almost as tall as Kyle.

"Well, he's likely to be a while at it," he rumbled, waving his drink in Nihs' direction. "Those Kol can really talk." He said to Kyle, "I don't think we were ever formally introduced." He held out a huge hand. "Rogan Harhoof."

"Kyle Campbell," Kyle said timidly, shaking one of Rogan's fingers.

"While we're waiting for our green friend to come back to us, why don't we talk about you for a moment?"

"I'm not all that interesting," Kyle said quickly, who at the moment was feeling this keenly.

"Really," Rogan said shrewdly. "You know, I bet there's a lot of people out there who would disagree with you. If it turns out you *are* from another world, you might just be the most interesting person alive right now."

"Great," Kyle said gloomily.

"Better you know it now and have time to get prepared. There's a lot to this world, and not all of it wants to give you a hand up when you fall out of the sky. Not only that, but you need to decide what you're going to do with yourself."

"What do you mean?" asked Kyle, who was feeling slightly miffed.

"Well, what are you going to do?" Rogan asked seriously. "Are you going to try and find a way home?"

It was as though Rogan's words had burst a dam in Kyle's mind. Suddenly, the thoughts were flowing faster than Kyle could process them. He hadn't thought seriously of home…of Earth…since he had gotten here. How *was* he going to get home? *Could* he? Did he even want to? His immediate thought was no—after all, all that was left for him on Earth was to hit rock bottom, which he had been in the process of doing when he had come to Loria. Why not just stay here? He didn't know much of this world yet, but he was curious to find out more—more curious, in fact, than he had been for a long, long time about anything.

As he thought more of his predicament, however, it became progressively more ludicrous to him. What was he *thinking*? He was standing on the deck of a flying ship in the company of a man with four ears, a small gremlin who talked of magic, and a giant Minotaur who drank Kool-Aid. Every particle of his being screamed at him that this couldn't be true, that he had to be dreaming, or drugged, or *something*. But what could he do but accept reality? Right now his past life—the *Caribia*, the Atlantic Ocean, and his home, Cleveland—existed only in his mind. What was there left for him, anywhere?

He snapped out of his reverie and noticed that both Rogan and Lugh were watching him.

"I imagine it's a lot to think about, all at once," Rogan said in a kind voice.

Kyle nodded; he couldn't think of much to say.

The Minotaur was scratching his chin. "Well…we can ask Nihs when he's done with the overhead, but you probably heard from him that the scientists here don't believe in the existence of alternate worlds. However, that's not to say that no one here studies them. I'd say a good first step would be to find a Kol who knows what he's talking about and see if he has any theories. You might find someone in Reno, but you'll probably want to travel to the Kol's homeland and get a whole council thinking about it—the more Kol involved, the better the chance of you getting something useful."

"What's Reno?" Kyle asked.

"It's the biggest city in the world," Lugh answered. "It's to the northeast of here. Everyone ends up in Reno at some point during their lives. You'll meet some funky people, but if you're looking for anything, you can probably find it there."

"Are you headed there?" Kyle asked him.

Lugh tilted his head back and forth. "Eventually. We've got some business around here first, but we were thinking of stopping there afterwards anyway."

"You want to make that stop," Rogan said firmly. "The *Ayger* needs the rest. It'll finally give me a chance to make some thorough repairs."

"Okay, well," Kyle said, having reached a conclusion, "I can just tag along until we reach Reno—if that's fine with you—and then I can try to make my own way from there." Kyle felt good for saying this, even though he wasn't truly aware of what the statement meant. Above anything, he wanted in some way to be capable, to retake control of his life. Lugh, Nihs and Rogan seemed like nice enough people, but he didn't want to cling to them as some hopeless foreigner who couldn't do anything for himself.

Rogan, however, shot him down immediately.

"Don't be daft," he said flatly, "unless you're some kind of superhuman, which I'm pretty sure you aren't, you wouldn't last a day here knowing nothing about this world. Besides," he added, leaning forward, eyes boring into Kyle, "when you say *make your own way*, do you mean to try and find a way home…or to start up a life in this world?"

Kyle stared at Rogan incredulously. How was it possible that Rogan had sensed his intentions so perfectly? Could the Minotaur read minds?

Rogan appeared to be further insightful, "Boy, I may be a Minotaur and I may be a sailor, but I'm not stupid. All I have to do is ask myself, 'if I found myself in a new world, where nobody knew me and the slate was clean, would I be in a hurry to go home?' Unless your world is a million times better than this one, I'd say you probably want to stick around and see the sights, eh? At least for now."

Kyle bowed his head, partly because Rogan's insight was extremely humbling, but mostly because of the truth of the Minotaur's words. Kyle had been telling himself that he would immediately find someone who could help him get home; he was therefore amazed at himself when he found that this was not his true intention at all.

"All right," he said. "I didn't leave much behind when I came here. Besides, this has never happened to anyone else, right? So I should find out about this world…maybe there's inventions and things that could be useful back in my world." He appealed silently to Rogan and Lugh, hoping they would help him justify his decision.

Lugh shrugged. "Hey, we're not blaming you, mate. Rogan's right— I'd do the same thing if I were you."

Kyle let out an explosive breath. For some reason, even though he was still bone tired from his sickness, he felt better than he had in years. Finally, finally, he was going somewhere.

"Well, that's settled, then," Rogan said, heaving himself to his feet. "Why don't you stick with us for the time being and if we come across anything about your home, all the better. Reno's on our way, so we'll poke around for details once we get there."

"You don't have to—" Kyle started, shocked at the suggestion that he stay with them, but Lugh held up a hand.

"Hey," he said, "we don't abandon people who need help. Besides, it's not like you're just going to sit around and watch. You'll make yourself useful—at least once you've toughened up a little." At this, Lugh winked. "No offence, it *could* just be because you're sick, but it looks like a good sneeze could knock you over right now."

"Hey, I used to be a database developer," Kyle said defensively. "It wasn't a particularly aggressive job."

"I'm going back to the engine room," Rogan announced, draining the last of his drink and setting it down. He nodded to Kyle. "Welcome to Loria, little one. I'm sure you'll have a blast."

"Thanks." Kyle said with a slight laugh.

Rogan nodded once more and lumbered his way back downstairs, leaving Kyle with Lugh and the spaced-out Nihs.

"So what is it that you guys do, exactly?" Kyle asked Lugh.

"We're adventurers," Lugh said grandly, sticking his thumbs in his belt. "The only worthwhile career in the world! Do you have adventurers in your world?" he asked, seeing his expression.

"If you define 'adventurers' as 'people who go on adventures', then yes. Somehow I don't think it's the same thing, though."

"That's right. Adventurers—well, some people would call us mercenaries, but that's not right, exactly. People post jobs at these outposts—we call 'em hideouts—and then adventurers can take them on. They usually involve fighting something, but they can be anything, any problem that someone can't fix on their own." Lugh shrugged. "The pay is good, and you get to travel and fight; of course, there's always the chance that you'll take on a job that's too tough for you and get killed, but nothing's fun without a little risk, right?"

Kyle was amazed. "There's that much stuff to fight in the world?"

"Well, yeah. If someone wants to be escorted somewhere, or they need some rare material gathered…there's always monsters, one way or another."

"Monsters?"

"Yeah. You don't have them in your world?"

"No. They're just myths, like Minotaurs."

"Well, they sure exist over here. And there's always more of them. No matter how many are killed by adventurers or soldiers or whatever, more always show up."

"Wow," Kyle said, "sounds kinda crappy."

"Eh, it's not so bad. I mean, people like Nihs and I would be out of a job if they got killed off. Besides, they usually stay away from civilization; you just have to be careful if you go wandering around on your own."

"So if I'm going to be staying with you—does that mean I'll be fighting too?"

"Well, yeah," Lugh said, sounding surprised. Catching Kyle's expression again, he continued, "don't worry, we're not going to throw you into anything you're not ready for. I can teach you what I know about fighting and Nihs can teach you about magic—or, at least, try to teach you about magic, if you turn out to be as bad at it as I am."

"I probably can't use it," Kyle said, thinking about what Nihs had said earlier. "I've got that weird reaction thing."

Lugh scratched his chin. "True," he said, "that could be a problem. Oh well, no point worrying about it now—oh, Nihs' back."

Kyle, too, noticed the absence of the shimmering sound that he had already become accustomed to. When he turned, he saw Nihs rising to his feet, dusting himself off.

"Well?" Lugh asked.

Nihs shrugged. "I asked about the effects of *reursis*. Apparently, no-one's ever heard of it causing memory damage, although one Kol near Santrauss said that he'll probably tire easily for about ten days after a case so serious."

"Great," said Kyle.

"That couldn't have taken you that long to ask," Lugh pointed out. "What kept you?"

Nihs sighed. "The political situation in Reno is getting worse."

"*Really?*" Lugh groaned.

"It's nothing new, really. Just all the Kol there are talking about it. Sounds like the tussles in the streets are getting worse and the police are having a merry time keeping everything under control."

"So Sanka and Livaldi are finally having it out?" Lugh asked.

Nihs snorted. "Both are making sure not to say anything too direct.

They're just sniping at each other under the table. A lot of the people in Reno are calling for the Buorish police to intervene and put at least one of them behind bars, but Sanka's too popular and Livaldi's too powerful."

"Excuse me," Kyle interjected, unable to remain silent any longer, "but what are you talking about?"

Nihs sniffed. "Just a stupid turf war in Reno. Don Sanka is the governor of the city—he's a Lizardman, a retired adventurer, and very popular. Recently, though, James Livaldi—he's the owner of a huge weapon manufacturing company—has started flaunting his power and money, and has made it clear that he disapproves of the way Sanka runs the city. Livaldi has a lot of influence and a lot of weapons; it's obvious that he wants control of the city. There have been fights between their supporters."

"Who's the good guy?" Kyle asked.

"We don't take sides," Lugh said quickly, "as adventurers, that is. Rulers come and go, and we travel too much for it to matter, anyway. That being said, Sanka probably gets the sympathy vote. Livaldi's a genius, but he's also sort of a bastard and a racist to boot."

"Aren't we going to Reno soon?" Kyle asked apprehensively.

"Oh, yeah," Lugh said, waving his arm dismissively, "but it's a huge place; as long as we stay away from the city core we'll be fine. Besides, smart people don't usually pick fights with adventurers—not to mention that the Buorish police will be more fanatical than ever right now. The Buors are the most lawful people you've ever met, and they won't stand for things getting out of hand in the city."

"They sound like pretty intense people."

"That's pretty much them in a word," Lugh agreed.

"Anyway," Nihs said, straightening his shirt, "all this doesn't matter right now. Do the job that's in front of you—that's the adventurer way. We can worry about all this once it starts to affect *us*. Right now, Lugh and I have a job to finish. Once we've done that, we'll stop at Reno and we can see what's what and have the *Ayger* repaired properly."

"Plus we can buy Kyle some adventurer swag," Lugh said.

One of Nihs' eyebrows shot up. "Oh?" he said, staring at Kyle, who looked away. "So you've decided to come with us, is that it?"

"Just for now," Kyle said, "if that's not a problem. I just thought, since I'm here, and no one else has ever had anything like this happen to them…well, it would be a waste not to stay for a bit."

"H*mm*. Well, I don't blame you. But," he said, holding up a finger, "if you're going to join us, that raises a couple different problems. Do you know how to fight?"

"I was a database developer," Kyle said pointedly, and then remembered that neither Nihs nor Lugh would know what this meant. "No," he added.

Nihs looked him up and down.

"I thought not," he said. "No offence, but right now it looks like a stiff breeze—"

"Yes, thank you," Kyle said angrily, as Lugh laughed. "Honestly, I can't look *that* weak. It's not like I'm old and feeble or anything."

"No," Nihs said seriously, "but it also looks like you've never trained your body. I'd say your CAL is around five, maybe six at the most."

"My what?" Kyle passed a hand over his forehead; he was now feeling tired once more, and was sick of all the new things he was being forced to learn.

"It stands for combat aptitude level," Lugh explained. "We usually just call it 'threat' or 'combat level'. It is basically a way of measuring how strong you are in a fight. The Buors came up with it."

"So what does it mean that mine is five or six?" Kyle asked.

"Well, it means that you're half as strong as someone who's a ten," Nihs said.

"What are Lugh and you, then?" Kyle asked.

"We haven't had ours tested for a while," Nihs mused. "Last time I checked, I was a thirty- eight and Lugh was a thirty- four."

"Thirty- five!" Lugh said indignantly.

Nihs rolled his eyes. "Lugh, you got thirty- four twice and thirty- five once, it doesn't take a genius—"

But Kyle had been doing some math in his head, and he interrupted him. "Wait," he said to Nihs, "if I'm just five and you're almost forty, that would mean that you're eight times stronger than I am."

"Yes," Nihs said plainly.

"Oh, come on!" Kyle said, snapping slightly. "How am I supposed to believe that? It's not possible—nothing your size could be as strong as a human!"

Kyle had spoken quickly, and without fully realizing what he had said—but he instantly regretted it once his mind had caught up with his mouth. Lugh had closed one eye in a strange sort of wince, and Nihs' expression had gone stony. Kyle once again noted that the term 'human' didn't seem to go across well with the others.

"Look, friend," Lugh said, clapping him on the shoulder, "we're okay with what you said since we know that you're not from here and you're a little confused—but don't go around saying stuff like that once we get to Reno, okay? It's a good way for you to end up head- first in a trash can."

"I'm sorry," Kyle said, deflated.

"Hey, don't sweat it," Lugh said easily, "just keep that in mind for the future."

Nihs had been eyeing Kyle in a calculating way. "I don't know how things work in your world, but here one of the most basic, fundamental laws of the universe is that anything is possible, and that magic knows no limits. If I start with a strength of one, and a day's training gets me to a strength of two—doesn't it logically follow that, if I trained for ten days I'd have a strength of ten, and so on until, if I were immortal and trained until the end of time, I could become infinitely powerful?"

Kyle was almost struck dumb by what he thought to be Nihs' extremely faulty logic. "No way!" he said. "You can't just keep getting stronger constantly, you'd reach a peak at one point—"

"Peak?" Nihs asked, his eyebrow rising again. "Your world must be *really* different. Over here, as long as you keep going, you'll keep getting stronger…there's no *peak* until you decide that there is. In any case," he added, suddenly rolling up his sleeves, "your first statement—that no creature my size could be as strong as a human—I think calls for a bit of an eye-opening experience." He spread his legs slightly and raised his tiny fists in a fighting stance. Beckoning Kyle, he said, "come, hit me."

Kyle stared in incredulity at the minuscule creature that was challenging him to a fight. Suddenly he felt very nervous. "I don't want to," he said truthfully.

Nihs grinned. "Ah, so you're not totally stupid after all. That's good.

Now, don't worry, I'm not going to bruise you up while we're trying to get you better. I just want to prove a point."

Kyle looked miserably down at Nihs, now acutely aware of how out of shape he was.

"I don't suppose you'll take no for an answer?" he asked hopefully.

Nihs shook his head.

Kyle sighed. Well, he might as well go for it—it wasn't as though he had any reputation to live up to in this world.

His punch was not the most splendid in the known universe; Kyle had never taken any kind of martial arts or boxing class in his life, and so his form was quite amateurish. He at least had the presence of mind to make it a jab, and not a wild swing of the like that were seen in movies. It was, all told, quite strong and fast considering, and aimed with decent accuracy at Nihs' face.

Nihs blocked it. His arm snaked up with inhuman speed and his palm smacked against Kyle's knuckles. Kyle watched in amazement as the tiny creature held his arm at bay, and then slowly started to push it back towards him, muscles the size of grapes bulging on Nihs' arms. Finally Kyle lost his balance and swayed backward, while Nihs rose from his stance, looking pleased.

"All right," he said kindly to Kyle, not pointing out the fact that he had just out-muscled a creature three times taller than he was, "I think that's enough for today. Kyle, why don't you go and rest some more— nothing interesting is going to be happening on this ship for a while, and you need all the sleep you can get."

"But it's morning!" Kyle protested, gesturing at the golden light that was now streaming in through the picture window. He did, however, feel very tired, and just thinking about the fact made his shoulders droop.

"Your body doesn't know that, and it doesn't care," Nihs said pointedly, "besides, Lugh and I never wait for night to sleep. Sleep when you're tired, eat when you're hungry—am I right, Lugh?"

"He's right," said Lugh.

"But—"

"*Rest*," Nihs said firmly, now positively shoving him toward his room. "There will be plenty of time to talk later. There's a lot to this world, and your brain can't process it all in one day."

Aware of the truth in this, Kyle allowed himself to be harried into his room. He shut the door behind him only to have Nihs knock on it a split second later.

"The bathroom's two doors down on the left," the Kol told him, sticking his head into the room. "You can grab a toothbrush from the drawer under the sink—we have plenty—just please, *please* remember what color it is." He scurried off.

Kyle, laughing despite himself, dragged his feet (it was amazing how the tiredness had crept up on him) to the bathroom. It wasn't huge, but still larger than the average bathroom in a house. It featured a massive counter of white marble set at about chest height, with another, smaller counter at about knee height next to it—apparently, this bathroom was meant to be both Minotaur- and Kol- friendly. An enormous shower set into the corner, also white, provided proof of this.

Kyle found the toothbrushes—the drawer under the sink was literally crammed with them. It reminded Kyle of the dentist's back on Earth, where they had an endless supply of disposable toothbrushes for their patrons. The only surprise was that they didn't seem to be made of plastic, but of some strange material that was almost like glass. Kyle briefly wondered whether they had plastic in Loria.

He found a block of a pale green, mint-scented substance on the counter; it was set on a small dish and a tiny carving knife was resting next to it. After gingerly poke-, smell-, and taste-testing it, he carved off a small chunk and brushed his teeth with it, sincerely hoping that he was right in assuming that this was what passed for toothpaste in Loria. He later experienced a brief moment of panic when he drank from the tap without thinking of what might be coming out of it—his fears were unfounded, though, for it seemed that the denizens of this world drank water just like everybody else.

Once he had rinsed his mouth, he did something that he rarely had done back on Earth—he leaned down and splashed water on his face, partially to clean it, but mostly for the feeling of it; the coldness, the wetness, but above all the *realness* of the water, and by extension that of the world he was in. When he looked back in the mirror, he was shocked to see himself—Kyle Campbell, the same man he had always seen in the mirror—

standing there before him. The same faded clothes, the same lank black hair and mossy beard, the same glassy blue eyes; his familiar features seemed strange and alien surrounded by Loria's atmosphere.

He smiled ironically at himself, or rather, at his reflection—he could barely identify with the man in front of him.

"Well, Kyle," he asked himself, "what have you gotten yourself into this time?"

Smile fading, he waited for an answer, but none came. Sighing, he turned and left.

He walked back to his room and slid under the white covers, resolving to stay awake and to think about the bizarre turn his life had just taken. As soon as he lay down, however, the drowsiness swept over him, and he was asleep within minutes.

Kyle could vividly remember his first day of school, kindergarten to be exact. It had been a particularly cold September morning, so his mother had carefully bundled him up before they left the house. She had been a quiet, graceful woman with strawberry blonde hair, as caring and as considerate as a mother could be. However, despite her constant reassurance, tiny five-year-old Kyle still had his misgivings about the entire 'school' business. It worried him that he would soon be in close proximity with over twenty kids his age, while he had only ever met the occasional friend one at a time. Wouldn't the noise and confusion be horrendous? Kyle had a hard time imagining so many kids piled into a single room, where there would be a limited amount of toys and snacks to go around.

It wasn't just that, of course. Kyle had been struck with the same fears as every child before him had: that he wouldn't fit in, that he would get lost, that his teacher would be mean, that his mother would forget him and he would be stranded at school. With one thing and another, he wasn't too eager to leave the house that he had come to associate with ultimate peace on Earth.

Once he had been armored to his mother's liking, she had taken his hand and the two of them had walked to the school, which was only a couple of streets away. Equipped with his backpack, lunch box, bobble hat and mittens, he surveyed the bleak stone building before him, which was already teeming with students. It didn't look too promising, and Kyle's fear became more pronounced.

"Don't worry," his mother reassured him, "I'll walk with you to your classroom."

And so they had penetrated the throng of people, Kyle scurrying along after his mother, his hand gripping hers for dear life. The noise made by the students outside fed his fear more and more; every shriek, every shout, and every laugh that stood out from the general noise spawned one more butterfly in Kyle's stomach.

Once they got inside, Kyle felt a little better; it was warmer, and quieter, and the walls were decorated gaily with artwork done by the students. The colors brightened Kyle's mood, and he asked his mother hopefully if he would be making paintings like the ones on the walls.

"Of course," his mother said, smiling, and he felt much better.

"You'll love it," she had continued, heading down the halls, "you'll learn all sorts of things and make friends and paint paintings. It'll be a lot of fun."

This comment, however, did not have the desired effect on Kyle; his fears now arose again. What if he didn't like the other kids here? What if the things he was supposed to be learning were too hard?

Before he could ask her about this, however, she stopped in front of a classroom.

"Room 225," she read. "This is your classroom, sweetie."

Kyle was now near panic. His mother was going to leave him in this class, and he hadn't asked her all the questions he had to ask. Suddenly it seemed like there were so many things he didn't know—he wanted nothing more than to run away from this school and go back home, where everything was familiar and safe.

"Mom…Mom," he stammered, near tears, unable to voice this wish.

She kneeled down before him and stroked his face, pushing his hair out of his eyes.

"Listen to me," she said, gripping his arms. "You'll do just fine. Miss Hazel is very nice, she'll make sure nothing happens to you. Just be yourself and play nice."

At that moment, Miss Hazel appeared in the doorway, smiling. Kyle had to admit that she *did* look quite nice; slightly older and more wrinkled than his mother, she reminded Kyle of a kind aunt or grandmother.

"Is that little Kyle?" she asked, also kneeling down. "Why don't you come inside? We've got plenty of toys to play with."

"I'm allowed to play?" Kyle asked in a tiny voice.

"Of course!" Miss Hazel said, laughing. "We do every day."

Kyle looked back at his mother for aid. She was smiling. She pulled him into a smothering hug and then gently nudged him toward the class.

"Go on," she said softly, and Kyle allowed himself to be led inside by Miss Hazel. "I love you," she added, before she vanished from his view.

Kyle awoke completely convinced that he was still five years old and entering kindergarten; it took him a couple panicked seconds for him to remember where and when he was.

The events of the previous day washed over him as he lay in bed, along with a huge feeling of relief. Though he hadn't minded kindergarten after all, it wasn't something he particularly wanted to relive; finding himself once more a grown man of twenty-six, alert and competent, had been extremely reassuring.

Not so reassuring was Kyle's awareness of all the events that had just taken place. The cruise, the whirlpool…and now this strange world—which Kyle seemed still to be within, as he had woken up in his bed on the *Ayger*. After replaying his odd conversation with Nihs, Lugh and Rogan in his mind, the encounter seemed all the more ridiculous and surreal—yet his memory confirmed that it had taken place.

Kyle lay in bed for a while longer, organizing his thoughts. It was not an easy task. At the forefront of his mind was the decision he had made, and the promise that went with that—that he was going to stay in Loria, for a while at least, and become an adventurer with Lugh, Nihs and Rogan. At the time, it had seemed like such a good idea.

Finally he was unable to keep himself in bed for any longer, being too full of nervous energy. He vaulted out of bed and made his way back to the helm of the ship, noting that it had gotten dark again while he slept.

I go to sleep at sunrise and wake up at night, Kyle thought to himself. *I guess warping between universes causes some pretty brutal jet lag.*

As he reached the end of the hallway that opened onto the helm, Kyle heard Lugh and Nihs talking in subdued voices. He hesitated, wondering whether it would be impolite to walk in on them.

His pause in movement meant that he could now focus on what the two were saying, and, as though it had been amplified, Lugh's voice now drifted clearly toward him.

"Do you think we can we trust him?" the Selk was asking.

"Honestly, Lugh, if you ask me that one more time…" Nihs' nasally voice sounded irritated as usual.

"Well, if you would just give me a straight answer, then I would leave it alone."

"I've told you, I can't *give* you a straight answer. Everything we've tested so far points towards him being legitimate, but it never hurts to be too careful. We can't rule out the fact that this might be a deception of some kind."

"What would be the point of deceiving us, Nihs?"

"I never said that *we* were the ones being deceived," Nihs said darkly.

There was a pause, and then Lugh said, "What does your gut tell you?"

"Oh, please." Nihs sounded highly agitated.

"Come on. Tell me. You must have a gut feeling about all this."

Nihs didn't answer, and so Lugh continued, "You know what I think? I feel like he might be legit."

There was a brief silence, and Kyle imagined Nihs shaking his head.

"I want to believe that, but I'm not going to get too excited yet. Let's just finish this job and get to Reno. We can ask around there; maybe something will come up, maybe it won't. We can head on to Proks afterward and I can put the question to the council. If no one there has any theories…" He left it hanging.

"Why don't you ask the overhead about it?" Lugh asked.

"We've been through this. If I ask the overhead, news is bound to get out, and quickly. Before you know it everyone in the world will know about

Kyle, and not all of them will be too happy with the idea of his existence. If that happened, the people most in danger apart from Kyle himself will be *us*."

"Good point," Lugh mused.

At this point, Kyle made a decision. He took a couple steps backwards and then deliberately stepped loudly into the room. As he had guessed, both Nihs and Lugh's voices died away when they heard him coming.

"You're up," Lugh said brightly, turning around, and Kyle was impressed to hear how natural his voice was.

"Right at the crack of nightfall," Nihs remarked blandly.

"That's right," Kyle said, copying Nihs' tone. "I think my biological clock is messed up."

"It's just the after-effects of your *reursis*," Nihs reassured him. "You'll get better eventually."

"Great," said Kyle, injecting a little sarcasm into his voice for the use of 'eventually'.

There was a brief pause in which none of them could think of something to say, and then Nihs said suddenly, "You heard us talking, didn't you."

Kyle was completely taken aback. "Uh…"

"You can admit it, you know. It's not like we're going to throw you off our ship for eavesdropping."

Judging from the look on Lugh's face, he had not realized that Kyle had been listening in. He rallied quickly, however, and managed a wink. "Yeah, nothing wrong with a bit of healthy eavesdropping. Start honing skills like that and you'll be an adventurer in no time."

"All right," Kyle admitted, "I did hear, but I didn't mean to. It's not like—" but Lugh held up a hand to stop him.

"Go no farther. Anyway, I guess now that you've heard us, you know a bit of what we're thinking."

"I don't blame you for doubting me," Kyle hastened to say, speaking primarily to Nihs. "I have a hard time believing it myself. I don't know what I can do to help prove my story, but…well, I owe you guys, so if there's anything I can do—"

"Okay," said Lugh, "first of all, you don't *owe* us anything; you didn't ask for our help and besides, helping people is part of being an adventurer."

"Secondly," Nihs continued, "the trick about the whole deal is this: *we* don't know what you can do to help either. In the entire history of Loria, there's no recorded case of someone coming here from another world. We have no idea where to start proving that your story is true—or figuring out how to get you back. Now, I know you've decided that you want to stay for a while, but I still think it's a good idea to start gathering information about how you came here—*if* you came here—and how to get back. If it turns out there's an easy way to send you back, all the better. You don't have to take it right away if you don't want to."

"I get it," Kyle said. "It makes sense, really."

Nihs seemed pleased by Kyle's agreeability. "Well," he continued, "if we're going to do it that way, I think that the first thing we should do after we stop at Reno is—"

"Go to the Kol's homeland and ask a council," Kyle finished. "Rogan mentioned doing that…and I heard you talking to Lugh about it," he added delicately.

Nihs nodded. "That's right, and after that…well, we'll just have to keep our eyes open and see what we can see. But if I'm to be truly honest," he added, in a serious tone, "I'll say that I don't think it's going to be as simple as all that. Something tells me that an event like this has to have happened for a reason. We don't know what, yet, obviously, but I think you'll find that you won't be leaving this world as quietly as you came."

"Is that a premonition or something?" Kyle asked, still unsure as to how magic apparently worked in this world.

"I don't do premonitions," Nihs said. "Call it a hunch."

They stood in silence for a moment, and then an appliance over at the kitchen let out a soft beep.

"Oh," Lugh said, "that's me." He strode over to the miniature set-up and removed a dish that was balanced on what looked quite like a simple stove, although the heating plates were elevated slightly, completely solid and golden in color. When Lugh removed the cover from the dish, it was revealed to contain two small items of food that looked like a cross between hamburgers and Jamaican patties.

"Do you want something to eat?" Lugh shot over his shoulder, pausing in the act of turning the stove off.

"Um, sure, I guess," said Kyle, who was in fact ravenous.

Lugh nodded, leaving the stove on, and removed from what Kyle assumed to be a freezer two more of the strange sandwiches, wrapped in paper. He set them up on the stove and then caught Kyle's expression.

"Adventurer-style cooking," he said, grinning, holding up one of the sandwiches, "Nothing in the world quite like it."

This was a joke that Kyle could immediately identify with. Living by himself, he was intimately familiar with what people called 'bachelor cooking', which involved a lot of leftovers, instant food, and take-out sessions.

While Lugh was preparing the food, Kyle said to Nihs, "So, if we're going to the Kol's homeland right after we visit Reno, there's not going to be much time for, well, being adventurers…right?"

"Oh, we won't go straight there," Nihs said, "we'll find some way to work a trip there into our adventuring. That's a useful tip if you ever find yourself going solo: never waste anything, and that includes time and things like a ship this size," Nihs made a wide gesture, "or you'll never get ahead in the world. Hopefully we'll be able to find someone who just wants passage to Proks—that's the Kol capital city—which will make the trip there pay for itself. *Or*, we might find a job whose location happens to be near our flight path to Proks, and we'll make a little detour along the way."

"Oh."

Lugh, meanwhile, had finished heating up the strange sandwiches for Kyle, and carried them over to him on a plate.

"Thanks," Kyle said gratefully, and in an unusual act of bravery, he took a bite *before* he asked what was in it.

It was, in fact, very good. It did remind him of those cheap patties one could buy in a meat store, although there was also a suggestion of egg and cheese, along with a strange yellow sauce that Kyle couldn't figure out whether he liked or not—it tasted rich, like mustard mixed with mayonnaise, but was so light that Kyle felt he was swallowing fog.

Having decided that it was good, Kyle asked, promising himself that he would keep an open mind, "what are these made out of?"

"Bwah meat," Lugh said, "and egg and cheese. And sauce."

"I'm okay with the egg and cheese," Kyle said, "but what's a bwah?"

"A monster native to the savannah south of Reno," said Nihs. "It looks kind of like a large duck with fur. They're very tame for monsters, and they're breedable, so their meat is cheap."

Kyle decided that the whole of the thing didn't sound too offensive, and he was starving besides, so he continued to eat with gusto. Another question came to mind.

"What makes this ship run?" he asked Nihs.

"A type of magical engine called an Ephicer engine," Nihs replied. "Why? Do you have similar ships in your world?"

So Kyle had been right about that—the machines here ran on magic. "We do," he said, "but they run on gas, not magic."

Nihs looked at him blankly. Guessing that Nihs probably thought he meant 'gas' as opposed to 'liquid' or 'solid', he added, "It's a type of liquid fuel refined from oil. I'm not sure exactly how it's made," he continued, scratching his head. "I think it's compressed decomposed plants or something—it's created naturally underground; we drill for it."

"Gas and oil," Nihs repeated, his expression distant. "I wonder if there's any of it underground in Loria," he added. "We've never mined for anything of the sort, you see—we've never had to. I wonder how it compares to Epicher-based engines," he mused. Kyle could see a fanatical light glowing in the Kol's eyes.

"I don't know how your engines work," Kyle said quickly, "but chances are it's better than gas. They're terrible for the environment—right now, everyone's trying to figure out better ways of running machines."

The Kol shot him a strange look. "The environment?" he asked.

"Yeah. It's because you have to burn the fuel in order to use it, right? So it releases all these gases into the atmosphere." Something occurred to him. "Do you have something like an ozone layer on your planet?"

"An ozone layer? Never heard of one."

"It's like, a layer of gas that surrounds the planet...it filters the sun's rays—"

"Oh!" Nihs said, "it sounds like the ether—a layer of perfect magic particles high in the sky that separates our atmosphere from space."

"Right, exactly," Kyle said, pleased that his comparison was going to make sense, "that sounds pretty similar. Well, our ozone layer is made of, well, ozone, and it reacts badly to the type of gas released by engines. So it's been getting thinner recently because there's so much fuel being burned on Earth."

Kyle had expected a negative reaction from this, but he never expected such a look of horror to pass across Nihs' face.

"But…but…" the Kol stammered, eyes wide and glued to Kyle, "isn't that…really bad? I mean…what will happen if the layer thins too much?"

"It's already happening," Kyle said cynically, "the sun's rays are being filtered less and less, so the average temperature of the world is going up. It's making the ice around the poles melt more and more, which is raising the sea level—yeah, it's a big production. They call it global warming."

Nihs' expression had gone from one of fright, to one of incredulity, and had now settled on something vaguely accusatory.

"And the people on your world know this is happening?" he asked sharply, "and they still use gas-based engines?"

"Well, yeah," Kyle said a little uncomfortably, "by the time people realized what the engines were doing, they were everywhere—the economy would've collapsed if everyone had been forced to stop using them. And like I said, people are researching other types of engines now that they know better."

"But—" Nihs started, looking scandalized, but Lugh interrupted him.

"Hey, give him a break," he said reasonably, "it's not *his* fault. And it's not like *we* were the ones to invent Ephicer engines—who knows? Maybe we just lucked out. Maybe if things had happened just a little differently, *we* would be using gas engines, too."

"But do you know how much of an uproar it would've caused once people found out they were damaging the ether?" Nihs said pointedly. "The Kol and the Buors would have banned them right away—they wouldn't have been allowed to keep being used."

"But there *are* no Buors and Kol in his world," Lugh pointed out.

"That's exactly what I mean," Nihs said darkly. Kyle was shocked to see the transformation that Nihs had undergone; his tiny fists were balled and a shadow had fallen over his face. It looked as though his eyes were about to shoot sparks any second.

Kyle looked fearfully at Lugh, who sighed. His expression, too, was grave, but at least it was also benign.

"Nihs," he said firmly.

Nihs seemed about to say something, but at that moment the crystal on the control panel lit up and Rogan's voice sounded in the room.

"Lugh? Anyone up there?"

Nihs shook his head and scurried over to the control panel.

"All I can say is," he said with his back to them, "I'm glad I don't live in your world." He climbed his stool and put a hand on the crystal. "Yes?" he asked Rogan.

"What was that all about?" Kyle asked Lugh quietly.

"Humans...well, they don't have the best reputation in our world," Lugh said apologetically. "Of course, we didn't know how they behaved in your world compared to ours—for all we knew, they were a totally different deal. But that story about the engines...well, it sort of confirms our worst suspicions, if you know what I mean. I've learned to deal with stories like that, but for a Kol...well, they're a lot closer to magic and the Earth than we are, so hearing stories of abuse like that can really rub them the wrong way."

"Right," said Kyle mildly, although he felt a strange feeling growing in his chest that might have been shame or affront. So humans in this world were considered...*what?* he wondered. He remembered the look that Nihs had given him when he had found out that Kyle's world was one-hundred-percent human. Between that and his embarrassingly low CAL or whatever it was, he wondered if there was anything else in this world that could possibly make him feel more worthless.

"I've got the engine up and running," Rogan was saying through the communicator. "Were you guys planning on pulling an all-nighter or do I get some rest?"

"What do you think, Lugh?" Nihs called over his shoulder.

Lugh scratched his chin. "We're pretty close to where that unicorn was supposed to be," he said, "so I don't see why we shouldn't just wrap it up tonight."

"You're going to go unicorn hunting in the dark?" Rogan's voice sounded skeptical.

"Best time for it," Lugh said brightly.

Rogan sighed. Over the crystal's interference it sounded like a rush of static.

"All right, then. Fire it up whenever you're ready, Nihs. Try to make it a smooth takeoff; you tend to veer to the left and I think that's part of what's harming the converters."

"I'll do my very best," Nihs said in a voice saturated with sarcasm. He took his hand off of the crystal and transferred it to the throttle, while removing a small object from his pocket with the other. He set it into the control panel and with a low hum, the ship sprang to life.

"Everyone ready? No hot drinks you need to put down? Okay…"

The humming of the engine grew very loud and high-pitched as the *Ayger* took off. The floor shook slightly and Kyle felt it rock beneath his feet; it was nothing like as intense as the rocking of the *Caribia*, however.

"Hey," said Lugh to Kyle, "why don't we go out on deck? The view's quite something while we're taking off."

"Sure," Kyle said eagerly.

"Oh, don't worry about me," Nihs called from the wheel, his brow furrowed in concentration. "I'll be fine right here, sailing on my own."

"Great, glad to hear it," Lugh said. He strode down the hallway that contained Kyle's room.

"The deck's this way," he called.

They passed through the door at the very end of the hallway—it was a serious construct made of golden metal and Kyle was reminded of the door that led to the deck of the *Caribia*.

The deck turned out to be a tidy affair at the aft of the ship. It was teardrop-shaped, Lugh and Kyle having come out of a door at the flat end. There was another door to their left, which Kyle assumed connected to the other hallway inside. Extending out from the pointed end of the deck was a massive finlike structure, which Kyle assumed was the rudder. The whole thing, including the railing of the deck, and (when he looked behind him) the bridge, was made of the same glossy, golden material.

The noise of the engine outside was quite a bit louder, but nowhere near as loud as a plane. Kyle could see large flaps on the rudder tilting back and forth as Nihs made minute adjustments back in the cockpit, no doubt in order to achieve the perfect takeoff that Rogan had requested.

Lugh strode over to the railing; Kyle followed him. He peered over the edge and was indeed impressed by the view offered. As the ship rose,

Kyle could see the trees close to him falling away gently. Though night had fallen almost completely, the moon was very bright, so Kyle could clearly see the rippling surface of the lake in the near distance.

He craned his neck to absorb as much of the view as possible. Just as when he had first looked through the front window of the *Ayger*, he was struck with a strange, yet wonderful feeling as he gazed upon the world of Loria. For some reason, the forest beneath seemed greener than any on Earth, the hills seemed hillier, even the lake seemed lakier. Kyle felt like someone who had finally gotten glasses after needing a prescription for a long time.

"Not bad, eh?" Lugh said beside him, and Kyle jumped.

"Yeah," he managed to reply, "not bad at all."

He felt elated, the wind was cool on his face and he seemed to be leaving all his worries and doubts on the forest floor beneath him. Feeling much better in himself, he said, "Rogan mentioned unicorn hunting."

Lugh nodded. "That's what our job here is. One of them has been spotted about fifteen minutes' flight west of here. They're from the land of the Elves, see, but occasionally one will get lost, or sick, or chased by another monster and end up where it doesn't belong. With most monsters that's not a big deal, but unicorns have a lot of powerful magic to them. They mess with the environment around them when they're not in Elfland."

"So you're supposed to kill it?"

"Sometimes that's what has to be done, but there's a group behind this job that's offering to cart it back to where it belongs. We just have to catch it."

Satisfied with this explanation, Kyle lapsed once more into silence, or at least tried to—but there were so many questions he still wanted to ask.

"You don't mind me asking all these questions, do you?" he asked Lugh in light of this.

Lugh laughed easily. "You kidding me? You dropped in here from a completely different world; of course there's a ton of stuff you want to know about."

"In that case," Kyle said, reassured, "why is everything in this ship made of gold?"

Lugh smiled. "It's not gold, unfortunately. It's *tigoreh*, an alloy the Buors and the Kol discovered. It's really conductive to magic, so it's used everywhere in Ephicer machinery."

"What is that, exactly?" Kyle asked before he could stop himself.

"You'd have to ask Nihs for all the lurid details," Lugh said, staring out over the lake. "I only understand the basics of it. An Ephicer is a certain kind of magical rock. Up until recently, it just seemed like they generated magic constantly, which was great, but they didn't do much else. A while back, though, some smart cookie found out how to make Ephicers absorb and store magic as well as release it. That's pretty much how Ephicer machinery works; you rig it up so that the Ephicer inside the machine releases the right amount and right kind of magic when you want it to, and absorbs it otherwise. They can absorb magic straight out of the air, but they do it faster if you connect it to *tigoreh* wiring. Think about a tree with roots spreading out from it, and that's pretty much how it works."

"So," Kyle said, looking around him, "all this...the whole ship...is gathering magic and sending it to the engine?"

"That's right," Lugh said happily.

Kyle thought about this for a while. "But if you have all these ships sucking magic out of the atmosphere, isn't there less and less magic in the air all the time?"

Lugh started to laugh, but then stopped himself. "Sorry," he said a little awkwardly, "I'm sure the question makes total sense to you, but for someone who grew up here, well, it just sounds funny. Anyway, you can't destroy or create magic—"

"You can only alter it," Kyle finished automatically.

Lugh gave him a look. "Now, how did you know that?"

"We have the same theory about energy on our world."

"Right," Lugh said, "I'm sure Nihs would go all gaga if you told him that, but personally I don't see the tease in it. I mean, if a rule works for one universe, it only makes sense that it would work for another, right?"

"Why not?" said Kyle, shrugging.

"Anyway," Lugh went on, "all you're doing with an Ephicer-based engine is moving particles around, the same thing you're doing when you work magic. Like I said, I don't really know what I'm talking about, but as far as I understand it all the magic ends up coming around again and being refreshed. I do know that you can't have too many ships pass over one spot or stay running there for too long, or you drain the useable particles before they have a chance to replenish themselves."

Kyle nodded, deep in thought. He could see, now, why Nihs and Lugh had been shocked at the idea of gas. From what he had heard, it looked like the people here had engines that ran on an endlessly renewable resource and left no lasting footprint whatsoever on the world. In a word, they were perfect.

They'd be no use back on Earth, Kyle thought to himself. *There's no magic there.*

They stood on deck for a couple more minutes, Kyle finishing off the last of his second bwahwich. His stomach was agreeably full, his face was pleasantly cool, and the scenery around them had not ceased to be beautiful. The world seemed to make a bit more sense out here, and while Kyle was still aware of the strange and somewhat frightening predicament he had landed himself in, it didn't bother him so much anymore.

He heard the sound of static behind him and turned to see a blue crystal like the one on the control panel set into the wall.

"Hello? Are you two quite finished out there?" Nihs' voice sounded even more nasally over the communicator.

Lugh laughed and walked over to the crystal, putting his hand on it.

"Could be, why?"

"We're getting close to the coordinates our employer sent us. I'm going to touch down soon, and then we can pile out and get hunting."

"Right," said Lugh, "I'll see you on the bridge."

"Uh," said Kyle uncertainly, "am I going to be going with you guys?"

Lugh eyed him thoughtfully. "I thought you should at first, but now I'm thinking that you should probably sit this one out after all. It's not a super dangerous mission, but we will be working at night, and you're not exactly at one hundred percent. Rogan'll probably stay back, too. He can take care of you."

Kyle would never admit it, but he was relieved to hear this. As exciting as the prospect of unicorn hunting sounded, Kyle still felt weak from his fall, and was all too aware of his lack of experience.

They went back to the helm and met up with Nihs, who was scanning the forest around them for a place to touch down.

"Please tell me you're putting it down *past* that mountain," Lugh said over Nihs' shoulder, pointing.

Nihs rolled his eyes. "That's a *hill*, not a mountain, you baby."

"It looks craggy. Are hills usually craggy? I don't think so."

"It's a hill, Lugh."

"Fine. Please tell me you're putting it down *past* that hill."

"*Yes*, I am. Don't you have someone else to bother?"

"Actually, no."

Nihs sighed. "So Rogan says he can start training Kyle while we're out looking for that unicorn."

"Why would you assume that Kyle isn't coming?" Lugh demanded, apparently offended on Kyle's behalf.

Nihs rolled his eyes. "Oh, please, Lugh, really? You were seriously considering taking a complete newbie—who just recently recovered from a serious case of *reursis*—on a level thirty mission?"

"You don't learn anything just sitting around," Lugh said in a hurt voice.

"I agree. For instance, you won't learn what happens when you take someone who's never held a sword before on a night-time hunting trip."

Lugh opened his mouth to retort, but Kyle cut him off.

"Don't worry about it," he said to Lugh. "It's fine, really, I don't mind." He turned to Nihs. "We had decided that I wouldn't be coming anyway."

"Well," Nihs said in a satisfied voice, "it seems as though even Lugh can make a smart decision every once in a while."

Lugh stuck his tongue out at him.

After they had flown over the hill Lugh had pointed out, Nihs found a large clearing to land the *Ayger*. As he was touching down, Lugh exited through a door on the wall behind the control panel. As Kyle watched him step down a staircase beyond the door, he noticed that the wall was decorated with a huge, colorful map.

"Is that Loria?" Kyle asked in wonderment.

"Yes," Nihs said without taking his eyes off the control, "that's the

Ayger's map system. It picks up signals from cities and other ships, so it can show us where we are in the world."

"Wow," Kyle said, approaching the map. It was colored vibrantly on what seemed to be a kind of glass plate, with seas that were very blue and continents that were mostly green, although there was some brown, white and beige—it was a topographical map.

Kyle took in the shape of the continents; it felt strange to see such a familiar thing as a map showing an alien world, blandly proclaiming the world's existence. To the west was a large continent mostly north of the equator. Much of it was brown, white and gray, with only the southern tips and bits near the coast colored green. At the center of the world map were two continents stacked on top of one another, like the Americas—the north continent was almost completely green, but most of the southern continent was the color of sand. To the east was a small, blob-shaped continent, very close to a greater one.

Kyle peered closer: he could see that points of interest were labeled with small black letters edged with gold; just as with a map on Earth, there were larger names that Kyle assumed were those of countries and continents. The names of the continents seemed quite uninspired: *Westia* was written across the large continent to the west; the two continents in the center were together *Centralia,* although the more interesting names *Ren'r* and *Ar'ac* seemed to apply to the north and south portions, respectively; the small blobby one was labeled *Nimelheim* and the larger one next to it was *Eastia.* There were large, pure white continents to the extreme north and south, just like on Earth. Both were labeled *The Ice Fields.*

Kyle raked his eyes along the map, taking in the names. He found a yellow arrow that he assumed to be the *Ayger* at the northern tip of the Ar'ac continent. Remembering what Lugh had said about Reno's location, he looked to the northeast and found a large yellow dot labeled *Reno* right on the land bridge between the Ren'r and Ar'ac continents. He also found Proks, near the southeastern edge of Eastia. The only other name that meant anything at all to him was one next to a small, round island off to the north and east of Eastia, which was *Buoria.*

"I'm guessing that Buoria is where the Buors are from?" Kyle asked Nihs.

"That's right, and you're pronouncing *Buors* wrong, it's 'boo-or', not 'bwor'."

Ignoring the correction, Kyle commented, "Their homeland really isn't too big, is it?"

"Not only that, but the island itself is a grim place. It's a giant caldera, nothing but rock, ash, and dust. That's part of why they're such noble people; they've always been forced to work together and to survive in such an unforgiving homeland."

"Huh," Kyle said, and he continued to peruse the map.

Nihs landed the ship soon after. Lugh returned wearing a set of leather armor, and something made of *tigoreh* belted to his waist which looked like a large dagger. He was carrying a small bundle of cloth, which he threw to Nihs.

"Thanks," Nihs said, unraveling what turned out to be a strange garment that looked like a pair of sleeves with no shirt to go with them. He pulled it on just as its appearance suggested—the sleeves were wide and billowy, colored gray and black.

"This is our adventurer swag," Lugh explained, catching the look on Kyle's face. "Those mutants that Nihs is wearing are called wizard's sleeves, they help with channeling magic."

"So you fight with magic?" Kyle asked.

"I do most things with magic," Nihs replied smugly, shaking his sleeves into a more comfortable position.

Something occurred to Kyle. "Do you think I'll be able to learn magic?" he asked, thinking of what he had talked to Lugh about before.

Nihs regarded him thoughtfully. "I'd say not," he said slowly, "but first, we don't actually know anything about how this world works with you, and second, the fact that you can eat, drink and breathe in this world without having problems makes me hopeful. After all, you're consuming magic by doing that. Of course," he added, "even if you could use magic, chances are you wouldn't be skilled enough at it to make it worth your while."

"Hey, that's not exactly fair," Lugh said. "Humans aren't as bad at magic as most people think. They're better than Selks, anyway."

"Which isn't saying much," Nihs smirked.

"Quiet, you, or I'll punt you," Lugh said.

Kyle couldn't help but smile as he listened to the two snipe at each other. He had only just met them, but he already felt as though he was included in what was obviously a strong friendship between Lugh and Nihs. He was also excited by the prospect of magic, and the optimism expressed by Nihs.

A second later he nearly jumped out of his skin when a low voice said behind him, "So, you two are leaving now?"

Rogan had come up from the engine room and entered the bridge quietly. Kyle danced out of the way so that he wasn't in the Minotaur's line of fire.

"That's right," Lugh said, adjusting his belt. "Try not to blow up the ship while we're gone."

"Look who's talking," Rogan said, folding his enormous arms. "What's the plan for catching that unicorn?"

"It shouldn't be hard to track out there," Lugh said. "The ground's nice and soft and we'll see it from a mile away in this light. Then Nihs can lure it with magic."

"That's the plan, at least," Nihs said. "It should follow me right onto the *Ayger* if all goes well."

"Hmm," Rogan grunted. "Well, have a good time. Try not to be out after dark."

"Oh, you're funny," Nihs snipped. He passed by them and went through the same door Lugh had just used.

Lugh followed him a moment after, though he turned in the doorway and nodded to Kyle. "Good luck," he said.

"You, too," Kyle said awkwardly.

Lugh winked and left after Nihs. The ship instantly seemed quieter once they had left.

"Ahh, peace," Rogan sighed contentedly, obviously feeling the same way. "Don't get me wrong, I love those two, but there's something about having the whole ship to yourself, you know what I mean?"

"Yeah," Kyle said quietly. Normally he would have liked the quiet and the loneliness, but he didn't feel nearly as confident with himself in this world as he had on Earth. At home Kyle had felt like the only person who knew what was going on; here, he was painfully aware that he knew almost nothing about how things worked. Not for the first time he wished he could get his hands on a drink.

"Well," Rogan said, suddenly changing tack, "I hear that I'm supposed to start your training while those two are gone. I'll admit that it's a good time for it—the ship's empty and the engine is in pretty good shape. Are you up for it?"

"Yeah, of course," Kyle said, who was feeling much better than yesterday and was eager to learn in any case.

Rogan nodded. "All right, then, follow me."

They passed through the same door that Nihs and Lugh had gone through; a staircase led downwards which took them to the floor below the bridge. They were in the middle of a medium- sized, T-shaped room; doors lined every wall.

"How big *is* this ship?" Kyle asked, studying the doors.

"This is pretty much it," Rogan said, striding forward. "The food storage and the stables are behind us—all these doors on the side are bedrooms—and this is the ballroom ahead of us. Of course, we use it as a training dojo."

"This ship has *stables*?" Kyle asked incredulously, "and a *ballroom*? What kind of ship is this?"

"It's a luxury liner," Rogan said with a hint of amusement, "for nobles to entertain guests and have parties. Lugh won it off of a rich friend of his, and now he just uses it to travel and show off."

"He *won* it?" Kyle asked. "I bet his friend was real happy."

"They still bring it up every time they see each other," Rogan snorted. "It's a running joke between the two of them. At least, Lugh jokes about it. Ellander—that's his friend—hasn't accepted that Lugh's got it for good. He keeps hoping he can win it back from him someday."

"I would, too," Kyle said reverentially, looking around.

"I've sailed a lot of ships in my time," Rogan nodded, "but the *Ayger* is one of the best. It *was* the best of its kind when it was built…the next big step in ship technology. Better ships have been built since, but only just recently, and the *Ayger* is more than three years old."

They went through the large set of doors and entered a spacious room that was obviously the ballroom-cum-dojo that Rogan had mentioned. It was bright and there was a lot of space to go around. Kyle noticed a stack of chairs and folding tables in one corner that mutely spoke of the room's previous use. The far wall was completely mirrored, and the three others were barely visible behind several racks of weapons and piles of equipment. There were even some training dummies and punching bags, and a couple targets—both of which looked somewhat singed—were hung against one wall.

Rogan folded his arms once more and glanced around the room, shaking his head.

"Those two have got too much stuff," he said disapprovingly, "although, I guess for our purposes that's not such a bad thing. Now," he said to Kyle, "do you have any experience with combat at all?"

"Uh," Kyle said, racking his brains, "I don't think so."

"Never practiced any kind of martial arts?"

"No," said Kyle, feeling miserable about it.

"Ever done archery, or sports of any kind?"

"I did a bit of archery in school. I was decent at it. I'm not really a sports guy."

"Hmm," Rogan said, and Kyle was grateful for the Minotaur's acceptance.

"What did you say your job was back in your world?" Rogan asked.

"I was a database developer," Kyle said gloomily.

"That doesn't sound like anything we have here. What did you do?"

Kyle had been afraid that this question was going to come up.

"It might be hard to explain…do you have computers in your world?"

"Never heard of one."

"Okay, how about…circuitry?"

"Our machines use *tigoreh* wires to conduct magic," Rogan said, "so yes."

"Okay, well, a computer is like…an artificial brain made with super complicated electrical circuitry, right? We use them for almost everything these days, because they can perform calculations faster than a human can, and they can store a lot of information. And that's where I come…well, *came* in…I worked on keeping the information that computers stored organized."

"Hmm," Rogan said again, "that actually makes a surprising amount of sense. Those computers sound like quite something…maybe we could have a use for them over here. Anyway, that's not what we're here to discuss. We're here to discuss your adventuring career.

"So it sounds like you have essentially no combat experience whatsoever, which is good in a way, because it means we have a clean slate, but is bad in a way, since it means that you have essentially no combat experience whatsoever. Now, adventurers generally try to specialize in certain types of combat, be they magical or physical; they usually work in groups, and in a group it's better to have different people who're really good at one thing than a bunch of people who're mediocre at everything."

"Makes sense," Kyle said.

"As you meet more adventurers, you'll find that they tend to use certain terms to describe certain styles of fighting. Nihs' a spellcaster, and since his specialty is elemental magic an adventurer would refer to him as a mage—but Nihs can tell you more about that when he teaches you about magic. Lugh fights with a sword in a mishmash style from Centralia, so they call him a fighter. I fight as most Minotaur do, with an axe, in a style that came from the plains, so they call *me* a warrior. And so on.

"In any case," Rogan went on, "while ideally you would be trained into something that would complement the abilities we already have in our team, we can only teach you what we know. Now, humans don't make the greatest warriors, so I think our best bet is to train you to be another fighter. Think you could get used to fighting with a sword?"

"Wait a minute," Kyle said, looking around the room. "A sword? Are your weapons really only that advanced?"

Rogan's bushy eyebrows shot up. "How advanced should they be?" he asked.

"You don't have…guns or anything?" Kyle, mostly because of what he had heard about Ephicer engines, was already thinking that the technology of this world was further ahead than that of Earth.

"We do have guns," Rogan said, "they're good weapons, and they have their uses, but a gunner doesn't stand a chance against a good swordsman."

Kyle opened his mouth to argue, but then thought better of it. Clearly, things worked differently here.

"How come?" he asked instead. "In my world, a gun is definitely a better weapon than a sword."

"The effectiveness of a gunner is limited by the quality of his weapon," Rogan said. "The best gunner in the world can't do much damage with a mediocre weapon. By contrast, as a swordsman gets stronger, they fight better no matter which weapon they're using. Guns just aren't strong enough to take on some of the creatures that adventurers have to fight; it takes the combined strength of the weapon plus that of the fighter himself to do that."

Something clicked in Kyle's brain. "Nihs said that there's no such thing as peak condition in your world."

"That's very true. Once you know that, you can see why skilled adventurers choose to use weapons whose effectiveness relies on their own strength."

"Yeah, I can." Kyle thought of himself, who Nihs had estimated was around one-fifth of his strength, and felt miserable.

He surfaced from these thoughts to find that Rogan had walked over to the wall near them, and was perusing the weapon racks set along it.

"Let's start you with a sword at first and see how you fare. If you don't take to it, we could try giving you a spear—Lugh knows something about fighting with them…maybe you'll make a good archer, too, we can try that out…" He turned back to Kyle. "Feel free to look around, I think you can be trusted not to hurt yourself."

"Am I looking for anything specific?" Kyle asked.

"Don't bother. You don't know what to look for, you'd probably end up with a weapon that you're not ready to use."

Kyle was too excited to be offended, and walked to the wall across from Rogan and let his eyes travel across the equipment there. Stepping around a pile of what looked like body padding, he found a small rack of weapons that looked similar to the one Lugh had been wielding. They were all different shades of gold, from a bright yellow to a darker color that was more like bronze.

"Are these weapons made of *tigoreh*?" he asked, taking one down. It looked like a fat, heavy dagger whose blade was made of many different little files of metal; it was completely golden, except for a small blue gem set into the pommel, which glowed faintly.

"There's *tigoreh* mixed in with the metal of the weapon," Rogan called over. He was rummaging around behind a group of dummies. "*Tigoreh's* color is very strong, so it looks like there's more in it than there is. You can't make a weapon completely out of *tigoreh*, it's too soft."

Kyle observed the weapon for a little longer, and then asked the question he had really meant to ask. "What *is* this?"

"That's a sword, a retrasword—a retractable one. That's what the *tigoreh* is in there for; it lets the Ephicer in the pommel gather enough magic to retract and extend the blade."

"Oh," said Kyle, surprised. He peered at the blue gem in the pommel; so that's what an Ephicer looked like. He realized that the gems in the *Ayger's* communicators were probably Ephicers, as well.

"How do you extend the blade?" he asked Rogan, looking for some kind of button on the handle.

"It's intent-driven," the Minotaur explained. "The user has to hold the blade and will it to extend. Just make sure to point it away from you if you try."

Kyle, unconvinced that the sword was capable of knowing what he wanted, held it by the handle and thought, *extend*. Nothing happened. *Extend!* he thought with more conviction. The blade remained stubbornly short. Kyle felt quite foolish. Maybe the sword wouldn't work for him since he wasn't from Loria…or maybe his mind just wasn't strong enough.

At this thought, he held the sword up to his eye and glared at it. No way was he going to be ignored by an inanimate object.

Extend! he thought furiously, giving the handle a hard squeeze.

At once, with a hissing sound like an air lock being opened, the sword flashed white and a fountain of light shot out of the top, accompanied by a repeated clanking sound; the handle grew hot for a split second, and Kyle yelped and almost dropped it. When the light faded, the multitude of small metal files had stacked on top of one another to form a shining golden blade and a crossguard had grown outwards from the handle.

"Whoa," Kyle said in wonderment, staring at the sword he was holding. He felt pleased with himself. His enthusiasm waned, however, when he realized that the sword was really quite long and heavy. Carefully he let the tip drop to the ground.

Uh, retract, he thought to the sword, staring down at it.

The blade obliged, flashing white-hot again and falling back into the shape Kyle had started with.

"That's neat," he said to himself, examining the blade again. "Hey," he called over to Rogan, "do I get to use one of these?"

"Not yet," Rogan said, stepping out of the piles of equipment with a fistful of weapons in either hand. "Retraweapons are tricky to use, their weight distribution is odd and they're not as durable as normal weapons. We're going to start you at the bottom and work your way up." He stepped to the middle of the room and set all the weapons he was holding down with a clatter. He sat down and beckoned for Kyle to join him as he began to arrange them on the floor.

Kyle sat down across from the heap of weaponry, eying Rogan cautiously. The Minotaur looked much more frightening when picking up and arranging sharp objects as though they were pencils.

"All right," Rogan said, "now, I'm assuming that you know nothing about weapons."

"Basically," Kyle said.

"Good. It'll make it easier for you to accept how they work here. In Loria there are several different ways to forge a weapon, most of them rely on a process called weaving, which was discovered not too long ago…I think it's been about fifty years. Anyway," he held up a sword that looked almost like a medieval European longsword, but with some slight changes that suggested modern refinement, "this is a sword forged normally, without any weaving. It's a pretty high quality one, but unwoven weapons—flat weapons, they're called—don't exactly measure up these days. They're cheap, which is good, but they're delicate compared to woven types."

He set the sword down and lifted up another. This blade was gray, slightly darker than normal, and the coloring and sheen had a strange texture that looked like thatch.

"This is a sword forged using cross weaving," Rogan said. "Notice that the blade is darker and looks almost wavy. These weapons are much, much tougher than the flat types—usually five to ten times so."

"How are they made?" Kyle asked.

"As soon as the blade has been cast into the right shape, while it's still hot, the metal particles that form it are aligned by magic, so that they end up woven around each other. They're not literally woven out of metal—that's impossible, obviously—but the end result is essentially that."

"Okay, makes sense, I guess."

Rogan gave a small laugh and picked up another weapon.

They went through three more types of weaving: spiral weaving (which made the weapon more receptive to enchantment), and web and grid weaving (used for weapons with bigger blades, such as axes). Rogan told him it was, as yet, impossible to weave a retraweapon, which was why they were considered easily breakable.

He then motioned for Kyle to get up, and went through the numerous swords he had picked out, getting Kyle to hold and try out several to see the differences between them. He also described a couple types that neither Lugh nor Nihs had managed to collect during their adventures. By the end of the lesson, Kyle's arm was sore and his head was spinning. He never would have guessed that the art of making a weapon and then subsequently sticking it into someone could be so complicated.

"And that looks like all the ones we have here," Rogan said finally, taking from Kyle what he had called a straight sword, which looked like an unbent katana. "Now," he said, pulling from the pile a thin, crosswoven sword that Kyle had tried before, "we can actually get down to some training."

"That wasn't it?" Kyle asked incredulously.

"That was the theory portion," Rogan said in an amused tone, handing the sword to Kyle. "Now we do the practical."

Rogan selected a thick wooden staff from one of the weapon racks and squared off in front of Kyle, shoulders hunched in a combat stance. Kyle held the sword awkwardly, apprehensive. The last time he had gone up against one of the denizens of Loria, a two-foot-tall creature had thrown him off-balance. Kyle was not looking forward to finding out what Rogan was capable of doing to him.

Rogan, again demonstrating his acute ability to interpret feelings, said, "Don't worry, I'm not going to beat you up—you'd learn nothing from that...except tolerance for pain, I suppose, but you'll develop that naturally anyway. Now, stand with your legs apart on an angle, right foot forward. When fighting without a shield, always keep your weapon hand closest to the enemy; it lets you block and strike faster, and your body will turn naturally to make a smaller target. Bend your knees a little more…"

Under Rogan's instruction, Kyle drilled sword techniques. Rogan twisted his staff to catch each blow—Kyle noticed that the hard wood had already been notched by previous training sessions. Rogan kept a constant stream of instructions flowing during their sparring, his brow sweaty with concentration. He ran Kyle through techniques for striking quickly without becoming exposed; they practiced footwork and controlling distance from the enemy; finally, with a series of blows that left Kyle's sword arm aching, Rogan taught him how to block effectively.

Kyle was gasping for breath by the end of their training session. He had not exerted himself so much in years. His right arm had gone numb with fatigue and he sported a couple bruises from when he had been to slow to block. Rogan, too, was panting, although not nearly as much. He surveyed Kyle critically as the student sank to the floor, completely drained of energy.

"You're in really bad shape," Rogan said in a voice that sounded more concerned and surprised than unkind.

"Yeah," Kyle said from the floor—given the circumstances, it didn't really make sense to deny it—"yeah, I guess I am."

"Even most people who've never fought before in their lives are in better shape than you," Rogan continued in the same tone. "Do you eat well?"

"No," Kyle said frankly, "and I drink a lot."

Rogan shook his head. "Even still," he persisted in a thoughtful voice, "maybe in your world…ah, no use worrying about it. If we keep on like this you'll be fit in no time, and once you start going on missions with Nihs and Lugh you'll just keep getting stronger."

"Great," Kyle said from below him, his voice little more than a breath.

Once Rogan had peeled him off of the floor, the two went back to the bridge, where Rogan tossed Kyle a large bottle of water and then promptly began quizzing him on everything he had been taught. He seemed pleased with how much Kyle had retained.

"You have a good memory, at least," he said. "That's good. It's easier for a smart person to train their body than for a stupid person to train their mind. Besides, it's no use teaching you if you don't remember what you've been taught."

Kyle nodded at this compliment and slid into a sitting position on the floor, his back to the wall.

Kyle had been convalescing on the bridge, enjoying the darkness and the silence for half an hour when the communicator on the dashboard lit up and Lugh's voice sounded through the room.

"Hey, anyone there? Hello?"

Kyle, who had been drifting in a sea of thought, started, but Rogan went over to the control panel at once. He placed his huge hand on the crystal.

"You got the unicorn, then?"

"Yeah," Lugh's voice sounded harassed, "but it's really jumpy and Nihs' having a hard time keeping it calm. Could you lower the ramp?"

"Sure thing," Rogan said, and he pushed a couple buttons on the control panel. Kyle could hear the sound of machinery working somewhere below them.

"Thanks," Lugh said, and the crystal's glow faded.

It was about fifteen more minutes before Lugh and Nihs returned to the bridge. Lugh's hair was rumpled and his arms and legs were smeared with mud; he had removed his armor and was looking thoroughly disgruntled. His expression, however, was nothing compared to Nihs. The Kol was a tiny ball of fury when he stamped into the room. He, too, was muddy, and his expression was thunderous as he took off his wizard's sleeves and wrung them out on the floor.

"*Oi!*" Lugh said angrily, but Nihs ignored him.

"*Tesh*ur," the little creature said with vehemence, and Kyle could tell that this was not a nice statement.

"Never…again," Nihs continued, throttling his sleeves as though they had mortally offended him. "I'm going to kill whoever set that mission up…no way was that only a level thirty…da*sha!*"

"I think you two need a drink," Rogan said, laughing. "When Nihs starts swearing in Kollic you know the mission went badly." He made his way over to the kitchen and set a pot on the stove. "Hot chocolate?"

"Yes, please," Nihs and Lugh simultaneously said with conviction.

"How about you, lad?" he asked Kyle.

"Sure," Kyle said, who had now cooled down quite a bit after his training session. He could hardly believe that something as simple as hot chocolate existed in this world—or that people as patently 'tough' as these adventurers drank it.

"So," Rogan said, as he pulled down some mugs onto the counter, "let's hear the rant. What went on?"

Lugh flopped against the wall with a sigh. "First of all," he said, "it took forever to find the damn thing. It was all rainy and muddy out; we couldn't see a foot in front of our faces. We basically ended up finding it by accident."

"And it immediately bolted," Nihs added. "Twice."

"And the second time it almost ran me over," Lugh said bitterly, showing off his mud-spattered clothes.

"It was still nervous as anything even after I managed to charm it," Nihs went on. "We had to move at a snail's pace all the way back to the ship, and then getting it to climb the ramp…ugh."

While they had been talking, Rogan had filled their four mugs (Nihs' looking like an eggcup) from a pot on the stove, and returned to the center of the room, passing their drinks around.

"Thanks," Kyle said, and he took a sip. He realized instantly that hot chocolate in Loria was not quite the same as hot chocolate on Earth. Though it was predictably richly sweet, it also had a spicy, burning aftertaste that made it feel as though a fire had been lit all around him. It was shocking at first and slightly off-putting, but Kyle felt the taste growing on him as he continued drinking. He felt himself becoming pleasantly drowsy as he listened to Nihs and Lugh harp about their mission.

"And how was *your* day today?" Lugh asked him brightly at one point, cutting Nihs off.

"Pretty good, I guess," he replied sleepily. "Rogan taught me about swords."

Rogan guffawed. "He seems to have some decent natural talent," he said appraisingly, "even though he's horribly unfit—sorry, Kyle, but it's the truth."

"No offence taken."

"Anyway, I'm thinking he'd do best as a fighter. I was considering archer, but—"

"I don't like archers," Lugh said, "they're expensive."

"Yes," Rogan agreed, "and none of us are very good at archery. It's not a job where it pays to be mediocre, and we can't teach him to be any better than that."

"Yes, fighter is best," Nihs agreed, "apart from the fact that both soldier and warrior are trickier styles, we have the most equipment for a fighter lying around."

"I think you should try teaching him some magic, as well," Rogan told him. "Firstly to see if he can even do it, and secondly because it never hurts to understand how it works, even if he doesn't use it himself."

Nihs let out a breath in such a way that suggested that he was less than thrilled at the prospect of attempting to teach Kyle magic. He agreed, however, adding that if it turned out that Kyle exploded when he tried to do magic, it would be better to find out sooner than later.

Kyle was too tired, and too elated at the idea of learning magic, to be bothered by this jibe. He finished his hot chocolate, which had only tasted better and better as time went on, and then spent a moment or two staring at the sky through the front window.

"How long is it until morning, do you reckon?" he asked.

Lugh went over to the dashboard, apparently to check a clock on it. "S'bout three and a half hours until sunrise. Why, thinking of turning in?"

"Yeah," Kyle said honestly.

"Good idea," Nihs piped up. "Hopefully you'll wake up at a half decent hour and you can start synchronizing yourself with the passage of time here."

Kyle muzzily nodded in agreement. He had just realized that time probably worked differently on Loria, but was too tired to get into another conversation on the topic. He bade the three of them goodnight and shuffled off to the bathroom. After brushing his teeth with his blue toothbrush (he had made a point of remembering the color as Nihs had instructed), he went to his room and flopped on the bed. He was so tired that he didn't even have time to get comfortable before he fell asleep.

One year older, an entire ten months of kindergarten under his belt, six-year-old Kyle was now facing a new trial: first grade.

Once he had gotten used to it, kindergarten had not been so bad. He had had a couple tiffs with his fellow students, many of whom Kyle found rude, loud, mean, or any combination thereof, but he had made a couple of friends as well, the quieter kids, who sat in the corners of the room when everyone else was playing. Kyle had taken immediately to Quentin, an extremely shy, blonde boy who had turned out be to quite smart; he did everything with gravity and calculation, from his schoolwork to his playing. Alex had light-brown hair cut into a bouncy mop on his head; he was louder than both Kyle and Quentin, and had a tendency to get overexcited, but he admired Kyle greatly and so usually followed the latter's lead.

Kyle himself was a serious, intelligent young boy whose black hair contrasted sharply with his pale skin; his blue eyes were piercing and once he got used to the ropes of kindergarten, he had moved about the class with more purpose and surety than any other student. Kyle had found to his joy that what was taught in kindergarten was not hard at all; his mother had already gone through much of it with him at home, and everything else was laughably easy anyway. He soon grew a reputation among his fellow students for being one of the smartest in the class, along with Quentin and a quiet girl with dark brown hair whose name Kyle could never remember. The other students often went to him for help with their work, and he was always one of the first to finish and have free time to play.

Despite his last year's success, all the old fears were cropping up in Kyle's mind with the advent of first grade. After all, kindergarten hadn't been *real* school. He asked his mother often about school, and her answers always followed the same pattern:

"It'll be just like kindergarten. Don't you worry about it; remember how much fun kindergarten was? You were one of the best students there. It'll be the same in grade one, you'll see. You'll do wonderfully."

Kyle was somewhat reassured by his mother's confidence, though a dark cloud of doubt still floated in his mind.

When the first day of school finally came, Kyle followed the new path to his classroom, this time in a group of students herded by their teacher. He had approached this situation with no small amount of trepidation, but his mother had assured him that as long as he kept an eye on the teacher, he'd be fine.

He did so, but once he got inside there arose a problem he hadn't foreseen. The hallways were much more crowded than the outside, and Kyle still could not recognize his new classmates. He followed the line for a while, but then a couple people passed in front of him and he suddenly didn't know where it had gone.

He panicked. He looked around himself wildly, all the confidence gained from a year of kindergarten gone. He was lost, there was no doubt about it. They had come in through a different door than the one he had used a year ago, and this hallway was completely alien to him. The ceiling seemed higher, the people taller, and the hallway bigger.

Someone jostled him, and said, "Get out of the way, dork."

This simple insult was enough to sap every last ounce of confidence and hope from Kyle. Crying openly, he shuffled quickly out of the way of the press of people; chattering students, serious-looking teachers. He reached the wall and wedged himself in the corner between it and a row of lockers, determined to make himself as small as possible. He didn't know what to do except stand there and cry, waiting for the hallway to empty of such frightening people.

It finally did after what seemed like an eternity. Kyle poked his head out of his corner cautiously. He stepped into the middle of the hallway, hiccoughing.

There was no one there. The silence was at least better than the loud students, but now Kyle was faced with another problem—he had no idea which classroom was his.

Kyle felt himself starting to cry again as he contemplated his options. He could try knocking on a random classroom door and asking the teacher inside, but as soon as he thought of it, he imagined himself knocking on the door of an eighth grade classroom only for it to be answered by a grim-faced, unfriendly teacher. She would scowl at him for interrupting the class, and the older students would laugh at him, and he would have to run away…

What would happen to him if he just waited here? What if he missed the whole day of school? Probably everyone would have made friends already, and learned plenty of things. He'd arrive in class the next day, and no one would want to talk to him, and he would be lost while the class built on what they had learned.

As he sobbed, stuck in the agony of indecision, he heard footsteps coming down the hallway towards him. He froze like a deer in the headlights. Who could it be? A teacher? Maybe they could tell him where his class was…or maybe they'd be angry with him for being where he didn't belong! Should be hide?

Before he could do anything, however, the owners of the footsteps rounded the corner in front of him. It was two grade eight boys, who were walking down the hallway side by side, laughing.

Kyle cried and cringed. He could think of nothing to do.

As they approached him, however, one of them suddenly stopped and said, "Hey, are you all right?"

Kyle looked up blearily at the tall boy in front of him. The boy's expression was concerned.

"You lost, little guy?" he asked, leaning down at him.

Kyle was too petrified with fear to do anything but nod minutely, saying, "Uh huh."

He heard a sigh above him and the boy he was talking to knelt down in front of him.

"Do you know what number your classroom is?"

"No," said Kyle in a voice the size of an ant.

"How about your teacher's name?"

"I can't remember," Kyle said again, starting to cry even harder.

"Hey, chill out…what grade are you in?"

Kyle held up one tiny finger.

"Okay. What's your name?"

"Kyle," he mumbled.

"Okay, Kyle. Follow me, squirt. We'll help you find your class."

Kyle was too terrified and too distraught to argue, so he plodded along behind the two boys, who were now talking quietly.

"Grade one…that's either Miss Baker or Mrs. Moreland, right?"

"I think so."

They made a left turn and one of the boys knocked on a classroom door. A small woman with blonde hair answered the door.

"Hey, Miss Baker…we've got a lost kid here. Is he one of yours? His name's Kyle."

"Oh, yes!" Miss Baker said at once, stepping out of the classroom to look at Kyle. "We were wondering where he was, he was the only one absent…how do you do?" she asked Kyle.

Kyle just sniffled and looked at her.

"Oh, you poor dear…don't worry, you're here now."

"Am I in trouble?" Kyle asked tearfully.

Miss Baker laughed warmly. "No, of course not. Here, come inside, we were just settling down. Thank you so much," she added to the eighth graders that had brought Kyle in.

"No problem," the one who had questioned Kyle said. "I remember I was scared shi—I mean, sorry—really scared when I was in grade one."

"Thank you," Kyle mumbled, looking at his feet.

Miss Baker looked impressed that Kyle had thought of saying thank you all on his own.

"Don't worry about it, squirt," the older kid said, ruffling his hair. The two boys left, leaving Kyle with Miss Baker.

"Come on in, sweetie," she motioned, holding the door for him.

Feeling much better than he had all day, as though the hair tousling by an older student had somehow blessed him, Kyle stepped into the classroom.

Kyle awoke with the strange feeling that reality had dropped away from him. For a moment, all seemed black, and he floated in limbo. Was he really back in first grade, being led to his new classroom by a couple of kind-hearted eighth graders?

But reality came back to him, and his room seemed to materialize around him. Of course he wasn't. The truth was much stranger; he was stranded in an alternate universe, and in his room on the airship *Ayger*.

Kyle reflected on this as he swung himself out of bed. He thought it strange how quickly he had adapted to the fact that he was now in another world. He had eaten a sandwich made of bwah meat and had a sword fighting lesson with a Minotaur, and yet somehow these facts did not seem so strange anymore.

He tramped his way to the bridge to find that morning had come, golden light filtered through the picture window and Nihs was again piloting the *Ayger*. Clearly they had taken off at some point during the night.

Nihs twisted around at the sound of Kyle's footsteps.

"Morning," he said jovially.

"Is it morning?" Kyle asked, yawning.

"Yep," the Kol said in a satisfied tone. "Looks like you're starting to adapt."

"Great," Kyle said, then asked the question he had thought of a couple hours earlier, "how does time work in this world?"

"Well, you see, it goes forward, and things happen in it."

"Very funny. I mean, obviously you have a sun, and I guess the world orbits around it, but how do you measure time? Do you have hours and months and years and stuff?"

While they were talking, Lugh climbed the stairs from the observation deck. He nodded once in acknowledgement to Kyle and then listened silently to their conversation, freezer in hand.

"A good question," Nihs admitted. "Let me think. Well, we have seconds, which pass like..." he tapped the wheel rhythmically.

"Sounds the same as our seconds," Kyle said.

"Well, sixty of them make a minute, and sixty of *those* make an hour."

"All the same as our world," said Kyle, amazed that this was so.

Nihs felt the same way. "Interesting," he said, "very interesting. Well, there are thirty-two hours in a day, two periods of light and two of darkness, about eight hours each. That changes depending on the time of year."

"Okay, that's new, we only have twenty-four hours in one day, and it's only light and dark once."

"Ah, so your world must rotate along a linear axis," Nihs said enthusiastically. Kyle had noticed that Nihs tended to drop his sardonic manner whenever they were discussing the differences between their worlds.

"Yeah…well, I guess so…why, how does your world rotate?"

"Oh, yes!" Nihs said, slapping his forehead. "Of course you've never heard that story…ah, it's so easy to forget that you know nothing about this world."

"Why? What story is it?"

Nihs bobbed his head back and forth. "It's not so much a story as part of one. Basically, at one point in this world's past, about a thousand years ago, the world was hit by a gigantic meteor." He jerked his head back towards the map of Loria. "You can still see the impact crater on the world map…it hit in the northwest of Westia. It threw up a cloud of dust that blocked out the sun for years. It was the toughest and the most desperate time in the whole world's history. Most of the races almost died out, and then there was a huge war…but I'm getting into the part of the story that doesn't matter. Basically, this world used to have a normal orbit, but it was thrown off by the meteor's impact. Now the world spins on itself in a figure-eight pattern. The sun crosses over the equator twice each day, and this cross moves east across the world as the year goes on. That's why each day has two periods of light to it."

"Wow," said Kyle. His gaze travelled back to the map. He looked at the large snowy shape of Westia, and its gray, mountainous northwest. He tried to imagine a meteor big enough to change the orbit of an entire planet.

"So…the days are different. How about weeks, months and years?" he asked.

"I don't know about weeks," Nihs said, "but there are eight months to the year that correspond to the position of the sun's cross relative to the center of the world; there are thirty-four days to each month. Sometimes we refer to seventeen days as a half-month."

"Close enough to our world. We have twelve months and there's about thirty days in each one."

"Funny, isn't it," Nihs said, scratching his chin, "how we have similar measures of time, and even the same names for them, but they're slightly different to each other."

"Yeah, it's wild," Lugh said, again demonstrating his complete lack of interest in the subject.

But Nihs' comment had made Kyle think of something else, something that he couldn't believe he hadn't thought of before. "Hang on, what language are you two speaking?"

Lugh and Nihs looked understandably quite surprised.

"We're not speaking any language," Nihs said. "We're just speaking."

Kyle didn't know what to think of this. "What? You can't be speaking without a language. That's what speaking *is*."

Nihs looked shocked. "So in your world," he asked in amazement, "there's no such thing as speaking without language?"

"Of course not. So what do you call what you're speaking now?"

Nihs shook his head. "It's not *called* anything, except for talking. It's because it's not a real language...it's just desire for communication put into the form of sound. Every member of the ten races is born with the ability to learn it. I just assumed that you had done so as well."

Try as he might, Kyle couldn't wrap his mind around this. "But how are we using the same words? I'm speaking English—the language I spoke back on Earth...I mean Terra."

"Perhaps you are," Nihs said with a shrug. "But you're in Loria now, and *we* hear something that *we* understand. It's a gift given to all the intelligent life of the world—a type of magic, I suppose you could call it."

Kyle rubbed his forehead. "Okay, so magic makes it so that everyone in this world can understand everyone else. That makes sense, I guess."

"You shouldn't question it so much," Nihs said a tad reprovingly. "Just be thankful that it works for you as well as it works for us. I suppose that's a good sign, really—more proof that you have the ability to adapt to this world."

Kyle nodded, deciding to let it drop, especially in light of the minor explosion Nihs had had before about the ozone layer. "Right," he said. "So, where are we headed next?"

"Oh, that's right, we haven't told you yet," Lugh said. "Guess what? A free contract just opened up in a town near here. The adventurer's guild estimated the level at anywhere from ten to forty, which means that you'll be able to come with us this time!"

Kyle felt a little thrill of both eagerness and fear. He wanted to go with the others, to find out about the world, and to prove himself...but he couldn't help but worry that Lugh's confidence in him was misplaced. He stopped himself, however, from asking about it, as his dream about his six-year-old self swam to the front of his mind:

"*Am I in trouble?*"

"*No, of course not!*"

It was a childish thing to ask, he decided. If they thought he was ready, then he would have to make himself ready. He wouldn't be a liability to this group. Instead, he asked, "What's a free contract?"

"It means that as many adventurers can take it on as they want, like a group effort kind of thing. Normally missions are reserved for the group who takes them on first; other groups have to wait for a deadline or until the first gives up. A free contract is first come, first serve, the more the merrier. Sometimes there's no reward but what can be gained from the mission itself."

"So what's this one going to be?"

"A goblin settlement's been discovered in an abandoned mine near this village," Lugh explained. "A bunch of adventurers are gathering up to flush them out before they start causing trouble."

"Why, what trouble?"

"Nothing yet," said Lugh. "Goblins live in all the little nooks and crannies of the world, right? Caves and such. Loria's full of caves—legends say that it's possible to travel all around the world without ever seeing the sun. But that's where you get some of the nastiest monsters—and creatures like goblins are always popping up where you don't expect. Once they get a foothold in a place like this mine, they'll spend a bit of time building up their defenses and whatnot, and then they'll start bugging the people living in settlements nearby. They steal stuff, mostly, like food and small animals, but if you don't get rid of them, before too long they'll actually start attacking people."

"So we're going to go into the mine and just kill a bunch of goblins?" Kyle asked.

"Got it in one," Lugh said brightly, then catching Kyle's look, he said, "hey, don't feel bad for them. They're sneaky, mean little bastards, and if we don't do something about them they'll do something about us."

"Lugh is right," Nihs said from the wheel. "Not only that, but no matter how many goblins you kill, there's always more of them. Adventurers have tried to extinguish them before, and it's never worked. Empathy is an admirable trait in a warrior, but you can't let it get in the way of the job in front of you."

Kyle nodded mutely. Though Lugh had already described what being an adventurer entailed, it jarred him to hear the two of them talking about what sounded like mild genocide with such lightheartedness.

"And with that," Lugh said grandly, stepping over to the kitchen to deposit his empty glass, "would anyone like a fried egg?"

"Hah. Sure," Kyle said, thinking that a fried egg was likely to be safe no matter what crazy animal it came from.

As Lugh performed some complex alchemy to get the egg frying (Kyle could see from its size why Lugh had only offered him one), and a piece of toast grilling, Kyle asked Nihs, "So how far away is this village we're headed to?"

"A few hours' flight from here. Everyone who shows up is going to spend the night preparing in the village and then attack together in the morning. Speaking of which," he directed at Lugh, "after he's done eating, you should take him down to the dojo and give him another training session."

"Sure thing," Lugh said brightly, lifting an egg-flipper in acknowledgement.

After Kyle ate (the egg, apparently from a birdlike monster called a gricks, was quite good, if a bit powdery), the two went the dojo, once more leaving Nihs lamenting on the bridge by himself.

"He really doesn't care about being left alone," Lugh said with a smile, as they descended the stairs. "He's just being a pain."

While they were crossing the lower level, Kyle instinctively turned his head in the direction of the stables. It had just occurred to him that somewhere on the ship was a captured unicorn. Despite himself, Kyle felt tremendously curious; he couldn't believe that such a creature could be so close.

Lugh caught his distraction. "Want to see the unicorn?" he asked, smiling.

Kyle tried to act offhand. "Sure."

Lugh laughed and led him along the corridor, talking as they went.

"We won't be able to get too close to it, not without Nihs there to distract it. They love magic, see—everything from Elfland does. They're neat creatures, but they're kind of unpredictable, and they spook easily. Okay, here we are."

Kyle could feel a tangible change in the atmosphere as they approached the stable where the unicorn was being kept. The air seemed to be thicker and darker, as though saturated with some odd energy. When they finally got close to the stable itself, Kyle's mouth fell open.

He had never been a huge unicorn enthusiast back on Earth, the creatures being as patently 'girly' as they were. But this creature was unlike anything he had ever seen on a primary school girl's lunchbox. It was a horse with a horn—that much was obvious, but at the same time it seemed to be something more. The creature's coat was a milky white; its mane, tail, and hair around its hooves were darker. They shimmered in the dim light of the small stable, shifting and changing color in an eye-watering way. The horn upon its head was three feet long, and looked like it was made from iridescent mother-of-pearl—white a first glance, but at different angles appearing to shift through all the colors of the rainbow.

The creature eyed them warily as they looked, whinnying. It was beautiful, there was no doubt about that, but it was also somewhat frightening. The air around the unicorn seemed somehow warped by its presence. Its outline glowed, and Kyle felt himself feeling strangely woozy after being near to it for too long. It caught Kyle's eye, and he felt himself being pulled toward its gaze, as though the unicorn's pupils were holes that he had fallen through into darkness.

"Interesting creature, huh?" Lugh whispered.

"Yeah," Kyle whispered back, mesmerized.

"I've never been to Elfland," Lugh went on, "but apparently everything there is like this. You can just feel the magic coming off of it in waves…anyway, we should probably get on with your training. We'll have to come down here again later and feed the thing."

They left the stables and moved on to the dojo. Kyle couldn't believe the difference in the atmosphere—the light seemed stark and bright, and the air thin.

"It's not often we use this place anymore," Lugh said. "I've forgotten we had all this stuff. What sword did you use yesterday with Rogan?"

Kyle rummaged around before he found the same thin, dark gray blade as before. He held it up for Lugh to inspect.

"Hm, a slim sword. I can understand why Rogan chose that one for you, seeing as none of us had seen you fight before...but you'll quickly outgrow that one." He perused the weapon racks and selected another sword, also crosswoven, slightly shorter with a thicker blade.

"A middle sword," he said, handing it to Kyle. "Still pretty light, and with a lot more cutting power than a slim. You'll tucker yourself out quickly using this one, but you'll get stronger faster, and that's what we need right now."

Kyle took it, and indeed felt the weight of this weapon much more keenly than the other.

Lugh, meanwhile, had taken a pair of round shields from a nearby pile. They were made of wood, but their frames were metal and they, like the swords, showed distinct signs of modern improvements applied to medieval weaponry.

"Fighters don't often use shields," Lugh said, as he handed Kyle one, "seeing as their job is to be fast and hard-hitting, not weighed down with a giant hunk of metal—that's a soldier's job. But, we want you to learn as much as you can as fast as you can, and the same goes for building muscle. Personally I find dual weapon training to be a waste of time in rookies like you, so the best way to make sure you're not lopsided when you finally start beefing up is to get you to carry a shield while we're training."

Kyle adjusted the shield on his arm, following Lugh's instructions, and then they set to sparring.

Lugh built on some of the things that Rogan had taught him, and added a few tips on how to use the shield correctly. Kyle could already tell that he was improving, though he did tire very quickly with both the shield and the new sword in hand.

At one point, Kyle's arms were aching so much that Lugh actually knocked the sword out of his hand with a fairly weak blow, so they took a brief hiatus, Lugh giving Kyle some water from a sink at the back of the room. He talked constantly even while they were breaking, in part of the different techniques they had gone over, and partly of what to expect in various real fighting situations.

"Having straight-up strength is good," he said at one point, "but knowing your limits is just as important. A big part of being an adventurer is picking your battles and recognizing danger that you won't be able to handle. When we go on this mission tomorrow, you shouldn't be in any danger *unless* you put yourself in it. For adventurers of our level of skill, caution is the most important thing. Even when you get stronger, it never pays to get cocky."

"Trust me, I'm not going to get cocky," said Kyle, struggling to force his words out his parched throat. "I'll probably be in the back throwing up."

"Don't sell yourself short," Lugh said seriously. "Rogan was right, you might not be too tough now but you're learning fast. I think you'll make a fine fighter once you've trained up a bit—and once the effects of your *reursis* wear off completely."

They rested a little longer, and then resumed sparring. Kyle had gotten a minor second wind, and his will to improve drove him on through his fatigue.

"You're getting better!" Lugh called to him over the clash of sword-on-shield. A second later, he sped up and hit harder, clearly holding himself back less in light of this improvement.

Kyle was taken aback by Lugh's sudden burst of strength, but he soon found his own body quickening to match the new challenge. It was extremely wearing and his whole body ached, but he pressed on, determined to keep fighting until he collapsed.

Then a strange thing happened. Acting on a sudden strong impulse, Kyle jumped back out of the way and held his sword out to the side at arm's length. A strange glowing filter passed in front of his eyes and his mind started buzzing. Time seemed to slow down. He felt himself twirl the blade once in his fingers, and then dash at Lugh with a speed he didn't know he possessed. Lugh's eyes widened and he hastened to raise his shield, reinforcing it with his other hand. When Kyle's blow landed on it, it was with a resounding crash that shot sparks and nearly threw Lugh off of his feet.

Trembling with adrenalin, Kyle lowered his weapons, incredulous.

"What just happened?" he asked, panting.

Lugh, however, was pleased. He threw his sword and shield to the ground and sat down, massaging his wrist.

"Your very first gaiden strike!" he said brightly, also breathing heavily. "Congratulations!"

"What...?"

"A gaiden strike is like... a releasing of combat energy in the form of a blow. See—well, Nihs will go into this more when he teaches you about magic—but magic is all around and inside us, right? And it's affected by everything that happens nearby. The magic that's around people engaged in combat sort of...aligns itself to make itself more warlike, if you know what I mean. Combat energy, in other words," he scratched his chin, "it's hard to describe to someone who doesn't understand how magic works, but basically this combat energy builds up in you as you fight, like, like—"

"Static?" Kyle suggested.

"Yeah, sort of like that. Well, once it builds up past a certain point it's dying to be released, and so it forces its way out of your body in the form of a gaiden strike. It takes some getting used to, but you learn how to control them and release them in ways that benefit you. It's just a part of combat, like everything else."

"Wow," Kyle said, sinking to the ground. The gaiden strike had set his blood boiling, but the rest of his body overruled his sudden urge to keep fighting. "Why did I spin my sword before I hit you?"

"That's part of what a gaiden strike is. It's hard to explain, but—think of it as almost like a spell instead of just another sword swing, right? It's a release of magic, and it only works under the right conditions. Magic likes a good show, and without doing anything special before a gaiden strike there's nothing to make it—well, special."

"'Magic likes a good show'? You talk about it as though it were alive."

"Well, it made us, didn't it?" Lugh said.

"But still—"

"Look," Lugh said patiently, "I don't know how things work in your world, but our world is completely controlled by magic, right? Once you understand how magic behaves, you'll see why things like this make sense. Granted, I don't get it entirely either; that's something you want to ask Nihs about. He's always going on about how all the magic in the world is connected and how what people think can change how the world works."

Kyle considered this. "That's really weird," he said.

"You get used to it. Think you're done for today?"

"For now, anyway," Kyle said gratefully, glad that Lugh had been the one to make the suggestion.

They threw their equipment down and walked (or in Kyle's case, staggered) back to the bridge, where they found Nihs just as they had left him, at the wheel of the *Ayger*. The tiny Kol's head was swaying back and forth slowly, and he was singing quietly what was obviously a song in another language. He stopped, however, when he heard Lugh and Kyle enter the room.

"How did it go?" he asked, flipping the autopilot on and plopping down on his stool.

"Pretty well," Lugh told him, heading over to the kitchen to pour them some drinks. "Kyle got a gaiden strike on me."

"Really?" Nihs sounded impressed. "I wouldn't have expected that so soon from someone who reacts to magic so strangely—if at all."

"Could it be that I'm adapting to your world?" Kyle asked.

Nihs regarded him thoughtfully. "That may be the case. I wonder…could your nuclear soul be converting itself into a magical one as a reaction to your new world? Oh, I *wish* I could sense auras!"

"Maybe we'll meet someone in Reno who can," Lugh said. He brought Kyle a huge glass of ice water, who accepted it gratefully.

"I don't doubt that we will," Nihs said. "The question is, would we be able to trust them with Kyle's secret?"

Lugh shrugged. "So I think you should try to squeeze one magic lesson in before we land today. Don't worry," he said to Kyle, "it won't be tiring…in fact, it'll probably give you an opportunity to sleep."

"Oh, very funny," Nihs said scathingly, "you should be a comedian. *Tish*." The word was almost like a hiss.

"I know what that one means," Lugh said accusingly.

They chatted on the bridge for a while more, Kyle recovering from his training session. Rogan had apparently mentioned the idea of computers to Nihs over the communicator while Lugh and Kyle had been sparring, and so Kyle spent the better part of an hour attempting to explain them in detail to Nihs. It was oddly amusing, if a little frustrating.

"I still don't understand how all those things can be accomplished with only on-and-off switches," the Kol said irritably at one point.

Kyle passed his hand across his forehead. "I don't know everything there is to know about it, not many people do. But it all comes down to figuring out how to represent different types of data."

"But converting say, a picture into a string of binary digits must be horribly inefficient," Nihs said, demonstrating what Kyle thought to be a frightening intellect. "If each...what did you call them? The dots of light that make up an image?"

"Pixels."

"Pixels, right...if each pixel can be any of, say, ten thousand different shades, and each one is only a fraction of an inch across...then a single picture would take..." he nodded his head slightly and stared into space as he performed some mental calculation, but Kyle, who was more familiar with computers, beat him to it.

"Several million bits to store, yeah," he said. "But that's just the thing. Because of how computers work, that inefficiency doesn't matter; a couple million bits is nothing. You could store a hundred books' worth of data on a card *this* big," he said, and held up a thumb and forefinger about a centimeter apart.

"I won't say I'm not impressed," Nihs admitted. "Technology like that is unheard of in Loria."

"And to think that there's nothing but humans in his world," Lugh pointed out. "No Kol or Oblihari to help them figure it out."

Nihs nodded silently, his expression distant.

Kyle, who by now could read the signs, laughed. "I bet you're dying to get your hands on a computer now, aren't you?" he mocked.

Nihs stuck his tongue out at him.

They sailed until what Kyle estimated to be late afternoon, eating lunch on the bridge and making idle chatter. At one point, Lugh turned to Kyle. "Think you could handle some magic training now?"

Kyle gulped down the bite of what was approximately a savory doughnut that he had been chewing. Excitement welled in him. "Of course!" he said eagerly.

Nihs made a small sigh, and then set the wheel on autopilot.

"All right, then," he said, and vaulted down from his stool. "Do you know where we're going?" he asked Lugh.

"Nah, I think I'll just do circles over this valley until we run out of fuel and crash." Lugh grinned, taking the wheel and turning the autopilot off.

"You slay me," Nihs said in the most un-humorous voice he could muster. "Let's go," he said to Kyle, who followed him down to the dojo.

As soon as they had entered the now-familiar room to Kyle, Nihs strode into the center of it and wheeled around to face him, arms crossed.

"Magic," Nihs said, and Kyle caught a glint in his eye. "Magic is the driving force behind our universe. It runs our machines, it gives us our powers, but most importantly, it makes up every last one of us—our bodies, our minds, the ground on which we stand, our food, our hopes, and our dreams. Once you understand magic, you understand the world. That being said, people who have spent their lifetime studying magic have yet to discover all of its secrets. By comparison, the time I have to teach you about it is pitifully short. All we can do is run through the basics as fast as we can, and look bit at how magic is used in combat. Hopefully this will be enough to give you the edge you'll need to survive in the adventuring world. Sit down," he added, though it was more of a consideration than an order.

Kyle noticed at once that Nihs was speaking very fast, and as though he were a professor in a lecture hall who had memorized his subject. He sat, leaning back against a pile of shields and armor, determined to understand everything that Nihs said.

"Now, many rules and behaviors regarding magic have been

unearthed over the years, but there is one rule that dominates them all, and, to those that truly understand it, helps to explain every other theory in the world. The rule is: there are no rules."

Kyle snorted before he could stop himself. Nihs shot him a scathing look.

"Sorry," he said at once, "I'm sure it makes sense, it just caught me by surprise."

Nihs sniffed, apparently mollified, and went on.

"It seems a simple enough statement at first, but as you study magic further, you'll realize just how profound it really is. You see, magic by nature is wild and unpredictable; we try to nail it down with philosophy and science, but the truth is, it only follows these rules when it feels like it. *Any* rule has the potential to be broken at any time. "Now, if magic as a substance is defined as absolutely anything present in the known universe, an ever-changing and ever-adaptable mass of energy, then what is magic as an act?

"Magic as an act is defined as the projection of a desire of the caster, a request for the universe to change voiced loudly enough that the universe obeys, rearranging itself to the caster's will. When you cast a spell, you are doing nothing more complicated than asking the universe to change a small part of itself—say, a fire you want lit or a wound you need healed. If your will is strong enough and provide the universe with enough energy to make the change, the change will be made."

"Hang on," said Kyle, "that sounds pretty abstract. You talk about making a request to the universe like it's an old pal you're trying to bum money from. Not even your world could work that way. Things can't just change, can they? The power has to come from *some*where."

"I can see you're more of a practical person," Nihs said. "Some people are happy to believe that the universe is simply receptive to their demands; they realize that there probably is some scientific basis to what they're doing, but they don't bother to understand it."

"Isn't that a pretty big liability?" Kyle asked.

Nihs put a hand to his forehead. "It *can* be," he said, "but you're forgetting the most important rule already. *There are no rules.* The people who don't bother with the scientific side of magic do so because they believe—and rightly so—that it's not as important as the *magical* side of magic."

Kyle sighed, trying to take this in. "So what you're saying is that magic makes sense scientifically, but only *after* it makes sense magically."

"Yes!" said Nihs, clapping his hands. "I'm glad you've managed to grasp that so quickly. That being said," he continued, now pacing and waving his hands enthusiastically, "a big part of being able to weave magic is conviction. If you don't believe that it's going to work, it won't. So, in order to satisfy your imagination, I'll describe the process of casting a spell, seen from a scientific viewpoint.

"I've already told you that anything in this universe is comprised of a combination of any of these three: body, mind and soul. Animals, monsters, and members of the races such as ourselves have all three." He jabbed a finger at Kyle's chest. "Your body is your physical self, composed of the four elements." He did the same to Kyle's forehead. "Your mind is your mental self, composed of electrical signals that travel through your body and grant you intelligence." Finally, he made an airy, round motion with both hands that seemed to encompass Kyle's entire reclining form. "And your soul is your magical self, an aura of particles aligned to your core essence, a magical blueprint of Kyle Campbell in distilled form."

"Except that I might not have one," Kyle couldn't stop himself from saying.

Nihs chewed his lip, staring at Kyle through narrowed eyes.

"Perhaps," he said, "although now I think that the truth is likely far more complicated. I don't think you would be able to survive in this world if you truly didn't have a soul. Besides, when I gave you a magic infusion, you reacted to it poorly, but your body accepted it in the end. I don't know if you'll be able to perform magic yet, but I'm starting to become hopeful that you're adapting to our world."

It was not the first time that Nihs had mentioned being hopeful about Kyle's future in magic, and by now Kyle was dying to try some for himself. The threat of experiencing the same burning sensation he had encountered earlier didn't bother him in the least. He reasoned that he had lived through it twice, and would do so again if it meant being able to attempt some magic.

Nihs, however, did not seem too pressed to move on to the practical part of their lesson. He resumed pacing, and recommenced his monologue.

"Magic as it is used by the races, both in and out of combat, is grouped into four main categories, much like those that study it. There is one category that corresponds to each of the three components of living beings, as well as one that involves control over living beings themselves.

"Elemental magic is the magic of the physical world. This is the type of magic that I, as a mage, specialize in. The four sub-categories of this type correspond to the four cardinal, or primary, elements: fire, air, water and earth. All physical matter in the universe is composed of some combination of these four elements. Does that make sense?"

"Yeah, I know about the whole fire-water-air-earth thing," Kyle said. "That's how alchemists in our world used to think the world worked."

"You're implying that they were wrong," Nihs said.

"They were. There's something like a hundred and thirteen elements discovered now, and chemists keep discovering more."

"Interesting," Nihs said, tapping his chin. "It's been conclusively proven that our world is in fact based around these four elements, so it's not a matter of our research being behind yours...but it's odd, don't you find, that our elemental theory shows up in your world's past?"

"Yeah, it is, but that doesn't really tell us much, does it?"

"I don't know," Nihs said, sounding pleased at this. "I think that it must be significant *some*how...but that can wait."

"Yes," Kyle agreed quickly, eager to move on.

"So that's the physical side of things. The mental side of things is covered by a domain of magic called mysticism—the three sub-categories are time, space and sense. They refer to the different ways in which the mind observes and documents the world; in other words, how any one object or event in the universe can be distinguished from the others."

Kyle said, "As in, when it happens, where it happens—"

"Yes, and how it is experienced and observed by the universe around it. You'll find that any event can be completely described by knowing all of these things.

"Mysticism gives you power over the state of reality as well as over the minds of others. By manipulating time and space a mystic can teleport and transplant objects; by manipulating sense they can alter the perceptions of others. This type of magic is not as immediately rewarding as elementalism, and it is much more difficult, but it can be extremely effective in the hands of the right mystic and in the right situation."

"I can imagine," Kyle said fearfully. He now fervently hoped that Nihs would teach him some way of defending himself against magic. The thought of an enemy being able to mess with his senses was quite disturbing.

"Onto the third type. This is magic that affects the soul, and as such, it is much less regimented than the other types. This is the magic of magic itself, not magic seen through the filter of the physical or mental world. It is called color magic. This is where some more magical theory comes into play, so try to pay attention.

"I've said that magic affects and is affected by the world around it. You see, at any given point in time a magical particle possesses certain properties; these properties can be changed, however, when it is exposed to other, stronger or more numerous particles. Over the years, scholars have unearthed two important theories related to this phenomenon.

"Firstly, magic remembers. Even if a particle changes into a hundred different things in a day, it remembers each and every one…and it remembers those forms that had more power behind them or that it spent more time being.

"Secondly, magic communicates. It seems that magic particles can affect each other even from a great distance. Scholars believe, in fact, that all magic across the entire universe is connected. Now, put those three things together, and see if you can tell me why color has so much power in this world."

Kyle thought about it. Old problem-solving skills that he had developed as a computer programmer started firing up. *What do we know…what are we trying to prove…*

Nihs had said that color was powerful in Loria. Why would that be? All magic affected other magic, everywhere, and it remembered what it had been before…

"What does it mean when magic remembers being a certain thing more than others?" Kyle asked Nihs.

Nihs smiled. "It means that it's more predisposed to become that thing again; it takes less energy to become something that it remembers strongly."

So memory had something to do with it. But if one particle remembered something in particular, then wouldn't all particles? So if someone set one thing on fire, then wouldn't all magic in the entire universe want to become fire just a tiny bit more than anything else? *But, hang on…if* thoughts *were made out of magic, as well, then wouldn't what people thought affect all magic in the world?*

"Hang on," he said suddenly, "that's what Lugh meant when we were talking about my gaiden strike. He said that what people think can change reality…does that mean that people's thoughts can actually change how the entire universe works?"

"Yes, yes!" Nihs said excitedly, motioning for Kyle to continue.

"So then color…well, people think different things about different colors, right? Like, they think that black is evil and white is good…and green means life and red means love, and stuff like that. So…does that mean that, in your world, white actually *is* good because that's what people believe?"

Nihs clapped his hands once loudly and bowed.

"Well *done*," he said, "very well done. To be honest, I'm stunned. Usually you have to spoon-feed that idea to rookies. You just described the law of connotation, albeit crudely. The law states that perception can change reality, just as reality changes perception. Color has power because some of the strongest perceptions in the world involve hue: green is lucky, blue is the sky and sea, orange is wealth, red is passion…Wizards, by channeling magic of specific colors, have power over these perceptions. This gives them more adaptability than mages."

"So why don't all mages just study color magic?"

"Because it's much harder than elementalism," Nihs said. "Remember that the caster's own imagination needs to be able to visualize the magic happening. It's much easier to manipulate objects in the physical world than it is to weave colors. Our subconscious minds understand the natural world—things they can see and touch—much better than they understand connotation and common perception."

Despite Nihs' confusing and long-winded explanation, Kyle felt that he actually understood what the Kol was saying. He remembered something else, from before.

"When I got my gaiden strike on Lugh, he said something about them not working if you don't show off first—"

"Yes, that's right," Nihs said, "you probably did something with your sword before you struck him, right? You spun it around or threw it in the air?"

"Yeah, why is that?"

"It's the power of connotation. Of *course* an attack that has a lot of twirling around and flashing lights is going to be more powerful than a normal one, right? It works on the same principles as color magic. Gaiden strikes are fancier than normal attacks because that's what people—and so the universe—expects. Connotation is like a river carving a trench, understand? Every time an event unfolds in a certain way, the more likely the *next* event is to happen the same way. Finally you get such a deep trench of connotation that it's impossible for any similar event to end up anything else."

"So when you get a gaiden strike, the universe forces you to show off first?"

"Exactly. If you keep studying magic, you'll hear the word 'connotation' thrown around more times than you're comfortable with. It's because this law is one of the most important in magical study."

"Okay," Kyle said, feeling as though the worst must be over, "what's the last type of magic?"

"Well, we've covered elementalism, which is power over the physical world, mysticism, which is power over the mental world, and color magic, which is power over the spiritual world, or simply put, pure magic. As I've said, these three types correspond to the three components of a living being. The last type of magic incorporates all these—it is self-magic, or the magic of power over living beings. The three sub-categories are body, mind and spirit, and a person who studies it is generally called a healer. It is worthy of note that the term 'healer' is misleading, since self-magic grants both the ability to heal *and* to hurt others."

"So…that's it? They can heal and hurt living beings."

"Yes," said Nihs. "It may seem simple, but it is a profound and profoundly powerful branch of magic. No other user is able to so directly affect other living creatures."

Kyle rubbed his forehead. His temple was starting to throb, and his enthusiasm for magic was starting to ebb. "Okay, I get it. There are four types of magic users. What now?"

Nihs gave him a long look. "You know," he said, "there's a lot to magic. I don't know a tenth of it, and you don't know a tenth of what I know. I'm trying to fill you in on common knowledge about magic, so you'll know what other people are talking about...unless you weren't concerned about fitting in here," he added with obvious reproach.

Kyle sighed, but quietly. "I'm sorry. I just thought—"

"That it would be all lights and explosions?" Nihs asked shrewdly. "As I said, magic only relies on science when it's in the mood, and there's such a thing as an instinctive spellcaster, but I think it's important to at least understand some of the theory.

"Now, one last lesson and then we can try to get you casting. How does one cast a spell?" He turned to one of the targets hanging on the wall and narrowed his eyes. He widened his stance and drew back his arm. As he did, Kyle felt a strange pulling sensation, as though a small implosion was taking place around Nihs. A red glow seemed to surround the Kol, particularly his drawn-back hand. A moment later the glow had evolved into a ball of flame, which Nihs threw submarine-style at the target. It connected with a moderately loud *whoomph* noise, burning out a second later.

Kyle had to resist the urge to whoop. Even watching Nihs perform the magic was strangely exhilarating.

"Now," Nihs said, smoothing down his shirt, "I want to draw your attention to certain things. I'm sure you noticed a pulling feeling as I was preparing the spell, like a warm wind blowing towards me?"

"Yeah."

"That was me channeling magic. Imagine your soul as a sort of Kyle-shaped container for magic. Just as your lungs accept and filter air from your surroundings, your soul is always gathering, filtering, and releasing magic. When you cast a spell, you're accelerating this process: you open your soul wide to fill up with magic, then you align it to your desire using willpower. If done correctly, when you release it again, it'll be released in the form of the spell you wished to cast. The red glow around my body was excess magic burning itself off. You see, when magic is under pressure, it takes the path of least resistance in order to discharge, just as electricity does. The more magic you can manage to bottle up inside your soul without it releasing itself, the more impressive spells you'll be able to work."

"Sounds simple enough," said Kyle. "You build up magic, you force it to change to what you want, and then you release it again."

"More or less. That explanation will suffice for now. Now, why don't you get up, and we can see if you can actually use some magic."

This was what Kyle had been waiting for. He stood up hastily and faced the target that Nihs had attacked.

"Try to mimic what I did," said Nihs from beside him. "See if you can conjure a basic fireball and hit that target. The most important thing is to visualize. If it helps, try to imagine what I just did and supplant yourself in my place. Try to pull the magic towards you with your will…feel yourself getting hotter, feel the heat gathering itself in your hand until it bursts into flame, and then throw it at your target. Imagine it happening however you like; just find a mental image that feels natural and clicks. Go ahead," he urged, when Kyle did nothing but stare at him.

"That's really all I have to do?" he asked, a bit nervously.

"That's all."

Kyle licked his lips and faced the target once more. It had looked so easy when Nihs had done it. Now, standing upright and preparing to do it himself, Kyle merely felt rather foolish.

"Just believe that it will work," said Nihs from beside him. "Imagine what it'll feel and look like. You just saw me do it; don't let your mind convince you that it won't work."

Kyle nodded, staring the target down. *Okay*, he thought. *Uh…*

He tried to imagine a multitude of tiny particles drawn towards his presence…he remembered the warm wind that had blown around Nihs and imagined a similar one brewing about him. At first, he merely felt stupid, but then…

It started as a flicker at the edge of his vision. Then the particles *were* there—a swarm of tiny lights, like pixels on a computer screen. As they gathered around him, their light became stronger, until a red aura glowed all around him. He felt himself becoming strangely heavy, as though the air around him had grown thick, and the edges of his vision grew darker. It was bizarre and surreal—Kyle couldn't believe it was happening.

As quickly as the feeling had come, it dispersed. Kyle's vision cleared up, and the particles vanished from his vision like the aftereffects of a camera flash. He looked at Nihs inquiringly, feeling suddenly cold and exposed after the heavy feeling's departure.

"That was definitely something," Nihs said approvingly. "I felt a little pull. Try again."

And so Kyle did. *Fire, fire, fire*, he repeated to himself. The feeling swept over him more quickly this time. His vision went dark, he felt heavy, he saw the particles, and this time they did not stop, but began massing at the edges of his body, creating a red glow.

But wait, they should be building up inside me, not around me—

Even as the thought flickered through his mind, the feeling of magic building up instantly vanished. He returned to the mundane world once more.

"What happened?" asked Nihs.

Kyle briefly described his experience. "You don't think it's because I'm rejecting the magic, do you?" he finished worriedly.

Nihs shook his head. "Definitely not," he said, with such conviction that Kyle was reassured. "We already know that your self accepts magic, if a bit reluctantly. Try to imagine that the red glow is somehow saturating you with magic by being around you, like a fire heating water through a metal pot."

"Why?" Kyle asked.

"Because you've built yourself a mental block that we need to get you to bypass. You see, this is both the blessing and the curse about working magic. Your own mind sets the difficulty of what you're trying to do. It's only as hard as you imagine it is. If you find yourself trying to imagine something that doesn't seem possible, change what you're imagining."

Kyle was dubious about this, but he said nothing and started accumulating magic once more. He got once more to the red glow, and tried to imagine it giving him magic through induction…but it was as unsatisfying and as frustrating as trying to drink a thick milkshake through a thin straw. He gave up after a few seconds and released what little magic he had managed to build up.

"I thought that would help," Nihs said thoughtfully. "Okay, try to imagine that the heat is burning you up from underneath, like a real fire…"

Kyle tried again and again, constantly changing his method of visualization based on Nihs' recommendations. Some of them seemed briefly like they were going to work, but Kyle invariably failed when his concentration broke or a part of his mind convinced him that it was a lost cause. It didn't help that, as he tried more and more, he seemed not to be getting any better, and was in fact getting worse. Soon he could barely even start to gather magic before it dispelled a fraction of a second later. It was like trying to scoop up water with a sieve.

Nihs remained patient, but Kyle grew more and more irritated. He was furious that nothing specific seemed to be going wrong, and yet he was downright failing to do what Nihs had done so casually and easily before. At first he tried to convince himself that he simply couldn't use magic because of his world of origin, but after a while he was sure that it was a matter of him not being good enough. It finally ended with him yelling in frustration and flopping to the ground, seething.

Nihs regarded him, blank-faced, as he ground his teeth and swore under his breath. After a long moment, he said, "Okay, new plan. Get up."

Kyle did not move.

"I said, *get up*," and there was a snap to Nihs' voice that Kyle had never heard before. It cracked like a whip over his head, and he reluctantly stood up.

"Good. Now, forget everything I've told you. Just forget it. Don't worry about it, it's just cluttering your mind. Have you forgotten?" he asked a second later.

"Yes," Kyle said through gritted teeth.

"Good. Now, look at the target."

Kyle did so. It stared back at him inoffensively.

"Imagine yourself where the target is."

It was as though a door had opened in Kyle's mind. Vividly, he saw his own countenance appear in front of him, as clearly as though he was looking into the *Ayger's* bathroom mirror. He saw his own lank hair and his stubbly beard. He stared into his own glassy blue eyes, which glared back. He remembered how often his gaze had been bleary and bloodshot. He saw the permanent sneer on his face and the lazy posture with which he held himself.

Suddenly, rage started boiling in Kyle's chest. It set fire to his limbs and caused a red mist to descend in front of his eyes. He hated himself, he hated what he had become; he wanted to hurt himself, to punch his own stupid face, to shake himself. *No, that isn't enough…it would take a destructive blast—*

The feeling was building in him before he knew it. What had been a trickle before was now a torrent. The red mist gathered around him as he pulled great sheaves of magic towards him; the particles travelled from all over his body to build in his right hand, which he had raised above his head. They teemed over his skin like a mass of insects, all jostling for the best position. The world for him went dark. Kyle heard a ringing in his ears. His hand caught fire; a halo of flame burned all around him, but didn't harm him. And then he hurled the fire at his image thirty feet away. He watched the fireball soar through the air, crackling, until it passed through his suddenly insubstantial self and struck the target behind it.

Kyle stared at the target, dumbfounded. Light returned to his vision and the world grew mundane once more. For a second, it had become a terrible and exciting place, where fire leapt from fingertips and the impossible became possible. Normal light now seemed bland in comparison to the textured darkness of the world of magic.

Nihs, too, was staring, though at Kyle. He nodded and laughed encouragingly.

"Well done! I had a feeling that would work. So you *can* use magic, after all!"

Yes, thought a part of Kyle's mostly stunned brain, *I can use magic.* What a wonderful feeling it was to know this.

"We need to make sure that there are no side effects of your magic use, Nihs said. "Do you feel strange at all? Any pain anywhere? Can you feel that burning that you felt before?"

Kyle did not know how people usually felt after using magic, so he decided to report on everything. "I feel…fine," he said, finding that it was so. "Great, in fact," he added, grinning as he savored the feeling. It was as though every cell in his body had just been exercised and then rested instantly. Then he noticed a strange feeling in his core. "Only…"

Nihs' attention perked up.

How to describe it? "It feels sort of…round," he said, gesturing to his chest.

Nihs' eyebrows teleported upwards. "Round?" he repeated, in a tone carefully crafted to not sound mocking.

"Yeah…like a round weight in my chest, like a bowling—like a heavy ball." Kyle knew the feeling, even if he didn't know how to communicate it. It was the feeling of something that normally felt good, but that had gone slightly wrong or a little too far; it was like a masseuse that had pinched a muscle a little harder than he should have.

"A round weight," Nihs repeated again, this time looking thoughtful and slightly worried. "Does it hurt at all?"

Kyle shifted his weight around to get a better feel for the odd sensation in his chest. "Nope," he said after a moment, "just feels a little weird is all."

Nihs bit his lip. "Well, considering that and everything else, why don't we end the lesson for today. You pay attention to that weight—if anything changes at all, I want to know right away, alright?"

"Alright," Kyle said meekly.

They made their way back to the bridge, which was deserted; Lugh had apparently given up steering the *Ayger*, and so the wheel turned gently on its own.

Nihs sighed when he took in the scene on the bridge. "That man can't keep at one thing for five minutes. It's no wonder he's no good at magic." He checked their position on the *Ayger*'s map.

"We're almost there, too. Lugh would've had us in a holding pattern over the town all night if he'd had his way."

Nihs moved his stool back into position, clambered up it and touched the communicator crystal.

"Lugh? Lugh, where are you?"

A second later, Lugh's cheery voice sounded through the room. "I'm out on deck. I gather you two are done, then?"

"Yes, and our trip practically is, too. Do you plan on landing us sometime tonight?"

"All right, all right, keep your pants on. I'll be there in a second."

Nihs harrumphed, jumping down from his stool and made his way to the far side of the room. He pulled a book from a small shelf that Kyle hadn't noticed before, sat down, and browsed through it without another word.

Kyle felt it would be rude to talk to Nihs when the Kol so obviously wanted peace and quiet, so he wandered to the control panel instead, which he had never had the opportunity to examine before.

Set into the panel around the wheel were four glass rectangles that looked like small TV screens, each showing a seemingly random shot of a horizon. It was only after he caught a glint of golden wing in two of the screens that Kyle realized they showed the view from different parts of the *Ayger*.

Several other screens and dials dotted the control panel; they all seemed vaguely recognizable, and yet strangely foreign. A simple counter right next to the wheel was probably a speedometer, but what was the other strange dial next to it whose increments were not numbers, but colors of the rainbow?

"Thinking of just landing us yourself?"

Lugh's voice sounded so loud and so close to Kyle's ear that he jumped. Lugh laughed as he spun around, arms half-raised in a defensive stance.

"Not exactly the fastest reaction time," Lugh said appraisingly, as Kyle lowered his hands, blushing, "but it's nice to know that you're starting to pick up some kind of instinct. Here, I'll take that," he added, reaching past Kyle to grab the wheel.

"Soo," he said, as he switched off the autopilot and peered through the picture window, which was now becoming dark again, "how did the training go?"

"I'm not sure," Kyle admitted. "I don't know how quickly people usually pick up magic."

"Good point," Lugh agreed. "Hey, Nihs, how did Kyle do?"

Nihs had not looked up from his book since opening it, and he did not react now. His tiny face was set in concentration and he held the book extremely close to him, as if the proximity would allow him to absorb whatever information the book held.

Lugh shook his head. "I swear, when he gets in the zone it's like he's on another planet—OI! NIHS!"

Kyle expected Nihs to jump and look up immediately, but it was still a painfully slow process to watch the Kol tear his eyes away from the book as though they were bound together.

"Yes?" he said after three seconds.

"How did the training go with Kyle?"

"We found out that he's capable of using magic, which was more than we could've hoped for. It took him a while, but I think he'll be decently powerful once he gets into the right mindset."

"That's good news," Lugh said cheerfully. He said to Kyle, "You sound like you're better off than me, anyway. And you didn't feel the need to scream and thrash around afterwards?"

"No," said Kyle, "I felt pretty fine."

"How's that weight doing, by the way?" Nihs asked.

"Weight?" Lugh asked.

"Just a weird feeling I got when I used magic," Kyle explained. He looked down and felt his chest. "I can still feel it, but it's gone away a little."

"That's good…I think," said Nihs. "That means we can probably write it off as an aftereffect of you using magic in this world. Hopefully it's not harmful."

Kyle noted the 'I think' and the 'hopefully' in Nihs' statement, but decided not to say anything.

At that moment, Rogan's voice sounded over the communicator. "What's going on up there?" he asked gruffly. "Why haven't we landed yet? Or has Nihs become such an able helmsman in the past thirty-two hours that we *have* landed and I just didn't notice?"

"Very funny," Lugh said, placing his hand on the crystal. "We haven't landed yet. I put the ship in autopilot for a bit while Nihs and Kyle were training."

"Autopilot? Murdon's horns, Lughenor, do you want to sleep under the stars tonight?"

"Oh, come off it," Lugh said dismissively, "there can't be *that* many adventurers showing up for this gig."

"There doesn't need to be. This town we're headed to is supposed to be tiny, isn't it?"

"Is it?" Lugh asked carelessly. "I forget who posted the job."

"It was the city of Donno," Nihs said quietly from the corner of the room, his face back in his book.

"There you go," Lugh said, then he seemed to actually think of what Nihs had said. "Wait, that can't be right. I would have remembered *that*. Besides, Donno's not exactly small."

"As far as I understand it, the job was posted by the city on behalf of one of the farming villages in the Donno region. They're making the base of operations a hideout at a small crossroads close to the mine where the goblins have shown up. That's where I set the autopilot to."

"Ah, Nihs, you're a genius. There's still the problem of the unicorn in the basement, though."

"I've made all the arrangements on the overhead," Nihs said in a smug voice. "They're meeting us there, they'll pick it up when we reach the hideout."

"Great, thanks," Lugh said, although Kyle caught the wryness in his voice. "Pay attention to that," he added to Kyle in a whisper. "The Kol are useful people to have around, but you pay for it in smart remarks."

"I heard that," Nihs said from the corner, although he didn't sound particularly offended.

As they came closer to their destination, Kyle walked down to the observation deck to enjoy the view. The hilly country they had been flying over had tamed somewhat, and fields of crops were now visible parts of the topography. Kyle identified a couple of roads, which were little more than dirt paths. He also noticed a few buildings in the fields and clustered at places where the roads met. It gave him a strange thrill to see these familiar hallmarks of civilization in an alien world. He realized that Lugh, Nihs and Rogan were the only three people he had met in this world so far, and none of them were human.

"What race lives around here?" he asked in light of this.

Lugh gave a small laugh. "That's the wrong sort of question to ask around Reno. That city's got the biggest racial diversity in the entire world, and the region around it is no different. You get a lot of humans, since there's a lot of them in general, and a fair number of Selks and Chirpa, because Reno's their kind of place. Recently a lot of Lizardfolk have moved in because of Sanka; you get Kol and Oblihari because it's easy to run into new ideas...and of course, there's the Buorish police."

"Is policing the *only* thing the Buors do?" Kyle asked.

"It's the thing they do best," Lugh answered, "and with the Buors that's saying something. They do do other stuff, although there's not many of them that choose to work away from home; besides, not many people like Buorish tradesmen, since as soon as you show a Buor how to do something they instantly become better than you at it."

"Oh, don't say that," Nihs snipped from his corner, "it's not...*entirely* true."

Lugh laughed.

Kyle, who was as always burning with questions, asked, "What are the Oblihari like?"

"They're sky people," said Lugh, and then he assumed a prim scholarly air: "hailing from the forests and valleys of central Eastia, the bird people known as the Oblihari are renowned for their natural curiosity, openness to new ideas, and skill in craftsmanship."

"They're bird people?" Kyle asked, shocked.

"Yeah, but try not to go around calling them 'bird people' all over the place. It's not an insult or anything, but it's not exactly the height of manners either."

"Oh."

They arrived at their destination half an hour later. Kyle, looking out of the picture window, saw a small cluster of buildings below what could almost be called a village. Though it was now quite dark, yellow light spilled out of almost every window. Beyond the crossroads, the countryside rippled upwards into a small mountain range, as it so often did in this part of the world.

"We're touching down now, Rogan," Lugh said into the crystal.

He was answered with a very loud and unconvincing yawn.

"Oh, shut up."

Kyle kept his face pressed to the window as they touched down. He strained to see signs of life in the small settlement nearby. He was very eager to meet other people from this world—for some reason he felt that encountering someone other than Nihs, Lugh and Rogan would prove Loria's existence once and for all.

It was far too dark to see clearly, although Kyle did think he could see a couple dark shapes weaving their way through the houses.

Lugh landed the ship on the outskirts of the—for lack of a better word—village, and an oppressive silence filled Kyle's ears as the many electronics that ran throughout the *Ayger* shut down.

"Allrighty then," Lugh said, removing what Kyle now assumed to be the key from the control panel and stuffing it in his pocket, "let's see if we can find us some lodgings."

"Hang on," Kyle said, "can't you just sleep on the ship?"

"We could, and have before," Lugh said, "but see, the ship has the disadvantage that you're the one who needs to make your bed in the morning, and besides, we'll be stopping in town to chat with the other adventurers who showed up."

"Plus we're just *rolling* in cash, aren't we, Lugh?" Nihs asked snidely, looking up from his book.

"You can't take it with you," Lugh said. He said to Kyle, "we're approaching ground zero for meeting other people from this world. We need to make sure you know how to act."

"Fair enough," said Kyle.

"All right. First of all, try not to act *too* green. We can introduce you as a rookie that we're training up, which is true, but it still won't help if you stare at everything you see. Just be prepared for everything and try to brush it off. If everyone else isn't worried, neither should you be."

"Should we make up a name for me? You said you had never heard my last name before."

"We don't need to bother," Lugh answered. "First, because everyone who's never heard your name will just assume it's uncommon, and second, because a good half of adventurers end up making up their own name at some point. I've heard much weirder than 'Campbell' in my time. Where did you get that name, anyway?"

"It was my father's name," Kyle said.

"And where'd *he* get it from?"

"It was his father's name, too."

"Oh, one of *those* names. Well, that's good. That's what you can tell people. It saves you the effort of making up a story about where you got it."

"Okay, so what about my past?" said Kyle. "People are going to be able to tell that I don't know anything about this world, and then they're going to question any story we come up with."

Lugh took a bit longer to answer this one. "Hm. That is tough. Any ideas, Nihs?"

Nihs' eyes were already distant in thought. "Why don't we just tell them that he fell out of the sky and when we picked him up, he had lost most of his memory? People will believe that. When spellcasters start fighting you see stranger things than people falling out of the sky, and it's well known that head trauma can cause memory loss."

"So basically we tell them everything, except replace 'came from another world' with 'lost memory'."

"Essentially," Nihs said, clearly pleased with himself, "we basically defend ourselves by saying we don't know what happened to him, and neither does he since his memory's gone."

"Sounds good," said Kyle, "but what happens if someone reads my memories the way you did?"

"You're not allowed to read other people's memories without their permission," Lugh said at once. "It's considered as bad a crime as physically attacking them."

"Oh."

Nihs snapped his book shut and followed the two of them downstairs, where they were joined by Rogan in the T-shaped room before the dojo.

"Are we kitting up before we leave tonight?" the Minotaur asked them.

"Yeah, sure," said Lugh. "No point going back to the ship tomorrow morning."

Rogan nodded, and they passed into the dojo. Here, Lugh grabbed the leather-looking armor and the retrasword that Kyle had seen him wearing before, while Nihs picked up his wizard's sleeves from a corner. Rogan rummaged around in the back, emerging with a massive web-woven axe slung across his back.

"Oh," said Lugh, when he spotted Kyle standing around the entrance of the room looking awkward. "I guess we need to get you some armor, huh?"

"Armor?" Rogan said. "What about his clothes?"

Only then did Kyle realize that he was still wearing the clothes he had on when he fell off the *Caribia*: blue jeans and a white t-shirt underneath a faded blue-buttoned shirt. At first it struck him as odd that he was still wearing the same clothes, but then he realized that there was no reason why he shouldn't be. He briefly checked his pockets to see if anything was left in them, but they were empty. With a pang, he remembered that he had lost his phone on the night of the storm. In any case, his outfit was painfully and obviously different from what the others wore.

"Oh," Lugh said, coming to the same realization. "I hadn't thought of that."

The three of them stood still, thinking, while he fidgeted. He hated the feeling of being a problem.

"You know," Rogan said eventually, "I don't think it's that much of a problem after all. Once he's got some armor on chances are no one will notice what he's wearing, and if they do, who's going to mention it? You know what the fashions are like in Reno; things come and go almost overnight."

"Good point," Lugh said, "but at least take that overshirt off. It'll get in the way when you put armor on. All right, let's get you kitted up."

"I've never trained with armor before," Kyle pointed out nervously, balling up his buttoned shirt and throwing it in a corner. "Is that going to be a problem?"

"Nah, I'll just give you a couple bits and pieces to help keep you alive. Shouldn't be too uncomfortable. Let's see...I think you should use that middle sword I gave you before. Slims just aren't any good against any kind of armor...and..."

He wandered off into the piles of equipment, talking to himself. He returned shortly after with the sword he had mentioned, as well as some hard, leatherish armor similar to his own, and two belts. Lugh helped him as he put on a pair of pauldrons, a small chest guard, and a set of greaves that ended at the knees.

"That'll keep safe the important bits of you," Lugh said, "and leave the rest of you free."

"My arms feel exposed," said Kyle, who felt just as embarrassed over this as he did vulnerable.

Lugh observed him critically. "You're right," he said, "one second."

He scavenged a pair of fingerless gloves from the room, as well as two tubular constructs that was made of rough material. Throwing them to Kyle, he said, "I don't think you're ready for full gauntlets yet, so we'll do it this way instead. Pull the armguards over your elbows. The gloves will help you grip, and besides, seeing an adventurer without gloves makes me uncomfortable. As for the belts, the small one goes around your waist and the big one goes over your right shoulder. You attach the big one to the small one to keep it from moving around."

"What's this?" Kyle asked, holding up a golden, metallic rectangle a foot long and three inches wide. It was polished and sleek, and it had a small Ephicer the size of a blueberry set into a corner.

"That's a magnet sheath," Lugh explained. "It'll sit right next to your neck when you put the belt on. You stick your weapon to it when you're not using it. The Ephicer in it charges the magnet, and it's intent-driven, so the magnet shuts off when you trying to detach the sword."

"Oh, neat."

He put the belts on and then gingerly placed the blade of his sword on the sheath. The two snapped together with a *clink*.

"A bit sloppy," Lugh said, "but you'll get the hang of where to put it as you use it more. You should probably practice with it a bit now, to get used to sheathing and unsheathing it."

Kyle tried removing the sword; the second he had gotten a grip on the hilt, the magnet died and Kyle felt the sword's weight transfer to his hand.

"That's neat." He sheathed the sword again.

"Oh," said Lugh, "and you'll need this." He handed Kyle a small object that turned out to be a flat dagger with a curved blade. It was in its own regular sheath.

"A smart adventurer always carries a dagger with him as backup," Lugh said, as Kyle attached the sheath to his left hip. "They're handy tools in any case; even if you never use it to skewer someone, you can always use it to cut loaves of bread."

"Right," said Kyle, laughing.

They left the dojo and proceeded to the rear of the ship, where a ramp had been lowered that led to the ground. First time standing on Lorian soil, thought Kyle as they disembarked. All told, it felt exactly the same as the soil on Earth.

Lugh turned briefly and held up the *Ayger*'s key in the direction of the ship. Kyle saw that it was one of the now-familiar golden constructions charged by a single blue Ephicer. The key flashed briefly and the ramp began to rise.

"All right," Lugh said, stowing the key in his pocket, "let's go meet the locals."

Kyle felt distinctly nervous walking side-by-side with Lugh, Nihs and Rogan. He was painfully aware of his own weakness and lack of knowledge about Loria. His companions, outfitted in all their equipment, suddenly looked much more like gritty, hard-eyed mercenaries and less like the relaxed, funny people he had gotten used to. Not only that, but he was about to meet other people from this world for the first time, and he had very little idea of what to expect.

Weaving in between the dark buildings, they came across another group of adventurers chatting in a small circle, near some golden machines that looked like a kind of vehicle. There were three men, all dressed in similar light-looking armor and carrying swords and daggers. At first Kyle thought they were humans, but then he noticed that they, like Lugh, had four pointed ears.

The first Selk's head whipped around rather quickly when he heard Lugh's group coming, but relaxed when he saw who it was.

"Oh, hello," he said, nodding his head. His eyes flickered from face to face. "You here for the goblin mine, too?"

"That's right," said Lugh. "Do you know where everyone's meeting up?"

The Selk looked to his companions, as though for support, before answering, "Yeah, the hideout's a tavern off that way; all the adventurers are staying there for the night."

"Great, thanks," said Lugh, and they went on their way.

Kyle caught up to him and fell into stride beside him. "Were those people Selks?" he asked.

"Yeah, but a different kind from me. I'm what you would call a sea Selk. Those were town Selks."

"They looked a lot more like humans," Kyle said.

"Yeah, they do. Here's a good tip to remember: if you're ever in any doubt as to someone's species, just look at their ears. No two races have ears that are alike."

"Thanks," said Kyle, "I'll keep that in mind." He paused in thought. "Funny how they know where everyone's staying, but they're not heading there."

"Town Selks never make a decision early if they can help it," Lugh said. "They'll probably slink in after everybody else has already shown up. They're probably trying to figure out a way to turn a profit before the night's up."

"What could they possibly be thinking of?"

"A little advance on their reward, maybe? A bit of casual burglary around town?"

"They're *thieves?*"

"Well," Lugh said, "their leader looked more like a fighter. The two others were probably thieves."

"So…a thief is just another type of adventurer?"

"Of course," Lugh said, sounding surprised. "They're pretty often necessary to have around; there are a lot of missions out there that become a heck of a lot easier when you have someone like a thief around."

"Makes sense," said Kyle. "But what about the whole, you know…thieving thing?"

Lugh shrugged. "They know what they're getting into when they steal outside of a contract; the Buorish police come down hard on thieves that get caught just stealing willy-nilly."

"So it's fine to steal if you're working for someone?" Kyle asked, disbelieving.

"Well, no, not exactly," Lugh said, bobbing his head, "but usually when you're working a contract the steal-ee is under the Suspension of Rights anyway, so they don't have to worry about it."

"The Suspension of Rights? What's that?"

"It's a Buorish law," Lugh said, "It works just how it sounds; as soon as someone living under Buorish law commits a crime, they lose all of their rights as a person. That means that no one can get in trouble for committing a crime *against* them until they're pardoned. The original idea was that it gives witnesses and victims of crimes the ability to fight back however they want. But the thing is, since the Suspension of Rights lasts until the criminal is caught or turns himself in, there are a good number of people walking around right now who technically have no legal protection. Since the first thing a Buorish court does when you complain about a crime against you is check *your* criminal record, most people tend to keep quiet when someone nicks their stuff."

"Wow," said Kyle, thinking about what this law entailed, "that's pretty intense stuff. So that means if you, like, litter on the street, then people are allowed to kill you for it?"

"Well, no, littering wouldn't do it. But pretty much anything from stealing upwards, and yeah, you're free game. Like I said, it jives nicely with the way adventurers work. It encourages civilian justice, as it were."

Kyle wasn't sure if he liked the sound of this or not.

They travelled in silence through the houses, and eventually emerged at the main crossroads, a large square lit by lamps outside and the glow from windows. Kyle could tell that this was probably quite a lively spot by day; he noticed several market stalls, various golden vehicles and a few horses tethered in outside stables. Judging from the signs over the buildings facing the square, almost everyone was some kind of store, restaurant or hotel.

"You still use horses in your world?" Kyle asked, nodding his chin to one of the stables.

"Aye," Rogan said. "We have Ephicer machines for moving around quickly, but horses are still popular in some parts of the world…particularly those that can't pay for expensive machinery. Of course, adventurers use them as well—a good horse can be trained, and made stronger and faster. A machine can't. There's no Ephicer-based machine that exists these days that can match the speed of a good horse."

"What!"

"You're thinking in terms of your world again," Rogan said. "Over here, there's no limit to how strong a living creature can become, remember?"

"Oh," said Kyle in sudden realization, "and that applies to horses, too, I guess?"

"Of course," Rogan said. "Adventurers who choose to travel mounted usually pick a single horse on purpose, so that the horse becomes stronger and faster with them as time goes on. I've seen horses that can outrun the wind."

They passed through the dark town square and wove through the back roads. Eventually they ran into two more groups of adventurers.

The first was a pair of humans, a young man and woman that must have been younger than Kyle. The man had a sword belted to his waist, a shield strapped to his back and was wearing armor similar to Kyle's. The girl wore softer clothes and carried a simple wooden staff. He noticed that they, too, seemed quite intimidated by the company that Kyle kept, and he got the feeling that they were rookie adventurers, as well.

Lugh had clearly noticed this, for he greeted them with a particular note of kindness. "You doing the goblin mine bit, too?" he asked.

"Yeah," said the man a little nervously, while his companion hung back. "We were just looking for the tavern where everyone's supposed to be gathered."

"You're headed in the right direction, or so we've heard anyway. I think it's that big place back there." Lugh jabbed his chin casually ahead of him.

"Oh, thanks," the man said, with a slight tremble to his voice.

They walked together for a while, Lugh chatting with the newcomers. It turned out that they were called David and Emil, and were brother and sister. David had learned something of being a fighter from his adventuring friends, and his sister had shown aptitude with healing magic. This, apparently, was their second job on their own.

"...And the last time we had our CALs tested—well, the only time, really—I was an eight and my sis was a six, but that was a while ago, and I figure that with a healer a level ten mission shouldn't be a problem?" David somehow managed to make this statement sound like a question.

"You're absolutely right," Nihs piped up from below them. He was trotting along at quite a pace, having to take five strides for each of Lugh's. "Users of self-magic always score lowly on CAL tests, and besides, there will be other adventurers around. As long as you keep Emil safe, you should have no problem."

Emil smiled shyly as Nihs acknowledged her with a nod, and mumbled something about not being that good.

"Oh, go on!" David said, "you're a great healer. You should be more sure of yourself..."

"Let's hope we're somewhere else when they get cold feet," Lugh whispered to Kyle. Nihs, having overheard, aimed a kick at him, but Lugh shrugged it off, adding quietly, "You know I'm right, Nihs, look at them, they're the greenest—"

At that point, they ran into the second group of adventurers, and Kyle had to bite his tongue to keep his expression stony. From a road to their left emerged three creatures that looked like lizards that had learned how to walk on their hind legs. Their faces were bright green, scaly and smooth; their eyes glowed yellow and shone with intelligence. One of them wore heavy plated armor and carried a sword and shield. One wore scaled armor and carried a spear, and the last wore a loose-fitting blue garment that looked almost like a multi-layered kimono—Kyle assumed that he must be some sort of magician, since he carried no visible weapon.

The metal-plated creature in front had had his head turned to talk to one of his companions; it was such that he almost bumped into David and Emil, who both jumped and let out little noises of surprise.

"Oh!" the lizard-man said, swiveling his head towards David, "ssorry, amigo."

"No problem," said David, sounding as though he had just swallowed his tongue.

"Excellent," Lugh whispered to Kyle. "Snakes. They're a kind of Lizardfolk. Some of the nicest people you'll ever meet; not too bad in a fight, either. Hello there," he said jovially to the leader. "Goblin mine?"

"That'ss right," the Snake said, inclining his head, "good pickingss, we heard, and we were in the area, sso..." he shrugged, clearly meaning to indicate, 'why not?' His voice was sibilant, but surprisingly high and boyish.

Lugh nodded. "Doesn't seem to make any sense to turn down jobs that are close by. Never know when you might hit a gem, am I right?"

The Snake laughed his approval. "Sso," he said, turning his head this way and that. His gaze fell on the large building they had been heading for. "That'ss the place, iss it?"

"We think so," Lugh said. "We were just heading there. Name's Lugh, by the way. The big one is Rogan, the small one's Nihs, and this is Kyle," he finished, clapping him on the back.

"Sorry if I look a little slow," said Kyle, feeling strangely confident. "I'm new to the whole adventuring thing."

To his surprise, the Snake laughed amicably and patted him on the shoulder—or, at least, it was intended to be a pat, but the Snake was quite densely built and it was more of a thwack.

"A newbie, eh? No worries, amigo, we all sstart somewhere. You'll pick it up in no time. If adventuring was hard, adventurers wouldn't be able to do it, eh? Hahaha!"

Kyle found himself laughing alongside Lugh and the Snake. There was something strangely charismatic about the green creature, though what exactly that was Kyle couldn't figure out.

After David and Emil had been introduced, the Snakes' leader went through their names: he, Qon, was a fighter; his friends were Doru the soldier and Sali the mystic.

"You're a mystic!" Nihs said enthusiastically, when Sali was introduced. "I've never had the pleasure of meeting an authentic Snake magician."

"And hopefully, come tomorrow, you don't have the opportunity to ssee an authentic Ssnake magician have his arsse handed to him," Sali said wryly.

"Oh, I'm ssure a couple of goblins will be no trouble," Doru said, punching his companion on the arm. He said to Emil, smiling, "Bessides, what can go wrong with a healer on your sside?"

Emil blushed furiously at this and stared at the ground.

"I'm still just learning," she said in a tiny voice.

"Better a trainee than none at all," Doru said, wagging a finger. "Healerss are rare enough these days, we adventurerss have to take what we can get."

"Hear, hear," said Lugh.

Their fleshed-out group went down one more street, and emerged facing a large building, built and decorated in a style that Kyle could only call 'authentic'. Care had obviously been put into the design of the building so that it looked like an old-fashioned tavern. There was even a swinging sign over the door. Yellow light spilled out of every window, and Kyle could hear the muffled sounds of conversation coming from inside.

"Ah, hideouts," Lugh said, breathing deeply as though enjoying the air, "you can always spot 'em from a mile away."

Qon sniffed. "They always think they can draw uss in with the whole russtic country tavern bit."

"Well, they can, can't they?" Lugh asked.

Qon dropped his miffed air immediately and laughed. "Home ssweet home," he agreed.

The inside of the hideout had been decorated in such a way as to match the exterior: the ceiling was low and beamed, the air was thick and dark, and there was even a fireplace with a pair of horns mounted over it— although it seemed unlikely that these horns had belonged to any creature that Kyle would recognize. While the building was designed to look authentic, there were some obvious modern touches. The floor wasn't dirt or straw, but a clean and weathered hardwood, and while the fireplace did seem to burn with real wood, most of the light was coming from *tigoreh* lamps mounted on support beams throughout the room.

Across from them was a counter behind which a human barman was serving drinks; the rest of the hideout was filled with round tables around which the groups of adventurers were clustered.

Kyle's first thought was that he had never seen so many different weapons in a single place before. All the adventurers were armed and armored, though no two were alike; Kyle saw swords, spears, axes, staves, knives, bows, and several other weapons that he not only could not recognize, but also could not understand. A tough-looking human with dark eyes sitting near to them had propped up against his chair what looked like a large black toboggan.

"Hey, check it out," Lugh murmured to him, jabbing him in the side and nodding towards toboggan-man. "That guy's a hero."

"What does that mean?" Kyle whispered back, since he assumed the term must mean something different in Loria.

"A hero is a type of adventurer. It's what we call a fighter who's been promoted. They fight with composite weapons—that's that big black thing he has. They're pieces of equipment that can transform and work like several different weapons at once."

"Woah," Kyle said, casting a quick glance at the hero. He did look very foreboding. He wore medium armor that was colored dark blue, and had blonde hair that was cut very short. Though he didn't look particularly tall, he was very muscular.

"What do you mean by 'promoted'?" Kyle asked.

"Oh, right, I never told you about that—well basically, as you get stronger you reach a point where you start to improve more slowly, right? When you hit that point, you won't get much stronger until you promote—that means going through some kind of trial so that you can unlock more of your potential. It works differently for everyone…but you have to be pretty strong to even attempt it, and once you promote, you're really getting into the big league of being an adventurer."

Kyle caught the strange tone to Lugh's voice, and so chose not to say anything further. He appeared uncharacteristically intimidated, and Kyle thought it had something to do with the fact that Lugh himself was a fighter.

Instead, Kyle let his gaze travel around the room. Most of the other adventurers—Kyle estimated that there was about two dozen of them—seemed to be either human or Selk, although there were some exceptions. There were two Lizardfolk apart from the Snakes that had come in with them—their scales were red, and they were heavier and more naturally armored than Qon, Doru and Sali. There were a couple Kol here and there, perched on tall chairs or actually sitting on the tables.

Nihs scurried up Rogan's back and came to stand on his shoulder, peering through the crowd. "I think I see our employers. I'm going to go talk to them, I want that unicorn off of my conscience as soon as possible."

"Good idea," said Lugh as Nihs dismounted. "I'm going to go get some drinks."

"No booze, Lugh!" Nihs told him sternly as he disappeared into the crowd.

"Yes, *mom*. Sheesh."

"So adventurers don't drink?" Kyle asked him once Nihs had left.

"Oh, we drink," said Lugh, "you just have to make sure to save it for *after* the mission is done. It's funny how many adventurers get that wrong."

"I can ssee an unclaimed table in the corner over there," said Qon, nodding his head. "Want uss to grab it for you? Might as well sstick together, eh?"

"Sure thing, thanks," said Lugh. "Want me to get you something from the bar?"

"I don't mind if you do," the Snake replied happily.

As the Snakes made their way to the back of the room, with David and Emil trailing along awkwardly behind them, Lugh, Kyle and Rogan approached the bar.

"You're for the goblin mine, too?" the barkeep asked them in a harried voice.

"That's right," Lugh said. "There's four of us in our party, plus two humans and three Snakes that just came in."

"Lordy," said the barman, passing a hand across his face. "I didn't expect nearly so many of you. I was thinking fifteen, twenty people at the most."

"You do still have room, don't you?" Lugh asked.

"Should do, I've got space for about fifty, provided there aren't too many Minotaurs, saving your presence, sir," he said, looking at Rogan.

"No offence taken," Rogan rumbled. "At least these days people acknowledge the fact that we tend to take up more room than a human."

"So you'll be wanting a room, then?" the barman asked, pulling a register out from under the counter. "Who's the fourth person in your party?"

"A Kol," Lugh said.

"Alright." He flipped through the register's pages, running his finger down a few. "Ah, you're in luck. I've got one big room left, two Minotaur-sized beds and two human-sized. A bit pricey, but unless you want two separate rooms that's all I've got."

Lugh shrugged. "Can't ask for any better than that. We'll take it. Oh, and we'd like some drinks, too…"

They found their five fellow adventurers sitting around one half of a wooden table. The Snakes had worked their charming magic on David and Emil, who were chatting with Doru and seemed much more comfortable than before. Kyle set down the tray on which their drinks were placed (as the newbie, the task of carrying it had fallen to him), and they took up the rest of the seats at the table. The drinks disappeared alarmingly fast from their resting place as soon as the tray had touched the table.

"Sso," Qon said, wielding his freezer, "I was just ssaying, among uss we've got four fighters, a ssoldier, a warrior, a mystic, a healer, and that Kol of yours…he'ss a mage?"

"That's right," Lugh said.

"Not a bad ssplit, eh? It's a sshame we're not all travelling together."

"That's true," Lugh said thoughtfully. "It is pretty perfect, isn't it? Maybe a bit big, and heavy on the fighters, but you don't usually get such a good group together these days."

"True that," Doru said, "the jobss always get smaller in dayss of peace. Nothing like a good war to create, ah, *employment opportunities* for us adventurerss."

"Careful, now," Sali interjected, "keep talking like that and these people will think you're ssome kind of warmonger."

"Monger? No, I've never monged war. I wouldn't even know how, but what I ssay is the truth."

Kyle let his mind wander as the others talked. Though the Snakes were nicer than he ever could have expected from people with green scaly skin and yellow eyes, he still felt awkward and nervous around the other adventurers. The armor and sword he was wearing felt unfamiliar and uncomfortable, and he was starting to think about what would be expected of him tomorrow. Sure, the training sessions he had had with Lugh and Rogan had gone well, for the most part, but when it came right down to it, would he be able to use the sword on his back to strike down another living creature? He had never seen a goblin before, but surely killing any creature, even one as foul as everyone claimed the goblins to be, would come as a blow to him.

Of course, there was the fact that he might not even have what it took to fight a goblin. He had never been on any kind of sports team or practiced any kind of martial art. He tended to avoid people and confrontations of any kind whenever he could. *In other words*, he thought to himself bitterly, *I'm a coward.*

He heard a sound like a continental shift beside him and Rogan's horned head appeared in his peripherals.

"What's eating you, lad?" the Minotaur asked him in a surprisingly quiet voice.

Kyle looked left and right before answering. "I feel like I don't belong here," he said. He had given up lying to Rogan; the Minotaur always seemed to know what he was thinking, and could certainly tell when he was lying.

Rogan nodded slowly, bringing his drink to his mouth. "A lot of new adventurers get that. Just look at David and Emil there; they look like fish out of water. I bet you're wondering if you have what it takes to be a fighter."

"Well, yeah," Kyle said.

"I thought so. Now, you listen to me: there's only one person who decides if you're got what it takes, and that's you. Anyone can be an adventurer, so long as they've got the will. Sure, you might not be as strong or as fast as you'd like, but that's something we can work on. The drive to learn and to grow more powerful—that's what you need to bring to the table on your own."

Kyle stared gloomily into his glass. "Right."

He looked to his left to find that Rogan was observing him. "What?" he asked, trying to keep the rudeness out of his voice.

"You didn't seem too happy to hear what I had to say," Rogan said. "I don't think I need to say that that's not the usual effect."

Kyle said nothing. He had just remembered something about his training session with Nihs. He saw that the Minotaur was still staring at him. He felt like the red eyes were boring into him.

"I feel like I should talk to Nihs about it," Kyle said, trying to avoid the subject. "He might, well, understand more...er, I guess..." his voice petered out pathetically.

Rogan laughed lightly. "Nihs is a smart lad, but there are some things that he just can't understand—such as the fact that not everyone in the world is as arrogantly self-confident as he is. I understand more than you think. Try me."

Kyle pursed his lips before saying, "when Nihs was trying to teach me magic, I couldn't get the hang of it no matter what I imagined or how I thought. But then he told me to imagine myself where the target was, and—"

"It worked right away," Rogan finished for him.

Kyle looked down. "Yeah."

Rogan took a large breath. "Now, I know what you're thinking, but that doesn't mean what you think it does. You don't hate yourself; no one does. All that it means is that you are your own greatest critic, you're the only person that can drive yourself to do things. Most people, in order to motivate themselves, remember a childhood figure like a parent, or they think of someone they love or of some other goal. You think of yourself, which means that you alone are capable of spurring yourself on. Depending on how you play it, that can be a great strength—or a deadly weakness."

Kyle stared once more into his glass. A part of him felt that what Rogan was saying was complete nonsense, but another suspected that the Minotaur knew more about him than even Kyle could understand.

"Why are you so good at telling what people are thinking?" The question was out of his mouth before he could stop it.

At this, Rogan laughed. "Minotaur are herd creatures. In the early days of our race, we spent all of our time running in massive packs across the Ar'ac continent. We've learned to think as a group and to be empathetic towards others—we think not of our own good, but of the good of the herd."

"Seems like every race here has some sort of ability," Kyle said. "The Kol can all talk to each other, the Selks can hear the sea and Minotaur can read minds. Can the humans do anything?"

"I'm afraid not. I suppose Nihs and Lugh haven't told you the story of the races?"

"No," Kyle said, fighting to keep his voice cool.

Rogan said, "Each of the ten races on Loria were born resembling humans. They came into existence one at a time, starting with the Kol. Each was born in a different part of the world, and they all adapted and changed to suit their environment. The Minotaur were born on the plains, so they evolved thick fur to protect from the sun, hooves so that they could run far in search of food, and horns to defend against predators out on the plains." He touched the ivory horns at his forelock. "The humans were the last race to come into existence, or so the legends say. They were born in the center of the world, and so when they looked around them, they saw all the other races and what they had become. They wanted to change for themselves, but couldn't decide what they wanted to be. Finally, they took so long to decide that they didn't change at all."

"Great," Kyle said, "that makes me feel really good." This time he didn't even try to keep the anger out of his voice.

"You should never bemoan who you are or where you come from," Rogan said, and his voice grew suddenly hard. "I just finished telling you that you alone hold power over what you become. If you let yourself be weighed down by whatever nonsense you believe about your race, or about yourself, then you'll never get anywhere. There was a time in our past that the Minotaur were considered no better than animals by many of the other races. We were killed for our pelts and horns, and captured to be put into slavery. But this was our past, not our present. Where would we be now if every Minotaur born remained convinced that slaughter and slavery was what they deserved, what they were made for? We cannot change the past, or the pasts of others, but we can shape our own lives. All it takes is the will to make the world a better place."

Shocked at how passionate Rogan had become, Kyle said nothing. He sought solace once more in the depths of his drink and thought, *You need to learn to think before you speak.*

"How could anyone ever think of the Minotaur as animals?" he asked. He had meant the question as a sort of peace offering towards Rogan.

The Minotaur took another gallon-sized gulp of his drink. "It's amazing, how when you expect to see the world a certain way, things tend to look that way all the more."

Nihs soon returned. He threw the *Ayger*'s key to Lugh and climbed onto the table beside Kyle, where he sat cross-legged.

"Talked to our employers," he said, after he had nodded to the Snakes and picked up his drink. "Took them to the *Ayger* and they took that unicorn off our hands. Thank goodness that's over."

"Ahh," Qon said, "sso you are the ones that own that large airsship on the outsskirts of town?"

"That's right," Lugh said, the pride obvious in his voice.

"Where did you—" Qon began, but at that moment, a loud thumping sound coming from the center of the room drew everyone's attention.

They all turned in their seats to see that the source of the noise was at the table belonging to the hero they had observed earlier. The three town Selks they had run into in the streets were standing around it, appearing nervous at the attention.

The hero rose to his feet and squared his shoulders. "All right, everyone," he called, "we've got the map of the mine here. We're going to go over our plans for tomorrow. Gather round!" He sat down.

Kyle looked to Lugh for instructions. The latter shrugged.

"Let's go over, I guess," he said. "We don't want to be the ones who screw everything up tomorrow."

Other groups, too, were making their way towards the hero's table. As they rose, Doru muttered something to Qon, who said, "Ahh, yess, of coursse."

"What was that?" Lugh asked.

"We recognize that hero," Qon said. "Doru jusst reminded me. His name is Reldan. He workss many jobs around thiss area. He is known for being somewhat proud of himsself."

Lugh shook his head. "I don't know where it's written in the Hero Guidebook that you have to be an arrogant ess-oh-bee, but I seem to hear that a lot about heroes."

"Well," said Qon, "if you ever promote into a hero and become an arrogant esss-oh-bee, I promisse to sslap you ssilly."

"Thanks," Lugh said, laughing.

They joined the circle of adventurers that were now clustered around Reldan's table. The hero was sitting in front of the map, his composite weapon still propped against his chair.

"All right," he said, placing a hand on the map, "this is the mine we're going to be raiding tomorrow. This—" he indicated an irregular line running along the bottom of the map, "is the face of the mountain we'll be entering the mine by. Notice that there are four entrances. The door far to the left is the smallest, and the farthest from the main part of the mine— that's where we think there'll be the least number of goblins, so the level for that door is ten. The two doors in the middle are both thirties; the one on the left leads into the storage chambers. That run will likely be lucrative, but it's also likely that there will be a lot of guards. The two doors on the right lead into the main part of the mine. Thanks to our Selkic friends here," he motioned lazily at the three town Selks, who looked none too pleased about being singled out, "we know for a fact that the goblin chieftain is living in a large room accessible from the far right entrance. That run is a level forty.

"So the plan for tomorrow is pretty simple. All the different groups are going to head up to the mine at the same time; we'll split up and each take a different entrance based on our levels. The routes get shorter as you go from left to right, but they also get tougher. If the timing goes well, we should all end up near the chieftain's rooms at the same time. We can all team up and tackle the last rooms together. We think that there's probably around two hundred goblins in the mine right now; we don't expect to run into every single one, but you can see how that can make for a lot of fighting. As long as everyone moves carefully and slowly, it should be a piece of cake." He looked around. "Any questions?"

One of the red Lizardfolk that Kyle had seen earlier shifted to the front.

"What kinnd of goblinss are we dealing with herre?" His sibilant accent was much more rough and gravelly than that of the Snakes. Every word seemed drawn from his mouth under extreme duress. "What kinnd of equipment are they ussing?"

At this, Reldan turned to one of the town Selks beside him, obviously expecting him to answer. The Selk squirmed slightly, as though the others' attention was a hand that was grasping him.

"Well," he said, when it seemed that no one was going to rescue him, "they look like, you know, typical wood goblins. Or swamp, maybe. Yeah, more like swamp. Pretty small, maybe about five feet? A lot of them have makeshift armor—leather, chain, stuff like that. Maybe half of them have weapons, a lotta swords and axes, and the rest are just using mining tools. They—"

At this moment, the door of the hideout swung open and the Selk broke off, his stance immediately turning wary as though he was preparing to bolt. The adventurers all turned on the spot to see who had entered the room.

A man stood in the doorway; Kyle could tell that he was a human by his round ears. He was dressed in what looked like the Lorian version of a suit—it was colored a dark green that was almost black, buttoned tight and military-looking. He carried a heavy *tigoreh* case in one arm and a clipboard in the other. He looked older than Kyle, around thirty, and his expression was one of poorly concealed superiority.

Noticing the adventurers' eyes on him, he flashed a smile towards the large group and strode into the room. As the light shifted on his suit, Kyle saw that there was an emblem emblazoned over the right breast; a purple bird whose wings were curved in such a way that they and its extended neck formed a stylized 'M'.

The silence in the room was oppressive as the man made his way to a table near Reldan's and set his case down on it. He carefully spun the case so that its clasps were facing the adventurers, and flashed another smile.

"Hello there," he said, in a voice of carefully sculpted friendliness, "I believe I've found the group that's taking on the goblin mine mission tomorrow?"

Reldan had stood up and was now at the front of the group. "That's right," he said, "what's it to you?"

The man's grin remained fixed as he shifted his attention to the hero. "I come on behalf of Maida Weapons," he said breezily, "to wish you all good luck on your mission tomorrow and to offer you an edge in the upcoming fight."

Ah, so he's a salesman, said a part of Kyle's brain, and the rest of it agreed.

"So you're selling weapons?" Reldan asked aggressively, jabbing his chin towards the *tigoreh* case.

Again, the man's grin did not falter. He inclined his head politely and reached for the clasps of his case. "Not selling, donating. Maida Weapons would like to extend its friendship towards the world's adventuring community—as such, we are starting a campaign to donate thousands of weapons to adventurers such as yourselves."

"What'ss the catch?" one of the red Lizardfolk asked.

The man's grin widened. "There is no catch. This is merely a promotional campaign. Think of it as advertising for Maida Weapons' upcoming releases in weapons technology. Of course, it's a win-win situation: I'm offering you for free what people will have to pay for in a few months' time." With that, he unlocked the clasps on his case and swung it open.

Kyle, like most of the other adventurers, craned forward to see what was inside. There, nestled in black velvet, was what was unmistakably a gun. It was golden, and definitely wouldn't have been confused for a gun found on Earth, but there was no questioning the object's purpose. It was about three feet long and looked like an assault rifle.

The man pulled the gun out of the case and held it across both hands so that everyone could see it. It gleamed alluringly, light dancing off of its golden finish. Emblazoned along the body in blocky purple italics was the word 'Maida'—the 'M' was the same bird-shape as the one on the man's jacket.

"The new Eagle 3 assault rifle," the man said, his words seeming to shine like the gun itself, "capable of firing more than twice as fast as the previous model, with a short-term fuel cell life that is more than four times longer than that of the Parrot." He reached back into the case and pulled out a small object that looked like a cylindrical phial full of Freezer; its contents were blue, viscous and incandescent. There was a golden contact at either end of the phial; the man inserted one end of it into a cavity along the bottom of the gun's barrel and it slid into place with a *click*. Although Kyle knew little about guns, it was obvious that this blue phial was some sort of clip—which meant that the man in front of them now carried an armed assault rifle.

The man transferred the gun to one hand and hefted it, point upwards, striking a pose that showed off the weapon's magnificence.

"The Eagle fires eight rounds a second for up to ten consecutive seconds, each bullet boasting a Buorish Damage Rating of over fifty. The weapon is also extremely light, weighing only…"

Kyle felt Lugh nudge him. "What is it?" he whispered.

"Remember when we were talking about the politics in Reno? The whole Sanka versus Livaldi thing?"

"Yeah."

"Maida Weapons is Livaldi's company. See what he's trying to do? Adventurers have always been in support of Sanka, since he's an old one of them; Livaldi's obviously hoping that by pulling stunts like these, he'll win the adventurers over. Fat chance of that. Just watch what happens here."

"…a deadly effective weapon overall, and one that would normally cost upwards of six thousand nells," the Maida salesman was saying, "offered to any of you who wish to have one, today, for free. It would surely make quick work of anything you would encounter tomorrow. Who's interested?"

Kyle expected at least one or two bites, but the adventurers who were facing the salesman all seemed unimpressed.

"No one?" the salesman asked, sounding artfully surprised. "No one at all? How about you, sir? Simply using this weapon could have the effect of raising your threat level by nearly twenty points. Are you sure?"

This was addressed to David, who just shook his head mutely and stepped backwards.

The salesman's eyes continued to scan the group. They flickered over Kyle, and then stopped and flickered back.

"And how about you?" he said, flashing his smile again. "You have the look of a new adventurer…you'll be much more of a threat to your enemies with a Maida weapon at your side."

"No, thanks," Kyle said, keeping his expression blank and his voice flat, "I'm training to use a sword."

As he was saying it, his eyes and those of the salesman locked for a split second. In that moment, Kyle was suddenly struck by a strange feeling. His vision seemed to grow dark around the edges and time slowed slightly. He felt keenly the presence of the round weight in his chest, something that had gone away almost completely since his training with Nihs. He saw a sparkle in the man's eyes, and though he knew it couldn't be happening, he got the impression that the man was reading his mind.

Then Reldan spoke, breaking the spell. "And this is all just goodwill on the part of Livaldi, is it?" He asked, leaning forward and leering.

"Of course," the man said, his gaze finally leaving Kyle. "Maida Weapons—"

"Wants to make money." The one who interjected was a Kol who was perched on his Selkic friend's shoulder. He looked somewhat like Nihs, but his skin was paler and his build stockier. "They wouldn't just give away millions of nells' worth of equipment if there wasn't something in it for them. There *is* a catch, no matter what you say."

"As I said," the man said silkily, addressing the Kol, "this is a promotional and goodwill campaign, designed to help showcase Maida's new products—"

"Most of your customers are large-scale organizations, aren't they?" the Kol interrupted again. "I doubt that you need to use showcase marketing to sell weapons to *them*."

"Fuel cells are exsspensive." This was Doru. "What happenss when all of our shiny new gunss need replacement ammo? I ssuppose we'd have to buy from Maida Weapons then."

There were noises of assent from the other adventurers.

"You're under no obligation to continue using the weapon once the original fuel cells have run out," the salesman talked over them. "You can throw the gun away, if you wish."

"Oh, yess," one of the red Lizardmen said scathingly, "once we'rre all ssoftened up and have forrgottenn how to usse a *rreal* weaponn."

This time the noises of assent were more pronounced. The man's smile had not faded, but it evolved a glassy quality as he listened to them.

Reldan stepped forward, picking his composite weapon up from the ground. "You listen to me, Maida snake. Real adventurers aren't interested in your shiny hunks of junk. Better to fight with your fists than to become a slave to your weaponry. Am I right?" he directed to the group behind him.

A couple people said "yeah!" and Kyle heard Lugh say "hear, hear" beside him.

Reldan had reached a hand towards his composite weapon. His hand closed around a piece of metal jutting out from the top and he pulled on it, drawing a large black sword out from somewhere in the weapon's depths. The small pieces that made up the black mass clinked and snicked quietly as they rearranged themselves. Now the remainder of the composite weapon was in the shape of a shield.

Reldan held the sword out at arm's length, point up.

"A real weapon is alive," he said, glaring at the salesman from behind his sword, "it grows with you. As you get stronger, it gets stronger with you, until there's no one else in the world that can use it the way you can. A gun doesn't grow. A gun doesn't live. A gun is no weapon for an adventurer, and neither is any of Maida's garbage. You can tell your boss Livaldi that."

This time the noise coming from the adventurers was more of a cheer. Kyle didn't participate, but took the opportunity to watch the others. He saw that, like himself, David and Emil were hanging in the back, not making any noise, their faces fearful.

The Maida salesman's expression did not change. He waited for the noise to die down and said simply, in a voice of fabricated warmth, "Well, if any of you change your minds, I will remain at my ship until tomorrow. Good luck to all of you."

As he turned to place the rifle back in its case, his gaze swept once more across the group of adventurers. On Kyle it lingered for a moment. Kyle thought he saw the man's smile widen slightly as he looked away.

Once the salesman had left, the tableau held for a few seconds, and then Reldan sheathed his sword.

"All right," he said, turning back to his table, "that should be enough. I'm going to sleep. If anyone needs more information, talk to our Selkic friends here."

And without another word, he climbed the stairs to the second floor.

"Well, that was interesting," Lugh said, once they, the Snakes and David and Emil had regained their seats. "Looks like Maida's trying to get on the adventurers' good side."

"Well, they're not doing it very well," Qon said in a satisfied voice. "Livaldi will never undersstand uss the way that Ssanka does."

"And yet his influence grows by the day," Nihs said quietly. "Sure everyone knows that adventurers are supposed to be against firearms, but the truth is a lot of us are willing to sell our souls to Maida for the extra edge. Fifty BDR per bullet? There would have been a stampede if we hadn't had our pride holding us back."

"True," Qon said sadly. "All we can hope is that traditional weaponssmithing keeps pace with Maida's new gadgetss."

"Lugh," Kyle said, his face pensive.

"Yeah, what is it?" Lugh asked him.

"Was that salesman using magic at all?"

Lugh stuck out his jaw. "Probably. I'm the wrong person to ask, though. Hey, Nihs."

"Yes?"

"Kyle wants to know if that sleaze ball was using any magic."

Nihs looked surprised. "You could tell?" he asked Kyle, sounding impressed.

"Yeah, sorta," Kyle said evasively, not wanting to mention the weighty feeling in front of the others. "It seemed like he was sort of making everything…shine."

Nihs nodded. "He was using charming magic, just keeping a weak aura up in the background to help make his pitch more successful. But he made a mistake in showing up in the first place. Nothing can help you if your audience is biased against you from the start."

"Thiss is true," Sali said, who had been listening, interested. "Now all of uss are jusst going to go on about how Maida tried to bribe uss."

"Yes, it does seem very stupid," Nihs said, scratching his chin. "Livaldi's supposed to be a genius, it seems strange that he would make such a basic mistake. He should have known it would be a waste of effort to try and get on our good side that way."

They talked for a little while longer, Kyle mostly keeping his own mouth shut and his ears open. He found himself warming up to the Snakes even more; already they seemed like old friends. He recognized that David and Emil were the kind of people that Kyle would have looked down on had they been on Earth; however, feeling so lost and out of place himself, he found himself unable to criticize them.

They ordered food at the bar, since none of them had eaten for a while, and then they bade the others goodnight and made their way to their room. It was very large and ran along the front wall of the hideout, so they had a view of the small square below. The human-sized beds were more or less equivalent to what could be found in a hotel back on Earth; the Minotaur-sized beds, however, were nothing short of enormous. This room, too, had been designed to look centuries old, but the bathroom was modern and quite spotless, and the lights were Ephicer-powered.

Nihs hopped up on his bed, which was far too large for him, and bounced up and down. Lugh sat down on his similarly oversized bed with a sigh (he had taken the other Minotaur bed) and began removing his armor, piling it unceremoniously off to one side.

As Kyle sat down and followed suit, he saw Nihs settle down and enter the overhead, a circle of light shimmering around him and making his outline blur. Kyle watched his swaying motion for a few moments, and asked of the others, "So? What now?"

Lugh shrugged and flopped backwards on his bed. "Nothing," he said, "we're officially off duty. So how did you find the other adventurers?"

Kyle propped his pillow up against his headboard and leaned back on it. "I liked the Snakes," he said drowsily, "which is funny, really…I never would've expected snake people to be so nice."

Lugh nodded. "They're good folk, and some of the best friends you'll ever make once you earn their trust."

"I'm concerned about that couple, though," Rogan rumbled quietly from his bed. "The siblings. They'll be doing the level ten run with us. I hope we can count on them."

"Well, all I can say is, if there's any hand-holding that needs to be done tomorrow, you're doing it. I don't have the right temperament to deal with newbies. Not you," he added quickly, nodding to Kyle, "you're green, but at least you know enough not to show it."

"Speaking of green, why do the Lizardfolk use the word 'amigo'?" Kyle asked.

"It's a term of endearment," Rogan said. "That's what they call their young. Why?"

"In my world, 'amigo' is the Spanish word for 'friend'," Kyle said.

Lugh rolled his eyes theatrically. "Another similarity? Come on, Kyle. Old hat."

Kyle stuck his tongue out at him.

Rogan reclined on his bed, an awe-inspiring movement that made its supports creak. "That Reldan seems quite full of himself," he said conversationally.

Lugh sniffed. "Let's face it, if I were that powerful I'd be full of myself too. I wish I could use a composite weapon," he said wistfully.

"Why don't you go through some intensive training and get promoted?" Rogan asked. "Your level is in the thirties now, it wouldn't take too long to work yourself up to a promotable level."

"Eh," Lugh said dismissively, and Kyle noticed that there was a tone to his voice that he hadn't heard before.

Nihs returned from the overheard not too long after. He let out a large sigh and began to construct something like a nest around him, using his pillows and blanket.

"What were you doing?" Lugh asked.

Nihs settled into his little den. "Gossiping," he said casually. "I told everyone about that Maida salesman. Apparently Livaldi's employees have been pulling the same stunt all around Centralia."

"Is it working?" Lugh asked.

"A lot of adventurers are refusing the same way we did, but the new Eagle *is* impressing people. And, apparently Maida's hinted that they have an even more powerful weapon ready to be released; some kind of super accurate long-barreled gun."

"A sniper rifle," Kyle said at once without thinking.

The others stared at him.

"A what rifle?" Lugh asked.

"A sniper rifle," Kyle repeated. "That's just what it sounds like. Long-barreled, super accurate. We have them in our world."

"Hum," said Nihs. "Anyway, it's causing quite a stir. The Buorish police have started giving Livaldi the Look again, but they can't do anything since he's not doing anything wrong. He says it's just normal marketing, and how can they argue with that? A lot of Kol on the overhead suspect foul play, though."

"Doru said that the ammo for the guns is expensive," Kyle said, "so they're probably giving away the guns for free in the hopes that they'll make it up with the ammo. What kind of ammo do your guns use, anyway?" he asked curiously. "Doru mentioned fuel cells, right?"

"Yes," Nihs said, "a fuel cell is a special phial containing a mixture of crushed Ephicers and various liquids; they don't last as long as a solid Ephicer, and they can't contain as much charge, but it's much easier to regulate a fuel cell's magic output, and the charge builds up more quickly. A gun has one solid Ephicer at the back of the barrel which works as an accelerator. A pellet of magic from the fuel cell builds up in the barrel and then gets fired along its length by the accelerator."

"In any case," Rogan said, "I'd say that Doru and Kyle are probably right. To Maida, getting those guns in circulation is the most important part. After that, it doesn't matter who's actually using them so long as someone's paying for the fuel cells."

Lugh yawned widely and pointedly. "As interesting as all this is, I think we can afford not to worry about it now. Big day ahead of us tomorrow, right? Let's try and get some sleep, huh?"

They all agreed, and as Lugh turned off the lights they all settled down in their own way. Nihs nestled down in his constructed den, taking up about a tenth of his bed, and Rogan rolled over onto his side, facing away from them. Lugh leaned back with his arms behind his head and his legs crossed at the ankles; he stared up at the ceiling as though looking at the stars.

Kyle, who was now feeling extremely tired, lay silently and thought back on the previous day. It had been his longest by far. And tomorrow promised to be even longer, so long as he didn't get himself killed by a goblin…

He tried to be worried about what he was getting into. He tried telling himself that being stranded in a strange world with a group of mercenaries was cause for alarm, but he just couldn't. The bed was warm and soft and Kyle was exhausted. He soon drifted off into sleep.

It was difficult to say whether or not Grade 1 had gone well for Kyle. Certainly he had proved himself as adaptable and as intelligent as he had been in kindergarten. All in all it had gone quite well, with the exception of a few hitches.

For instance, there was the matter of homework. They had been doing simple sums in class when Miss Baker had told them, to Kyle's surprise, that she had more for them to do, to be completed once they got back from school. She gave them little booklets and told them to have the first page of sums done for tomorrow.

Kyle simply couldn't wrap his head around the idea. He raised his hand.

"Are we doing these tomorrow?" he asked, thinking he must have misheard.

Miss Baker smiled kindly at him. "No, dear. You'll do them tonight, at home."

Kyle was confused. "Are you going to come over to our house to help me?" To him, the idea of completing work when there was no teacher present was completely alien.

This time Miss Baker laughed. "No, honey, I won't be there. You'll do them all on your own. Your parents can help you if you have any trouble."

"My parents can help me?" Kyle asked incredulously.

"Of course," Miss Baker said.

This had been enough to assuage Kyle's concerns for the time being, however, once he had gotten home that night, another problem had arisen. He opened the first page of his workbook to see no fewer than twenty problems staring back at him, all the same difficulty and some the exact same as the ones they had been doing in class.

He brought the booklet to his mother and showed it to her like an accountant presenting some faulty papers to their boss.

"Why do I have to do these?" he asked her.

She took the booklet from him and looked at the problems. "It's practice, dear. Miss Baker wants to make sure that you know how to do them."

"But...but..." Kyle was having problems arranging his thoughts. "But I *do* know how to do them."

"Well, then," his mother said with a small smile, "they should be easy for you, shouldn't they?"

"But why do I have to do them if I already know how?"

"I told you, dear," his mother explained patiently, "it's so that Miss Baker knows."

Kyle was shocked. Couldn't he just *tell* Miss Baker that the problems were easy? Didn't she trust him?

Desperate, he tried another angle. "But there's so many of them!" he said, "it'll take forever to do them all."

"Well," his mother said, "if you're good at them, then you'll be able to do them quickly, won't you? Listen, Kyle. All the other students have to do this as well. I'll help you if you need me to, but you need to get these problems done."

Kyle was now near tears. He felt betrayed by his mother, whom he had expected to be on his side.

"But I don't *want* to do them!" he wailed.

His mother was unsympathetic. "Well, you have to," she said firmly.

It ended with Kyle in tears, distraught and defeated. His mother set up a little desk for him in his room, and he eventually settled down and did the problems. All in all it wasn't too bad, except that Kyle had felt it to be a huge waste of time. He skimmed through his homework easily, and then went back downstairs to where his mother was.

"Done already?" she asked. "Let me see your homework book."

Kyle couldn't believe his ears. Did his mother not trust him, either?

She opened the first page of Kyle's booklet and scanned it quickly.

"Well done," she said, smiling, handing it back to him, "it's perfect. Now that wasn't so bad, was it?"

Kyle said nothing, not wanting to anger his mother now that she was so kindly disposed towards him. He thought, however, that while it hadn't been so bad, it certainly could also have been better.

"Hey! *Hey!"*

Kyle woke muzzily, Lugh's insistent whispering sounding uncomfortably loud in his ears.

He opened his eyes to see that the room was still fairly bright; though night had fallen completely, there were many windows into their room and the light from the stars and moon shone in.

Lugh was propped up on his side, watching Kyle with an expression that was half concerned, half irritated.

"What is it?" Kyle asked him, yawning.

"Do you always do that?" Lugh whispered.

"Do what?"

"Talk in your sleep. You've been doing it for the last fifteen minutes."

Kyle stared at him, incredulous. "I don't talk in my sleep!" he whispered indignantly.

"You *didn't* is what you mean, because you sure were just now. I was afraid you were going to wake up Nihs and Rogan."

Kyle risked a glance behind him. Nihs was curled up in his den at the very top of his bed, and a rhythmic noise like waves crashing upon a distant coast coming from the bed beyond Lugh indicated that Rogan too was asleep.

"You weren't asleep?" Kyle asked Lugh. "How long has it been?"

Lugh shrugged. "Maybe half an hour? I don't fall asleep quickly. Anyway, what's up? Were you dreaming?"

Kyle thought of what had been going through his mind. "No," he said.

Lugh shrugged again. "Well," he said, "you should try and get back to sleep. You can't afford to be dragging your feet tomorrow."

Kyle nodded, laying back down, this time facing away from Lugh. He had never before been caught talking in his sleep, and he found the experience somehow shameful. He wondered if he had been saying anything coherent, but he wasn't about to ask Lugh that.

Come to think of it, I've never dreamed as often as I have been these days…

On Earth, his dreams usually consisted of situations that always ended with someone he knew chasing him down the streets of Cleveland, but even those dreams were few and far between.

He pulled his covers up over his head, brooding. He felt embarrassed, and silently promised to himself that he would never talk in his sleep again. As he lay there, he repeated to himself: *I will not talk in my sleep. I will not talk in my sleep. I will not talk in my sleep…*

Kyle awoke to a general hubbub. At first, his mind was too confused to take in what was going on. As his senses lined up for another day of bringing information to his brain, he realized that the source of the noise was Nihs, who, being the first one up, had apparently taken it upon himself to make the others' awakenings as rude as possible.

Nihs climbed up onto Kyle's bed and jumped up and down.

"Up you get, lazybones! That mine won't raid itself!"

"Get outta here," Kyle complained, leaning up groggily. A pillow sailed at high velocity into his vision and hit Nihs squarely in mid-jump, causing him to topple over the side of Kyle's bed.

"Act your age, Nihs," Lugh said from his bed, which was now a pillow short. His golden hair was frightening in its unkemptness. He mashed his face into his remaining pillow and seemed unwilling to move.

Rogan, meanwhile, had propped himself upright and was sleepily pulling on various bits of armor from beside his bed.

"Let's hope your energy holds throughout the day, little one," he rumbled. "You'll likely need all of it before the mission's done."

Nihs, after being hit by Lugh's pillow, had scurried back onto his bed and now sat there with an amused expression on his face.

"You should be worried about yourself, not me," he said smugly. "*I* don't have any armor to lug around."

Kyle sat up and swung his feet over the edge of his bed. He said nothing. Somehow, the gravity of what he was about to do had hit him overnight, and he was now feeling horrible butterflies in his stomach. *Going into an abandoned mine and killing a bunch of goblins? What was I thinking?*

And yet a small part of him told him that he would be fine. It was true that Kyle seemed to pick up quickly what it took others a long time to figure out. Oftentimes in the workplace he had been frustrated by the incompetence of not only his co-workers, but his superiors as well. Despite everything, Kyle couldn't help but feel confident and even a little bit excited; perhaps he would prove to be as skilled in the world of adventuring as he had in the world of database development.

Kyle geared himself up, feeling more excited and nervous all the while. They eventually had to wait for Lugh to get up and put on his equipment; Rogan had to grab him and lift him bodily from his bed in order to get him moving.

Once armed and armored, except in the case of Nihs, who only had to slip his arms into his wizard's sleeves, they headed downstairs. When Kyle caught sight of all the other adventurers gathered there, his excitement mounted even more. Some were eating, some were talking, many were tending to their equipment. Kyle spotted Reldan, who was sitting in a corner trying out his composite weapon. As Kyle watched, the hero sheathed a sword back into the black mass and pulled on a different handle—this time, the weapon that emerged was a black-bladed axe.

"Joint's jumpin'," Lugh said ironically, as he surveyed the scene. "How about some breakfast, everyone? I think I see the Snakes over there…why don't you guys join them, and I'll have the barman bring us some grub."

They sat down at the Snakes' table, who greeted them sleepily. All three of them seemed very tired and reluctant to move.

"M-m-morning, amigo," Qon said, yawning hugely and showing off rows of teeth. "Fine day for ssome killing, eh?"

"As fine as any could be, I suppose," Rogan said, sitting down ponderously.

"You'll have to f-f-forgive uss, amigo," Doru said, who had been slumped over the table. "We Lizardfolk are not used to waking up sso early in the morning. Ssleep until the ssun sstops climbing, that'ss our way."

"And a fine way it is, or would be, if the rest of the world slept for as long," Rogan agreed, laughing.

"Hear, hear," Doru said faintly. Sali snored.

Lugh returned with breakfast shortly after; it consisted mainly of bread with various spreads, some of which were even recognizable by Kyle, some eggs and fried Bwah meat, and a kind of gray glop that, to hear Lugh describe it, seemed to be similar to porridge. Kyle ate indiscriminately, trying everything. Apart from the fact that he was very hungry, he felt almost that he was proving his own bravery by asserting his dominance over Lorian cuisine.

It was quite good, really, even the gray glop.

David and Emil showed up towards the end of their meal. Both were looking extremely nervous. Lugh waved them over to their table.

"Oh, no," David said, "did we miss breakfast? We woke up late…"

"No worries, lad," Qon said, patting the seat beside him, "there's sstill time. Sit yoursself down and get ssome food in you."

David and Emil only had a couple minutes to eat before Reldan stood up and made his way to the center of the room. The chatter died down as he caught everyone's attention.

"The raid will be starting soon, if no one has any objections," he said, turning to look at each group in turn. "Is everyone ready? No one missing?" When no one spoke, he said, "Good. Let's go," and he made his way out of the hideout.

"Prat," Lugh muttered under his breath, as the other adventurers filed out, "thinking he's in charge of everyone just because he's the strongest."

"Well, if someone's going to be in charge, it might as well be him, I suppose," Rogan said calmly, draining the last of his drink. He slapped Lugh on the back. "Come, Lughenor, let's not miss the rush."

Lugh grunted, but got to his feet; Kyle hastened to follow him. Nihs had climbed once more onto Rogan's shoulder, and remained perched there as they went outside. Kyle figured that Nihs must have done this many times in the past, since Rogan did not seem bothered by the free ride he was giving his companion.

The adventurers trooped together in a large mob towards the nearby mountains. A path led first straight toward the mines, then zigzagged up the side of the mountain as the ground got steeper. Kyle was turning his head this way and that, taking in every detail; the sun was bright and the landscape was very interesting. Again and again he got a strange feeling looking at the world of Loria—everything seemed so perfect, designed deliberately to look foreign and exciting. The local plant life were all similar to that of Earth's, but subtly different in way that made Kyle want to examine every tree and bush.

There were many signs of habitation along the path that they followed. As they made their way up the side of the mountain, they came across various constructions and discarded mining equipment, most of it made of simple wood and iron.

"No *tigoreh*," Lugh noted, running his hand along a large piece of scaffolding. "Talk about old. Any mine worth the effort was renovated using *tigoreh* a long time ago. This place must've been empty for what? Thirty, forty years?"

"If not more," Rogan agreed.

A small, childlike part of Kyle's mind was very excited at the prospect of exploring an old abandoned mine. He twisted his shoulders in order to get a feel for the sword on his back. Though he was still frightened, this feeling was almost completely eclipsed by his eagerness to finally get adventuring.

At one point, the path they were following widened into a large landing, and the group slowed to a stop. To their left, built into the side of the mountain, was an old wooden doorway. Scattered about outside were several smaller tools, a bit of tent canvas and even the remains of a fire pit. Clearly, this landing had been used as a camp by the miners more than once.

Reldan was having a quick conversation with the town Selks. One of them nodded, and Reldan turned to the rest of the group.

"This is the first door," he called out over their heads, "level ten. Who's running this?"

"That's us," Lugh said, striding forward.

The only other people who opted for this door were David and Emil. They looked relieved to see that Lugh's party would be going with them. Lugh's expression was one of carefully crafted neutrality.

Reldan spared them all a glance. "All right," he said to Lugh, who he must have assumed was in charge, "you'll have more running to do but less fighting than the other groups, so you should show up in the chieftain's chamber at about the right time. Good luck in there."

"Thanks," Lugh said drily.

Qon walked over and clapped him on the shoulder. "Happy hunting," he rasped, nodding to each of them in turn. He winked when he got to Kyle. "I have a feeling that adventuring will agree with you." His gaze flickered to David and Emil, who were hanging behind. "I'm ssure I don't need to warn you about those two," he said quietly. "Ssali thinks that Emil showss much potential in the field of magic, but that will mean little if her will, or that of her brother, doesn't hold. Be careful."

"Thanks, Qon," Lugh said, much more genuinely, bringing his own hand up to rest on the Snake's shoulder. "We'll keep an eye on the siblings. Hopefully they won't be too much bother. Good luck yourself in there. Kill a goblin or five for me."

"Will do," Qon said, flashing a grin.

The group began to move on, and the Snakes turned and left. Sali nodded to Emil before he joined the others.

"Well then," Lugh said, walking over to the mine door and swinging it open, "everybody ready?"

"As always," Nihs said, as Rogan nodded.

"Yeah," David said in a slightly broken voice.

Kyle considered the question honestly. Something was rising in him that he did not understand. He didn't know how he felt about what he was getting into, but whatever else he was, he wasn't scared. He reached up over his shoulder and drew his sword. The sound of it ringing as it scraped against his sheath pasted a grin on his face that he couldn't get rid of no matter how hard he tried.

"Let's go kill us some goblins," he said.

Lugh drew his own retrasword and the blade hissed as it sprang into life.

"Spoken like a true adventurer," he said approvingly.

The door opened into a dark, narrow passage not quite wide enough for two people to walk comfortably beside one another. Torches lined the walls, and yet none of them were lit.

"Allrighty then," Lugh said cheerfully. "Kyle and David, you're up front since you need practice. Nihs and I will go after you. Then Emil. Rogan, you can cover our backs. Sound good?"

"No complaints," Rogan rumbled, drawing his axe. This movement almost dislodged Nihs, who raised his hand.

"Um. Objection. Does that mean that I have to walk?" he asked.

Lugh gave him a look.

"I wouldn't want to slow the group down," Nihs said in a voice scintillating with innocence.

Lugh rolled his eyes. "Fine, then, you big baby," he said, "I'll carry you, okay? Are you happy?"

Nihs grinned broadly and slid down off of Rogan's shoulder. He scurried over to Lugh and shimmied up his side until he reached the same vantage point that he had been occupying on the Minotaur.

"Excellent," he said, settling down on Lugh's broad shoulder. "All right, let's go!"

Lugh made a face. He said to David and Emil, "You two okay with being apart?"

David looked to Emil, obviously waiting for her opinion.

After a moment, she nodded. "I'm sure you know best about how we should go."

"Thanks. Well then: Kyle and David, front and center. Keep your eyes open. If you have to fight before the tunnel opens up, go one at a time and don't get in each other's way. The goblins we'll run into around here won't be a problem for either of you. Your biggest concern is accidentally hurting each other. Call your kills if you have to."

As Kyle walked past Lugh to get to the front of the group, the former grabbed his arm and said in a low voice, "You okay?"

Kyle nodded and kept moving. He drew up alongside David, who inclined his head awkwardly.

"Hey," Kyle said. He took in David's body language in a split second and recognized it instantly. He had seen it many times before in the workplace. It was that of someone who was contemplating something unpleasant and who was stalling for time in the hope that someone else would bail him out. "I'll go first."

David shot him a grateful look.

They stepped into the mine, Kyle crouching low and holding his sword. David followed him, with Nihs and Lugh behind them both. Emil stepped inside nervously, clutching her wooden staff. Rogan came last, his enormous bulk bent low in order to fit inside.

Kyle hadn't gone twenty paces when we heard Nihs say, "Hang on a second."

He turned around to see the Kol lift a torch from its bracket and clasp the top of it in his hands. There was a *whoomph* and the torch caught fire. He passed it to David, who handed it to Kyle.

"Thanks," he said, and held it in his left hand, sword still in his right.

The tunnel led straight into the mountain, its width unchanging and the ground was level. Kyle, however, was excited. He held the torch ahead of him and scanned the ground and walls, ears straining to hear any sort of noise coming from deeper in the mine.

The path remained unchanged for another ten minutes, by which time Kyle's enthusiasm was ebbing slightly. He was spared boredom, however, when the tunnel suddenly opened into a small chamber. There were two lit torches here, and they illuminated a crude wooden table around which lay a good amount of discarded mining equipment. The table itself featured a couple plates, utensils and mugs, some of which looked recently used. Bags of flour and a few wicker baskets were stashed behind the table.

There was room in the chamber for them all to stand at once, so Kyle waited for the others to catch up to him.

Rogan strode over to the table and picked up one of the plates. "Goblins have been here, and not too long ago," he said, setting the plate down. "Less than a day ago, I'd wager."

Kyle looked around, his mind buzzing. There were three tunnels leading from the room apart from the one they had come through. Wanting to do something on his own, he checked down the tunnel to their left while the others were occupied. It was more of a doorway than anything else, and it opened into a small, boring room that contained more storage containers and old mining tools.

"Anything interesting in there?" Lugh asked him when he returned.

"Don't think so, unless you wanted a new pickaxe. Which way do we go?" he asked, wanting to get moving as soon as possible.

Lugh checked each of the tunnels in turn, then bit his lip. "Forward, I should think. We're supposed to be running the perimeter of the mine, and if I remember the map correctly, this passage should curve all the way around and end up to the chieftain's place."

"Yes, that's right," said Nihs from his shoulder. "Now let's get a move on, we don't want to be late for the big fight."

The tunnel they went down was wider and brighter than the other, enabling Kyle and David to walk abreast. Kyle discarded his torch, feeling somewhat disappointed that it hadn't been very useful.

They walked for a bit longer before Lugh suddenly stopped them up. "Wait!" he hissed. "Do you hear that?"

Kyle froze, straining to hear what Lugh was talking about. Then he heard it: scuffling noises coming from the tunnel ahead, as though creatures were walking and dragging their feet. Even as he made out the noise, a peal of guttural laughter reached his ears.

"Goblins," said Lugh at once. "Probably only a couple. Don't try fighting them together! One of you take them on. Everyone else, stand back."

Kyle didn't even wait to discuss things with David; he strode ahead, raising his sword, his heart racing. *This is where I see if I have what it takes...*

They advanced cautiously down the tunnel, which was now curving noticeably to the right. The ceiling had opened up, so it seemed almost as if they were skirting a large boulder which formed the right wall. The noises coming from the tunnel got louder. The goblins were talking to one another, in burbling voices that made Kyle think of bubbles bursting on the surface of a swamp. He was now prepared to see the goblins appear at any moment. He had never seen one before...he wondered what they looked like. *Were they—*

And there they were, suddenly, horribly, without any warning. They had been walking side by side as David and Kyle had been. Both of them wore short, simple swords and one of them carried a torch. They were small, about half a foot shorter than Kyle, and their garb was a mismatch of cloth and armor. They wore dirty red tunics over their makeshift equipment and each had a small leather cap perched on their head. Their faces were angular and wizened, looking almost pinched; ears, nose, chin and brow all stuck out at different angles. Their skin was a kind of pasty, brownish green.

Kyle took all of these details in a split second, as well as two important facts: one, they were looking at each other, and neither had noticed him; two, their weapons were sheathed.

Kyle never would have known that any instinct he possessed was powerful enough to spur him into action the way that he was. Before he knew it, he had jumped forward, sword already raised to strike the torch-carrying goblin on the right.

They did see him, as he was flying towards them. He heard noises of surprise as they reached for their weapons, but it was too late for the first goblin. Kyle's blow caught him across the chest, and he fell backwards even as Kyle wheeled to face the second one. It had drawn its sword and Kyle was just fast enough to catch its first blow, which had been aimed at his head. He threw the goblin's sword off of his own and made his own cut at stomach level. The goblin blocked this, screeching, and riposted, sword plunging at Kyle's own chest. He knocked the blow aside awkwardly and managed to catch the goblin on the upswing; it yelped in pain and lowered its guard. Acting on instinct, Kyle allowed his sword's momentum to spin him all the way around. His sword rose and then fell, catching the goblin on the shoulder as his turn completed itself. The goblin slid to the ground, gurgling, blood spilling from the wound Kyle had inflicted.

He heard a ragged cheer from behind him. He turned around, panting, adrenalin pumping through his veins, to see that Lugh, Rogan and Nihs were all applauding him.

"Nice work!" Lugh said enthusiastically, striding forward and clapping him on the shoulder. "Are you sure you haven't done this before?"

Kyle didn't say anything. He didn't yet trust himself to speak. His whole body was shaking, although not with fear. He felt as though there was a fire in his chest, a fire that had sparked into life upon their entry into the mines and was now being fed by his victory. He felt a sudden strong urge to flex his muscles and punch the air.

He surfaced from his thoughts to see Lugh watching him with a smile on his face.

"Quite a rush, isn't it?" he said. "You'll get used to it as you fight more."

Kyle grinned viciously. *Fighting more…what a good idea.*

Rogan had shuffled past them and was now kneeling, examining the two dead goblins. He stood up and held out their swords for Lugh to see.

"Short, steel and flat. Not in bad condition, though, considering it was goblins who were using them. Maybe worth a hundred nells each. Worth keeping?"

Lugh sighed. "Normally I'd say no, but that Selk at the hideout said that a lot of them aren't even using swords. We might regret it if we leave these two and they turn out to be some of the best loot here."

Kyle heard this conversation through a layer of fog. He was replaying the battle over and over in his mind. Two goblins he had killed! He didn't feel at all remorseful or sick, as he had feared he might; as nice as this was, it did disturb him slightly. Had he secretly been a bloodthirsty person all his life and just never realized it? Surely, feeling a bit of regret after killing two living creatures would have been natural and healthy?

Try though he might, however, he couldn't force himself to feel sad about the goblins. He would never tell Nihs or Lugh this, but secretly he thought this might be because he was in Loria—though he had been in this world for several days, it still didn't seem completely real to him, and a small part of him felt as though his actions had no consequences.

He shook his head and brought his mind back into focus. He could think about all of this later, when they were safe.

They set out again, this time with David in the lead. His expression was determined. Clearly, he wanted to prove himself after seeing Kyle meet with such success.

Lugh drew up beside Kyle as they walked. The path had straightened out again, and was getting wider by the minute.

"You feeling okay?" Lugh asked him, as they passed through a largish chamber that featured a deep shaft in one corner.

"Yeah," Kyle said in a voice that still shook slightly.

"No shortness of breath? No sudden attack of cold feet?"

"Nope," Kyle said, smiling thinly.

Lugh gave his shoulder a shake, causing Nihs to chitter with annoyance.

"See?" he said. "What did I tell you? I *told* you he looked like a natural. Keep that up and you'll be a pro in no time," he added to Kyle.

Kyle's smile returned, and this time refused to go away. Between killing the goblins and receiving praise from Lugh, he was in a very good mood indeed.

The passage they were heading down had now gotten much wider and more interesting, showing many more signs of habitation and mining activity. Rooms and other tunnels branched off from the one they were following. Here and there, a shaft or a slide would lead to the deeper part of the mine; they saw abandoned carts and rails set into the ground. There were more tables and benches, a crude door or two, even the occasional wooden wall dividing a chamber in half.

"Those two we ran into back there were probably sentries," Rogan said in a low voice, axe clutched in his hands, "which would explain why they had swords and were so far away from the others. I think we'll start running into the bulk of them now."

Kyle's heart beat faster. He started checking every room and passage they passed, expecting to see one of the muddy green creatures appear around each corner.

They eventually did run into another group, although it wasn't Kyle who saw them first. They had entered a chamber which was cut in half by a rickety wooden wall with a door set in the middle. The wall didn't extend all the way to the ceiling, and so the sounds of goblin chatter coming from its other side were quite loud.

Lugh pressed a finger to his lips and stepped forward quietly. He leaned towards the wall, listening. After a moment, he turned and held up three fingers. He tiptoed back to Kyle and David.

"Two for you," he whispered, nodding at David, "and one for you," he said to Kyle. "They're probably sitting around a table. David, you go for whichever is closest to you; Kyle, you take the farthest. Then David can kill the last one and we can move on. Are you two ready?"

Kyle nodded at once, his fingers gripping and re-gripping his sword. David swallowed nervously, holding his own sword tightly and rotating his shield arm. He nodded, too, after a moment.

"Good," Lugh mouthed, and then crept back to the door. The handle didn't turn; it was a simple round of wood that had been nailed into the frame. He put a hand on it, then nodding one last time to the two others, swung it open and jumped out of the way.

"Yaaah!"

Kyle didn't know why he yelled—his only excuse was that it seemed like the right thing to do. He ran through the door quickly after David, who, Kyle noticed, despite his nervousness, moved with practiced precision.

The table was ahead of them and to the right; it was rectangular, with a long bench along each side. Two goblins were seated on the side closest to them, and a third sat on the other side of the table. This was the only one that Kyle had eyes for. He sprinted past David and to the right around the table, sword raised to strike.

His goblin reacted the fastest, since it had been facing the doorway when Kyle and David entered. It drew a small knife from its belt and made a quick swipe at Kyle's stomach; his momentum was too great and his sword too heavy to stop this blow, and he felt a horrible stab of pain in his core as the knife connected. His own blow, carried on mostly by his sword's weight, fell near the goblin's shoulder—it raised its knife arm quickly and instinctively to block the strike, but miscalculated. Kyle's sword fell across both its arm and its shoulder. Snarling with rage, it drew back its knife and plunged it again at Kyle, this stab catching him near the armpit.

Kyle's body was panicking and pain was lancing through him. He felt afraid for the first time that he might lose a fight. He was also, however, feeling a strange urge about his arms—for some reason he wanted to clap his hands together in front of him. Even as he struggled with the goblin, the feeling got stronger and stronger, and he felt his arms starting to move towards one another of their own accord, as though drawn by magnetism.

He fought back this feeling with difficulty and tried to focus on the battle at hand. The goblin had drawn back its knife again, and seemed to be calculating a third strike. Not having enough room to swing his sword, Kyle reached forward and pushed the goblin back by main force. It was amazingly light, and staggered backwards, almost losing its balance. Kyle pulled himself together and jumped, swinging downwards. The goblin tried to block the blow, but its knife was too small to be effective; Kyle caught it on the shoulder. He pulled his sword away and struck the goblin again on the upswing; as he did, he felt another urge, one that he at least understood. He jumped back and felt his sword spin in his hands, a roaring filling his ears. His gaiden strike was a stab that slammed the goblin backwards as though it was a wall of force. It was lifted off its feet and fell to the ground, unmoving.

Kyle turned, gasping in pain. He saw that one of the other goblins had already fallen; David was sparring with the last, which was wielding a pickaxe. As Kyle watched, David caught a blow on his shield and countered the recoiling goblin with a sword swipe that knocked the axe out of its hand. With a look that was half grim determination, half revulsion, David followed up with two swift chops that felled the goblin at once.

"Nice work," Kyle said dizzily. His vision was starting to swim. The pain in his chest and shoulder was blossoming.

He heard footsteps and then Lugh's voice: "Oh, shit, Kyle's hurt. David, you okay? Good. Somebody grab Kyle…"

Kyle felt large, warm hands grab him and lift him gently onto the table. Once he was laying down, his vision's spinning slowed somewhat and Rogan's face became apparent in front of him.

"Stay with us, kid," the Minotaur rumbled. "Don't worry, we'll patch you up. It's not too serious…Emil, do you think you can help him?"

Kyle saw Emil walk up close to him and touch his chest nervously.

"Um," she said, "I think so. Um. But I need to take his armor off…" her voice petered away weakly.

"I'll do that," Lugh said kindly. "Rogan, if you could just lift him off his back…great."

Kyle winced in pain as Lugh undid and then removed his chest piece and pauldrons. The Selk examined them and then set them aside with a snort.

"Bloody useless, if a goblin can slash through it. I should just get rid of it."

"He was just unlucky," Rogan said, shaking his head. "He ran into the first blow and the second was a stab. No armor made of hide could stop a puncture wound like that. In any case, it would have been much worse had the armor not been there."

"Uh," Emil said timidly once his armor was off. "I think his shirt should come off, too. Sorry."

"You don't have to apologize," Lugh said. He stepped back and observed Kyle critically. "How attached are you to that shirt?" he asked him.

"Not very," Kyle said.

Lugh nodded, and then drew a knife from his pocket and slashed Kyle's shirt open.

"I'm assuming you have a spare or two on you," Lugh said to Rogan.

"Should do."

Emil moved closer to Kyle and touched his chest gingerly. The tip of her wooden staff tilted downwards to hover over the wound.

"Okay," she said to the world at large. She looked terrified. "I'm going to try now. Um. Please stand back."

The others obliged, Lugh's expression matching Kyle's thoughts—it was not one that inspired confidence.

Emil narrowed her eyes until they were almost closed, and started whispering to herself. For a second, nothing seemed to be happening. Then the tip of her staff, her free hand, and the wound on Kyle's chest, all started to glow white. Kyle felt the atmosphere change as the magic started working. Everything seemed bright and stark, and a high, pure note sounded in his ears. His own vision started whiting out as the lights grew more intense. Kyle felt as though the whole world was being healed, not just himself; everything was white and pure, and Kyle felt blissfully detached from the aches of his own body. For some reason, when his head tilted to the left and he caught sight of Emil, she looked extremely beautiful to him.

Then the magic faded, and the world slowly went back to normal. Kyle felt as though the wound on his chest was being pinched, or set on fire, or something between the two. When he leaned forward to catch sight of it, he saw that it was nothing more than a scar.

"Well done," he heard Nihs say.

"Yeah, good job, Emil!" David said encouragingly.

Emil smiled bashfully and then moved her attention to the puncture wound on Kyle's shoulder.

"This one's more serious," she said, looking downcast. "I'm not sure if I'll be able to heal it completely…"

She worked the magic again and Kyle resurfaced to find that he was feeling much better. His vision no longer swam, and he now felt merely tired. He sat up and twisted his shoulder to bring the wound into view. It was now a large scab, still looking somewhat serious and bruised but no longer bleeding. He rotated his shoulder and found that it barely hurt.

"Great!" Kyle said happily, the after-effects of the magic making him slightly light-headed. He looked at Emil, who still appeared much more attractive than he remembered. He put it down to the magic and tried to ignore it.

"Thanks!" he told her.

She didn't seem too happy. "I'm sorry," she said miserably. "If I were stronger, I could have healed that easily…"

"For goodness' sake, don't worry about it," Nihs said. "It's more than any of us could have done. We might have had to call the mission off if it weren't for you."

"Your powers are amazing," added Kyle, who was still rotating his arm. "I've never seen anything like them."

Emil smiled again, mumbling thanks to the ground in front of her.

Kyle jumped off the table and grabbed the shirt that Rogan proffered to him. It was an oddly shaped light green affair that seemed to have been designed for someone much larger than him. He looked at the strange folds of cloth in dismay, realizing that he had no idea how to put it on.

Oh, shit, he thought. *Think fast.*

"Uh, Lugh," he said, wincing artfully. "I'm still kinda sore. Sorry, but could you…?"

To his relief, Lugh seemed to understand immediately. He strode over and helped Kyle into the shirt, saying in a low voice, "quick thinking. I guess there's no way you can prepare for every eventuality, eh? For future reference, *this* part folds under *that* part, then you tie it with *this*. They make 'em like that so that people from different races can wear them. There you go," he added in a louder voice, and then helped Kyle back into his armor to maintain the facade.

They set off again after Rogan took the one goblin's knife—the other two hadn't had any real weapons. Kyle was feeling slightly drained after being healed by Emil, but quite well otherwise. His respect for both siblings had shot up after their fight; David, after all, had gotten through the skirmish without so much as a scratch. He could tell that the others felt the same way. As they walked, Lugh fell into pace beside David, and Kyle overheard him congratulating him on his fighting.

They pressed on. The passage they were going down was now less of a tunnel and more of a succession of chambers—they were getting closer to the main section of the mine.

Soon the sounds of goblin presence once more drifted to the group's ears. Their burbling voices carried far in the silence of the mine. Kyle thought it sounded like a great many goblins.

Lugh stopped, head tilted, listening. "There's a lot of them this time. Sounds like at least a dozen; there must be some big room up ahead." He nodded sideways at Nihs and said to Rogan, "I think us three should handle this one, wouldn't you say?"

Rogan cricked his neck back and forth. "We should try and get *some* fighting in today," he said reasonably. "We don't want our skills to atrophy completely."

"Right," Lugh said, grinning. He said to David and Kyle, "You stay in the back this time, with Emil. Only get involved in the fight if one of them breaks away from us and goes after you, understand?"

Kyle and David nodded mutely. Kyle, for one, was excited to watch Lugh and the others in action. He imagined that their fighting skills must be very impressive if Lugh was casually suggesting a three-on-twelve battle.

The group rearranged itself so that Lugh, Nihs and Rogan were in the front. Kyle, David and Emil walked more or less abreast in the back.

"This is quite something, isn't it," David said.

Kyle just nodded, although inwardly he was chafing. *Why does everyone always want to talk to me?*

"You look like a natural at this," David pressed admiringly. "And this is your first mission, too, isn't it?"

"Yeah," Kyle said. Before he could stop himself, years of social programming kicked in and he asked, "It isn't yours, right?"

"Sort of. Emil and I have run missions before as part of another group. But just small stuff. This is our second time working alone—well, sort of alone, I guess. We—"

"Ssh," Lugh said gently, putting a finger to his lips. He pointed to the passage ahead of them, clearly intending to say, 'they're close'.

The group advanced cautiously, trying not to make any noise. The sound of goblin chatter was certainly getting much louder, to the point that Kyle thought their stealthy measures were quite unnecessary. They reached a wooden door set into the cave wall ahead and Lugh leaned against it, listening. Light was filtering through the cracks in the door, indicating the room beyond it was brightly lit.

"They're in here," Lugh said in a low voice. "Sounds like even more than I thought. Twenty at least. We weren't supposed to run into this many...obviously there's more goblins in here than the guild thought."

"Will you be able to fight them all?" Kyle asked concernedly.

"Oh, for sure," Lugh said. "It would take a lot more than twenty goblins to get the better of us. I'm just afraid that we won't be able to block them off from you and Emil; you'll probably have to deal with a couple. Are you ready for that?" he asked seriously.

Kyle wanted to say immediately that he was, but he didn't want to be responsible for getting the group in trouble. He rotated his wounded arm and gauged his own strength honestly, while David said, "Yeah, I'm fine."

Kyle made his decision. "I should be fine, if David's fighting with me," he said, nodding to his fellow fighter. "I'll be more careful this time, I won't get myself hurt."

Lugh gave them both a long look. "All right," he said, and that was that. He turned back to the door and crouched down low, trying to see through the cracks. "It looks like they've built some kind of dining hall. They've got a bunch of tables set up." He shifted his stance, cramming his face against the door. "Oh, good! The room's below us—there's a set of stairs past this door leading down to it. That'll help you two defend it if any goblins come after you."

He stood up and squared his shoulders. He put his back to the door with his hand flat against it, preparing to swing it open. "Everyone ready?" he asked. "Here goes..."

Light spilled into their antechamber as Lugh pushed the door open. He disappeared through it in a flash, sword in hand, sprinting down the rickety wooden staircase beyond it. Rogan barreled through the entrance after him. Shrieks and cries coming from inside the room indicated that the goblins were now aware that they were under attack.

The sounds of battle met Kyle's ears as he and David rushed to occupy the doorway. They stood at the top of the stairs, observing the battle below. The room was as Lugh had described, a large chamber inside which had been arranged many tables and a couple small fires. Lit torches were set into the walls, their light added with that of the fires' meant that the room was brightly illuminated.

The center of Kyle's attention, however, was the fight taking place at the bottom of the stairs. Goblins were swarming towards Lugh, Nihs and Rogan, who were fighting alongside one another in an expanding fan formation. Lugh's golden blade flickered and flashed as the Selk swung it with more speed than Kyle had ever seen; Lugh himself was spinning, jumping, kicking, and overall fighting with a sort of deadly, calculated grace. Rogan was swinging his axe in wide circles, keeping the goblins at bay, threatening to brain whichever one was foolish enough to approach him. He advanced slowly, herding the goblins backwards.

Nihs, meanwhile, was hanging back, between Lugh and Rogan; he was immobile, and an aura of power surrounded his tiny being. Red light spilled towards Nihs' location. As Kyle watched, the Kol ran straight up Rogan's back and vaulted off of his shoulder, sailing over the crowd of goblins, his entire body glowing like a beacon. Nihs twisted his body in mid-air and pointed his hand at the ground—a massive ball of fire struck the ground underneath him, exploding with a detonation that felled five goblins at once. Nihs' momentum, which he seemed to possess in impossible quantity, carried him to the far edge of the chamber, where he landed and started to attack the group of goblins from behind, sparks flying from his fingertips.

Watching his companions fight was terrible and awe-inspiring. It seemed as though the laws of physics had no hold over them. They moved with surreal speed and strength, decimating the goblins even though they were heavily outnumbered. Rogan caught a goblin with an upward swing that lifted the unfortunate creature fifteen feet in the air, a moment later, Lugh jumped just as high in order to avoid an attack.

Nothing and no-one on Earth can fight like this, Kyle thought. Lights of every hue and intensity were flashing on and off around Nihs; he was surrounded constantly by an aura of magic, and his arms blurred as he wove spell after spell. Rogan's axe moved at a speed that was unnatural for something so large, and Lugh looked nothing less than untouchable.

Kyle was noticing something else, however. Even though numerous goblins were dying everywhere, their numbers did not seem to be diminishing. They continued to pour in from the dark corners of the room, where Kyle assumed were more tunnels—there were far more than twenty of them.

David had noticed this, as well. "Look at them all! There's a lot more than twenty—are they going to be all right?"

Kyle had no answer for him. He had no idea what his companions were capable of. Should they run down and try to help?

He was spared making the decision. Lugh's fighting had taken him towards the center of the chamber, and so it enabled a small group of goblins to get past him and move towards the staircase. One of them pointed at Kyle and David, and it, and two of its kin, ran up the stairs, weapons bared.

"Let's go!" Kyle shouted to David, sword raised.

They met the goblins at the top of the stairs beyond the doorway. There was enough room for the two of them to stand and fight side-by-side. The goblin that Kyle engaged was wielding a makeshift weapon that looked like a sharpened spade—it was slow and clumsy, and Kyle had the height advantage besides. He stepped back easily from the first blow and caught the goblin just below the neck; it toppled backwards into its companion, who stepped over its body to take its place. Before it could act, however, David rammed into it from the side with his shield, knocking it sideways off of the staircase.

"Thanks," Kyle said as they regained their positions.

David smiled for the first time that Kyle had seen. There was a glint in his eye as he clanged his sword and shield together, awaiting another attack.

Kyle, too, focused his gaze once more on the staircase. He was distracted, however, by the same urge he had felt before—his hands were trying to put themselves together of their own accord again. His body was trying to convince him that it would be very comfortable and natural, like lying down when tired. He fought it back, fearing it. He had no idea what was causing it, or whether or not it was dangerous.

He was pulled out of his reverie by a shriek coming from behind him. A spasm of fear shot up his spine as he realized that it was being made by Emil.

Both Kyle and David wheeled around to look, and both cried out in fear at the same time: four more goblins had somehow gotten behind them and were advancing on Emil, who was holding her staff out in front of her in defense.

"You get them!" Kyle shouted at once to David, his analytical mind being one step ahead of the rest of him. "I'll cover the front!"

With a furious, animal yell that caught Kyle completely by surprise, David launched himself past Emil and bowled into the group of goblins, hacking away madly at them. Kyle couldn't afford to watch, however, he turned his attention back to the staircase ahead of them.

His heart sank in dismay. Lugh had been absorbed further into the brawl, which was now raging all around the room. The goblins had stopped swarming in, but there were so many of them that the entire chamber was densely packed. No fewer than eight goblins had just shoved their way past Lugh, and were already at the foot of the staircase.

Kyle hefted his sword, his heart beating in his throat. For the first time that mission, he truly feared for his own life. He wouldn't be able to fight eight all by himself. What could he do? Call for help? His gaze flickered across the room, and he picked out the shapes of Nihs, Lugh and Rogan. All three were fighting several goblins at once, and were surrounded on all sides.

The goblins were halfway up the staircase. Kyle thought he heard the one in front cackling.

Mentally he steeled himself. There was no way out, nothing he could do except fight as well as he could. There was no point in thinking about what would happen if he lost.

Even as he told himself this, his mind started to run away from him. What if he died, right here and now, in this strange world, slain by goblins? Would they then move on past him, and kill David and Emil? Would Lugh,

Nihs and Rogan hold a funeral for him? How about back home on Earth? Maybe they already thought he was dead over there, his body having gone missing during the storm.

One of the goblins on the stairs made a noise, and Kyle's attention snapped back to them. He took in their faces, their armor and weapons, the way they moved. He thought, with amazing clarity, *these things are going to kill me.*

Suddenly a feeling of great serenity and confidence welled up inside Kyle. In that instant, he knew that there was a way to defeat all of them; he had known it all along, he just hadn't recognized it for what it was.

The urge built in Kyle's arms again, this time so strongly that it couldn't be ignored. He didn't try to resist it; instead, he sheathed his sword on his back, getting it out of the way. His hands slapped together, fingers pointing forwards. Kyle felt a tingling that started in his chest and travelled down his arms to his palms. He saw silver-white sparks of light coursing across his arms, flowing and leaping like fish in a river. Light consumed Kyle's forearms, sparks joining together in his hands until they were incandescent.

A beam of what looked like molten silver shot out from between Kyle's palms, extending three feet out from his hands and then stopping. The sparks swirled around it, glowing so brightly that Kyle almost had to close his eyes. Finally the glowing died down somewhat, and Kyle looked at what was in his hands.

It was meant to be a sword, that much was obvious, although it didn't look like any sword Kyle had ever seen on Earth or Loria. It was composed not of a single piece, but of several curved and twisted shards of silver metal. They all floated, apparently unattached to one another, in such a way that they formed a crude sword-like shape. Blue light shone from the empty space in the middle of the construction, it was as though the silver shards had been glued to this central beam, this *idea* of a sword.

Set into the crosspiece of the sword was a single diamond-shaped blue gem, although it was not an Ephicer—it was dull and dark, like a regular sapphire from Earth.

A wonderful feeling filled Kyle's soul. The sword was extremely light, and yet carried with it an unmistakable aura of power. Kyle had no idea what the sword was, or where he had gotten it from, but he did know that he was very glad to have it.

The goblins were hanging back, suddenly looking fearful. Kyle felt that he knew why. With the sword's appearance his fear had dissipated entirely; he barely hesitated before he leapt forward and struck.

The sword was unstoppable. Every time it connected with one of the goblins or their weapon, there was a small detonation like a firecracker going off, silver sparks flew, and the weapon shattered or the goblin died instantly. The sword was as light as a toy and Kyle felt no recoil whenever he struck a foe. He cleft his way through them easily, swinging left and right.

After he had killed the first five, the remaining three tried to escape him, but Kyle advanced ruthlessly down the stairs, forcing them to back up into their companions behind. Desperately they tried to fend off his blows, but it was no use—no weapon survived a single attack from Kyle's mystery blade.

Kyle felt another gaiden strike building in him. He leapt backward from the goblins and lifted his sword until it was directly in front of his face. His eyes snapped shut for a second, then he opened them and leveled his glowing weapon at the pack of goblins ahead. He saw the eyes of the goblin in front widen in fear as it realized what was going on, and felt a brief pang of sympathy for it as it raised its hands to protect itself...but he was no longer in control of his own body. He dashed towards the group, his sword glowing brighter than ever. When he struck, a huge wall of force exploded outwards from the swing's arc—the goblin, and five more around it, were lifted from their feet and sent flying backwards.

Kyle looked left and right, ready to engage any goblins that were left, but the battle was drawing to a close. To his left, Lugh quickly cut down the three goblins that he had been fighting, then made his way over to Kyle. Kyle smiled and opened his mouth, ready to accept praise for his goblin-slaying skills.

Lugh, however, did not seem very happy. "Where's David and Emil?" he shouted at Kyle as he ran past him to help Rogan.

Kyle's heart sank. Of course he had left David to fight four goblins on his own. In his elation, he had forgotten that the other fighter possessed no magical sword.

He turned and sprinted back up the stairs, fearing the worst, but when he crossed the threshold into the antechamber it was to find David sitting up against the cave wall, panting, while Emil tended to a wound on his arm. Four dead goblins lay beyond them.

"You killed them all?" Kyle asked incredulously.

Emil turned and looked at Kyle with shining eyes. "You should have seen it," she said in a voice thick with emotion. "It was amazing."

David's eyes had widened when he saw Kyle. The latter saw the glow of his newfound sword reflected in David's eyes.

"Speaking of amazing," he said in a breathless voice, "where did you get that sword?"

Kyle examined it, drinking in its beauty.

"I don't know how I got it," he said, hypnotized. "It sort of grew out of my hands. I'll have to ask Nihs about it after, I guess."

"Wow," David said, and then gasped in pain as his arm spasmed.

"This is the best I can do," Emil said to him, binding it in cloth. "When we get back to town, a more skilled healer can heal you completely. How are the others doing?" she asked of Kyle.

"Hang on, let me check," he said, and ran back to the top of the stairs.

The battle was over. Dead goblins littered the floor, and Nihs, Lugh and Rogan were picking their way through them, looking into the dark corners of the room to make sure that there were none left.

Lugh squinted up to the staircase and spotted Kyle. He cupped his hands to his mouth and called, "Hey! You okay?"

"Yeah," Kyle called back.

"How about David and Emil?"

"David's been hurt, but he should be fine. Emil's okay. How about you?"

Lugh spread his arms to indicate the destruction around him.

"Pretty good, considering. Hang on, we're gonna come up and take a look at David. Don't move him."

The three of them made their way back up the stairs. All three were panting; Rogan was massaging his wrist and Nihs was working out a crick in his neck.

"I'm getting too old for this," Rogan lamented, then he stopped and stared at Kyle.

"Nice sword," he said in wonderment. "Where did you get that?"

Lugh and Nihs, too, were noticing the glowing sword in Kyle's hands for the first time.

"Wow!" Nihs said, his brown eyes wide, "you never told us that you had a soul sword!"

"I have no idea what that is," Kyle said honestly, lifting the sword up to his face. He noticed that his right palm seemed glued to it. He couldn't let go of it if he tried. "It just grew out of my hands during the battle. What is it?"

"A soularm is a special kind of weapon that you weave into the fabric of your spirit," Nihs said in an awed voice. "They can't be separated from you and you can draw and retract them whenever you want. They're extremely rare," he added, his voice almost accusatory. "The process of integrating a soularm into your spirit is very difficult, not to mention expensive. How did you get that one?"

"I don't know," Kyle said. "I was hoping *you* could tell *me*."

"Hmm," Nihs said, tapping his chin. "I don't know much about soularms myself, but I've never heard of one just showing up inside someone's spirit. In any case, we can worry about it later," he said firmly, with an undertone that said to Kyle, *not in front of the others*. "In the meantime, you should probably try not to use it. Apart from the fact that we have no idea where it came from, you'll never get any stronger if you use a weapon like that to fight normal battles."

"Okay, fine," said Kyle. "Sounds great. Only one problem. I don't know how to get rid of it."

He waved his arm enthusiastically, keeping his hand open. The sword remained fixed to his palm. The only way he was able to move it was by grabbing it with his other hand, and this just stuck it to his left palm, instead.

"I think soularms are supposed to be intent-driven, just like retraweapons," Nihs said, his eyes still fixed on the soul sword. "Try just willing it to retract."

Kyle did so, and at once felt the urge to put his hands together again. When he did, the sword slid easily back into his palms, turning into a volley of silver sparks that dissipated along his forearms.

Both Nihs and Lugh watched the process hungrily. Lugh sighed and shook his head.

"That's so cool," he said enviously. "You lucky duck. Why can't I have a soul sword randomly pop up in my hands? Do you know how much easier that would make everything?"

"Look," Nihs said, "I don't know if the rest of you realize this, but there's still a mission going on. That was a big fight, everyone did very well, but we have more ahead of us yet. We need to hurry if we want to arrive in time with the others. We can't afford to lose focus," he added, shooting a look at Lugh.

The latter rolled his eyes. "Fine, fine. David, how are you?" he asked.

David had gotten up, but was unable to pick up his sword with his damaged arm.

"I'll be all right," he said, smiling at his sister, "thanks to Emil. But I can't fight like this. Sorry."

"Don't worry about it," Lugh said. "You killed four goblins by yourself, without some fancy-pants sword to help you—"

"Hey!"

"—which is more than we could have asked for. Rogan, why don't you hold onto his sword for him, and we can get going."

They made their way back down the staircase and across the room, where a similar stairs led up to another doorway. Kyle looked at the bodies of the slain goblins as they passed, trying to count them mentally.

"So how many do you think were here after all?" he asked Lugh.

"Hoo boy. Must have been over fifty. As it turns out, there were a couple other rooms all attached to this one. I didn't see them when I looked through the door. Sorry about that. It could have gotten the three of you killed."

"No worries. But there shouldn't have been this many on our run, right? So what happened?"

"Probably just misinformation," Lugh said, shrugging. "More goblins might've moved in since they checked, or we were just unlucky and some other group is going to find their path pretty sparse. No point worrying about it now, though. Nihs' right, we need to hustle it out right now if we want to catch up."

With this in mind, they moved at an accelerated pace through the next rooms of the mine, Kyle and Lugh in front, David and Emil behind them and Rogan and Nihs taking up the rear. The passages they went through grew slim once more, and climbed often. They ran into a couple more goblins, but between Lugh and Kyle these posed no problem. Kyle could tell that he was getting better with every single goblin he slew. Even though he was no longer using his soul sword, he found that combat was becoming easier and easier as he went along.

Finally they reached another doorway, at the top of a long ascending tunnel. There was light coming from beyond this one, too, but it was fainter. Lugh put his ears to the door and then peered through the cracks.

"I can't see anything," he said, "but I can hear fighting. We must be close to the others! Come on!"

He pushed the door open without waiting for them. Beyond it was a long pathway that sloped gently downwards and to the right. And it was a pathway, not a tunnel, since there was no cave wall to their right—the floor dropped off into a deep fissure fifty feet below. On the other side of the fissure was a large chamber, a massive cavern bigger than any Kyle had seen so far in the mine; it could easily have fit several houses. It was approximately dome-shaped, and the ground at the center of the cavern was flat. The path they were currently on followed the shape of the dome downwards. After two hundred feet, the path entered solid rock and became a tunnel once more.

Since they were on an elevated path, they had a perfect view of the chamber below. It was utter chaos. A massive skirmish was raging in all corners of the room—goblins were swarming everywhere, and the fifteen or so adventurers that had already arrived were battling them ferociously. Kyle could easily make out Reldan in the din—he was fighting in the direct center of the room, and was constantly clearing a space in the mass around him with his composite weapon.

"Hurry!" Lugh shouted at them, already sprinting down the pathway, sword in hand.

Kyle ran after him, struggling to keep pace with Lugh's massive strides. He heard a crashing behind him and assumed that Rogan was following them; when he turned to look, however, he saw that Rogan, with

Nihs still on his shoulder, was running directly towards the chasm to their right. When he reached it, the Minotaur performed a spectacular jump that launched him from the pathway—he flew nearly two hundred feet and landed on the platform where the battle was taking place. He instantly joined in, axe swinging around him as Nihs launched spells from his back.

Kyle turned his attention back to the passage ahead of him. Lugh had reached the cave entrance and disappeared beyond it. Kyle followed him, turning sideways to get through the narrow passage.

Inside, the cave opened into a small, wide room; it curved sharply to the right, and Kyle was just fast enough to see Lugh's golden mane disappear around the bend. He stopped to steel himself for the upcoming battle, taking deep breaths to slow his heart's pounding. David and Emil caught up with him, and they too stopped.

Kyle took in David's damaged arm and was about to tell them to stay put in this room when he realized that he was making the same mistake as before, and would essentially be leaving his friends for the goblins if he went on ahead. His heart sinking, he said instead, "Let's stay here. I'll fight off anything that tries to get in. Both of you, just stay back."

"I'm sorry," David said, sitting down and propping himself up against the far wall. "I went and got myself hurt, and now you're stuck here protecting us."

"Don't worry about it," Kyle said. "If I hadn't been such an idiot back there, this wouldn't have happened."

He went to the bend in the room to see what was around it. He was met by a rather wide opening that led directly into the large chamber, and then into the battle. He could see Lugh ahead of him, who had already been absorbed into the fray; close by him were the three Snakes, Qon, Doru and Sali. In the far distance he saw what might have been Nihs and Rogan, but the press of goblins prevented him from making out much else.

He watched the battle in awe, sword in hand. Goblin bodies were flying all over, weapons were clashing, and magic crackled constantly in the air. Occasionally Sali would cast a spell that would paint the air a different color and make Kyle feel strange, as though his weapon was suddenly lighter or his senses keener.

The other adventurers slashed, stabbed, parried, jumped, dodged and otherwise fought with the same unbelievable strength and precision that Kyle had seen before in his companions. Magic was everywhere—it lined the adventurers' weapons and traced the arcs of their slashes. Kyle could only assume that this was caused by gaiden strikes, or perhaps some other technique that Lugh hadn't yet taught him.

To Kyle's disappointment no goblins seemed about to make their way to the entrance he was guarding. Every time a couple of them got close, an adventurer would leap out of nowhere and engage them. Kyle, however, resisted the urge to rush into battle; no matter what, he would not be responsible for getting David or Emil injured again.

Although the battle was even larger than the one before, the adventurers were making short work of it. The goblins, despite their huge numbers, were melting under the adventurers' assault. Reldan in particular had claimed an unthinkable amount of lives; a ring of goblin bodies surrounded him, and yet he showed no signs of slowing down.

Finally there was a commotion at the far end of the chamber—the fighting continued, and yet Kyle could sense a shift in the goblins' and adventurers' attention. Kyle thought he could see a small group of goblins making their way down a path to join the fray, but his vision was blocked by the press of bodies.

Whatever the disturbance had been, it caused the battle to rage on fiercer than ever. The adventurers, who had started to push the goblins back towards the far end of the chamber, were now forced to retreat slightly as the goblins struck back.

One of them broke away from the battle and headed towards Kyle. Now that it was closer, Kyle could see that it wasn't like the creatures they had met before in the mine—it was slightly larger, almost as tall as Kyle, and armed with a spear.

Kyle nervously raised his weapon, unsure of how to engage an enemy armed as such. The goblin advanced on him in a crouch, jabbing the spear at Kyle to force him backwards.

Kyle parried one or two blows clumsily, and was considering drawing his soul sword to beat his foe when Lugh leapt out of nowhere and caught the goblin a massive blow to the arm. The goblin was launched sideways into the cave wall beside them, where it connected with a *crack* and slid to the floor.

"The chieftain's personal guard," Lugh shouted to Kyle as explanation. "We've drawn him out from his chambers. Reldan's dueling him now. Come on!" He beckoned to Kyle as he started to turn back into the fray.

"I'm guarding David and Emil!"

"They'll be fine, but we might not be! Come help!"

Kyle wasn't about to argue with Lugh. Heart thumping, he dashed after the Selk into the chamber ahead.

The main battle was a huge ring that lined the edges of the chamber. In the center of it all Reldan was fighting a massive goblin that had a net in one hand and a strange sword-like weapon in the other. They seemed evenly matched; Reldan was faster, and he dashed to and fro trying to find a gap in the chieftain's defenses, but the goblin was keeping him at bay with the swinging net, and his sword that had more reach than Reldan's composite weapon. Goblins and adventurers alike were giving them a wide berth.

The adventurers seemed to be having a tough time fighting the chieftain's guard. Although the goblins didn't seem particularly strong on their own, their spears' reach was significant and not many of the adventurers had weapons long enough to match them.

Lugh grabbed Kyle and pulled him close so that he could shout in his ear.

"Don't try fighting them from the front!" he said. "Find one that's already occupied and hit it in the back! You don't get points out here for fighting fairly! If one of us gets attacked, the other circles around it while it's distracted! Got it?"

Kyle nodded to show that he had; Lugh released him and the two joined in the fight. They circled the battlefield together, using Lugh's strategy to attack the guards from behind whenever they could. Oftentimes it was Kyle who would be harried by one of the spear-wielding goblins— Lugh, with unnatural agility, would quickly dash around it and cut it down.

Once they had freed up a couple more adventurers, the tide of battle began turning again. The goblins' spears were slow and hard to use against multiple opponents, and groups of two or three had no problem overpowering them.

They ended up reaching Nihs and Rogan at the far side of the room. Rogan was fighting a complicated battle against several guards; his axe was as long as the goblins' spears, but it was also slower, and he was struggling to keep them all at bay. Nihs was casting the occasional spell from atop Rogan, but his strength seemed depleted. He clung to the Minotaur's back like an infant, his head bobbing as though he were falling asleep.

Kyle and Lugh quickly started harrying the guards around Rogan—as soon as their focus wavered, the Minotaur immediately switched to the offensive and cut them down. Soon, all of them had fallen and the four reunited friends took a moment to recuperate.

"Lugh, you nuck," Nihs said, lifting his head up from Rogan's back, "why didn't you leap over that ledge?"

"The others don't know how to leap!" Lugh retorted angrily. "Someone had to lead them down the path!"

"Tesh*ur*," the Kol said in dismissal, his head falling back down as if he were unable to keep talking.

"What's wrong with him?" Kyle asked, concerned.

"He's been using too much magic," Rogan said, shaking his head. "We underestimated how tough these goblins were. I'm sorry, Lugh," he added, bowing to him, "that leap was reckless of me. I didn't even think of the others." Lugh just shrugged, as most of his attention was taken up by the rest of the battlefield.

"Whatever, we all got through it, so no harm done," he said. "Hey, it looks like we're winning—Reldan's still fighting the chief, though."

They ran over to the center of the chamber, where a ring of adventurers had formed around the battle between Reldan and the goblin chieftain. The rest of the chamber was now empty, all of the chieftain's guard having been slain.

They joined the ring of onlookers to watch the two foes spar. Neither seemed to have slowed since the fight began. The chieftain was still swinging his net and sword, keeping Reldan at bay while snarling away in its strange language. Reldan fought silently except for grunts and cries of effort. Sweat was streaming down his face and his expression was screwed up with concentration.

"Why isn't anyone helping?" Kyle asked Lugh.

Lugh gave a small laugh. "Cause of—oh, right, sorry," he said, apparently catching himself. "I keep forgetting that you don't know about...right. Okay, well, it's like...unwritten law, I guess. You're not supposed to interfere with another adventurer's fight except under certain conditions. In a duel like this, we can't help unless Reldan calls for it."

"Oh," Kyle said. It was still difficult, as he watched the two struggle, to keep himself away from the fight. Every time it looked as though Reldan might lose, Kyle felt the involuntary twitch of his hands as they tried to summon his soul sword.

It was only then that Kyle noticed who he was standing next to—it was Doru, the Snake.

"What'ss up?" Doru said, bobbing his head, when he noticed Kyle's attention on him. "Quite the fight, issn't it?"

"Yes," Kyle said, turning back to it, "it is. Who do you think will win?"

"We were jusst talking about that," Doru said quietly. "We're ssuprised, but it lookss like Reldan might need ssome help. Of course, he will not assk for it. We'll just have to ssee."

Doru seemed perfectly fine with the prospect of watching Reldan until it was possibly too late, but Kyle was disturbed. He was not fond of the hero, but he had no desire to see him get killed. Of course, there was also the question of what would happen if Reldan failed to kill the chieftain—he was, after all, supposed to be the strongest adventurer here. Surely all of them together would be able to slay it if Reldan fell?

As Kyle worried, the compulsion to draw his soul sword became stronger and stronger. He tried fighting it down, but the feeling was rising in him like bile.

Suddenly, Reldan's composite weapon got caught in the chieftain's net. He struggled to free it, but the chieftain quickly threw the net to the ground and stepped forwards onto it, pulling Reldan off balance. The chieftain raised his sword as Reldan freed his own from the weapon's depths—he blocked the crushing blow at the last minute, though his aim was wild and his arm was knocked aside by the attack. The chieftain raised his sword again as Reldan desperately tried to set his arm.

Kyle lost control over himself. He sheathed his sword and clapped his hands together, the silver sparks already flowing along his arms. A part of him seemed to understand the urgency of the situation—the glow gathered much faster than before, and the sword quickly grew from his fingertips and solidified.

He was aware of Lugh shouting something from behind him as he leapt forward, but there was noise filling his ears and he ignored it. He swung a huge overhand blow that caught the goblin on its sword arm. Just as before, there was a loud detonation when the sword connected and the chieftain screamed in pain as his arm was mangled.

The goblin jumped back to get away from Kyle and to bring both him and Reldan into its view. Kyle took the opportunity to cut at the net binding Reldan's weapon, which snapped and burned away under his soul sword's assault.

Reldan scrambled to his feet, tearing the rest of the net from his weapon. He was furious.

"What do you think you're doing?" he shouted angrily at Kyle.

There was no time for Kyle to even compute this—the goblin chieftain was rallying himself for another attack, and both Kyle and Reldan were forced to face him. The chief circled, eyeing Kyle's glowing weapon warily. While the creature's armor and natural hide were tough, a large amount of blood seeped from the wound inflicted by the soul sword.

The chieftain moved sideways towards Reldan; it was obvious that its intention was to attack the target that it had already almost defeated once. Reldan, however, wasn't about to wait for the goblin's attack. He ran forward, shield raised, and struck with his composite sword. As the two exchanged blows, Kyle darted to the side and slashed at the chieftain's leg. It howled again the second the sword touched its flesh. Kyle jumped backwards and looked up just in time to see Reldan sheath his sword and pull out his black axe. He twirled the axe in a figure-eight pattern about his body, and Kyle could actually feel the gaiden strike's presence. Reldan leapt high into the air, axe aloft, and then descended, dealing the chieftain a massive, crushing blow to the head.

The creature gurgled once, and fell to the ground with a clatter as the adventurers around them erupted into cheers.

Kyle, panting with adrenalin, watched as Reldan kicked the body of the goblin away from his axe and recovered the creature's sword. Despite the situation, he looked far from happy. He turned on Kyle, the goblin's sword in his hand.

"What the hell was that? I didn't ask for your help. What made you think I wanted you to step in?"

Kyle backed away, shocked and afraid. Reldan's dark eyes looked slightly mad. He found himself unable to speak. But a sudden voice piped up from the group of adventurers around him.

"Hey, now!" it called, and Kyle realized that it was Qon talking. The Lizardman had stepped forward and sounded indignant. "We all know you wouldn't have assked for help if your life depended on it."

"So?" Reldan snapped, wheeling on him. "That doesn't give him the right to get in my way."

There was a huge snort from behind Kyle.

"Get in your way?" Rogan said in a voice laced with contempt. "A couple more seconds and that goblin would have finished you off, Reldan."

"Hear, hear, you prideful *tish*!" a Kol within the crowd shouted. "You owe that man your life!"

Emboldened by this statement, several other adventurers started to talk at the same time, their voices running over each other as they supported Kyle.

Reldan spun in place as he tried to meet each of the shouted comments in turn. His expression was murderous. Kyle's mind was blank, and he said nothing as he let the arguments wash over him.

Finally the noise subsided. Kyle watched Reldan warily—the hero looked like he might attack at any moment.

"Fine," he said, spitting the word. "You want the stupid sword? You can have it."

And he tossed the chieftain's sword to Kyle before a word could be said. Kyle flinched at the movement, but instinctively caught the sword by the handle when it reached him, his soul sword hissing back into his arms. As the adventurers dispersed to comb over the goblins' corpses, Kyle finally found his voice.

"But I don't want—" he started, and he felt a hand clamp his shoulder, hard, and steer him backwards.

"Don't say anything," Lugh's voice sounded in his ear, "just come on."

"But—"

"Shush."

They re-joined Rogan and Nihs in an out-of-the-way corner of the chamber. Nihs looked slightly better than before, propped up against one of Rogan's legs. The Minotaur himself was sitting cross-legged on the ground, tending to his axe.

"Phew," Lugh said, once they were out of earshot of the others. He plunked down facing Rogan. "That was close. Kyle, what got *into* you? I had just finished telling you that you don't mess with another adventurer's fight."

"I'm sorry," Kyle said in a low voice, sitting down to his right. "I couldn't control myself. It was just instinct."

"I guess I can't hold it against you," Lugh said, "you're not used to fighting. And hey, it turned out all right this time. Just try to curb your heroic instincts in the future, okay?"

"Right," Kyle said in a small voice. He held up the sword that Reldan had thrown to him. It was silver in color and had a one-edged blade, although the blade was wide and straight instead of curved. It looked like a piece of machinery that was half-assembled. The blade was split open at several seams, exposing what looked like miniature hydraulic piping underneath.

"What is this?" he asked, holding it out to Rogan.

"That's a changesword," Rogan said, sounding impressed, as he took the weapon from Kyle. "They're uncommon. I didn't bother to mention them to you because we don't have one in the dojo. Basically, they're a type of intent-driven arm similar to a retraweapon. The difference is, while a retraweapon moves between one useful shape and one inactive shape, a changearm moves between two useful shapes." The Minotaur held the sword up and focused his attention on it. With a neat little *snicking* sound, the blade sank down, the hydraulics became hidden and the weapon was suddenly a short sword with a neat, unblemished blade.

"That's a good find," Rogan said approvingly, handing the sword back to Kyle. "It's high quality, and in good condition, too. Worth a good two,

two and a half thousand nells, I'd wager. That chieftain must have gotten it from some other adventurer he killed."

"So we'll sell it?" Kyle asked, extending the blade again for the fun of it.

Lugh laughed. "Sell something like that? Nah, it'd be a waste. You can use it," he said, slapping Kyle on the back. "After all, you earned it."

"I can use it? Really?" Kyle asked in wonderment. He studied the sword again. "But I have my soul sword, shouldn't one of you—"

Nihs raised his head. "You shouldn't be using your soul sword as your main weapon, for many reasons," he said. "We still don't know what it's capable of, or where it's from, or why you're able to use it. You need a normal weapon, and that sword should do nicely."

"Changearms are easier to use than retraweapons," Lugh added. "It won't take you long to get used to that one, and remember, we're trying to get you to improve as fast as possible."

Kyle considered the sword in a whole different light now that he knew it belonged to him. He found himself grinning as he thought, *this is my sword.*

The rest of the mission passed in a haze for Kyle. The adventurers spent a while searching the cavern as well as the chieftain's chambers for loot. Kyle, knowing nothing about the process, just hung back and rested. David and Emil joined him before too long, having gathered that the battle was over. Kyle, strangely thankful to see them, nodded politely as they approached.

"How're you feeling?" he asked David.

"I'm fine. I wish I could've been a help during the battle, though," he said, watching the other adventurers enviously. "Still, I guess I should be thankful that I'm alive."

Nihs, Lugh and Rogan returned soon after, Rogan with a huge pack full of spoils on his back.

"Decent haul," Lugh said happily, "even divided as many ways as it was. That sword of yours is definitely the main attraction, though. If I were Reldan I'd be pretty unhappy." He looked pleased at the prospect.

The adventurers eventually left through the far side of the chamber. Kyle assumed that this must have been the passage that Reldan's group had entered by. They trouped as a large mob outside; Kyle was astonished to see that it had grown dark in the time they had spent in the mine. Loria's stars were bright and plentiful, though Kyle didn't have the time to see if they were any different from Earth's.

There was a celebration at the hideout that night. Seeing as the mission was over, the adventurers no longer had any qualms about drinking, and so Kyle, happily in his element, was able to test out various types of Lorian alcoholic beverages to his leisure. He tried several simple mixed drinks that originated from the Selks and humans of Centralia—these were quite similar to those that could be found on Earth. Although the barkeep's selection was relatively limited, Kyle still had the opportunity to attempt a couple more exotic drinks as the night went on. He was enjoying himself immensely. He felt swelled up with confidence as a result of the night's events—other adventurers kept coming over to his table to congratulate him on his success. The hideout was bright and noisy with activity; adventurers talked, laughed, looked over their spoils, and recounted stories from their own runs through the mine. The room was full with the noise of plates and glasses clattering, adventurers talking and chairs scraping along the ground as people moved from table to table. Kyle, feeling amazingly sociable in his current state, chatted with everyone indiscriminately.

Oddly enough, while the other adventurers were impressed by Kyle's victory, many of them seemed equally impressed by David's fight against the four goblins.

"Well done!" It was the Kol that had spoken up in Kyle's defense earlier. He and his Selkic companion had rotated around to Kyle's table. He was Erai and his companion was Dezzela; the Selk seemed fairly quiet, but Erai was particularly talkative.

"What did you say your CAL was the last time you got it tested?" he asked.

"An eight," David said, obviously taken aback by all the attention.

"Hm! How long ago was that?"

"Maybe half a year?" David said, looking to Emil for support.

"Well!" Erai said pompously, "I think it's about time you got it checked again. Four goblins at once? That must put you at least at level fifteen. I wouldn't be surprised if you were getting close to twenty."

Kyle felt Lugh nudge him. He turned to look at him through bleary eyes.

"Reldan doesn't look too happy," Lugh said in a grimly amused voice.

Kyle peered over at the hero's table—Reldan had a drink on the table in front of him and was scowling.

"Sucks to be him," Kyle said happily, waving his drink.

"Did you drink a lot, back on your world?" Lugh asked.

Kyle thought about it for a moment. It was quite difficult. "Yes," he decided.

"Somehow, I'm not surprised. Well, this is your night, and we'll be flying all tomorrow, so no harm done. Try not to throw up. I'm going to bed." He left the table.

"See you!" Kyle called, raising his glass. He lowered it to eye level and noticed that it was empty. When had that happened?

"Tesh*ur*," Nihs said disapprovingly from atop the table. He was sitting cross-legged, nursing a tiny glass.

"Hey," Kyle said, "you're drinking, too."

"This is my only one," Nihs sniffed. "*Some* of us have to drive the airship tomorrow."

"There is such thing as autopilot," Rogan murmured from Kyle's other side, making him jump—Rogan was normally so quiet that it was easy to forget that he was there. "We did a good run tonight, you deserve a bit of a rest."

"Huh! You stick to your rules and I'll stick to mine, Rogan."

Kyle would happily have drunk himself under the table that night, but Nihs and Rogan managed to dissuade him. The huge Minotaur led him upstairs while Nihs hopped up after them, flaunting his sobriety. Lugh was asleep when they got back, so they shuffled carefully into their beds, making as little noise as possible.

Kyle lay awake for a couple moments, savoring the day's memories. He was infinitely pleased with himself—*so I do* have *what it takes to be an adventurer, after all.* Not only that, but he had won a sword to call his own and discovered another one, a powerful and dangerous blade that he didn't understand. For some reason, knowing that he could draw the soul sword whenever he wanted gave him a great feeling of satisfaction. No matter where he went, he would always be armed.

Braced by these thoughts, and by his drinking, Kyle soon fell asleep. His last thought before his eyes closed was, *I love Loria.*

Throughout the years following Grade One, Kyle proved himself time and time again to be an above-average student, in academics at least. His performance in the arts was quite variable, and he never managed to do very well in gym class, but in the fields of English, math, and science Kyle succeeded consistently. At the age of nine, he took part in a giftedness test with his fellow students and was found to be exceptional. His mother was understandably quite pleased, although Kyle approached the idea with a lack of enthusiasm.

"I don't have to go to a special school now, do I?" he asked his mother on one occasion.

She took a moment to answer, looking up slowly from the paper she was reading. "Not if you don't want to, dear," she said kindly. Kyle was still too young at this point to read the expression on her face; it would be a difficult one to decipher even for an adult.

"That's good," Kyle said happily at once, thinking of the friends he had made during his first four years of school. He was still friends with Quentin and Alex, the kids he had met during kindergarten, and was on good terms with a fair number of the other students. "I don't wanna go to some other school."

His mother gave him a smile, and then turned back to her reading. Just as Kyle was leaving the room, he picked up a sigh coming from behind the paper. He ignored it. His mother had been doing that a lot lately.

Although Kyle's teachers often went on about his intelligence, many of them had complaints to make about his work habits. It soon became obvious to the school that if Kyle knew he could get away without completing an assignment, he would do so. He scored highly on all of his tests and when he was set a graded assignment he completed it, but anything ungraded or unchecked would remain undone.

"We see it often in gifted students," a school counselor told his mother during an interview. "They find the normal curriculum boring and easy, so they don't try as hard as they could. It won't be a problem for now, but when he moves on to high school and university he might find himself falling behind. We need to make him understand the importance of good work habits for the future."

Kyle had sat in on this interview, being asked the occasional question and given the occasional instruction, but mostly just waiting in silence while his mother and the counselor conversed as though he wasn't there. He twiddled his thumbs in boredom and irritation as the two grown-ups discussed his fate.

"The best thing for him would be to move to a gifted school," the counselor finished. "There he'll meet other kids like him, and be taught by instructors that understand better how to work with an uncommon mind like his."

Kyle's mother seemed slightly flustered as she replied, "He…actually doesn't want to move to a different school." She said it timidly, as though she was admitting to an embarrassing fact.

"Ah," the counselor said pointedly. "Well, I'm sure you can discuss the matter and decide what's best for you. Most gifted students don't make the switch, and they usually turn out just fine."

Kyle's mother seemed harassed as they drove back home afterwards. "I've told you about how important it is to do your homework," she scolded Kyle. "Why haven't you been doing it?"

Kyle said nothing. He knew how the conversation was going to go. He had held it with her once before, two years ago, and his reasoning hadn't changed.

"Well?" his mother repeated, sounding unusually snappish.

Jolted into reaction, Kyle mumbled, "I don't want to. It's stupid."

"It's not stupid!" his mother said, with a conviction that Kyle had rarely heard before. "It's important that you learn how to work for later on in your life. School won't always be this easy."

"Then why can't I learn later?" Kyle asked, his own voice getting slightly louder.

"It's practice," his mother said in a strained voice. She ran her fingers through her hair. "You'll never get better if you don't practice. When things get harder you need to be ready for it, you might not have time to learn later, do you understand?"

"But—"

"No buts," his mother said firmly. "From now on, you're doing your homework, even if it means that I have to watch you to make sure you get it done."

Again, Kyle was far too young to catch the tone in his mother's voice, but this time, an adult easily could have interpreted it. It added quite plainly to the end of her sentence, 'and I don't need anything else to have to worry about right now'.

Kyle awoke slowly the next morning, his vision falling into focus as his eyes geared themselves up. He was groggy, and had a slight headache, but as always this was far better than it could have been for how much he had drunk. He was, however, slightly sore, and his chest and shoulder hurt him where the goblin's knife had struck.

He sat up, wincing slightly as his head twinged. Rogan was still asleep, but Lugh and Nihs were both awake, quietly gathering up their things and preparing to leave.

"Morning, sunshine," Nihs said mockingly when he saw that Kyle was awake. "You look pretty good for someone in your shape, I must say."

"I have a strong stomach," Kyle said sleepily, swinging his legs over the side of his bed. "What are we doing today?"

"Flying to Reno," Nihs said. "So you'll have time to recuperate. We should get there by later tonight, provided we leave early enough."

"Reno, huh?" Kyle asked, interested despite his tiredness.

"Yes. We've got a lot to do there. We need to repair the *Ayger*, sell our haul from that raid, buy you some equipment, and of course see if anyone can figure you out. Oh! Speaking of which," Nihs added, jumping from his bed to Kyle's, "could you draw that soul sword of yours for me? I never got the chance to take a look at it."

Kyle nodded, and put his hands together absent-mindedly. Already the motion came as naturally to him as scratching his head. The silver sparks flowed and leaped down his arms, and the sword appeared.

"Tesh*ur*," Nihs said, shaking his head. "That's amazing. I've never seen a soul sword up so close before."

With the sword's glow reflecting in his eyes, Nihs reached out to touch the blade. As soon as his hand got close, however, Kyle felt a sudden strong aversion to the contact. He jerked the sword backwards instinctively, yelping, "No!"

Nihs jumped back, alarmed. "What?"

Kyle was shaking his head. "I don't think you should touch it," he said. "It just feels like a bad idea," he added apologetically when he saw Nihs' expression. "I think the sword's trying to warn me not to let you do it. In the mine, everything I hit with it sort of…exploded."

"He's right," Lugh said, walking up to them, interested. "I saw it. It was almost as though the sword reacted to whatever it touched."

Nihs stared at the sword as though paralyzed. Kyle could practically hear the gears turning in his head.

He opened his mouth soundlessly, then closed it, then opened it again. "Kyle," he said, not moving his head as though afraid that the idea inside of it would slosh out, "can you feel that weight in your chest right now? The one you get after using magic?"

Kyle, surprised, shifted his stomach around. "No," he said.

"Retract your soul sword for me, would you?"

Mystified, Kyle did so. As soon the sword disappeared he realized what it was Nihs was after.

"I can feel it now!" he said, putting his hand to his chest. "So that weight is my soul sword? Is it supposed to feel like that?"

"I don't think so," Nihs said, his voice distant. "Normal soularms aren't supposed to be noticeable when retracted." He raised his eyes towards Kyle. "But your soul sword isn't a normal soularm!" he said excitedly.

"Uh, okay, so what is it?"

"Don't you see?" Nihs said, jumping to his feet suddenly. "You fall into this world and there's not a scrap of magic in you. When I try to revive you, you accept the magic but something in your body causes you extreme pain. Now, when you use magic, you feel this foreign presence in your core; and when your soul sword is drawn, the presence is gone!"

He spread his arms and looked from Lugh to Kyle and back, apparently expecting them to understand. When they obviously didn't, he let his arms drop to his sides in exasperation.

"*Tish*," he said, then took a deep breath. "Kyle's soul sword *is* his soul, the nuclear soul he had from before he came to Loria! The magical atmosphere of Loria must have compressed it somehow…pushed it into the center of his being. That's why it reacts to everything here. It's the same reaction we saw when I tried to heal Kyle with magic!"

"What?" Kyle said. "How is that possible? My soul just shrinks and then decides to become a sword? That's a pretty wild theory."

"Yes," Nihs said, "but it makes sense, doesn't it? Look, soularms don't just appear out of nowhere, and they don't make things explode. How could it be a coincidence?"

"Look," Lugh said, "let's just not worry about it for now, okay? Let's just assume that Nihs is right for now, and when we get to Reno we can ask about it then. Kyle, I'm going to veto you using that sword for now, unless it's to save someone's life. What with one thing and another, I don't think it's the greatest idea for you to be swinging it around right now."

"Fair enough," Kyle said.

"*Dasha*," Nihs said. "I wish I could experiment on it somehow. Maybe—"

A loud creak came from Rogan's bed. The huge Minotaur was sitting up slowly, rubbing the sleep out of his eyes.

"Hadfar's hooves," he rumbled discontentedly. "I don't suppose all of you could keep it down?"

"*You* should have been up a while ago; you're lucky we didn't wake you up earlier," Nihs snipped.

They gathered up their belongings and got dressed, and went downstairs. Some of the other adventurers were there, but most were still sleeping or had already left. There was no sign of Reldan, the Snakes, or of David and Emil. Erai and Dezzela were sitting in a far corner, eating. Erai waved at Kyle when he saw them.

"All right," Lugh said, "let's grab something to eat and then get out of here."

They did so, Lugh checking their keys in at the bar and ordering them breakfast. Their meal was a subdued affair. Tired and sore, the four friends ate in silence, conserving their energy. Kyle noticed that Nihs was eating ravenously, at least relative to his size. When he brought the subject up, Nihs told him that it was because he had used so much magic the day before.

"Think of it as burning calories," he said around a bite of toast, "except that they're magical ones instead of physical ones. Consuming food allows your soul to replenish itself faster."

After they ate, they trudged sleepily back through the tiny town towards the *Ayger*. Unlike the night when they had arrived, some of the residents were out on the streets today. Lugh's party attracted some attention, consisting as it did of four heavily armed adventurers, but no one approached them.

"That's the good and the bad side of adventurers being so widespread these days," Lugh said. "It's easy to get jobs and we get paid well, but everyone takes us for granted. Before the guild was formed, people would actually start to panic if goblins settled nearby. Now they just assume that a pack of adventurers will be around to take care of them."

"It's the price we pay for having such a stable career," Rogan said. "Besides, there's still room for heroes in this world—they just need to be bigger."

"I'd love to make it big one day," Lugh said wistfully, "not like Reldan big. Like everyone in the world knows my name big."

Rogan laughed deeply. "Every adventurer's dream."

Nihs, who was again riding on Rogan's shoulder, piped up. "I'd like a title," he said, and Kyle was amused to hear that the permanent sarcasm in his voice was gone. "That's not too much to ask. Nihs the Sage! Doesn't it ring well?"

"It does when you say it alongside Lugh the Hero!" Lugh said enthusiastically, drawing his sword and holding it up dramatically.

By this time, Rogan was guffawing loudly. "You're like children playing with sticks, dreaming of being great warriors. If you like those dreams so much, why don't you pursue them?"

"Someday," Lugh said, sheathing his sword. "I'm working myself up to it. How about you, Rogan?" he taunted, elbowing his huge friend in the stomach. "What are your plans for herodom?"

The Minotaur chuckled again. "I don't think it's in my stars to become a famous adventurer," he said, looking off into the distance. "I'm a creature of the plains, and sooner or later they'll call me back."

"Sure," Lugh said mockingly. "And when would that be?"

Rogan, however, said nothing, and so Lugh turned to Kyle. "How about you? You don't have to go back to your world if you don't want to. You could always stay here and become a famous adventurer with Nihs and me!"

This comment set fire to Kyle's mind. Suddenly, he saw his future stretching out in front of him. Somewhere in his mind, he had always told himself that he was just visiting here, and that he would be going home someday. The prospect of staying and dying in Loria had never even occurred to him. But now, the option presented itself to him for the first time as being viable. *I could just stay here, couldn't I?* He wasn't exactly leaving anything behind back home. What did he have to go back for? Unemployment and loneliness? And even if he got a job, what then? A lifetime of sitting behind a desk, working, just like the hundred other people around him. Here he could fight, he could cast magic, he could do something interesting with his life. The concept shimmered in his mind's eye like a golden bubble: Kyle, famous and powerful adventurer, battling the evils of the world with his companions, Lugh, Nihs and Rogan. Everywhere he went, people would know his name…

…And yet, even as he contemplated the idea, a strange feeling grew inside him. He looked up at the sky, his thoughts turning to Earth, his Earth, the planet he had left behind. Where was it now? Was it somewhere up there, lost in the sky? Even though he couldn't see it, a part of him could feel it, and he knew with a sudden certainty that it *was* there, somewhere, waiting for him to return. He could stay in Loria, if he wanted—but a part of him would always remain on Earth, calling him back home.

He looked at Lugh. "I don't know," he said, and he felt he'd never spoken a truer statement.

They made it back to the *Ayger* and deposited their equipment, Rogan taking up his place in the engine room while Nihs, Lugh and Kyle climbed the stairs to the bridge. Nihs twiddled the controls while they waited for the all-clear from Rogan. Kyle stood about awkwardly, suddenly aware that there was nothing to do. He remembered something that he had wanted to ask before.

"Lugh," he said.

"Yeah."

"When we were in the mine, Rogan did that jump across the fissure. Afterwards, Nihs was asking you why you didn't leap over it, and you said that the rest of us didn't know how."

"Oh, right, of course," Lugh said. "That's something I would have gotten to eventually during your training. Basically, there are a bunch of techniques that non-magical fighters have access to that consume magical power, but that aren't technically magic—like gaiden strikes. It's called metamagic, and it's different from normal magic because you don't need to be thinking about it or even know about it for it to work. A leap is a jump fuelled by metamagic; it launches you farther than a normal jump and stops you from hurting yourself when you land. There's also dashing, tumbling, soaring…other stuff."

"Soaring?" Kyle asked, his interest piqued. "It sounds like you're saying that people can fly."

Lugh nodded.

"No way!" Kyle said, then before he could stop himself, "that's awesome! How does it work?"

"All it takes is a strong enough being and some practice," said Lugh. "None of us can soar, though. It's the hardest kind of metamagic there is, only really powerful adventurers learn how. We can all leap, but only Rogan and I can dash, and only I know a bit about tumbling."

"What about them?" Kyle asked, now very curious and excited. "What are they exactly?"

"They're pretty self-explanatory, really. Dashing just means running super-fast. Pros can run along and up walls; I can't do that yet. Tumbling is changing direction in mid-air; flips, rolls, stuff like that."

"Can I learn how to do that?" Kyle asked. Lugh laughed.

"Sure, but not yet. Chances are it'll be a while before you're ready to leap. It's not like other things that you can start working at and then get better. You either can do it, or you can't; something just needs to click inside your body first. I'll tell you when I think you might be ready."

Kyle was impressed and once again filled with anticipation at the thought of what it was possible to do in Loria. He imagined being able to fly, whenever he wanted, just jump into the air and take off. The other metamagic techniques sounded interesting, too, but it was soaring that really caught Kyle's imagination. He was now more eager than ever to continue his training, as if he had needed any more motivation. But as much as his mind was willing, his body protested. He was tired and sore, and he had drank more than was good for him the previous night. He looked around for somewhere to sit, and found that there was none.

"Why don't you guys have any chairs up here?" he asked, finding it very strange.

Lugh shrugged. "I don't really know. I keep meaning to get some, but for some reason or another I always forget. You could sit on the bench on the observation deck, if you want."

At this point, Kyle's body overrode his mind. "Yeah, I think I'll do that."

A couple minutes later, when Rogan told Nihs that the *Ayger* was good to go, Kyle was not regretting his decision. The view offered by the picture window from the lookout deck was superb. In the short while that Kyle had been on land, he had forgotten what it was like to watch the ground fall away and scroll by beneath him, and to feel the booming of the wind around him as the ship fought with gravity and won. Kyle could understand, now, why Lugh was so proud of his ship; even being a passenger aboard it was exhilarating.

After a while, Lugh made them all some more hot chocolate, and Kyle went back up the stairs to the bridge. Nihs juggled his drink and the *Ayger's* wheel, listening to Kyle and Lugh chat about nothing much.

Rogan's voice sounded on the communicator. "The ship's wobbling like a cow in labor," the Minotaur complained. "What's going on up there?"

"Nihs has his hands full," Lugh told him happily, "we're drinking hot chocolate." He pretended to waft the scent of his drink through the communicator. "It's a shame you're stuck down there, Rogan, I would have made you some."

"Pah, you can keep you jibes and your hot chocolate to yourself, Lughenor, it gets hot enough down here as it is. You can tell Nihs to give up trying to steer the ship, though, and spare us all the stomach-ache."

"He's right, you know," Lugh said, once the crystal's glow had faded. "We're not going to get to Reno in time to do anything useful anyway, we might as well take it slow."

"Teshur," Nihs said, although he did switch on the autopilot and sit down on his stool.

"Why does Rogan call you Lughenor?" Kyle asked. "Is that your full name or something?"

"Yeah. He knows it annoys me, so he calls me that all the time."

"Do you guys have last names?" Kyle continued curiously. "Everyone I've met so far has only given me one."

"Yeah, we have 'em," Lugh said, "although we tend to ignore them when we don't need them. Adventurers usually only take one-word names; it leaves room to tack on titles afterwards. I'm technically Lughenor MacAlden, but I never use that name. Alden was my grandfather's name, see? Shortened from Aldenor."

"Just like how you shorten Lughenor to Lugh," Kyle said. "But then shouldn't it be 'Lughen'?"

Lugh winced while Nihs laughed. "Yeah, it should, but I hate that even more than I hate 'Lughenor'."

"Oh, okay."

Nihs saw Kyle turn to him, and pompously announced, "Nihs Ken Dal Proks. It means, 'Nihs of the Ken folk of Proks'."

"So your family's from Proks?" Kyle asked, interested.

"That's right. But Kollic families work differently than yours do. In fact, part of what makes us the Ken family is that we *are* from Proks."

"Huh," Kyle said. For some reason, the thought 'if I were a Kol, my name would be Kyle Campbell Dal Cleveland' ran through his mind. He shook himself mentally to dislodge it, embarrassed even though he hadn't spoken the thought aloud.

"Rogan told me his last name when we met," he mused instead, just remembering this detail.

"Rogan's less adventurer and more Minotaur than us," Lugh said. "We've gotten used to meeting other adventurers and ignoring our last names. From what I know, the Minotaur have a lot of pride about their homeland and upbringing and all that."

Another question occurred to Kyle. "How old are you?" he asked, then quickly backpedalling, said, "you know, if you don't…uh…mind me asking."

Lugh laughed. "We're not women, Kyle. I'm twenty-eight."

"I'm a hundred and six," said Nihs.

"What!" Kyle exclaimed.

Nihs nodded, smiling. "We Kol are very long-lived," he said, with a note of smugness. "Usually we live about five times longer than humans and Selks."

"You left out the part where you age more slowly, too," Lugh said pointedly. "Think of a Kol's life as a human's life stretched out across five times the distance. In human years, Nihs' actually the youngest one here…what would that make you, Nihs? Twenty-oneish?"

Nihs stuck out his tongue at him. "Use whatever kind of years you want, Lugh," he said, "it doesn't change the fact that I'm almost four times your age."

"Wow," Kyle said, his mind lost in thought. What would it be like to know that you had about four hundred years to live your life in? To live for an entire century, and to know that you had at least a couple more to look forward to?

"What did you *do* with all that time?" he asked Nihs.

The Kol shrugged. "You'd be amazed at how it adds up. I spent much of it studying in Proks, but mostly I just tried different things and went where I wanted when I wanted, and before I knew it…" he shrugged again.

Strangely enough, Kyle could see the logic in this. If he knew that he had so many years to waste, he imagined that he would spend his time much the same—taking it slowly, not bothering to rush anything in his life.

"How about Rogan?" he asked.

Lugh scratched his chin. "I think he's told us," he said. "How old *is* he, Nihs? For some reason I'm thinking thirty-three."

"Yes," Nihs agreed, "that sounds right."

"Wow," Kyle said, thinking of the hulking form of Rogan, "I actually imagined that he'd be older."

"Thirty-three is pretty old for a Minotaur," Lugh said, "they don't live for that long. About fifty, sixty years, usually."

"Oh," Kyle said, his voice subdued.

There was a slight silence, but Lugh saved it from becoming too awkward. "Well," he said brightly, clapping Kyle on the back, "how about you?"

"I'm twenty-six," said Kyle.

"Huh. Hey, we're always telling you about us…what about you? Your world…what did you call it, again?"

"Earth," said Kyle, then remembering the issue from before, said, "oh, right. I mean Terra."

"Right. So what's Terra like? You never really talked about it."

"It's…" Kyle tried to come up with something to say. *What* can *I say, really?* "It's not as colorful as Loria," he said, saying the first thing that came to mind. "It's sort of duller and…more serious looking, in a way. There's no magic; we just use machines for everything."

"We use machines as well," Nihs said, his voice expressing interest. "How do yours compare to ours?"

"I don't really know what your machines can do yet," said Kyle, "but if you don't have computers then ours are probably more complex. We do pretty much everything with computers. We can communicate with each other like you do with those Ephicers, and we can all send data to each other like you do on the overhead."

"The overhead is an ancient racial gift of the Kol," Nihs said. "It works by sending magical signals through the air. How can you replicate that with computers?"

"It's complicated," Kyle said. "We send signals through the air called radio waves. And we connect computers using special cables."

Nihs, having finished his hot chocolate, went back to piloting the *Ayger*, half paying attention to Lugh questioning Kyle about his world. Kyle did not want to talk much more, however, as it left an odd taste in his mouth to be discussing his life back on Earth. Eventually, Lugh seemed to pick up on this, and let the subject drop.

Kyle went out on deck, leaving Lugh and Nihs on the bridge. For some reason, he was craving isolation. He stood on the polished deck, leaning on the golden rail as he drank in Loria's topography. It was quite interesting: the countryside was now grassy and hilly, and there were many small lakes scattered about. In the far distance to the ship's left, there was a larger body of water.

Kyle tried to sort out his thoughts. He was in a strange mood. Memories from his past, both recent and distant, kept jumping out at him, and thoughts constantly flickered in and out of his mind. He wondered what it would be like in Reno, the largest city in Loria. What was the biggest city on Earth? Was it New York? For some reason he couldn't remember. He had been to New York before, and had found the experience interesting in a not entirely pleasant way. Kyle was an introvert by nature, and he didn't care much for people besides—for some reason, seeing the best and worst that people had to offer jammed into one huge city did not appeal to him. He wondered if Reno would be the same. What was crime like in Loria? To hear the others talk, the Buorish police seemed a force to be reckoned with. But did that mean that crime was low, or that such an intense police force was required because Reno was a crime-filled place?

He kept recollecting the mission he had run the previous night. He saw Reldan's axe rising and falling, and the red blood spilling from the goblins. He remembered Reldan's rage afterwards and the support of the other adventurers. Everything that had happened had seemed so natural at the time, but looking back on it, it all felt like a dream.

Acting on a sudden desire, Kyle drew his soul sword. He stared into the unwavering blue light that the sword gave off. It was very calming. Even though he knew nothing about it, he could feel that it was on his side. Of course, it was stupid—swords couldn't take sides. But something about the strange blade talked to him nonetheless.

Kyle surveyed the empty deck behind him. Slowly, he pivoted and swung the soul sword in an arc in front of him. The blade hummed as it completed its trajectory. It was lighter than air. He swung again, not knowing why he did it. Soon, he was fighting an imaginary battle by himself on the deck. He drew on all of the techniques that Lugh and Rogan had taught him, and improvised wildly besides. He remembered Lugh's graceful fighting style back in the goblin mine—he tried to mimic it as he danced about the deck, laying waste to invisible enemies all around him.

He sparred with the air around him for who knew how long; in the end, he stopped because he was winded and tired, all of his nervous energy was spent. He withdrew the soul sword, planning to go back inside, only to notice that Lugh was standing on deck, watching him.

He froze.

Lugh's arms were folded and he wore an amused expression on his face. When Kyle approached, however, he merely said, "Think you could stand another training session later today?"

"Sure," Kyle said, out of breath.

They went back inside silently, Kyle still not entirely sure as to what had just happened.

They ate lunch on deck, then sat and stood around, resting and talking little. For the first time, Kyle felt slightly bored. While being on the *Ayger* was a thrill in itself, one could only stare at the ground below for so long, and there didn't seem to be anything else to do on the ship. When Kyle brought this up with Lugh, the Selk just shrugged.

"We tend to sleep a lot while we're flying," he said. "We're usually tuckered out after having run a mission. When the engine's in better shape, Rogan comes up to visit us more often; sometimes Nihs sets the autopilot and we play cards. Do you have cards in your world?" he asked.

"Yes," Kyle said, "but they're probably different from yours."

"Yeah," Lugh said, "you're probably right. Well, once we get the ship repaired at Reno, we can teach you how to play."

"I won't be able to play for money," Kyle said, somewhat sullenly. He had enjoyed gambling back on Earth. "I don't have any."

Lugh laughed easily. "No worries, friend," he said, "another one of those unwritten adventuring rules is that you pool your money when you're travelling in a party, so there's no real point in us playing for money anyway. In any case," he added, "if you're getting bored, why don't we head down to the dojo and continue your training?"

Kyle, having eaten lunch and rested away his hangover, nodded. "That sounds like a good idea."

Once they had gotten to the dojo, Lugh selected some shields for them to practice with and they set about sparring, Kyle breaking in his changesword.

"The idea behind using a changearm," Lugh explained between blows, "is to switch between your weapon's two forms without stopping to think about it. As you keep using it, you'll get the feel for which form is more appropriate in each situation." He started controlling the distance between himself and Kyle in light of this lecture, forcing him to alternate between the long and short states of his changesword.

The changesword felt strange in Kyle's hands at first, having grown used to the middle sword in the short while that he had been using it, but the more he practiced with his newfound arm, the more he came to like it. The blade was aerodynamic and was made of stronger material than the middle sword; it took noticeably less effort to knock Lugh's blows aside, although the weapon was not much heavier. It was of course nowhere near as easy as using his soul sword, but he was resigned to the fact that he would have to give that weapon up for now.

The changesword snicked and clacked as it extended and retracted. Already, Kyle was getting used to the rhythm of the weapon. When Lugh got closer and Kyle began to feel claustrophobic, the blade shrank and instantly became lighter and more maneuverable. When Lugh stepped back, the blade extended to offer more reach and power.

They sparred for a quite a while, Lugh slowly picking up the pace to increasingly challenge Kyle. Finally, when they both started to notice a drop in their skill levels, they gave up. Lugh fetched them some water as Kyle collapsed on the ground, panting.

"You're definitely getting better," Lugh told him encouragingly, sitting down across from him. "Next time we'll start teaching you a little about combat energy and metamagic."

"Like gaiden?" Kyle asked.

"Yeah, sorta. See, I lied to you a little when I said that gaiden is the combat energy you build up while you're fighting. The truth is, gaiden's just *one* type of energy; there's a bunch of different combat energies, and each one builds up in a different way and lets you use different types of metamagic. Being a fighter means keeping track of all these energies and releasing them at the right times while you're fighting.

"And it doesn't even have to be in combat. Anything you do that takes skill and energy works that way. People who weave blankets and blow glass can work their own special skills in their craft. I don't really know how the philosophy works—it's the Oblihari that really study it. They have some fancy word for it. I think it's like *Quai Don* or something. It basically means that everything you do generates energy and that you can only become a master of your craft if you tap into it."

"That sounds like kung fu," Kyle said at once.

"Kung what?"

"Kung fu," Kyle repeated. "It's this eastern philosophy in our world. I don't think anyone in America really understands it all that well, but it's sort of like...every person who works a craft has their own kung fu, which is like a personal philosophy that makes them unique...I don't really know," he admitted.

Lugh, however, was nodding. "I don't really understand *Quai Don*, either, but it does sound sort of similar. But who's surprised by this point?" He laughing, spreading his arms. "It seems like everything in our worlds is related, huh?"

"Yeah," Kyle said vaguely. "Yeah, it does seem that way."

They sat in silence, and then Lugh got up.

"All right," he said, "let's rest for now. We made good progress today. Say what you want about the humans, they do pick stuff up fast."

"Really?" Kyle asked, standing up as well. "They do?"

Lugh nodded. "Have either of the others told you about the story of the races?" he asked.

"Yeah, Rogan told me. How all of the races were born in different places and developed different abilities?"

"That's the one," Lugh said. "So you know about which ability the humans are supposed to have, don't you?"

"Rogan told me they didn't have one!" Kyle exclaimed, miffed.

Lugh sighed. "A lot of people believe that," he said, "but some people go further and say that since the humans didn't gain any one ability, they learned how to pick up new abilities quickly instead. They couldn't decide on any one thing to be, right? So they learned how to learn. Now, obviously it's not as easy to see the effects of that when you compare it to, say, the Kol's overhead, so people are always arguing as to whether or not they really do learn things faster. I haven't been close to too many humans in my time, but from what I've seen, I believe it."

"Wow," said Kyle, shocked and pleased. *So humans do have an ability, after all!* For some reason, he found the knowledge profoundly comforting. Feeling much happier, he followed Lugh back onto the bridge.

A couple hours later, when Kyle had rested, Lugh took over the wheel from Nihs so that the two of them could commence Kyle's second lesson in magic. The Kol seemed reluctant at first, but Kyle noticed, as with the first time, Nihs' sardonic manner fell away once he got talking about his craft.

First, he had Kyle conjure a few more fireballs, to make sure that he still had the technique down. Kyle enjoyed this immensely; the feeling he got after using magic was a rush unlike anything he had ever experienced. Every fireball he cast made him feel powerful and dangerous—they lined the edges of his vision red and made blood pound in his ears.

"The effects of using magic on the mind," Nihs explained at one point. "Every type of magic has its own distinct feel, its own distinct connotation, that leaves an imprint on your psyche after it passes through you. It might feel good now, but it's not something to be taken lightly." Nihs said seriously, "Magic has many different and powerful effects on the world around it: on the user, on the user's target, and on the environment surrounding them. If you fail to understand these effects, you could end up paying a greater price for the spells you weave."

This was enough to catch Kyle's attention. "Why?" he asked, "what sort of things does using magic do?"

Nihs seemed pleased that his lecture had made an impression.

"All you have to do is consider what you are already feeling and extrapolate," he said. "As you cast more fire magic, your soul will slowly become more attuned to fire, not to mention more powerful. Soon, particles inside of you that would normally be unattuned find themselves becoming fire particles. As this happens, fire magic will become easier to cast, but you are also less protected from its side effects. Fire is the most destructive and warlike element...what do you think will happen to your personality if more and more particles inside your mind become attuned to fire?"

"You're saying I'll actually become a more aggressive person if I use too much fire magic?" Kyle asked.

"That's exactly what I'm saying. A spellcaster's ultimate goal is power, but that should never come before the ability to contain it. There are techniques you can learn to avoid losing your mind to the magic you weave, but nothing can prevent it entirely. To become a very powerful user of magic is to put a permanent strain on your soul...a strain that only becomes more pronounced as you gain more power.

"In any case, now that you've tried some fire magic we should work our way through the remaining three elements. It'll be useful for you to see and feel the difference between the types of magic. After that I can train you to become more powerful in elemental magic and teach you what I know about self-magic and mysticism—which isn't much. But the most important thing for you is to learn the different theories behind magic, so that you can better understand it and learn to defend yourself against it. Chances are you won't be using magic in combat most of the time—it doesn't often pay for an adventurer to try and juggle spells and swords at the same time. The more thinly you spread yourself, the weaker you become. Now..."

Nihs spent the rest of their lesson teaching Kyle some basic earth, water and air magic. He was met with decent success by the end of the day, but took to none of the new magic as well as he had to fire.

"People often find fire magic the easiest to use at first," Nihs said. "It works the best with most people's imagination. You'll most likely get over it as you keep learning."

He taught Kyle how to summon small stones and propel them forwards, how to cause small geysers of water to erupt at a certain location, and how to use air pressure to fashion small blades out of air. Even though it was harder than fireballs, Kyle found it amazingly fun. Seeing a geyser erupt or the air slice through something just because he had thought about it was extremely empowering. Each spell made him feel different after being cast; his senses brought amazing information to his brain as the elements danced around him.

"I have a question," he said.

"Ask away," said Nihs, who seemed pleased by how quickly Kyle was learning.

"Where do all these things come from?" He held his palm out in front of him and clenched his fist as Nihs had taught him. As he opened it again, magical light swarmed around his hand and a small rock grew out of his palm, where it remained, quivering slightly. "Like this rock," he said, holding it out to Nihs. "How is it possible that I just created that? Does it really just come out of nowhere?"

Nihs sniffed in a slightly smug manner. "You didn't seem to have any problems with that concept when you were using fire magic."

"Well...yeah," Kyle admitted, "but that's...different somehow. Fire's just...energy. This is a rock, it's a solid object."

"You need to rearrange your mind, I'm afraid," Nihs told him. "You're thinking like you're back in your world. This is Loria. Everything here is made of the same substance, remember? That rock in your hand is solid now, but in a second the magic that makes it up can become as insubstantial as a thought."

"But how does that *work*?" Kyle protested, his scientific mind rebelling against the thought. "Like, look. I can summon water now, right? So I'll never go thirsty again. I can just create it whenever I want! What's to stop people from doing that with food, or money, or anything?"

"You know," Nihs said, "instead of me just telling you, how about we try it out?" He walked over to the sink at the back of the room and retrieved a glass.

"Here," he said, standing in front of Kyle and holding the glass in front of him. "You cast a geyser, and I'll catch some of the water from it."

Kyle hesitated, shrugged, and focused his will on the floor in front of Nihs. A small jet of water burst up, rising three feet in the air. Nihs put his arm forward and filled the glass with water before the geyser dissipated.

"Now," he said, striding up to Kyle, "try drinking it."

Suddenly Kyle felt very uncomfortable. He started at the glass in Nihs' hand as though the Kol was offering him something mildly obscene. Even the thought of drinking the water slightly disgusted him.

Nihs was watching Kyle's body language, smiling knowingly. "Suddenly doesn't seem like the most natural thing in the world, does it?" Nihs asked. "Come on—try it. I promise it won't hurt you."

Very hesitantly, his entire being fighting him, Kyle grabbed the glass and took a tiny sip of the water. It tasted like nothing; it wasn't cool, or wet, or anything else besides. The only thing Kyle could say about it was that it was liquid.

"Bleh," he said, holding the glass out at arm's length. "Why is it like that?"

"Two main reasons," Nihs explained, taking the glass from him. "One, you were the one who cast that geyser, and magic that has passed through a soul once isn't meant to pass through that same being again right away. Life is all about the recycling and transformation of energy, and everything in this world comes around and is renewed—but eventually, not immediately. It is unhealthy for the same energy to pass through the same place again and again; I could give you an example of this on a more physical level, but I'm fairly sure I don't have to."

"You're right," Kyle said quickly. "I get it. Please don't."

Nihs nodded, and tipped the glass sideways, pouring the water onto the floor.

"Hey!" Kyle exclaimed, but Nihs just continued talking.

"The second reason is that particles charged through the act of magic are only transformed temporarily—to transmute something from one shape into another permanently is a much more difficult process. The water you created just now is only charged weakly. The particles remain water because your will remains bent on them, but as soon as your concentration moves on they will either return to being what they 'remember' from before, or they will dissipate into their current environment." Having emptied the glass, he shuffled back over to the sink to put it away, leaving Kyle staring at the wet patch on the ground.

"So that water is just going to go away?" he asked, once Nihs returned. "But I haven't been focusing on it this whole time, and I don't feel like I'm using magic."

"You might not have been thinking about it consciously," Nihs said, still looking smug, "but your will is still bent on it. What happened to that rock you summoned earlier, by the way?"

Kyle's mouth fell open as he realized the truth of Nihs' words. He checked his hands and the floor around him, but the rock was gone, nowhere to be found.

"And how about the rest of the water from that geyser you cast?" Nihs asked, sounding as though he was enjoying himself. "I don't see any streams of water flowing across the floor of the dojo."

Kyle couldn't believe it, but the Kol was right. Of any of the other rocks he had conjured, or of the other geysers, there was no sign.

"That, I think, should be the end of the lesson for today," Nihs said in a pleased tone. "Nothing that magic creates is permanent—remember that. If you do it properly, you can make something that will last a hundred years or a thousand—but you can't make it last forever. Kind of like everything else, really," Nihs added happily. "Let's go back to the bridge, shall we?"

When they arrived, the bridge was significantly darker than before—it was twilight outside. Kyle was surprised. He still had to get used to Loria's much shorter days and nights.

Lugh half-turned when he heard them approaching. "Right in time," he said happily. "We're going to hit Kena soon. Kyle, you'll want to see this."

"What's Kena?" Kyle asked.

"It's one of the sub-cities that surrounds Reno," Nihs said. "There are quite a few of them. They give people the opportunity to live close to Reno itself without being smothered by it."

"Yeah," Lugh agreed, "the races tend to clump together in their own sub-cities; it's like a little home away from home for them. Kena's one of the newer ones, it's mainly Selk and human...We're already near Donno, that one's older."

Kyle made his way to the observation deck to see what Lugh was talking about.

"Donno was the city that posted the job about the goblin mine, right?" he asked.

"Yep," said Lugh. "The regions around the cities are named after them. It's mostly farmland, and all the food ends up in Reno."

"Just like everything else," Nihs quipped.

"We're passing by Donno on our left," Lugh called down to Kyle, once he had made it to the deck. "You should be able to see it if you lean out and crane your neck."

Kyle did so, eager to see what a city looked like in Loria. The area they were flying over was getting flatter and wetter. There were still some small hills, although mostly only grass grew on them, and the small lakes were appearing more frequently. Several roads crisscrossed the area, curving around and between the patches of water. Small clusters of buildings often sat at the intersection of these roads. Getting closer ahead of them was a large expanse of water. Kyle could just barely see the opposite shore from his vantage point.

Kyle caught a glimpse of what must have been Donno before it vanished from sight. It was much larger than any settlement he had seen before. Illuminated only faintly by the setting sun, it showed up in Kyle's vision as a cluster of lights by the water's edge. Judging from the general shape of the city, it was built on a rather steep hill leading to the water, and some of the buildings were quite tall.

"Donno's not very interesting unless you like old Selkic culture," Lugh said from the wheel. "Half of the buildings are built like Selkic stone houses—what we used to make when we lived on the northern coast of Ren'r. If you want interesting, look there—that's Kena. Think of it as mini-Reno."

Kyle's eyes followed where Lugh was pointing, and his jaw dropped. Ahead and to their right was a large jumble of lights of every size and color;

it was so obnoxiously modern that for a second Kyle thought he was back on Earth. As they got closer to the city, Kyle could make out the general shape of the buildings. For the most part, they were tall, sleek and deliberate, the exact opposite of what Kyle had been expecting. Nothing in the city was the least bit medieval or old-fashioned; in fact, it looked even slicker and newer than any city Kyle had seen on Earth. From what he could tell, there were skyscrapers, high-rise buildings that looked like office towers and apartment buildings, and even raised highways. There *was* something foreign and strange about it, however—little touches that overall reminded Kyle in no uncertain terms that he definitely wasn't at home. The colors were more intense and the buildings' designs were strange and exotic. The roads in particular looked different and bizarre—most of them were bent and curved, and set high up from the city floor. They couldn't have been more different than the grid-like, land-locked streets of Cleveland.

"So you people have cars, then?" he asked.

"Cars?" asked Lugh. "What are they?"

"Land vehicles," said Kyle. "You use them on roads—"

"Sounds like runners to me," Lugh said. "That's what those roads are for, anyway."

"They're probably similar," Kyle agreed, now peering down at the roads to see if he could spot anything moving along them—he couldn't, however, as the angle was poor and they were still quite a good distance away.

"We're getting close to Reno now," Lugh said happily. "That ahead of us is Centralia Bay; once we're flying over it, we're on the border between Ar'ac and Ren'r. It narrows quite a bit after this. There's an island in the center of it, and that's Reno's core. It used to be all of Reno, until the city started spilling over onto the land around it."

By this time, Kyle's face was glued to the view in front of him. If that had only been Kena, a sub-city around Reno, then Reno itself must really be something to watch for.

There was a crackle of static from behind him and Rogan said from the engine room, "You should pull us up a bit, Lughenor, the Buorish police usually cruise higher than this."

"Right," Lugh said, and a moment later Kyle felt slightly heavier as the *Ayger* ascended.

Kyle turned back to the control panel as the ship rose. "So the Buorish police have airships?" he asked.

"That's right. They're always doing circles over the city, watching for airships coming in and basically being the police's eyes in the sky. They always want to get a visual on ships entering the city, so it makes it easier for everyone if you match their height."

"So you can just fly in whenever you want?" Kyle asked, turning his gaze back to Centralia Bay.

"Basically," said Lugh, "you have to go through some paperwork when you dock a big ship like this, but you're essentially good unless you're like a convicted criminal or something."

Kyle heard the sound of flesh hitting flesh and suddenly Nihs jumped up on the control panel, swearing in Kollic and hitting himself in the head.

"*Or* if you're someone who doesn't have an Iden card!" he shouted, in sudden realization.

Lugh's mouth formed an 'o'. "Oh, right!" he exclaimed, "that's going to be a problem, isn't it?"

Kyle opened his mouth to ask, but Nihs answered him before he had gotten the question out. "An Iden card is a special card that stores information about who you are. The Buors came up with the idea. You need one in order to use any public service."

"You guys have *identity cards* in your world?" Kyle asked, astounded.

"You don't need one to dock, though, do you?" Lugh said. "I'm the only one who needs it for that."

"Yes," Nihs snapped, "but what happens when we need him to join the adventurer's guild? Or use the hospital? Or something else? Someone's bound to ask for it eventually."

Lugh shrugged. "So we'll have to get him one," he said. "We'll make that our first stop. Anyone asks, we just tell them the story we would tell anyone else—we found him unconscious in a crater with nothing on him."

"Yes, but you know how the Buors are," Nihs sighed, rubbing his temples. "When we actually go to get him a card, they're going to ask questions."

"Well, we'll just have to deal with that as we come to it," Lugh said firmly. He had caught the expression on Kyle's face, who was feeling miserable seeing how much trouble he was causing.

Nihs did not seem reassured, but he let the subject drop. A moment later, a sight appeared ahead of them that drew all thought about Iden cards from Kyle's mind.

"Reno city," Lugh said, smiling.

They were approaching a large island in the center of the bay. The waterway had narrowed significantly, so it looked almost as though the island was plugging the flow of a giant river. Built upon it was one of the largest clusters of structures that Kyle had ever seen.

Closest to them was what looked like a single enormous construction made of *tigoreh*. Even in the twilight, the gleaming golden material was easily recognizable. As they drew closer it became apparent that this was some kind of port or industrial zone—the *tigoreh* formed railways, massive cranes, and large vehicles that wove between the structures. This entire section of the island was in constant movement as machines and vehicles ran full force, and even though it was nearing night time, the water in the area was thick with ships of every size, shape and color.

Behind the port rose building after building after building, each one more impressive than the last. Raised pathways wove between the structures seemingly at random, some of them reaching half the height of the tallest buildings. They were all lit with matrices of small blue lights—the effect was mesmerizing. As they got closer, buildings continued to appear at the edges of Kyle's range of vision. The far banks of the waterway came into view, revealing to be just as heavily constructed as the central island. Lights were everywhere; now Kyle could see small multicolored dots moving their way along the pathways. There were huge glowing signs, windows, streetlights. Kyle even saw lights in the sky—it took him a moment to realize that these must be other airships, circling the airspace above Reno city.

Just like when he had first stared out of the *Ayger's* picture window, Kyle was rendered speechless by what he was seeing. Rarely in his life had he travelled by plane, and even when he had, he had never seen a sight quite like this.

Lugh gave a small laugh when he saw Kyle's face. "It is quite something," he said.

At that moment, static came from the communicator crystal. Kyle expected to hear Rogan's voice, but instead the crystal glowed red and sounded a couple odd, reverberating notes. Kyle was slightly startled, but Lugh just put his hand on the crystal as always.

"This is the Buorish police," a polite, male voice sounded from the speaker. "You have entered official Reno airspace. Please state your name, the name and registration number of your craft, and your intent regarding Reno city."

Lugh answered casually, "This is Captain Lughenor MacAlden of the airship *Ayger*, registration number eff-ee-six-four-eight-two-one. Requesting permission to dock."

"Thank you. One moment please."

Kyle found himself looking at the outlines of the ships ahead of them—*is the voice on the communicator coming from one of them?*

After a moment, the policeman said, "Very well! Your ship has been approved for docking. Your landing bay code is eight-thirty, the coordinates are being transferred to your ship's map system now. The cost of docking your ship has been prepaid to the ship's profile, however please note that any additional costs involving the upkeep of your craft will not be covered. As captain of your vessel, you will also be asked to present your identification upon docking. Please be prepared to do so."

"Will do," Lugh said, winking.

"Thank you," the voice said again, and the crystal faded.

Kyle's mind had been blown somewhat by the onslaught of formality. The voice that had sounded on the speaker had oozed crisp politeness and professionalism.

"So," he said, as the *Ayger* started to veer to the left and descend, "what kind of people are the Buors, really?"

Both Nihs and Lugh laughed.

"Kinda throws you off, hearing one of them talk for the first time, doesn't it?" Lugh said. "They're not all like that, though. That guy was just acting super formal because he's an aircraft controller."

"You should say they're not all *that bad*," Nihs noted. "I've yet to meet a Buor who talks entirely like a normal person."

"What do they look like?"

Lugh shrugged. "No one knows," he said. "They wear full armor all the time, no one's ever seen what a Buor looks like."

"What!" Kyle protested. "That's impossible! Someone must have seen one at *some* point!"

"Never," Nihs said with a tone of satisfaction. "Or at least never in such a way that they can provide proof. There are always rumors going around to that effect—that someone has finally seen a Buor unmasked! It was a popular prank to play on the overhead a little while ago. People have said that they look like rats, or that they're insects, or that they're just humans or Selks in armor. But the Buors are very careful with their secret, they've never officially slipped up."

"I wonder what they have to hide," Kyle said. "Why is it so important to them not to be seen?"

Both Nihs and Lugh shrugged this time.

"They've made plenty of statements about it in the past in the world of diplomacy," Nihs said. "It's always the same talk. They say that they have their reasons and that they wouldn't insist on it if it weren't absolutely necessary. Since the Buors are very useful people to have on your side, most people are okay with that."

"Hmm," Kyle said. He was now more eager than ever to finally meet one of these mysterious people. He tried to superimpose the voice he had heard over the communicator onto the image of a knight in full armor. It didn't work.

"But they wear full armor all the time?" he asked. "Doesn't that, you know, suck?"

"Not for the Buors, apparently," Lugh said. "They evolved in a place where the only resource available was metal. They learned how to make clothes out of steel before they learned how to make clothes out of cloth."

"It's true," Nihs chipped in, "what we consider to be 'armor' is often just regular clothing for a Buor."

"What does their armor look like, then?" Kyle asked.

"Oh, just you wait and see," Nihs said, flashing a grin.

The *Ayger* descended swiftly, guided by Lugh and by the coordinates that the traffic controller had given them. They approached a massive *tigoreh* structure that dominated the western side of the island.

"That's dockside," Lugh explained. "It's all cranes and pulleys and ramps and stuff for getting ships and cargo out of the water…and out of the air. We're headed in there," pointing to one of several large edifices that looked like man-made caverns. Each stood on its own, facing the coastline, and seemed to be divided into several different areas for ships to dock in.

"That's the airdocks," Lugh said. "A lot of people call 'em the honeycombs since that's what they look like. Biggest and most advanced in the world. Of course, how could they not be, Reno being what it is." Kyle noticed that Lugh was talking quite a lot—he seemed to have appointed himself tour guide of their arrival in Reno. Kyle didn't mind, since he was curious about everything, and Lugh volunteering the information saved him the trouble of asking questions every two seconds.

Delicately, the *Ayger* made its way towards one of the larger honeycombs, sailing smoothly inside the huge building. The process took a decent amount of time—Lugh was flying very slowly, making sure not to bump into the walls of the hangar. Though it was fairly bright within the structure, it was still darker than outside; the artificial light coming from numerous *tigoreh* lamps was not enough to compete with the twilit sky and Reno's cityscape. The world inside the honeycomb was made of metal— catwalks lined the walls, and heavy pulleys and chains hung from the distant ceiling.

Lugh touched the *Ayger* down on a large platform made of wire-mesh material. The landing was surprisingly soft.

"And we're good," Lugh said, placing his hand on the communicator crystal. "Welcome to Reno city! Hey, Rogan, everything all right down there?"

"Mm-hm," the Minotaur affirmed, "smooth landing. Ahh, I can't wait to get to work on the ship with some real equipment. I'll be up in a second."

Lugh twiddled with some of the *Ayger's* controls as Nihs started rummaging in the bookshelf.

"All right, let's see," he said to the world at large, "what will we need? Money…"

"You can stop there for tonight," Lugh said. "We should just find somewhere to rest and wait until tomorrow to do our errands."

"If we're going to do that, why don't we just sleep on the ship?" Nihs snipped.

"Rogan's going to want to start working on the engine tonight," Lugh said, passing a hand through his hair. "It's going to be louder than loud. Besides, this is Kyle's first visit to Reno city! We should get out and experience the culture."

Nihs snorted. "We should bring our weapons, then," he said snidely.

"Don't worry about him, he's just being a nuisance," Lugh said to Kyle in a low tone. He scratching his chin. "Although it probably isn't a bad idea to carry our weapons after all. I usually do when I'm in Reno anyway."

"That's necessary?" Kyle asked in a worried tone, "and *allowed?*"

Lugh nodded. "Oh, yeah, everyone's allowed to bear weapons in Reno, as long as you don't actually fight someone with them. There are rules about who's allowed to carry what, too, but those aren't usually enforced unless there's a problem. It's not really necessary, but it doesn't hurt. Most of the people who go around armed are adventurers, and these days it always helps for people to know that you're one of us."

Rogan strode onto the bridge, bringing Kyle and Lugh's swords with him. As Kyle buckled on his changesword, he listened to Rogan and Lugh talking.

"I'll have a word with the workers here," the Minotaur said. "It shouldn't be too hard of a job to get everything working the way it's supposed to, but I'll have to hire some help if you want it done quickly."

"That's fine," Lugh said, waving his hand, "do what you have to do to keep the *Ayger* running. We're going to walk around a bit and sleep off the ship tonight."

"That's probably a good idea."

They trooped onto the deck outside to find that the hangar workers had already installed a small ramp for them to disembark. One of them stood on the catwalk to greet them—he was a town Selk with unkempt red hair kept out of his eyes by a grimy bandana. He looked like every automotive worker Kyle had ever seen. His face shone slightly with grease and sweat, and his clothes were utilitarian.

"Day to you," he said brightly, giving a lazy sort of salute. He spoke with a strange accent that sounded almost Australian. "That's a mighty fine ship you got there! It is yours?" he asked, laughing.

"Yep, it's mine," Lugh said, dangling the *Ayger*'s key. "I think we're going to need some repairs."

"Not a problem," the Selk said, drawing a cloth from his pocket to wipe his hands with. "What do you need for it?"

Rogan stepped forward. "It's got some damaged converters, and the engine needs some general work. I can lead the repairs myself, but I'll need a couple helpers to get it done."

"Absolutely o'course!" the worker said brightly. "Why don't you show me to the engine and we can talk details?"

Rogan nodded to the others. "Have a nice outing. Keep your eye open for anywhere we could sell our stuff."

"Will do," Lugh said, clapping Rogan on the arm. He turned to the Selk workman. "Is there any paperwork I have to fill out?" he asked, in a tone that translated his words into: 'where's the paperwork that I know I need to fill out?'

"Oh, right!" the Selk said brightly, jumping. He scooted over to a nearby wireframe table that had been bolted to the catwalk and returned with a small binder. He flipped through a couple pages and handed Lugh the book and a pen.

"Name and registration number, signature goes here," he said, pointing at the fields. "And I'll need to see your Iden card."

Lugh filled out the paper and then flashed his Iden card to the worker. It looked quite like a credit card back on Earth, except that it was made of a translucent blue material that almost looked like glass. Kyle couldn't see what was written on it, however, since the worker nodded once he saw it and Lugh stowed it swiftly away.

They left Rogan with the town Selk and made their way towards the far wall of the hangar. The catwalk they were walking on was quite thin and minimalist in design, with only a simple piped railing keeping them from falling over the edge. Kyle peered down to the hangar floor—it was a huge, blank space far below.

"It's a shame we had to arrive at night, really," Lugh told him as they made their way outside, "as it is we've just got time to do a quick tour and then turn in for now. Now remember, try not to act too shocked at anything you might see, okay? Just assume that everything's normal unless Nihs or I tell you otherwise."

"Feel free to gawk, though," Nihs added from Lugh's shoulder. "Everyone does that the first time they arrive here."

They stepped out into the cool summer night and Kyle immediately started following Nihs' advice. By itself, nothing in particular was too spectacular, but the overall effect was overwhelming. They had come out on the side of the honeycomb that faced the city; the back of it had been covered with metal platforms and staircases so the people leaving all of the hangars could make their way to ground level. They were high up off the ground, allowing Kyle a good view of the city ahead of them.

Directly in front stretched a massive, wide avenue that Kyle assumed was the main road of the city. The buildings that lined it got taller and taller into the distance, and signs and lights bordered it on all sides. To the right of this road was a park-like area, and beyond that, lining the waterfront, were the rest of the docks. Apart from the park, buildings stood on every available surface, and the high, airy roads wove between them.

"We're stuck on ground level for now," Lugh said, "but just wait until you learn how to leap and dash. Nothing is more fun than free-running along Reno's rooftops and jumping from road to road."

"You've done that before?" Kyle asked, immediately burning with desire and jealousy.

Lugh laughed. "Once or twice. It takes a lot of guts—missing a leap might not kill you, but it hurts, and people don't tend to like free-runners that much."

"Is it illegal?"

"Vaguely. Free-running itself isn't technically a crime, but if you're caught on private property or smash into something the police will nail you."

"But they wouldn't be able to catch a free-runner, would they?" Kyle asked. "Because they wear armor all the time?"

Lugh shook his head and Nihs laughed.

"Don't make the mistake of thinking that, friend," the Kol said, wagging a finger. "A Buorish policeman in full armor can move faster than most other people can in nothing but their underpants. All policemen can dash and leap, and some of them can soar, as well."

"Wow," said Kyle. He wasn't so sure he wanted to meet a Buor anymore.

They made their way down the catwalk, along with a couple other late-night arrivals. Kyle tried not to stare, but whenever he saw an unfamiliar shape he was tempted to see what it could be. He made out several Selks, one or two Minotaurs, and a strange couple that looked almost like—

"Are those Oblihari?" Kyle whispered to Lugh as they passed.

"Yeah. Remember, no staring."

Kyle tried to eye the strange pair covertly. They both wore baggy, loose-fitting garments that he assumed must have been designed for use by bird people. It was difficult to make out details in the dim light, but he thought he saw the glint of a beak and the suggestion of a feathered arm.

Once they reached ground level, they made their way down the huge road that Kyle had seen before. Although the sun had now completely set and the sky was growing dark, the streets were still teeming with people. Kyle stuck close to Lugh's reassuring size as people passed by them heading in all directions. The road itself was fairly deserted, although occasionally a golden vehicle would zoom by, making a strange noise that Kyle couldn't describe, and leaving a rainbow-colored streak painted across his vision. He didn't manage to get a good look at any of these vehicles, but they seemed roughly car-sized, if not car-shaped. Kyle assumed these were the runners Lugh had been talking about.

There was simply too much to see with one pair of eyes. Kyle felt like a dog between two bowls of food. His attention turned one way, then another; in trying to take everything in all at once, he failed to truly take in anything at all, and so he walked the streets of Reno city in a daze.

Apparently, advertising had caught on in Loria as much as it had on Earth. Storefronts lined both sides of the road, their displays brightly lit and inviting, and massive signs were mounted high on buildings. Many of the stores were recognizable: here a clothing store, there a furniture store—but others were decidedly exotic. Some stores had signs written in different languages, and while there was usually a translation that Kyle could read written underneath, many of the words still made no sense to Kyle. Every once in a while they would pass a restaurant or something similar, and a blast of music would reach Kyle's ears. Strangely enough, this music often didn't sound very outlandish, and some of it was frighteningly familiar.

"Was that *techno?*" he asked in disbelief, turning back to look at the doorway they had just passed.

"Hmm?" asked Nihs.

Kyle pointed at the sleek blue sign over the door. The characters written on it were unreadable to him. "What kind of place is that?"

Nihs squinted. "Kol bar," he said dismissively.

Kyle was shocked. "The Kol have bars?"

"Oh, yes, we're famous for it. The music you heard is Ly music, it's all the rage these days. I enjoy it, but clubbing has never been very appealing to me."

"You're too old-fashioned, Nihs," Lugh joked, shaking his shoulder. "You've spent too much time in Proks."

"Hmm," Nihs said in annoyance, trying to keep his balance. "Were we just going to walk around the city until the sun came up again, or did you have a destination in mind?"

"Oh, give it a rest, we're in Reno!" Lugh said expansively, "Besides, the hotels aren't until farther down the road, you know that."

"There are plenty of hotels dockside," Nihs pointed out.

"Yeah, all the insanely expensive ones. You're the one who's always complaining about me wasting our money. Now hush, you're ruining the experience for Kyle."

Kyle couldn't help but laugh at the absurd conversation; however, while it was true that he enjoyed listening to Nihs and Lugh argue, he did want to see as much as he could of the city.

The road continued straight into the core of the city. It sloped upwards as the island rose out of the bay, then evened out into a large, paved square surrounded by buildings. Two enormous fountains faced each other from opposite corners of the square, and there were several round, stone benches sprinkled about. The architecture was obviously much older than that of the buildings they had passed earlier. The square was quieter than the streets had been, but it was still full of people and sound. Street musicians with strange instruments played near the fountains, and a couple late-night entrepreneurs were selling food and small trinkets from stalls.

"Outer square," Lugh said, putting his hands on his hips. "Most tourists only make it this far. I'm kidding," he added, seeing the look on Kyle's face, "but this *is* the main touristy part of town. There's usually something interesting going on here during the day—oh, hey, look, you said you wanted to see a Buorish policeman."

Kyle followed where Lugh was pointing. There, standing with his back to the fountain nearest them, hands gathered behind his back, was a Buor. Kyle didn't know what he had been expecting, but it probably wasn't this. The man looked exactly like a human—albeit a human clad from head to toe in charcoal-black armor. The panoply was lined with red, and the guard wore a sword-belt, sash and cloak of the same color. The cloak's hem was lined with gold, matching the red-and-gold crest emblazoned on the armor over the guard's heart. Kyle noticed that the guard was bristling with weapons—he had a long sword and a small gun belted to one hip, several pouches of equipment and what looked like a truncheon on the other, a dagger attached to his thigh, and a shield and a bow slung to his back.

The policeman's face was completely concealed; he wore a half helm with a triangle of red cloth hung across the front.

"Just one tug and someone would be able to see his face!" Kyle pointed out.

Lugh shook his head. "Buors all wear masks made out of metal, even when they're not armored. The red cloth is just for politeness—some people find the masks creepy, and I'm one of them."

"Oh." Kyle surveyed the guard again. The policeman's appearance should have felt threatening—the idea of a whole race who wore metal armor like clothes and went around masked should be enough to accomplish that—but for some reason, it didn't. Something about the guard's body language as he stood by the fountain suggested to Kyle that this was not an enemy.

The guard shifted his weight and looked around. Kyle was too slow to look away, and the guard caught him staring at him. He inclined his head politely. "Good evening," he said.

"Evening," Kyle almost yelped, taken by surprise. Awkwardly he turned his attention away from the guard and followed after Nihs and Lugh, who were snickering.

"Hey, give me a break," Kyle said in a low voice, once they had gotten out of earshot.

"Ahahaha, oh, I'm sorry," Lugh said, trying to stop himself from laughing. "That was pretty funny, though. Well, I can't really blame you, the Buors can be pretty intimidating until you get used to them. Just be thankful that they're on our side. Oh, and a word to the wise: if you run into a problem anywhere that there are Buorish guards, swallow your pride and get one to help you. They're the most useful people on Earth and they know basically everything about the city they work in."

They crossed outer square and continued their way down the main road. It had narrowed and quietened down, but was still quite busy.

Lugh pointed down the avenue. "You can see city core from here, or some of it, anyway. Those three ridiculously tall towers are the government buildings. There's also a ton of hotels and the boring stuff like the banks, and all the buildings belonging to the big companies. And Sky Tower."

"What's that?" Kyle asked.

"Livaldi's headquarters," Lugh said. "Remember him?"

"The guy who's fighting with Sanka over Reno?" Kyle said.

"Yeah, that's the one. He's building this giant tower right near the center of city core; that's Sky Tower. They're just putting the finishing touches on it now. From what I know Livaldi already works from there. When it's finished it's going to be the tallest building in the world. Anyway, is anyone hungry? We should stop and find a place to eat." He scanned the storefronts on either side of him.

Kyle *was* hungry. Now that Lugh had mentioned it, he felt it keenly. He let his gaze travel from store to store as well, even though he wasn't about to suggest somewhere knowing nothing of the city.

"Was that a weapon store we just passed?" he asked, turning back slightly.

"Yep," Lugh said, "we'll definitely want to spend some quality time checking one of those places out. Weapon stores are always a lot of fun. Hey!" he said suddenly, spotting a store on their left. He pointed, shaking his shoulders up and down in a passable mockery of an excited child. Nihs was almost dislodged from his bucking shoulder, and hung on angrily.

"What?" he demanded.

"Can we eat at Colors?" Lugh asked excitedly, "can we, can we?"

"Tesh*ur*," Nihs swore irritably, "*that's* what you're freaking out about? And are you insane? A meal at Colors costs about as much as we'll make from that whole goblin run!"

"Oh, don't be silly," Lugh said, "Kyle's changesword alone could pay for ten meals there. Come on, it's the Reno experience! When was the last time we ate there?"

"It was a while ago," Nihs conceded. "Fine, then. But what about Rogan?"

"Rogan's not really into fine dining anyway," Lugh said, starting to stride towards the restaurant. "He can go to some Minotaur place that serves simple food and lots of it and be happy."

The section of Colors that faced the street was minimalist but sleek. Everything seemed ultra-modern; it was all polished glass and bright metal, and the windows were dimmed. Above the doorway glowed a sign bearing the title of the restaurant. The letters were picked out by points of light of every color of the rainbow, so that the effect was like looking through a window into multi-colored space.

Music, voices, and style greeted them inside the restaurant. It was as Kyle expected—everything was clean, colorful, simplistic, and obviously expensive. While the outer walls were forced to be square, no such restriction was imposed on the inside of the restaurant; floors, walls, tables and counters curved and flowed wherever they wanted to. A black column ahead of them was at the center of the restaurant; a girl running a counter in front of it was assigning seating. Off to the right Kyle could see a very interesting looking bar—and not just because it promised to serve alcohol. High benches lined the outside of the room; minimalist café tables were set up everywhere else. The restaurant was quite busy, and while most of the patrons were Selks, Kyle saw a decent smattering of Lizardfolk and the occasional member of another race.

The girl running the counter turned out to be human. Kyle was almost shocked by this. Somehow, seeing such a familiar sight in such a strange, exotic city was very confusing. He was about to greet her as a fellow outcast before he remembered that she would be a Lorian, just like everyone else.

"Hello, and welcome to Colors!" she said charmingly as they approached. "Would you like a table?"

"Yep," Lugh said, "this is all of us."

"Okay." She reached behind her counter to retrieve a few menus. "A Selk, a human and a Kol…" she said to herself, as she drew them. "Would you like a table or a booth?" The question was passed around by the three of them.

"Table?"

"Table?"

Lugh nodded. "Table," he said to the waitress.

The girl smiled. "All right, please follow me!" and she strode off to their right, menus under her arm.

They sat at a small table near the front of the restaurant. It was fairly close to the bar, and so Kyle could see it and slightly around the black column—that was where the booths were. The table was made of a silverish metal and had a glass top; it had a bench installed all around it, like a picnic table. To Kyle's left was a strange bump in the bench, where it rose almost to the height of the table itself and then dropped back down. It wasn't until Nihs jumped from Lugh's shoulder and installed himself in this spot that Kyle realized it had been designed to be Kol-friendly.

The waitress distributed the menus and pulled out a notepad and pen.

"Can I get you something to drink?" she asked.

"Sure," Lugh said, "I'll have a Freezer with aquia." Aquia was a type of Selkic alcohol that Kyle had come to think of as approximately Loria's equivalent of vodka. He had enjoyed several such drinks during the celebration following the mine raid.

"Sure thing," the waitress said, taking the order down. "Which color Freezer would you like?"

Lugh's mouth opened. "They make different colored Freezers now?" he asked incredulously.

"Yep," the waitress said happily, "they just started experimenting with them. There's white, yellow, green and blue now, although green is the one that's really taken off so far."

"Really!" Lugh said. "Huh. Well, what's a green Freezer like? Have you had one?"

"Mm, I'd say it's not as refreshing as a blue, but it tastes better."

"Well," Lugh said, "I'll try that then."

"And I'll have the same thing," Kyle chimed in, as curious as Lugh was to try this new invention.

The girl smiled at him and then moved on to Nihs. "And you?" she asked. "We serve mind bombs now, would you like one?"

"Oh!" the Kol said, his ears perking up. "Really? Well then, yes, I would, thank you!"

The girl left, leaving the three of them to peruse their menus.

"Well fancy that," Lugh said at one point, "green Freezers. Isn't that interesting?"

"Fancy them serving mind bombs here," Nihs riposted. He had propped up his menu in front of him and was almost completely hidden by it. "I will say, I'm impressed by that."

"See, I told you it was a good idea to eat at Colors," Lugh said.

"What's a mind bomb?" Kyle asked.

"It's a drink the Kol invented," Nihs said. "It's made by imbibing certain liquids with energy from Ephicers. It boosts magical attunement and mental keenness for a short while."

"It makes you hyper," Lugh translated. "If you think Nihs talks a lot now, wait until you see him with a mind bomb or two inside him. Once when he was trying to work out a problem with some Kol on the overhead, he drank six at once, and talked to himself in Kollic for *three hours straight.*"

"Oh, I did not!" Nihs said angrily, poking his head out from around his menu as Kyle laughed.

"Did so. You probably just don't remember, I bet your mind was in a haze."

"Kyle," Nihs said firmly, "don't believe a word that he says."

The drinks arrived. Kyle and Lugh's were an interesting grassy color, translucent as the blue Freezers had been. Nihs' drink looked drastically different. It was sparkling blue, opaque, and thickly viscous. It reminded Kyle of some glitter glue he had used in crafts as a child.

"Mind bomb," Nihs said happily, indicating the drink, and then promptly started to consume it.

The green Freezers were really very good, and the already recognizable tang of aquia made his even more satisfying. They ordered food, Kyle picking something at random based on the philosophy that everything must at least be palatable at such an expensive restaurant. He ended up ordering some kind of seafood pasta that Lugh assured him would be good.

They sat back, drinking their drinks and talking about nothing much. Lugh and Nihs told Kyle a bit more about Reno's history, how it had been the first real aboveground city built in the world, and how many races had contributed to its building.

"That's why you see differences in style from district to district, and sometimes even from building to building within the districts themselves," Nihs said. Kyle noticed that the Kol had indeed become distinctly more chatty after working his way through the greater half of his mind bomb— which was a very large drink relative to Nihs' size.

"You said that Reno was the first real aboveground city," Kyle pointed out, "so what came before it?"

Nihs cracked a superior little smile. "The underground cities of the Kol, of course," he said, "starting with Proks. Before we surfaced and travelled west, we lived under the mountains of Eastia. There were hundreds of Kol settlements built underground before the first brick of Reno was laid."

"Wow," Kyle said. *So Proks is an underground city*...he was now very curious to visit it, as well.

Their food arrived, and they ate. Kyle's pasta turned out to be delicious—the sauce was something like Alfredo back on Earth, almost overwhelmingly thick and buttery. Small dark bundles of meat were distributed throughout the dish; after eating a couple, Kyle speared one with his fork and held it up to his face.

"This is good," he said, "what is it?"

Lugh looked up from his dish. "Scail," he said, stealing one off of Kyle's plate and eating it, "a kind of sea snail. Selks fish for them all the time."

After they ate, they ordered more drinks and Lugh paid a bill which Nihs refused to look at. Lugh sighed contentedly once they had left.

"I love that place," he said, then clapped his hands together. "All right, let's find us some lodgings."

They continued on their way up the road. Kyle was now getting too tired to take in many details. He did notice that the amount of people on the street was lessening somewhat, and the building frontages were less done up; he assumed they were starting to leave the touristy part of the city. The streets and buildings were still designed in an interesting manner— Lorians seemed to have an innate desire in their construction to make things as radical as possible. Some buildings had large stone staircases leading up or down to the front door, others were spaced in such a way that there was room for a small square containing a statue or fountain. Trees and planters lined the streets, and the ever-present raised roadways arced overhead.

They stopped at a moderately classy and expensive-looking hotel farther down the road. The front of the building was simple enough, while the lobby inside was bright and warm.

"This place looks good enough," Lugh said. "We'll only need it for a couple nights anyway."

"Couldn't we have stopped at a hideout?" Kyle asked, remembering the one they had stayed at in Donno. "Or is that a stupid question?"

"Not at all," Lugh said, "there are plenty of hideouts in Reno...problem is, there are plenty of adventurers, too. The hideouts are almost always packed."

They went inside the hotel, and Kyle hung about in a daze while Lugh talked with the man at the counter about getting them a room. It was amazing how quickly Kyle had come to take Loria's appearances for granted. There was something familiar about the design of the hotel that made Kyle think a little of home, but even the outlandish details that never would have taken place on Earth had started to look normal to him. The *tigoreh* chandelier hanging over the lobby, the tiny chairs and tables set up for the sake of the Kol and the massive equivalent for the Minotaur. Even the people in the lobby had been overlooked—Selks he now essentially treated as humans, and even Lizardfolk were becoming a common sight for him. He did, however, spot a group of men seated in a corner whose appearance was not familiar to him. Their skin was a dark, ruddy green, their hair was black, and large tusks erupted from their lower lips. Orcs, as he later found out. The person behind the counter was another human, a bored-looking man in his thirties. Again, Kyle was struck by an odd feeling seeing a human holding such a mundane position. He reflected on the fact that David and Emil had also been humans, but then again, the only time he had seen them, they had been slaying goblins and working magic.

Kyle tuned back in to what Lugh and Nihs were saying.

"…so give it one day to sell our stuff and get Kyle some equipment," Lugh said, "and another at least to do our other errands."

"You're probably right," Nihs said. "Better make it two nights, then."

They got the keys to their rooms and trekked upstairs. They had gotten two rooms side-by-side which were connected by a door—in one were two Minotaur-sized beds and in the other were normal beds. Lugh deposited his effects in the larger room and came over to Kyle and Nihs' room for a conference.

"We'll go visit Rogan tomorrow and see if the repairs on the *Ayger* are done," he said. "If so, he can come with us, and we'll sell all our stuff from the mine raid and get Kyle some clothes and things."

"And then during second sun we can try to find someone who knows something about Kyle," Nihs picked up. "That search might take a while. We should probably go pay a visit to one of the universities…there are always a couple of oddballs hanging around who study alternate dimensional theory."

By this time, Kyle was very tired. He tried to take interest in what Nihs and Lugh were saying, but his eyelids were drooping. He did, however, ask, "What's second sun?"

"That refers to the second period of daylight in a day," Nihs replied. "Remember how in Loria every day is split into two periods of light? We call the first one 'day' and the second one 'second sun' in order to avoid confusion."

"Uh-huh," Kyle replied, yawning, "it's a good thing, too, that's totally not confusing at all."

Lugh laughed and got up from Nihs' bed. "All right, let's get some rest, a lot of walking tomorrow. Night."

Kyle settled down under the covers, looking around the room he shared with Nihs. Again, he was struck by the contrasting feelings of familiarity and difference. All the components of a hotel room from Earth were there—desks, walls, bed—but there was something off with each one, some little detail or other that reminded Kyle in no uncertain terms of where he was. This got him thinking about his homeworld. *Homeworld— what a strange concept.* For all of his life, Kyle had thought of himself in terms of his hometown, his home country, but never his homeworld. He wondered what other people from Earth would think of Loria, and what they would do if they had found themselves in Kyle's position. Another strange thought struck him—what if it had happened before? It really was ignorant of him to assume that he was the first to whom this had happened. He thought of the strange whirlpool that had brought him here—maybe it had happened to thousands of ships in the past. Maybe the Bermuda Triangle was like some weird hotspot for these…portals to show up. And what about the other passengers on the *Caribia*? What had happened to them after Kyle had fallen off the ship? Maybe they had all ended up on Loria. There could be crowds of people running around who were originally from Earth.

Kyle considered bringing up these thoughts with Nihs, who was nestled in another makeshift den in the bed next to him, but he was tired, and wasn't sure if the Kol would be interested in his thoughts anyway. He told himself to forget about it and tried to fall asleep.

Fifth grade marked the beginning of some rough times for young Kyle. As he had hoped for, he had not changed schools as a result of his giftedness test in grade three, and so he got to see all of his old friends grow and change in interesting and sometimes none too pleasant ways.

Under the influence of newfound hormones, the grade five classroom became a hotbed of chaos and drama, particularly which revolved around the two sexes' sudden obsession with one another. While Kyle's introverted nature kept him, for the most part, far back from all of this, he too was not immune to the sudden shift in social dynamics. Feuds broke out between old friends and old groups of friends, rifts between the different social castes grew ever more pronounced. Suddenly 'he' was popular, and 'she' unpopular; 'he' a nerd, 'he' a jock, 'she' the 'hot one', 'them' the 'weird kids'.

Kyle's trio of Quentin, Alex and himself had more or less broken up. Quentin had not become more outgoing with time, and was not really worth the effort it took to hang around—he was extremely uneasy with how the other students had started to act, and so retreated always further into his bubble of schoolwork. Alex had become one of the most affected by changing personalities—he spent his time during recess schmoozing the 'cool kids', trying to integrate himself into their group. This left Kyle alone.

Sometimes he would still spend time with his old friends, although hanging out with Quentin tended to be boring, and hanging out with Alex tended to result in insults and mild bullying directed at the two of them. He sought out Mark, a boy whom he had known for years but never bothered to hang out with; the two of them spent many a recess staying out of other people's ways and talking about whatever happened to interest them. A girl from Kyle's class, Melissa, started to join the pair. She was a small thing in braces and glasses, although mildly attractive in her own way. Kyle liked her, but her presence made him uncomfortable. He wasn't used to dealing with girls.

It happened at the beginning of recess during the spring of grade five. Kyle was heading towards a group of trees that he, Mark and Melissa often sat under when Alex fielded him.

"Hey!" the brown-haired boy said in a tense, excited voice. "Rob's found a pack of cigarettes, we're going to try smoking them behind the portable! Want to come?"

Kyle stopped. His heart was beating furiously. Did he want to? Trying out smoking…he didn't even know if the cool kids did that on a regular basis. It could be that he was getting his big break…his chance to be more daring than anyone else in the grade!

He glanced briefly at the trees that were possibly concealing Mark and Melissa. He had spent the last hundred recesses hanging out with them…surely one couldn't hurt?

"Okay," he said.

He followed Alex behind the portable classroom, where a group of five of the cool kids were standing in a circle, looking around furtively.

Rob, a large blonde boy, held out the package to them as soon as they joined them. "Hurry, take one!" he said, shaking the package.

Kyle took one first. He turned the odd cylinder around in his fingers as Alex grabbed one nervously. He knew how to smoke, having seen his father do it often. Yellow end goes in your mouth, you light the white end and breathe in. Simple enough. He could do this.

He noticed that the other cool kids were also holding cigarettes, but no one's was lit. Everyone was looking to everyone else, apparently waiting for someone else to try it before they did. It was Rob, finally, who produced a cheap plastic lighter and lit his own cigarette. Everyone watched with baited breath as he took an inexperienced pull. He immediately fell to coughing, almost dropping the cigarette and doubling over, clutching his stomach. A couple of the kids looked shocked; Kyle certainly felt it. But when Rob straightened up again, he was laughing.

"Come on!" he said, offering the lighter to the others and still laughing. "Come on, try it!"

No one else stepped forward. Kyle made a decision.

"Here," he said, holding out his own. There was an 'ooo' among the other kids as Rob smiled and lit his cigarette for him. Kyle felt a thrill of excitement.

Hah. Take that. I'm the first one to try it apart from Rob himself!

It was disgusting. He coughed and hacked as Rob had done, while the other kids laughed nervously and Alex thumped him on the back. He felt like throwing the thing away, and certainly wouldn't have been looked down upon for doing so. After all, he'd been the first to try it apart from Rob. But he'd be damned if he let anyone else outdo him, so he finished the entire cigarette while the others got theirs lit and tried it out. In the end, he was proud of himself. No one else but Rob managed to finish theirs.

Mark met up with him as the students were filing back into class.

"Hey," the boy said, "where were you this recess?"

"Umm," Kyle said, "I had to stay in, I had work to do."

"Your breath smells funny."

Of course it did. Kyle had been trying to get rid of the smell for the entire rest of the recess. He secretly feared that it would never go away.

Kyle awoke itching to see more of Reno. He had been fatigued the previous night coming into the city, he felt as though he hadn't really absorbed anything of their first run through the streets. He looked around. It seemed early in the morning, and though it had gotten fairly bright in their room, Nihs was still asleep.

Kyle lay in bed for a couple moments, wondering what to do. He couldn't see anything that looked like a clock in their room, and probably wouldn't have known how to read a Lorian clock anyway. He didn't want to wake Nihs up if it was too early. The little Kol was curled up in a tight ball at the top of his bed. Kyle wondered if all Kol slept that way.

His problem was solved when he heard noises coming from Lugh's room. *He must be up as well.* Kyle got out of bed carefully and dressed quietly, then sidled over to Lugh's door and gave it a gentle knock.

"Yeah, come in!" the Selk's voice sounded loud and clear from the other side. *So much for that*, Kyle thought as he went in.

He was amazed at how much Lugh had managed to spread out during their one-night stay. It looked as though he had already been living there for at least a month. He was buckling on his sword as Kyle came in.

"Oh, it's you," he said. "Great, I was just about to go and wake you two up. Is Nihs up yet?"

"No," Kyle said.

"Excellent," Lugh replied, striding into Kyle and Nihs' room, "I love waking him up early, he always gets so pissed off...HEY! NIHS!"

After they woke a surly Nihs, they gathered their effects and stepped once more into the streets of Reno, making their way back down the road to the docks. Reno was different by daylight, and even more interesting than it had been the night before. The streets were teeming with people:

Selks, humans, Lizardfolk, Orcs, Minotaur. Kyle saw more of the Buorish guards—they all walked with the same steady pace, greeting politely everyone they saw, hands folded behind their backs. There were a lot of them.

Kyle also saw several creatures walking the streets that he couldn't identify. Apart from the fact that he still wasn't familiar with all of the races of Loria, the appearance of each race's representatives varied wildly. He soon noticed that Lizardfolk came not only in green and red, but also blue, purple, black, white and any color in-between. Dying of hair also seemed to be in style for all of the people of Reno who possessed it. Selks in particular rarely wore their hair in natural or even reasonable colors. The fashion was just as volatile, ranging from adventurers, armed and armored, to teenagers who wore their clothing colorful and radical.

Kyle caught himself staring more than once as they wove their way through the streets. There was activity everywhere. Runners shot up and down the main road, making their strange noises. Kyle could see them clearly now—golden and somewhat stingray-shaped, they were more like motorcycles than cars after all. For the most part they sat only one person, and were roof-less.

"Now we'll go and see if Rogan's finished with the repairs," Lugh said, "then we can bring that stuff we got from the raid and find somewhere to sell it. Then we can work on getting our newest adventurer some equipment."

"What about his Iden card?" Nihs asked from Lugh's shoulder.

Lugh tapped his chin. "You know," he said, "I was thinking about that. Should we even bother? In a couple days we'll be leaving Reno, and then we'll probably be going to Proks. No one's likely to card him that far east. We could probably get by without it."

"And what if Kyle decides to stay?" Nihs said. "Or what if we just can't find a way for him to get home? The longer we wait, the more trouble it will cause when we finally decide to get him a card. We should be thinking of the long-term here, in case Kyle ends up as a permanent citizen of Loria."

"Fine, fine," Lugh said, "we can do that first. But I'm blaming you if we end up under inquiry from the police."

This statement worried Kyle, although he suspected that Lugh was joking. But what worried him more was what Nihs had said. He had decided before that he wanted to stay in Loria, at least for a while, so why did the thought of living in Loria forever give him such a chill feeling? In an attempt to distract himself from his own thoughts, he went back to observing the city.

They made their way down to the docks and climbed back into the massive honeycomb shape within which was docked the *Ayger*. Once inside, they ran into the same Selkic worker from the day before.

"'Ello then," he greeted them brightly, as they approached. He waved his hand in the direction of their ship. "All done! Your Minotaur friend's inside, just buffin' up the engine."

"Brilliant, thanks," Lugh said. He was grinning as they climbed the ramp onto the *Ayger*, and sounded almost giddy as he spoke. "It's been ages since we've had her fully repaired. I can't wait to take her for a spin! Nihs, I call first!"

"Go right ahead," the Kol grumbled, "you can have second and third too, if you want."

Once inside, they took a route that Kyle was unfamiliar with. They went beyond the stairs that led to the bridge, and down another flight beneath them. Kyle assumed that these led to the engine room. He was proven right when they passed through an antechamber and made their way into a small enclave filled with *tigoreh* machinery.

Though the room was only dimly lit by a couple of lanterns that hung from the ceiling, the light gleamed off of every golden surface. The room was dominated by eight huge pistons, four on either side of a narrow catwalk. Each was nine feet high and four feet across, their bulk stretching down past the catwalk and up into the ceiling. They were inactive, all frozen in different positions, and some of them revealed a blue glow coming from within. The rest of the room was crammed with machinery: *tigoreh* pipes and wires snaked everywhere, and dials and levers seemed to be stuck wherever they would fit. It was clean and bright, but still so complicated and intense that Kyle's eyes watered as he contemplated the *Ayger's* huge engine. It didn't help that the room was cramped, and quite warm.

Rogan was working on one of the farther cylinders, astride a metal stool. He was reaching far up onto the top of the piston, tightening a bolt with a giant wrench. Muscles rippled along the Minotaur's arm as he struggled with the machinery.

Lugh folded his arms and squinted upwards, waiting politely for Rogan to finish working.

Rogan checked the bolt with his hand, nodded, and jumped down from his stool with a crash. Wiping his hands on a rag, he acknowledged Lugh and the others as though seeing them pass by on an afternoon stroll.

"Morning, Lughenor," he said, "Nihs, Kyle. Did our Selkic friend tell you that everything got done?"

"Uh-huh," Lugh said. "How'd it go? And how far back did it set us?"

"About four thousand nells," Rogan said, "but she's as good as new. Should be flight path-ready now. These two converters—" he banged the one he had been working on and the machine next to it with his wrench, "completely refurbished. We should be good for at least another four months."

"Excellent," Lugh said, grinning widely, "and not as bad as I would have thought. So what do you say? Are you up to seeing if we can make back some of that money? We were going to do some shopping today."

"Sounds good. I'll be with you after I get cleaned up. As it is, no one we trade with is going to want to stand downwind of me."

They went back to the bridge as they waited for Rogan to get ready. Lugh ran his hand lovingly along the control panel.

"So it'll be Proks next for us," he said excitedly. "We haven't been abroad in so long. We haven't been to Eastia since we met, right, Nihs?"

"That we haven't," Nihs agreed.

"How long ago did you two meet?" Kyle asked, suddenly curious.

"Seems like forever," Lugh said in a mock tortured voice.

"Nuck," Nihs shot at him. "I think it's been about two years?" he added seriously.

"Yeah," Lugh agreed, "just a little over, it was winter in Eastia."

Kyle allowed this comment to slide by; he felt that he wasn't ready to try and grasp how Lorian seasons worked. He was, however, reminded of something that Rogan had said earlier.

"What did Rogan mean when he said the *Ayger* was flight path-ready?" he asked.

"Oh," Lugh said, "it's a system the Buors cooked up. There are these specific trails set up that lead between major cities—it's like a path that you program into your ship so that it flies it automatically. The speed cap when you're flying a path is higher than when you fly manually, but your ship's condition needs to be right up there before they let you use one. We'll do it when we fly to Proks."

Rogan arrived, not armed with his battle-axe, but with a huge sack of weapons and equipment slung to his back.

"Oh wow," said Lugh. "I didn't realize we had so much. Are you okay to carry all that with you?"

Rogan shifted the weight of the pack around. "Don't you worry about me, Lughenor. Did you have anywhere particular in mind to go with this?"

"General Arms is in the market complex, which works out, since we need to get Kyle some stuff."

"*Or* we could go down river," Nihs said. "Which is closer to the Iden center," he added in scolding tones.

Lugh reached down and tapped him on the head, causing the Kol to swat at him angrily.

"*I* have thought of that," Lugh said. "I was thinking that we should get him some new clothes before we go in to get his card. That way we can say that he had no clothes when we found him and it's one less thing for the police to poke at. Normal people wouldn't notice what he's wearing, but the Buor working at Iden will."

Nihs opened his mouth to argue, then closed it. "That's…actually a good idea!" he said in tones of great surprise. "Well done!"

"I'm honored." Lugh said in a voice dripping with sarcasm. "Shall we go?"

Kyle followed the three of them back into the city, letting his mind wander. Again he marveled at his strange situation, but even stranger was the fact that he had adapted to it so quickly. He could be walking down the streets of Cleveland right now. Of course, he didn't know Reno city nearly as well as he knew Cleveland.

Suddenly, a wave of powerful homesickness struck him. He thought of his boring, dull life back in the USA. It had been so easy to take the familiarity for granted…now he was stranded in this strange world, which he knew nothing about, having to rely on the knowledge of his friends to survive. Back in his home city, Kyle had possessed a street savviness that was the envy of all of his friends. Strangely, he missed the jaded, cynical Kyle that he had left back on Earth. He felt like a child again in Loria—this was exciting to a point, but it also came with all of childhood's insecurities. He was struck by a sudden urge to just go home, curl up in bed and do nothing, something that seemed a far way off here in Loria.

"Kyle?" Lugh's voice penetrated his bubble of thought. He shook himself out of his daydream. The others were turning down a side street, and Kyle was about to go on forwards.

"Right, sorry," he said quickly, and followed.

Once they were off of the main road, Reno became disorganized. The streets were no longer straight and orderly, and buildings clustered wherever they wanted, shooting up into the sky like giant stalks of bamboo. No two were alike, and each and every edifice was festooned with signs and advertisements. Massive billboards and lit signs hung from every available surface, bearing down on a suddenly very tiny-feeling Kyle as they walked below. The streets teemed with people, and the raised roads soared overhead as though painted in the sky.

The atmosphere here was more relaxed in a chaotic sort of way. People appeared to loiter a lot and Kyle caught a couple of glimpses of younger Lorians. Vendors' stalls clustered everywhere, creating streets within the streets. No space was wasted: every inch of street was built on, used as a store, decorated, walked on. Runners were present, as well, though this didn't stop the roads from being covered with people. Jaywalking was a common practice in Reno—adventurers, workers, Buorish guards, and youth mingled, headed in every direction.

Kyle was drawn out of his pensive mood by the sights and sounds of Reno. There was simply too much input to his senses to be ignored. He was again hard pressed not to stare at the people around him; an Oblihari passed close by and he got a view of a crooked, feathered, and winged body, and a beaked face. A group of strange creatures dashed past them, moving swiftly; whooping and hollering as they wove in-between the crowds, jumping over stalls and catapulting off walls. They were clearly skilled in leaping.

"Chirpa free-runners," Lugh said, smiling. "Watch them."

Kyle squinted at the runners as they burned down the street. Already they were quite far away. Their bodies were furred, and long tails sprung from their forms. Several other people in the crowd turned to watch them, as well. Once at the end of the street, they ran straight up the wall of a building and vaulted onto the roof of a nearby, shorter construction. Kyle watched in amazement as they ran along its roof, leaping and flipping, and then jumped out of sight.

"What are the Chirpa like?" he asked Lugh, as they continued on their way.

"They're known as the feral race," Lugh said. "A lot of people call them the cats, but not all of them actually look like cats. They're great athletes, but they're lazy as all hell too."

"They tend to avoid work whenever they can," Rogan said in his soft rumble. "They're pleasure seekers, and don't like being tied down by jobs. They make good adventurers…those of them that can take the profession seriously, that is."

At this point, however, Kyle had ceased to pay attention. They had just rounded a corner onto a large square and had ended up face-to-face with the largest building, or rather group of buildings, that Kyle had ever seen. It was a massive complex that faced an equally massive square. The building sprawled to the left and right, spilling into huge wings and looking as though it had eaten the rest of the street. The face of it was a wall of glass and concrete, covered in signs and lights; huge columns framed the main entrance. Through the glass walls Kyle could see elevators moving up and down, and people walking on raised floors.

"Behold," Lugh said in a grandly sarcastic voice, "the Reno market complex."

"That's insane!" Kyle exclaimed. "How much stuff do you people need to *buy*?"

"Most people react in much the same way when they see the market," Nihs said, buffing his nails on Rogan's forehead. "Reno has a reputation for being unnecessary and indulgent. That being said, the market *is* an interesting place, and chances are that no matter what you're looking for you'll be able to find it there. So, what's our plan of attack?"

"First we should find a weapons shop," Rogan cut in, shifting the pack on his back. "It'll take me a good while to get rid of all this. And I should take your weapons when you go shopping, Lugh and Kyle. It's a little less acceptable in the complex to walk around wearing swords."

"Good point," said Lugh. "We could leave you to it and pick up some clothes and equipment. Oh! Should we get Kyle some new armor?"

"I brought the suit he was wearing in the mine," Rogan replied. "I can get it refurbished for him."

"Perfect!" Lugh said happily. "Always thinking of everything, Rogan. All right, let's go. Stick close, Kyle, try not to get sucked up by the atmosphere."

"Very funny."

"Who said I was kidding?"

The inside of the marketplace was no less spectacular than its outside. Kyle couldn't believe the feat of architecture that it represented; he'd never seen such a massive—or unique—shopping space before. Everything was lavish, polished and bright: glittering stores lined every single available line of wall, and booths were stretched along the lengths of every hallway. The hallways themselves were decorated with statues, benches, sculptures, and planters that held everything from miniscule flowers to entire trees. The tiled floor gleamed brightly, and sunlight poured in from the distant glass ceiling some two dozen floors up.

The place had no symmetry, and seemed not to have a sense of scale, either. While the floors of buildings back on Earth were always a constant height, here they were built wherever they were needed to accommodate the various races. There were places where next to a single, human-sized store, were two Kol-sized stores stacked on top of one another, equipped with their own small staircase and balcony. Staircases extended upwards and downwards wherever they wished, and fast-moving elevators were peppered about. The overall effect was one of splendid chaos.

Shoppers swarmed here, too. Kyle noticed that the average age was much younger than on the streets. The sight of Lorian teenagers struck him as very odd for some reason. Their group, composed as it was of a human, a Selk, a Kol and especially a Minotaur carrying a bag of weapons, drew quite a bit of attention. Kyle felt rather awkward and tried not to make eye contact with anyone.

For not the first time since he had arrived in Reno, Kyle found his senses overwhelmed by the sheer volume of details to take in within the complex. Storefronts, people, decorations, signs. Massive advertisements and sculptures hung down from the ceiling, and huge plants and works of art rose up from the ground floor.

Lugh provided commentary on each store to Kyle as they passed.

"Rabla's, a restaurant chain run by the town Selks. The food is crappy but cheap. Okidari, an Oblihari chain, their food is usually better but some of it's really weird. The Buorish Travel Company…yeah, the Buors don't bother with complicated names. They handle airship registration and flight paths, we'll use them to get out of there. Eyez. Uh, I don't know what that is. Must be new."

"It looks like a clothing store," Nihs said. "There's enough of them in Reno in any case."

"Probably," Lugh agreed. "The humans, Selks and Chirpa here are obsessed with clothes. It's annoying, but that's good for you, Kyle, we'll have plenty to choose from when we want to make you look like a local."

They ended up ordering breakfast from Okidari, while Rogan wandered off to find some place that offered its food in greater portions. The person who served them was an Oblihari. It was Kyle's first close look at one of their race. His body was feathered in dark gray and his face was dominated by a large beak. From what Kyle could see, he possessed both hands and wings—the wings hung from his forearms like overlarge sleeves, pulling back and revealing his inner arm whenever he reached out to grab something. The hands themselves were feathered and clawed. His body was bent and crooked, and his legs were skinny, bony affairs that ended in large claws. He was courteous and spoke in a calm, clipped voice. Kyle ended up with a bowl of what seemed to be egg soup; it was hot and well-seasoned, and very good.

After they ate, they continued on their way and came to a large store with a sign above in gold letters that read GENERAL ARMS. Kyle's eyes lit up as he took in what was displayed in the main window: racks and racks of swords and other weapons hung from floor to ceiling. The picture window glittered with polished metal. There were retraswords much in prominence, some of them retracted and others active to show off their golden blades. A rack of spears hung to their left, with Ephicers of different colors glittering at the base of their points. A massive decorated battleaxe, even larger than the one Rogan carried, was the main focus of the window. Daggers, handguns, and other small weapons Kyle could not name were scattered everywhere. A mannequin wore a suit of gilded metal armor.

"Try to contain your excitement, Lugh," Nihs chirped from Rogan's shoulder. "He always gets giddy around weapon stores," he confided to Kyle.

"Really?" Kyle said, rather distracted.

Nihs took in his vacant expression and snorted. "*Tish.* Another one! I don't see how you people can get so excited looking at a bunch of metal."

"So beautiful," Lugh said, ignoring him. He said to Kyle, "Come on, weapon stores are a bunch of fun. I'll give you the tour!"

The inside of the store was beyond what Kyle could have imagined. Every single surface from floor to walls to ceiling was covered with every kind of weapon that Kyle could dream of, and many he couldn't. Swords, spears, axes, daggers, bows, guns, staves, and shields of every description mingled with strange, exotic weapons whose use Kyle couldn't fathom. Lugh was talking excitedly to him the second they stepped into the store.

"Rogan probably told you about most of these, right? Those are the retraswords in the front...oh, look, mine is the same make as this one— this must be a new model. These spears are for soldiers like Doru, I learned a little about using one once. They're retractable, too, see? They keep more of the weapons for promoted adventurers in the back and in the basement, those are the coolest ones. Look at those bows—oh, here comes the owner."

The owner of General Arms was a male human, possibly in his forties. He was tall and well-built, with a dark brown moustache, bushy eyebrows and a square head. Kyle imagined that he must have been a retired fighter or a smith of some kind.

"Welcome," he said, his voice deep, "adventurers, I presume?" He noticed the pack on Rogan's back. "Are you selling today?"

"That's right," Rogan said, shifting to the front of the group. "We had a run through a goblin-infested mine the other day. Nothing fancy, a lot of flat weapons and some woven spears. In surprisingly good condition."

"But the real find was this sword of Kyle's," Lugh cut in before Rogan could continue. "Show him your changesword, Kyle!"

Kyle, surprised, drew his silver arm and handed it to the merchant. The man let out an "oho!" as he gripped the weapon.

"Can you appraise it for us?" Lugh asked, pride and excitement evident in his voice.

"That I can," the merchant said. His large eyebrows contracted as he squinted at the blade.

"Accida," he said, a moment later, "they're an older company, out of business now, but they made good changearms. This one's high quality, and in good condition, too. Maybe around fifteen, twenty years old…the usage level for these swords is twenty-five, but the damage level would be comparable to a level thirty weapon."

"Oh, nice!" Lugh said enthusiastically as the merchant handed the sword back. Kyle had no idea what the merchant had said, but he assumed it must be something good.

"Worth a good two thousand four hundred nells if you were willing to sell it," the merchant added, laughing slightly.

Lugh laughed, as well. "Good to know," he said, "but we'll be keeping this one, thanks."

"Well," Rogan said, "that weapon notwithstanding, are you willing to buy?"

The merchant smiled. "Of course! Between you and me, it's worth a man's time to stock plenty of low-level weapons these days. Heroes are becoming pickier about what they buy, but new adventurers pop up every day and they all need decent arms to start out with. Why don't you bring that pack over to the counter and we can start to sort through it?"

"Absolutely," Rogan said in an approving voice, lumbering forward.

"We'll just look around," Lugh said brightly to the merchant.

"Of course. At your leisure, friend."

The tour of the shop continued, Kyle drinking in the sight of each weapon and listening to Lugh's commentary. They made their way towards the back of the shop, and true to Lugh's word, the weapons became progressively more impressive and complicated.

"What the heck is that?" Kyle asked, pointing to a ring of metal that looked like a deadly hula hoop.

"Giant chakram," Lugh replied. "There's a kind of Elvish dance-fighting that uses those. I'm surprised they have one here, to be honest."

Lugh later stopped next to a wall, looking high at a row of bows.

"Remember the look of these," he told Kyle, pointing, "and be afraid when you see an adventurer holding one."

The bows were very strange. They were divided into three parts, two branches and a ring-shaped handle in the center, and had no string that Kyle could see. They looked sleek and impressive, and each had a large Ephicer set into the grip. Strange, screw-shaped arrows colored dark blue were arranged next to them.

"Those are ring bows," Lugh explained, "and they use a ton of Ephicer energy. The strings are purely magical, so they pass through anything but arrows made for them. As you draw it back, the bow spins around the ring and twists the string around the arrow, so it spins like crazy when you let it go. They can shoot arrows for miles, but you need insane upper arm strength to draw one. Snipers use them."

"Wow," Kyle said. "Wait. You said for *miles*? What would be the point? You wouldn't be able to see what you were shooting at!"

"*We* wouldn't be able to," Lugh said, "but it's possible to gain something called farsight through metamagic. If you want to use a ring bow, you learn how to see far enough for it to be useful. Don't ask me how snipers know how to aim at that distance though, because I haven't a damn clue."

They went downstairs. There were axes attached to chains, retractable lances, changearms far more impressive than what Kyle carried, and slim katana-like swords that came in bundles of four for some reason.

"Kinda scary, huh?" Lugh said as they went from display to display. "Awesome, but freaky. Some of the stuff that adventurers can do gives me the willies."

"I'll say," Kyle admitted. "Do I want to know why those swords come in fours?"

"Would you believe that there are heroes that can use all of them at once?"

"No!"

"Then forget it. Oh, look…composite weapons."

Kyle recognized the shape of these weapons from those that Reldan had worn; some were black, like his had been, while some were the gold of *tigoreh*, and others were different colors entirely. Each were in a different shape and size.

"They all turn into different things, see," Lugh explained, "for different fighting styles. Reldan's was an axe, sword and shield—some of these are two small axes and a big one, some are a sword, bow and shield. This one—"

Lugh stopped in front of a graceful-looking golden composite weapon. Two webs of blue magic stretched along its length, glowing faintly.

"Two swords and an energy shield." The Selk's eyes were filled with the weapon's light. "The shield's made from a web of Ephicer power, see, so the weapon itself can be smaller and lighter. If I ever became a hero, I'd use a weapon like this one."

Kyle was fairly good at reading people, but even if he hadn't been, the desire in Lugh's voice would have been obvious. In that moment, Kyle knew that whatever else Lugh wanted, there was nothing that he wanted more than to be a hero.

"I have a question," Kyle said, aware that it possibly wasn't the best time. "Are there two different meanings to the word 'hero'?"

"Yeah," Lugh said, his voice distant. "One of them is a promoted fighter like Reldan. But it also means any other type of adventurer that's been promoted. It's a little confusing. Think of it as the difference between being a hero by profession and a hero by status."

They went back upstairs to find Rogan and the merchant working their way through the weapons Rogan had bought. Nihs was sitting on the desk nearby, looking bored.

"We'll be heading off, then," Lugh said, waving to them and handing their swords to Rogan. "Coming, Nihs?"

"Yes, please," the Kol said, getting up and jumping onto Lugh's shoulder as they stepped out. "Weapons interest me even less than clothes do. Is that what we're doing next?"

"Suppose so," Lugh said. "Oh hey, we should get Kyle a haircut, too."

Nihs gave him an exasperated look. "Oh, Luuugh."

"No, think about it!" Lugh said seriously. "Everyone who has hair wears it scaled these days, especially humans. We want him to blend in as much as possible, right?"

Nihs narrowed his eyes and grit his teeth. "Hmph, I suppose so."

Kyle decided not to say anything. He was beyond pride at this point, he would just go with whatever Lugh and Nihs decided for him. He was, however, determined not to stay in ignorance. "What do you mean by scaled?"

"Like mine," Lugh replied, turning away from Kyle so that his large mane could be seen. Now that Lugh had pointed it out, Kyle could see that his hair was sculpted into a series of scales like those of a fish, each two inches long.

"How do they do that?" Kyle asked.

"You charge it with magic particles," Lugh said. "It's all the rage right now. If you want to fit in you really should get it done. Plus it'll get you babes." He winked.

"Oh, please," Nihs said.

Kyle let out a small, rueful laugh and then stopped himself. "Well," he said into the silence, "what first?"

"Haircut," Lugh said, pointing to a shop on their right. "At Lara's. It's a Selk place, I go there myself."

"Yes, once every hundred years," Nihs said, tweaking Lugh's mass of hair.

"Hush, you."

The inside of the store looked like every high-end fashion shop Kyle had ever seen. It was even more slick and modern than the inside of Colors. Pictures of beautifully done-up Lorians, mostly Selkic women, hung on the walls, and the entire place smelled of perfume.

"Pah," Nihs said, plunking himself down on one of the cushioned chairs that lined the storefront. "These places always smell so strongly. Why is that necessary?"

"You're a Kol," Lugh reminded him, "your nose is more sensitive."

A young town Selk made her way around the counter to approach them. She wore a short, multi-layered dress in green, and tall brown boots. Her face was meticulously made-up, both her lips and eyes done in greens that complemented her dress. Her hair, also scaled and dyed an orangey brown, was gilded by a green headband whose ties streamed down her back. It was a strange look that made Kyle think of hippie and Goth at the same time, and was shamelessly cutesifying. Even though he was aware of this, Kyle couldn't help but feel attracted.

She flashed them a dazzling smile as she approached. "Hi there! What can I do for you today?"

"Uh," Kyle said. He wasn't quite sure what he was asking for, and the musky perfume that the girl wore was rather distracting.

Lugh came to his aid, putting an arm around his shoulders. "A cut for my friend here," he said, "and a hair scaling. Whatever you think'll look good. He's from out of town, so we're trying to make him look like a Renoite. He's never had his hair scaled before."

The girl turned her attention to Lugh. "I remember you! You're Lugh, right?"

"Got it in one." Lugh touched a finger to his brow in a kind of salute.

The girl winked. "I can always recognize my own work," she boasted. She said to Kyle, "So you'd like to get your hair scaled, hm? What's your name?"

"Kyle," he managed to say, feeling quite overwhelmed.

She smiled sweetly at him. "Kyle, hm? Okay, then, Kyle, let's get you started. I'm Sel."

"Nice to meet you," Kyle said weakly, as he allowed himself to be led to the back of the shop.

The rest of the procedure passed more or less the same as a haircut back on Earth. Sel washed his hair and seated him in front of a mirror, set above a table equipped with various weapons of war. Kyle noticed that the normally familiar glow of Ephicers tended to lend an ominous cast to Lorian barbershop tools.

Sel chatted constantly with Kyle and Lugh, who had taken up a position behind the seat, as she worked. At first Kyle found it strange that Lugh was hanging by so closely; he assumed that he merely wished to schmooze the cute hairdresser. But then he realized that Lugh was once again being much more intelligent than he let on—he was distracting her and preventing her from asking Kyle too many questions about his life.

"I'm not going to cut it too short," Sel explained as she worked. "I'll scale it in thin strips and give it something that'll keep the wet look, I think that'll suit you just fine. Not many people can wear the dark look, but you've got the hair for it."

"Should we keep the beard?" Lugh asked, a look of amusement on his face.

"Mhm, I'll scale that too. Beards aren't really the thing right now, but I think I can make it work in your case. What do you think, Kyle?" she asked, leaning down to him.

"I don't know!" Kyle said, surprised. "I trust you."

Sel giggled and tapped his cheek jokingly. "Good boy, I like you."

After Kyle's hair was cut, Sel drew a sinister-looking *tigoreh* tool from her table. It glowed blue and looked like a scalpel.

Sensing Kyle's trepidation, she explained, "This is a scaler." She popped out its blue fuel cell and added another one colored black. "This is what'll make you look good. Unfortunately it'll also make you sterile."

"What!" Kyle jumped.

Both Lugh and Sel laughed, and Kyle sank lower into his chair, feeling foolish.

"Aww, don't feel bad," Sel said, starting to pull the instrument through his hair, "you'll forgive me when you see the job I've done!"

After the mysterious scaling procedure had been completed, Sel trimmed Kyle's beard and ran a tiny version of the scaling device through it. She brushed everything off and presented Kyle to himself.

"Well?" she said, "what do you think?"

Kyle looked…different. His normally lank, untidy hair had been tamed into something that appeared more sophisticated than neglected. The scales that had been put in it were much thinner than Lugh's, and so the effect was not unlike that of recently wetted hair. Kyle ran his fingers through it, deliberately upsetting the pattern. It snapped back into place once his hand was gone as though attracted by static. His beard, too, looked neater, shorter, and each hair pointed straight downwards instead of in every which direction. For one of the first times in a while, the sight of himself didn't make Kyle want to wince.

"Wow," he said in complete honesty and surprise, "it looks really good! Thank you!"

Sel grinned at him so widely that her eyes almost shut. "Told you I could pull it off. The scaling should keep for a couple months. Come by again when you're ready to try a new look. I would love to experiment on you. It's not often that you get humans with black hair in here."

"Sure!" Kyle said, then remembering himself, added, "uh, if I get the chance."

Sel winked at him.

They made their way back to the counter. Nihs, who had remained seated at the front of the store with his nose in a magazine, came scurrying up Lugh's arm and peered at Kyle.

"Not bad," he said with a clever smile on his face. "You're almost bearable to look at now."

"Why don't you get your hair cut?" Kyle riposted.

"I, if you didn't notice, don't have any hair, my young friend."

"Oh, that's okay!" Sel said brightly from behind the counter. "I could give your head a polish, if you like, or I could try scaling your ears."

"Excuse me!" Nihs said indignantly as the others laughed.

"I'm sure we could come up with something," Sel persisted

innocently. "Some kind of ornament for your ears, maybe. Or you could wear a wig! Just think, you could be the first Kol to have the new look!"

Lugh drew his wallet as Nihs fumed. "Allrighty," he said, "how much do I owe you?"

"Five kajillion nells. Just kidding. That'll be ninety nells."

"Ninety nells!" Lugh said in mock dismay. "Kyle, we're getting you a helmet as soon as we leave. That haircut had better last you forever. All right, here you go. Thank you!"

"Yeah, thanks!" Kyle added.

Sel smiled. "No, thank *you*. See you later, Kyle!"

Kyle caught himself smiling several times once they had left the barbershop, and felt rather ashamed about it. Somewhere between getting his hair cut, talking with Sel, and jabbing at Nihs, he had arrived at a good mood. He felt stupid for feeling so happy about such a simple thing as a haircut.

"Well, that was fun," Lugh said grandly as they walked. He nudged Kyle in the ribs. "And I noticed that you made a new friend."

"Huh?" Kyle said, trying to sound offhand. The stupid grin was creeping onto his face again. Feeling absurd, he tried to fight it.

Lugh, however, had noticed. "Sel seems to like you, wouldn't you say?" he taunted. "And you seemed pretty happy in there, too."

"Oh, please."

"Seriously, I haven't seen you smile so much since you got excited about killing goblins in that mine—ouch!" he cried in mock pain as Kyle stamped on his foot.

They wandered the halls of the market complex for a while longer, scanning the stores on either side. Lugh got excited on seeing a stall that sold a type of candy called poppits, and they ended up buying a bag of multicolored and multi-sized orbs that were like gobstoppers filled with sweetened soap suds.

"If you shtay in Reno," Lugh said firmly around a mouthful of candy, "you have to try the poppits. Well-known fact."

"That's disgusting," Nihs commented. "Besides, poppits aren't that good."

Lugh swallowed. "Says you. I saw you sneaking a couple when Kyle wasn't looking."

Down one of the market's wings was the fashion section, and it did deserve a section all to its own. Ads and logos bore down on Kyle from all directions; he was reminded of a documentary he had seen about rainforests, where all of the plants fought and struggled to catch the sunlight. The market was overgrown with clothing stores of every kind.

They paused in the lobby of the wing, contemplating the mass of culture like generals observing the enemy.

"Huh, it's bigger than I remember," Lugh said.

"It gets bigger every day," Nihs pointed out. "So, do you know where we're going?"

"No," Lugh admitted. "I've never had to worry about human fashion before. How about you, Kyle?"

"I don't know!" Kyle said. "I wasn't fashionable back on Earth, let alone here."

"Huh," Lugh said again. There was a long pause. He shrugged. "How bad can it be, right?" If they sell it here, it must be at least somewhat in fashion. I'm sure we can wing it."

"Great," Kyle said.

"Okay," Lugh said five minutes later, "this is pretty cool."

Kyle had to agree with him. He wasn't normally interested in clothes. As far as he was concerned, if it covered him up and at least somewhat matched the occasion, it was good enough. He wasn't in much of a position to compare Loria's world of fashion with that of Earth's, but he was hard pressed to imagine a place like this existing in one of Earth's malls. It was like the Vegas of clothes—lights, color, ads, and people were everywhere. Each brand of clothing had its own theme: a store named Tones only sold clothes colored in gradients, another sold layered clothing similar to what Sel had worn, and still another sold bright, multi-colored outfits that Kyle had seen some locals wearing.

"Everything is so bright," he said, squinting, "and so colorful."

"Color is very important in our world," Nihs told him. "It's something you'll have to be aware of."

Again, Kyle noticed the demographic here was much younger than outside. He felt strangely intimidated in the presence of people that could have been ten years younger than him; he was out of his element, while they were not.

They wandered the halls of the clothing stores aimlessly, Lugh pointing out various items to Kyle as they walked.

"See, the truth is, you can wear pretty much anything these days and people won't mind. We just need to get you out of those clothes you brought with you. I think I know where to get you some pants kind of like those things you're wearing."

"They're called jeans."

"Sure. Okay, how about this?"

They ended up grabbing Kyle a pair of black pants that closely resembled denim, and a softer cream-colored pair. They picked out a couple simple under- and over-shirts in various colors. They also bought a layered shirt from the Selkic store.

"Black seems to be your thing," Lugh told him, "but color is really in right now, it's best that you grab some of that."

As Nihs complained and commented on the state of Lugh's wallet, they also bought a pair of shoes and a pair of boots, and some fingerless gloves.

"Every adventurer needs a pair of gloves," Lugh said firmly, "except for spellcasters, of course. Pay attention to that. It's practically a symbol of office. Well, do you think that's enough?"

Kyle was overwhelmed that they had gotten so much, and felt absolutely miserable when Nihs opened Lugh's wallet and mockingly called into it, "Hellooo in there! Well, yes, Lugh, I think we're quite finished."

Lugh caught the look on Kyle's face and shook his shoulder. "Oh, come off it, Nihs, give Kyle a break. This is fun! Besides, it's not like we're using that money for anything. You can't take it with you, you know."

"I'm not planning on going anywhere just yet," Nihs pointed out. Lugh ignored him.

Kyle had wandered into a group of clothes within a section of the complex. He stood under a sign reading *Tear It Up*, looking through them. The theme of this store was ripping—shirts, pants and accessories were all designed to appear ripped apart and then sewn back together.

A certain coat caught Kyle's attention. It was black, and knee-length. The rip in it was horizontal; a white tear ran through the elbows and just above the waist of the torso. But the main feature of it was a decal stitched into the coat in silver—a stylized phoenix, its wings spread below the shoulders, dominating the coat's back.

As Lugh and Nihs caught up with him, Kyle took the coat off its hanger and tried it on. It fit comfortably. He looked at himself in a nearby floor-length mirror and to his surprise, did not immediately feel foolish.

"Am I insane?" he asked Lugh, "or does this actually look not too bad?"

His friend smiled. "Better than that, I think it actually really suits you! Try billowing the back out, like this!" Lugh made a sweeping motion with his arms, pushing an imaginary coat back and out.

Kyle copied the motion, throwing the coat out behind him. It made a satisfying *whoosh* sound and slowly settled back down. To Kyle's embarrassment, he found the silly grin creeping back onto his face.

Lugh said, "You know what, I'm sold. I think it's fate. Let's get that coat for you. Besides, it'll look good when you get to adventuring. It matches your changesword."

Kyle wore the coat with one of his white shirts and black pants as they left the store. Secretly, he was very happy with how everything looked. The coat in particular rested on his shoulders as though he had owned it for years, and he couldn't resist billowing it outwards every couple seconds. He felt much more in place knowing that he was dressed as a Lorian.

"Well," Lugh said, "let's go and find Rogan again; he should be finished by now. Then we can head down river and get Kyle his Iden card."

They found Rogan sitting on one of the benches in the complex, eating a huge meat sandwich. He waved them over and they sat down next to him.

"Nice coat," he told Kyle.

"Thanks."

"I take it your mission was a success, then?" he asked Lugh.

"Yep. We're all done. How did it go with you?"

"Eighty hundred nells all told." The Minotaur polished off the rest of his sandwich and brushed his hands together. "He took two hundred out of it to remake Kyle's armor. We'll be able to pick it up tomorrow."

"Eighty hundred!" Lugh exclaimed with delight. "That's a lot more than I thought."

Rogan nodded. "It was the spears that did it really—woven and quite new. Well, now that that's out of the way, what do we do next?"

"Iden card for Kyle. Tomorrow I guess we'll check out the jobs and head off to Eastia."

"Sounds good." Rogan rose ponderously, handing Lugh and Kyle their swords. "Let's get going."

They left the market complex and headed west towards the waterfront, strolling down the streets of Reno. Kyle felt more at home than he had before. It helped that the back streets were much less overwhelming.

Rogan fell into stride next to him as they walked. "This is an old Buorish part of town. That's why everything is made out of stone. Some of these roads still contain their original paving stones, laid almost a thousand years ago. That's why they say that Reno is both the oldest and newest city in the world."

Kyle was amazed to admit that he was capable of taking interest in Rogan talking about rocks. Everything seemed to take on a much more significant cast when spoken by the Minotaur.

"Rogan," he asked, "why is your currency called nells?"

"It's the Kollic word for 'two'," Rogan said. "You see, before the Kol made contact with the other races they had their own currency called the dolur—the Kollic word for one. After all the races came together, they decided to establish a common currency—the nell, you see?"

"Makes sense," Kyle said. He knew it was nothing new, but felt it necessary to say, "Our currency is called the dollar."

Rogan laughed. "Someone up there has a sense of humor, hm?"

"I guess." Another question came to Kyle, brought to mind by Rogan's comment about Reno. "What happened a thousand years ago? Lugh and Nihs told me about it a little. They said there was a meteor crash."

Rogan nodded gravely. "The Kol call it *Adaragem*—they have a special word for everything, as you'll find out when we reach Proks. The meteor hit Westia and blocked the sun for years—did Lugh and Nihs tell you that?"

"Yeah. They mentioned that there was a big war."

Rogan sighed. "It was a very dark time in every possible way. I suppose it's important to tell you about it. It still affects us to this day, and some people still haven't gotten over it. Remember, a thousand years is only a couple of Kol generations away. Do you remember being told that the races all appeared in the world one at a time, and that the humans were last?"

"Yes."

"Well, the first nine races arrived before the meteor crashed. The humans, last, arrived during *Adaragem*. The war that was fought was against them."

Kyle felt a slight chill in his stomach. "The humans? Why?"

"They wanted to take over the world. They were led by one of the most famous warlords in history, one named Wyvern. He's a historical mystery; he came out of nowhere after the meteor fell, and after he was defeated no one found his remains. The humans became a conquering machine under his command. The other races were unused to working together, not to mention war. No one's quite sure where or when the fighting started, but it's said to have ended where Reno stands now. Most of the other races ended up participating, though the tides only really started to turn once the Buors got involved. Their army was ages ahead of anyone else's, including Wyvern's—it still is, in fact. Wyvern himself, though, was rumored to be immortal. No one could figure out how he could be killed, until the Kol and Oblihari got together and came up with a solution."

"What was it?" Kyle asked breathlessly, totally caught up in the story.

Rogan sighed again. "They created artificial life forms with their magic. Killing machines, designed to destroy Wyvern and his army. Monsters that could fly and breathe fire."

"Dragons?" Kyle exclaimed.

Rogan gave him a piercing look from underneath his bushy brow. "Now how did you know that?"

"They're in our folklore," Kyle said. "They're probably the most famous kind of creature there is." He was slightly disappointed that it had turned out to be them, in fact.

"Indeed. Well, they certainly did the trick. Wyvern's army was overwhelmed by them, and one of them ended up finishing him off by the end, with the help of four heroes. In fact, they named the final dragon after Wyvern himself. But the Kol were ashamed of them—as a matter of fact, they still are. Don't bring them up with Nihs, or any other Kol for that matter, alright?"

"Why were they so ashamed of them?"

"You see, the dragons were miserable once Wyvern had been defeated. They were creatures that did not belong in the world and had no reason for existing. Most of them died out, but rumor has it that some are still alive. They are immortal, you understand, creatures of pure magic. The Kol made them that way, so that they could steal magic from the world around them and continue replenishing their soul forever. In any case, once Wyvern was dead, the war ended and the humans made shaky peace with the other races. They decided to build a city nearby the site of the final battle—that was Reno. Roads were built, technology was shared, and the ash cloud eventually cleared. The rest, as they say, is history."

Kyle asked, "Who were the four heroes? The ones you mentioned helped kill Wyvern?"

"It's a long story," Rogan said. "They were two Selks, a Kol and a Minotaur: Leffeselein, Riolua, Xeru and Maradus. It's said that Wyvern himself honored them as his rivals, and gave them the names that everyone knows them by: Lightstar, Warangel, Sunchild and Greatwolf. Little is known about them, just that all but Lightstar were killed by Wyvern before the dragon defeated him."

Kyle pondered over this, the names of the four heroes ringing in his mind. He could see, now, why Lugh was so obsessed with becoming a hero—he imagined being so important that he was given a name by his greatest rival, a name that would be remembered for centuries to come. The war interested him greatly; he wanted to question Rogan more about it, but settled for one last question.

"What was Wyvern like?" he asked. "If he killed three heroes and those dragons…"

"You have to understand," Rogan said, "just because the four were heroes in name doesn't mean they were heroes in power. Almost nothing is known about them, almost as little as Wyvern himself. Wyvern's a mystery. Some poor drawings and descriptions of him have survived, but apart from that, nothing. No one knows what he looked like, because the only people who ever wrote about seeing him only saw him in his armor. There are some theories that state he wasn't human at all. He fought with a weapon almost as famous as him, a double-bladed spear with the same name. It went missing after his death, as well as his remains. All that people know about him was that he was extremely powerful, and wanted mankind to rule the Earth. To give him credit, he is said to have been an honorable leader. As a matter of fact, he was the founder of the world's first order of knights."

Kyle found it strange that an event which had taken place so long ago could be considered so significant. Rogan had talked about the war with the gravity that someone from Earth might have talked about World War 2— but that had only occurred seventy years ago, while this had been an entire millennium.

They reached the Iden Office. It was a small, utilitarian building with the name written above in black letters.

"Okay, Kyle," Lugh told him before they stepped in. "Remember, we found you a couple days ago with nothing on you. You have no memory of what happened to you before. Don't lie about anything but that, though, be as honest as you can if he asks you any questions. Be polite, and talk as little as possible. Buors aren't particularly good at reading body language, but he'll pry at anything that doesn't sound logical. Anything I forgot to mention?"

"Not really," Rogan said, "the most important thing is to think before you speak and to be courteous. Buors believe strongly in reason, manners, honor and being genuine. Keep that in mind and we shouldn't have any trouble."

Kyle thought that this was rather a lot to ask of him, but he tried to juggle all that the others had told him as they went inside. It was a rather small place, also very clean and modern-looking but in a more humble and utilitarian way. The only person visible within was a Buor seated behind a white desk at the far end of the room. Kyle took a quick look around the office: notices, memos and maps of Reno marked in various ways covered the walls. Paper was everywhere, but it seemed to be an organized chaos, and the desk the Buor worked at was almost completely clean. Kyle found it strange to see a man wearing a full suit of armor working behind a desk. As far as he could tell, the Buor looked exactly the same as the guards outside, with the exception of the red and gold sash and cloak; this man wore a large blue scarf around his neck and shoulders instead. He looked up as they approached.

"Good afternoon," he said politely, setting his pen down. "May I help you today?"

"Yeah," Lugh said, "we need an Iden card made for my friend here. To tell you the truth, though, it's kind of a weird case."

"Oh?" The Buor turned to Kyle and back. "And what is this case, sir?"

"Well," Lugh shifted awkwardly. Kyle suspected that he was play-acting. "We're not sure. We found him out in the wilderness a couple days ago. He had nothing on him when we found him, and whatever happened to him made him lose his memory."

"Goodness!" The man asked of Kyle, "Is this true, sir? You can remember nothing of what happened to you?"

Kyle shook his head. "I remember my name, that's pretty much it."

The clerk pulled a couple papers in front of him and began writing. "And you wish for an Iden card? With respect, sir, I believe that in your particular circumstance the police, or perhaps the church or a hospital, might be of greater use to you. Have you taken any steps to seeing if your memory can be recovered?"

"Not yet," Kyle said.

"We've been talking about what we can do about it," Lugh said in a reasonable voice, "and we thought that looking into an Iden card might be the best thing to do first, right? We thought we could see if he had ever had one, and maybe get a temporary one just to make things easier?"

The Buor considered this. "There is something to what you are saying," he said. He addressed Kyle, "in any case, you seem to be of sound mind and body. What is your name, please? I will look to see if we have ever registered an Iden card in your name. And all of you, please forgive me, but I'm sure you will understand my desire to write a police report about this incident."

"Fair enough," Lugh said. The Buor nodded.

"Your name, sir?" he asked Kyle.

"Kyle Campbell," he said.

The Buor swiveled his chair around and opened a drawer full of files. He leafed through them and pulled out a wad.

"Have you ever dyed your hair, sir, or gone through other significant changes in your appearance?"

"I've had my hair scaled since I got here," Kyle said, "that's pretty much it."

The Buor nodded as he went through the files. "I have three Iden cards registered under the name Kyle Campbell, but none of them match your physical description or appear to be otherwise compatible with your state of affairs. It is possible that my records are not entirely up to date." He asked Lugh, "Please, where was it that Kyle was found?"

"Northern Ar'ac," Lugh replied, "southwest of Donno."

The clerk nodded again. "One moment, please," he said, standing up, "I must go and speak with my colleagues."

The man rose and opened a door into an office behind him. He stood in the frame as he talked to the people beyond it, so it was impossible to see what was inside.

"Ezki," he said, "please pass this message onto the overhead. A man named Kyle Campbell has lost his memory, and we are searching for any registered Iden cards that could match him. Human, black hair and beard, five feet eight inches tall, approximately twenty-five years old."

"Will do," came a voice from inside the room. Kyle could tell from its nasal tone that it belonged to a Kol.

The Buor addressed someone else inside the room. "And excuse me, Acclairiad, might I use you outside to fill a police report while I grant this man a temporary Iden card?"

Kyle's heart soared at this statement. Had he heard it correctly? Could it possibly have been that easy?

Another Buor followed the first clerk out through the door, and seated himself next to him. Now that Kyle could see both of them side-by-side, he could discern minute differences in the armor that the two wore. The new arrival wore a strange H-shaped scarf in yellow.

"This gentleman is the one who has lost his memory," the first clerk pointed Kyle out to his kinsman, "and these three are the people who claimed they found him. If you will please interview them, I will speak with Kyle."

"Of course," Acclairiad said. He took out a pen and several forms, and Kyle's three friends clustered around his desk to talk with him.

"Kyle," the first clerk said politely, moving himself to the left, "if you will come with me, I will give you a temporary Iden card that you can use while we and yourself search for a more permanent solution. It will grant you all of the innate allowances of a full card; however, it will be up to the discretion of those with which you use the card whether to accept it. I will leave a magical imprint of your story thus far on the card for this reason. I will also notify the kingdom of Buoria as to your position. Depending on how busy the courts are, we may review your situation and contact you again. Is this acceptable?"

Kyle's mind was spinning, but he imagined that Nihs and Lugh wouldn't have opted for this process if they thought it was going to be dangerous.

"Yes," he said, and felt he should add, "thank you."

The Buor nodded. "Now I shall need your name, and normally I would ask for some other personal information, but obviously considering your situation this will not do. For the sake of rigor, I will ask of you to recall what information you can. Can you remember your date of birth?"

"No, sorry," Kyle replied, feeling rather foolish.

"Not a problem. Your age?"

Kyle almost answered truthfully, then decided against it. "No," he said.

The clerk asked him several other things, all of which Kyle denied remembering. In the end the man settled for writing down Kyle's physical appearance and some of the information about the *Ayger*. He turned to the table behind him, which was laden with a couple strange instruments. He drew a blank, transparent card from a stack and set it into a vice-like machine, and turned it on. The arms of the vice glowed blue and the outline of the card became etched in the same light.

"When the machine is finished charging the card," the clerk said to Kyle, "I will ask you to clamp its surface between your forefinger and thumb, and hold it for several seconds. I will tell you when it is time to release it. Please draw your sleeves back and make sure there is nothing near your hand that might brush it."

Kyle did as he was told, shedding his black coat and holding out his hand. He wore nothing on it. He had never been one for jewelry or even watches back home.

The Buor was watching the machine intently. He took a couple objects which looked like chopsticks made of glass from beside it, switched it off, and delicately removed the card from its grasp using the glass sticks. He wheeled his chair around and proffered the card to Kyle.

"Now, please," he said.

Kyle pinched the card, half expecting it to be warm as if heated on a fire; however, it merely felt strange, almost as if it were made of water. The surface of the card shimmered and the blue light seemed to cluster around Kyle's fingers; he held it until the clerk indicated for him to stop. The man held it up to the light.

"Excellent," he said, turning back to his machines, "this will just take one moment." He fed the card into one of them and performed a couple activities which were blocked from Kyle's sight. He let his gaze shift to the left and saw his friends still conferring with Acclairiad. He felt a pang of worry and hoped everything was going well.

"There we are," his own clerk said a moment later, placing the new card on the table. He handed Kyle an instrument which looked like a pen made out of glass with a silver tip. "Just one more step. Please sign your name on the card here. Do not worry about what you are writing with or what you are writing on, simply sign naturally as though with a normal pen on normal paper."

Kyle did as he was told. The pen etched his signature into the card in glowing curves as he wrote. When he was done, the clerk passed the card through one last machine, which split it along its thickness into two identical cards. He stored one away and gave the other to Kyle.

"Your Iden card," he said, as Kyle marveled at it. "At this moment, since this is the first Iden card you remember having, I will tell you of the most basic things you need to know about the Iden service."

"Sure thing," Kyle said, still mesmerized by the sight of his card. It was still clear, although the blue light given to it from the machine permeated it. On its left side, where Kyle had pinched, was not a fingerprint but a kaleidoscope of angles and colors. Different lines and areas reflected in rainbows as Kyle tilted the card this way and that. His signature was in the top-right corner, written along the side in cursive was his name and personal information. The fingerprinted area revealed something different every time Kyle looked at it, it was as though several images were printed over one another. At one point he could have sworn he caught a picture of his own face. On the card's back was printed in more serious letters:

Kingdom Of Buoria

Temporary Iden Card

The clerk spoke to Kyle of the benefits and responsibilities of owning an Iden card; much of it was legal jargon that went over Kyle's head, but he did pick up some of what was said. As far as he could tell, an Iden card was used for almost everything: docking airships, using hospitals and banks, and essentially every other public service. They were sealed with a magic signature, and so it would be impossible to pass off someone else's card as one's own.

"And that should be all," the Buor finished.

"Great," Kyle said, "thank you very much."

"Not a problem," the clerk said kindly. "Only one thing more. I have a colleague who is qualified to perform memory checks. If it is alright with you, might he perform a quick scan of your memories, so that he may add his testimonial to your file? It will make things much easier when you are looking for a full card if we have that information in advance."

Kyle's mind immediately went into overdrive. What was the right thing to say? He felt there was no way he should allow them to see his memories; it would be a disaster if they realized he was lying. But wouldn't refusing to perform the check be just as suspicious?

"Umm," he said, looking over to his friends, "I'm sorry, would it be okay if...?"

The man seemed to understand his plight. He nodded indulgently. "Of course you may confer with your companions."

"Thanks." Relieved, Kyle walked over to where the others were talking with Acclairiad. They had finished filling out the police report, and were merely talking about recent news in Loria.

"Yeah?" Lugh asked him, as he approached. "All done?"

"Yeah," Kyle said, then in a low voice to the three of them, "he asked me if they could check my memory."

"Oh," Lugh said, the syllable loaded.

"I'm sorry," he said to Acclairiad, "could you excuse us a moment?

"We'll have to refuse, won't we?" he asked Nihs a moment later once they had stepped away. "They'll see his memories from Terra."

Nihs was thinking furiously. "Yes," he said finally, "but if my suspicions are correct...let them do it," he said decisively to Kyle. "And go now, quickly, before it looks like we really agonized over the decision. Lugh, chew me out later."

Kyle obeyed at once, walking over to the clerk and telling him. The Buor summoned his co-worker, Ezki, from the back room. He was a male Kol with a squashed and bored-looking face, seemingly older than Nihs by a fair number of years.

"I believe you know the situation," the clerk said to him, "this gentleman says his memory is lost. I thought it would be wise to perform a check ourselves before we forwarded his file to the court."

"A sound idea," Ezki agreed. He jumped up onto the desk and approached Kyle.

"Have you ever had your memory read before?" he asked him.

"Once," Kyle said, "my friend Nihs read it after they found me."

"Very well," the Kol said, placing his hands on Kyle's temples, "then you will know what to expect. Here we go…"

Just as before, Kyle felt his eyes snap shut of their own accord. Images flickered in front of his vision. He wasn't sure if what Ezki saw was what he saw, but he sincerely hoped that it wasn't. Surely the Kol would be able to tell that something was there, and that Kyle wasn't being honest?

A moment later, Kyle's vision stopped flickering and his eyes reopened. He saw Ezki step away from him, wearing a look as though he had just eaten something bitter.

"There are memories there, Derumnai," he told the clerk, shaking his head as though to clear it, "but they've been corrupted somehow. Nothing I saw made any sense at all. My guess would be that some powerful magic has scrambled them. I've seen similar illusions, but nothing quite like this. Perhaps a more powerful mystic would be able to identify the problem."

"Thank you," Derumnai said, inclining his head. "And thank you for your cooperation," he added to Kyle, while making some notes on the paper before him. "If you wish to recover your memory, I might suggest that you visit a doctor or a practitioner of self-magic; perhaps, as my co-worker suggested, you might also see a mystic. If you so desire, I could provide you with some names and addresses."

"Thanks, but no thanks," Lugh answered for him, striding over. "My friends and I know Reno well, we'll find our way around. Thanks for all your help, though."

"It was my pleasure." Derumnai inclined his head to all of them. "I wish you good luck in your endeavor, sirs. Please keep in mind that the Buorish police may eventually wish to contact you with regards to your situation and Iden card. Thank you for using the Buorish Iden Office."

"Wordy bunch of bastards," Lugh said, once they had left the office. "Real helpful, though, and no one will go out of their way more to be nice than a Buorish civil servant. So hey, what was with that whole memory thing? I thought we were doomed for sure. What gives, Nihs?"

Nihs smirked, pleased with himself. "I had a suspicion that they wouldn't be able to read Kyle's memories," he said. "For a couple reasons.

The biggest one is that reading memories requires the partial intertwining of the participants' minds and souls, and we know that at least one of those in Kyle's case doesn't work like normal."

"But you read my memory before in the *Ayger*," Kyle pointed out.

"I skimmed it," Nihs corrected, "I was just checking the seams between your memories for tampering. But I sensed resistance even then. I don't think I would have seen anything but garbage had I tried to look at anything specific."

"That seems like quite a flimsy theory to gamble on, if you don't mind me saying," Rogan said.

"Well, I was right, wasn't I?" Nihs preened. "And I was right about something else, too."

"And what would that be?"

Nihs grinned. "Remember what happened to me after I tried reading Kyle?"

"How could I forget?" Kyle said.

"Well, if you didn't notice, that didn't happen to Ezki when *he* tried it. That proves that my theory was correct—your spiritual makeup is slowly adapting to Loria's atmosphere! You're acquiring a magical soul!"

"And according to you his other one is being squished up inside of him," Lugh said. "Right. Well, that all sounds like a bunch of nonsense to me, although I guess you're gonna get some of that when you start jumping between worlds. At least we got out of there alive and hey, you've got an Iden card now!"

"Yeah," Kyle agreed, pulling it out and holding it up so that the surface shimmered. "I gotta admit, it's pretty cool."

"For sure! Hey, you're practically one-hundred percent Lorian now!" Lugh clapped Kyle's shoulder.

"Yeah," Kyle said again, his eyes lost in the depths of his shimmering card, "I guess so."

They wasted a bit more time in the city, and trekked back to the hotel they had checked into for the night.

"So tomorrow," Lugh told them as they conferenced in his room, "we'll pick up the armor, check out the guild for jobs that'll take us toward Proks, and see some people about Kyle's problem. I don't think we want a doctor or a healer, like our Buorish friend told us. What do you think, Nihs?"

"A doctor or healer wouldn't be able to help us," Nihs said firmly. "I think we can all agree that Kyle's state of health most likely isn't the problem here. I think our best bet is to ask some researchers at a university...someone who's looked into alternate universe theories. Maybe something will click and make sense."

"Sounds good," Lugh agreed, leaning back and yawning. "If not we can take it from there. One step at a time, right?"

Kyle and Nihs returned to their room and Kyle flopped down on his bed. Even though the day had been short in hours, he felt as though he had done so much. He looked to his right, where over a chair was hung his black jacket. Stashed away in one of its pockets was his Iden card.

Despite what Lugh had said, Kyle did not yet feel almost one-hundred percent Lorian. But as he drifted into sleep after participating in a mild bickering match with Nihs, he felt more at home than he had anywhere else for a long time.

The mad politics of Grade five eventually wore out as the years progressed, and the students settled into more measured lifestyles. Mark left school after Grade six due to his parents moving out of town; this broke up the friendship between Kyle and Melissa, and as a result, he saw little of her for the remaining years. He no longer had a close circle of friends. He hung out with whomever it was convenient to hang out with at the time, often not bothering and just being by himself. The days, months and years seemed to blend together for Kyle; he drifted through school as he drifted through his social life, lazily passing every course with above average but slowly slipping grades. He lived for simple joys such as eating, walking, and sleeping. He found school tiresome and boring and life at home depressing. His mother had not become more of an interesting person for him with time. She spent some days working various jobs which never lasted long and others apparently doing nothing. Their house, while not horrendous, was never very well kept and Kyle had learned a long time ago that if he wanted things like his laundry done, he had to do it himself.

He was now old enough to see that his mother was not a happy person. Since the source of much of her grief seemed to come from communications with her family and friends, to which Kyle was not privy, he did not know exactly why this was. But her constant sighs, forehead rubbings, and moments spent staring at the wall irked him nonetheless. He started to avoid her, the two of them keeping out of each other's way. Kyle was not interested in figuring out why she was unhappy; after all, she was his mother. What was he expected to do about it?

One day, Kyle was skimming through a book he had to read for English class when the phone rang.

"Mom, phone!" he called without looking up.

His mother bustled into the room, out of breath. "Kyle," she told him, "couldn't you have picked it up?"

"It'll be for you," Kyle retorted.

His mother said nothing, picked up the phone and walked around the corner with it. Kyle went back to reading. He would have done it in his room, so as to be less bothered, but he disliked his room for anything but sleeping. It was always untidy and felt like a prison.

His mother returned shortly. "That was your dad," she told him, putting the phone back. "He says happy birthday."

Kyle snorted. He didn't bother to say anything. The message might have been floating in front of both of their faces for how obvious it was. His mother waited for a moment, apparently to see if he would say anything else and disconfirm her assumption. When it became clear that he wouldn't, she sighed and passed her hand over her forehead.

"He said he might like to see you this weekend," she said.

"Why?" The syllable was loaded with derision.

"Kyle," his mother snapped, "he's your father. It wouldn't kill you to stay in touch with him."

"Mom, he doesn't care about me," Kyle's eyes bored holes in the book he was reading.

"Don't you dare say that! Kyle, he loves you."

"Whatever." Kyle snapped the book shut and got up. As he started to leave the room, his mother appeared to sag. Her shoulders drooped and she rubbed her forehead again.

"Where are you going?" she asked him.

"My room. I need to finish reading."

His room might have felt like a prison, he reflected, but sometimes that was better than having to deal with his mother.

Kyle woke to utter darkness; he had woken up early, for the sun hadn't even started to rise. He felt slightly perturbed. He would never have admitted it, but he felt almost afraid of the dark. In the dim light, his cushy hotel room here in Reno could have been his childhood room from back on Earth. He felt a sudden urge to turn on the *tigoreh* lamps in the room, to remind himself of where he was and to take solace in their warm glow. He expected to see Nihs asleep in his den; to his surprise, he saw the Kol sitting up in his bed, immobile. Kyle sat up slowly, and Nihs' head rotated toward him. The Kol's brown eyes glowed faintly in the darkness.

"Can't sleep?" he asked. His normally snide voice sounded different when he spoke so quietly.

"Yeah," Kyle admitted, feeling foolish.

"What were you dreaming about?"

Kyle said nothing for a moment. "I was talking in my sleep?"

"Yes. Do you do that often?"

"I never used to." Kyle forced himself to lay back down and sound casual. "Apparently I've started since I got here. I was dreaming about...Earth."

Kyle could not see Nihs' expression from where he was laying.

The Kol waited for a moment before asking, "Did you have a family, back on Earth?"

"Well, doesn't everyone?" Kyle realized that he had snapped. He looked away and said, "I was an only child. My parents didn't get along well. I haven't been in touch with my father. My mother's dead."

There was a long pause. "I'm sorry," Nihs said.

Kyle snorted. "Well, it wasn't the happiest little family anyway. We were never really close."

"And I am sorry about that most of all."

256

Studying the small figure on the bed, Kyle was confused. Was it really the same person he was talking to? Because sleep had made him groggy, he made bold to say, "You sound different."

"We Kol are actually nocturnal. Did you know that? We have trained ourselves to sleep during the night for the sake of the other races. But nighttime has always been different for us. Do you see stars from your world, Kyle?"

"Yeah."

"I recommend that you take a look at Loria's stars. The balcony door is open."

Kyle was about to refuse, saying that he had seen them before, but it felt strangely as though he had been given an order. He got up and made his way past Nihs' bed to the balcony door. He craned his neck and looked up at the sky.

"Yeah," he said, pulling back, "real pretty."

Nihs' voice had gathered a bit of its cynicism back, "You know, you're in Reno during early summer. I don't think it will kill you to go outside."

Kyle sighed and opened the balcony door. A warm breeze upset his hair as he went out onto the balcony and looked up.

He was no stargazer, but he could tell that Loria's stars were different from those of Earth. The familiar constellations were gone. Orion and the big dipper were nowhere to be found. Reno's light pollution was depriving Kyle of most of the view, but there were still a good number of stars in the sky, more than Kyle had seen in a long time. As they twinkled down at him, he received the odd impression that they were in fact the same stars that he knew, just recast upon a different sky.

He kept telling himself that he would go back inside, but something made him tarry on the balcony. Something about the stars, or about the warm breeze, or about the sight of Reno below. In the end, he must have stood there for at least ten minutes. When he went back inside, Nihs was still sitting in the exact same position, and remained so as Kyle made his way back to bed.

"Well?" he asked softly.

For not the first time since he had arrived in Loria, Kyle swallowed his pride. "It was nice," he admitted, rolling over so that Nihs couldn't see him.

His cynical side made him add, "Very calming. Grade-A therapy right there. I'm definitely cured."

Nihs said nothing for a long time. He finally said, "There is an old Kollic proverb I heard a long time ago. In fact, it was spoken to me the very first time I left Proks. It goes, 'you can't return to where you've been if you don't know where it was you left'. Of course, it sounds more graceful in Kollic."

"What's that supposed to mean?" Kyle asked sullenly from his bed.

"The same that everything else means—whatever you take away from it. You should try to sleep again. Believe me, Lugh is miserable to be around when he has energy and you don't."

The next day dawned slightly overcast, the partial blocking of the sun lending everything an odd gray tone. Kyle felt strange as he pulled on his clothes. He was itching to get moving.

Because it had been their last night staying in Reno, it took them a while to get ready to leave. Lugh in particular spent forever gathering up all his effects. They ate breakfast at the hotel and checked out, their destination Reno's city core.

"Do you know where Reno University is?" Rogan asked Nihs, as they walked.

"I've been there before." The Kol tapped his chin. "I'm not sure if I'll be able to find it right away, but I know it's in this general direction."

As they walked up the main street, the government buildings came into view at its far end. Off to the side, Kyle would occasionally catch a glimpse of a huge tower under construction. He assumed this must be Sky Tower, Livaldi's headquarters.

The streets and buildings became distinctly less touristy as they progressed. The barrage of ads that was the market district ceased, and instead many of the signs had a more utilitarian or political purpose. Kyle saw a couple billboards adorned with the face of an aged-looking red Lizardman. He gleaned from these billboards that the man was Don Sanka, Reno's governor. Larger, more serious companies posted their advertising here; Kyle saw many ads for Maida weapons in the mix.

"Oh, hey," he said, pointing one of these ads out to his friends, "look at that."

The others turned to where Kyle was pointing. On the billboard was graffitied:

Live James Livaldi

Reno's REAL governor

"Oh, I forgot about that." Lugh clucked his tongue. "We're heading into the Livaldi versus Sanka war zone. Kyle, if anyone asks, we're from out of town and don't care about the power struggle."

"But we are from out of town and I don't care about the power struggle," Kyle pointed out.

"Exactly. Just don't try to improvise."

"Is it really that bad? Why is this even happening? Livaldi isn't even running for governor, is he?"

"He isn't," Rogan said, "but he's undoubtedly Sanka's rival in every way but this. Sanka holds more political power because he's governor, but Livaldi is much richer. Some people argue that he does more to keep Reno running because of the money he brings in, and that the position of governor is a pointless one. It's an awkward situation, because no individual in the past has ever become powerful enough to challenge the governor's authority. That being said, don't be fooled by how much of an issue this seems to be. Reno's people are volatile, they'll forget all about this as soon as something more interesting to fight about pops up."

"The city core is an interesting place, though," Nihs added. "Read the graffiti; it has almost a folkloric role in Reno's makeup. They say that it is through its graffiti that the city speaks."

Kyle looked around. "There isn't that much of it."

"Just wait. There'll be more."

Nihs was certainly true to his word. As they walked it became impossible to see the walls for the messages painted on them. Some were signatures or pictures drawn for the sake of the art; others obviously had more purpose. Livaldi's color tended to purple and Sanka's was red. Their supporters battled it out on the walls of Reno city, drawing their messages over one another's. But they were by no means the majority.

"Hmm, interesting." Rogan nudged Kyle and pointed to a symbol scrawled in black on an otherwise blank wall. It looked like an upside-down V with two crooked lines attached to each end, as if the person had started to create a block letter but given up halfway. Despite its simplicity, it looked strangely deliberate.

"Wyvern's symbol," Rogan said. "The Wyvernus. I suppose you see a little bit of everything on these walls, hmm?"

"Why would that be there?" Kyle asked, "Hasn't Wyvern been dead for like a thousand years?"

"Wyvern does still have supporters in some parts of the world—humans, mostly, who believe in his philosophies even after his death. I doubt this was drawn by one of them, though, probably just some youngster who wanted to feel edgy."

They ended up having to ask a policeman for the location of Reno University. He directed them to the right of the path they had been following, to the far side of a massive park in the middle of the city. Kyle caught sight of many fountains, gardens, trees and paths as they skirted the edges of the park. Seeing so much green within Reno was odd. Kyle wasn't usually the type for parks, but it did seem appealing.

Reno University turned out to be an enormous complex of buildings situated near to the park; as such, most of the grounds around it were similarly green and almost as forested. It was another example of stunning architecture that left Kyle speechless: while there were some older buildings scattered about the University, the scene was dominated by a huge, cylinder-shaped building that was many stories high, and connected to the buildings around it by numerous branching walkways with glass banisters. The building was constructed of smooth gray stone, like concrete, and lined with *tigoreh*, making the entire edifice look like one huge Ephicer machine. Paths spidered out from it in every direction; they took one of these and soon found themselves on a raised walkway headed towards the building's core. Below them on their left side was a huge field that Kyle imagined must have been used for sports. Beyond this he could see another pathway leading to a large astronomy tower and a dome-shaped building whose purpose he couldn't divine.

As they drew closer to the cylinder, Kyle saw that what at first had looked like a straightforward structure was more complex than he thought. Many pathways and add-ons grew apparent as the building came more into view. There were even sections that looked as though they had latched on to the main building like mushrooms. The larger of these were supported by pathways or stilts, though the smaller ones hung frighteningly over empty space. Overall, he knew without a doubt that had it been up to him alone to navigate this place, he would have been lost within minutes.

The path they were walking along eventually split into three; one heading into the cylinder, the two others curving around it. There was a directory set up at the fork; they clustered around it, trying to decide where they should go first. A couple students passed by as they stood. Kyle saw that the racial makeup was quite diverse, though there there was an inordinate number of Kol and Oblihari. A pair of girls—human or Selk, Kyle didn't notice—passed by from behind them, and he thought he heard them whispering to one another and one of them giggled. He ignored it, though he realized that their group would probably draw a certain amount of attention inside the University.

"Well?" Rogan asked, "what now? Do we ask someone if they can point us in the direction of the nearest universal theorist?"

"Hmph," Nihs sniffed, "despite your sarcasm, I believe that is in fact the best thing to do." He pointed a clawed hand at the directory. "There's an information desk on the ground floor of the main building. They should be able to help us."

"Right," Lugh said, heading forward. "Let's get this over with."

"Do you really think that someone here will know something?" Kyle asked, as they walked.

Lugh nodded. "For sure. Trust me, people study the craziest crap here. All those theories about alternate universes might be a bit off the wall, but I'll bet you that someone here studies them anyway."

Their path squeezed them through a tall opening in the cylinder's glass face, and they emerged in a huge anteroom dominated by a spiral pathway that lined its sides. The roof was several hundred feet above them and made of glass. A kaleidoscope of light shone through it and painted a pattern on the far walls. Everything was new and polished—for not the first time Kyle couldn't believe how done up and intense every inch of Reno city was.

The walls of the structure were covered with doorways leading to other wings, pathways leading outside, and alcoves where study spaces had been set up. There were also a number of small elevators set into the walls at regular intervals.

Before any of them could move, there was a huge *whoosh* sound and Kyle nearly jumped out of his skin—a massive lift whose floor perfectly filled the space inside the spiral rose up from below, supported by a pneumatic *tigoreh* column, and carrying about twenty-five people. As they watched, one of the students riding it stepped right off it as it was moving, onto the spiral pathway nearby.

Kyle couldn't believe what he saw.

"Are you kidding me?" he asked in wonderment and shock, watching the lift ascend to the top floor. "Isn't that, like, *really* dangerous?"

"Eh, I'm sure it's not," Lugh said confidently, striding towards the empty space. He reached out into the abyss, and Kyle saw a blue disturbance in the air appear where Lugh's hand made contact with something invisible.

"Thought so," the Selk said, satisfied. "It's an energy field charged by Ephicers. I'll bet it only lets you get on and off when the lift is over ground."

Gingerly, Kyle stepped up beside him and peered over the edge. It looked as though nothing was there, and he got queasy looking at the floor so far below.

"C'mon," Lugh said, "reach a hand out, it's fun! It doesn't hurt," he added, and he put his arm forward again. There was a small electrical sound and Kyle saw a web of blue particles blocking Lugh's hand's movement.

Kyle carefully extended his own arm—the feeling he got when his hand struck the force field was a strange one, as though it were a window that carried a slight electrical charge. It didn't hurt, as promised; in fact, it felt kind of neat.

Rogan, laughing, drew up beside them. "So?" he said, "are we riding it down to the ground floor?"

They waited a while for the lift to come back down; it seemed not to want to stop for anything, so they had to jump onto it as it passed by. Kyle did so with extreme trepidation, but the maneuver went well and soon they were headed downwards. The ride on the lift was amazingly smooth, and it paused for a few seconds at ground level to let everyone get off and on.

"Why go to all that trouble?" he asked, once they were safely on land again. He watched the lift slide gracefully back up.

Lugh laughed. "That's Reno for you," he said. "The city won't be outdone in anything. Anywhere else the architect that came up with that would have been laughed away, but here they just say, 'why not?' After all, they've got the money."

They found the information desk tucked in a corner of the ground floor. As they walked towards it, Kyle was studying the tiled floor, trying to make out the significance of the multiple designs that adorned it.

Nihs noticed his interest, and said, "Do you remember what I told you about the four types of magic?"

"Yeah."

"The patterns on the floor are representations of them." He pointed each one out as he mentioned it. "The elemental compass, the event trinity, and the color wheel. The components—the symbol of the self—was drawn on the lift itself. The center of all magic, remember?"

"Right," Kyle said, his mind spinning.

The secretary at the information desk was an aging Oblihari woman, her frame crooked and her feathers gray. She eyed them tiredly as they approached.

"Hello," Lugh said cheerily, leaning onto the desk. The secretary looked at his elbow as though it were an ant scurrying across the desk's surface.

"Good day," she said eventually. Her voice was slightly warbly and very fussy-sounding. "How may I help you, sir?"

"We're looking for directions," Lugh said, unfazed. "Could you please tell us where we might find someone who studies universal theory?"

The secretary sniffed. "The spatial complex is in the southeast corner of the University," she said as though loath to divulge the University's secrets. "Ride the lift up to floor fourteen, exit from the eastern door, and turn right down the pathway to reach the Klio Nott building. Perhaps someone there can help you further."

"Excellent, thanks, mate," Lugh said, a smile fixed to his face. Kyle noticed that he had started to speak in an exaggerated accent like the one their Selkic repairman had used. "I'll 'ead down there right away, o'course." The secretary winced at 'o'course' as they walked away.

"You're such a child, Lughenor," Rogan reprimanded, as they rode the lift again.

"Oh, come on, that was funny, admit it."

"I didn't know you could speak with an accent," Kyle said.

"Absolutely o'course!" Lugh laughed. "Most Selks are born with it. Mine used to be a lot worse—it's worn off since I left home, thank goodness for that."

"It does make you sound like quite the tit."

"Shut up, Nihs."

Following the secretary's directions, they emerged from the fourteenth floor's entranceway and headed down a meandering path that, after weaving its way over the forest floor, touched down into a slightly older and less crowded area of the University. The buildings here were connected by ground-bound, curving stone paths, and while many of them still featured glass and *tigoreh*, some of them had obviously been built before this style came into practice. The whole area showed signs of careful sculpting and design; a couple of crossroads had been deliberately dressed up, encased by vine-covered lattices. Students walked to and fro. Just as before, Kyle could sense that their party attracted a couple of stares.

They ended up coming across an interesting duo of buildings towards the back of the grounds: a very old, stone building connected to a much newer and larger building of glass, concrete and *tigoreh* sitting next to it. A polished sign sitting out in front read:

-Spatial Complex-

Klio Nott Building

Adenwheyr Research Center

"That's interesting," said Nihs, poking his chin at the glass construction. "Adenwheyr sponsored that building. It's a Buorish company that makes weapons and Ephicer machines," he added to Kyle as explanation.

"Oh. I'm guessing that Klio Nott was some famous professor?"

"Mildly famous," Nihs said, shrugging. "He was a Kollic spatialist. He discovered some formula for the movement of particles or something like that."

"I see your years of education are really shining through, Nihs," Lugh said.

"Oh, hush. You should let me do the talking, by the way. I'm the only one who really knows what we're looking for."

"Suit yourself."

They ended up entering the Nott building. The décor made Kyle assume that it was in fact an old house converted for the sake of the University. The inside was small and poorly lit; the house was certainly showing its age, especially when compared to the blinding gleam of Reno's more modern areas, and particularly the main cylinder of the University itself. Rogan had to bow his head in order to avoid smacking into the rafters.

The very first room was a sort of anteroom and mudroom, with space to hang coats on the left and a desk on the right. The secretary here was a human woman, in her thirties or forties.

When Nihs asked her directions to anyone studying universal theory, she claimed ignorance but directed them to the office of a Kollic professor by the name of Karu Dun. They found it down one of the buiding's hallways.

Lugh knocked quietly on the professor's door. Beyond a fogged window Kyle could see a hint of movement.

"Come in!" a dry, slightly snide voice beckoned them.

Lugh shrugged and opened the door; Kyle followed him, but Rogan opted to stay outside considering the fact that his shoulders were too broad to fit in the doorway. Nihs hopped from his shoulder to Lugh's.

Karu Dun was standing on his desk, surrounded by papers. He had four separate boards covered with calculations set up and was going from one to the other, adding figures and crossing things out. The study was a very small space; books and papers were crammed everywhere they would fit. Behind the desk were two bookcases, both full, and stacks of books were clustered around them. The air was dry and smelled of paper. It was the kind of atmosphere that diluted sunlight and made time slow to a crawl.

As Karu had his back to them as they entered, they waited awkwardly at the front of the room for him to finish working. He finally did, and turned to peer at them through narrowed eyes. Kyle had not seen many Kol, but Karu seemed very old. His skin was whiter than Nihs', his face was wrinkled, and a tiny pair of round glasses were perched on his nose.

"Yes?" he drawled at them, "what is it? I am very busy."

"Excuse me, professor," Nihs said politely, "but we were wondering if there was anywhere nearby that we find out about alternate universal theory."

The professor's eyes narrowed even further. "Alternate universal theory? A waste of time, boy, just a silly thing that young students have come up with. Not a scrap of science behind it, mark me."

"I've heard that as well," Nihs agreed in classic suck-up-to-the-elderly style, "but I've been performing a study myself and for the sake of rigor I'd like to include some facets of the theory. I've never bothered studying it before, so I don't know much about it."

The professor made a face and removed his glasses to clean them. "You're not a student here, are you? What's your name, boy?"

"Nihs Ken Dal Proks. No, I'm not."

"One of the Ken folk, eh? I worked with one of them once, years ago, when I was in Proks. Dari, his name was."

"Dari is my father," Nihs said. Kyle caught the tone of his voice.

"Hm!" Karu's brow furrowed as he replaced his glasses. He peered intently at Nihs, who had started to look noticeably uncomfortable. "I knew Dari had children," he said, "but I don't remember you."

"I've been studying abroad for a while now."

Kyle was distressed at the sound of Nihs' voice. He seemed strangely shrunken, his voice quieter and more unsure. Kyle could only imagine why.

"Hm," the professor said again. There was a pause as he seemed to consider the situation. "Dari was a bright lad, had a good head on him, as I remember. You should be proud to be his son."

"I am."

"So, you said you're doing research of your own now?"

"Yes."

The professor moved his tongue about his mouth as though trying to dislodge a piece of food. "Hm," he said, his tone slightly more approving, "well, none of the professors here study that theory, so you'll have to ask some students, I'm afraid. A student of mine has been writing papers on the subject. He lives in one of the graduate houses."

The professor walked to the far side of his desk and leafed through a pile of papers. He pulled out a map of the University's campus and pointed to a building with his pen. "Here. His name's Yuma Fen. Name should be on the building. Load of garbage, if you ask me, but I suppose if you're interested…"

"Thank you," Nihs said, bowing his head. "Good luck with your studies, professor."

Karu grunted and turned back to his papers without bothering to see if the others had left. They filed out silently and only started talking once they had left the Nott building.

"Small world after all, eh, Nihs?" Lugh said. "That guy working with your dad!"

"My father has worked with many different people," Nihs said quietly. "He's quite important in the academic world."

Lugh seemed to take the hint, and didn't press the issue. "Well, that works out well for us, we got our directions. So we're looking for this Yuma guy. The house should be somewhere around here…"

The building Yuma was staying at turned out to be another house-cum-university conversion, a tiny little one-floor place sitting at the side of a pathway at the extreme edge of the campus. Its garden was overgrown and the house very dilapidated; a tarnished, cheap-looking bronze plaque attached to the front read:

Yuma Fen, Spatialist

Oklade Okaden, Philosopher

Universal Researchers

Nihs snorted slightly when he saw the sign. "That looks almost homemade. The University wouldn't have done that."

"Who's this Oklade person?" Lugh asked. "I thought it was just supposed to be the one guy."

"Karu probably doesn't have time for students who aren't his," Nihs said. "See, Oklade's a philosophy student."

"Well, whatever." Lugh walked up to the door and knocked. "If he can help us, then he's fine by me."

No one answered the door. Kyle's heart sank. They *had* to be home! He had gotten progressively more nervous and excited as their search had narrowed down. Though at first he hadn't been interested in the details of his world jumping, he was now dying for some answers.

"Hmm," Lugh said, and knocked again, louder. He put his ear to the door.

"I can hear people inside!" he said, and knocked even louder. "OI!"

Now Kyle could hear somebody moving about within the house. He heard someone shout, "Oke! Door!"

"I'm getting it!" another voice shouted back, and the door swung open to reveal a youthful Oblihari boy feathered in black.

"Oh!" He seemed to quail when he saw Lugh standing in the doorway. "Um, can I help you, sir?"

"Hey," Lugh said, "are you Oklade?"

"Uh, yes, that's me! Philosopher and universalist, at your service! You've heard of me?"

"Oh, yeah, sure," Lugh lied, "one of the professors told us about you. How about the other guy...Yuma...he home?"

"Oh...yes!" Oklade fidgeted for a moment, flustered about what to do, then kept the door propped open awkwardly with one clawed foot as he turned to call inside the house. "Yu! There are people to see us!"

"One second!" a voice came from the back of the house.

There was an awkward moment where Yuma did not seem likely to appear.

Oklade turned back to the others, his whole body seeming to twitch nervously. "So, what can we do for you?"

"We have some questions about the work you do here," Nihs said, smiling encouragingly. "Your studies in alternate dimensional theory."

"Oh! Really?" Oklade was both surprised and pleased. "Er...well! That's wonderful! Of course we'd be happy to talk about it...well...you see, most of the others here think that what we do is a waste of time..."

"Ah, well," said Nihs, as though the very thought was nonsense, "we're very interested. In fact, we think that your research might be able to help us."

"R-really?" Oklade stammered. "Well...that's excellent! Um, would you like to come inside?"

They filed in. It was fairly dark, as the *tigoreh* lamp in the living room gave off little light and the windows were overgrown with vines. To their left was a small, cramped kitchen, and to the right a sitting area. A hallway directly ahead presumably led to the bed and bathrooms.

The apartment gave the impression of being poorly cared for. Notes, books and waste such as food wrapping was littered everywhere. There was less clutter than in Karu's study, but considerably more disorganization. The dishes in the kitchen had not been done, and some looked as though they had been sitting there for quite a while. Clothes also hung neglected across a couple of chairs. Kyle recognized many empty mind-bomb bottles among the debris.

"Would you like tea?" Oklade asked, as he shuffled into the kitchen.

They accepted, and the Oblihari spent a moment locating and retrieving the different components needed to make the beverage. As he worked, a Kol who looked Nihs' age came out of one of the back rooms, calling to his housemate. He wore a simple suit of dark red and purple and had a pair of very complicated-looking *tigoreh* goggles strapped to his forehead.

"Oke, I told you not to leave the...oh! Hello," he said, seeing Lugh and the others. He did not seem quite as flustered as Oklade, but still revealed some intimidation. "You're guests? Would you like to sit down? I'm sorry, the chairs are kind of...here..." and he grabbed piles of clothes and papers from the chairs in the sitting room and threw them elsewhere.

"It's okay, we—" Lugh started, but seeing Yuma's bustle of activity decided to give up.

Oklade arrived as most of the sitting room had been purged, carrying six cups of tea of varying sizes on a tray. He danced back and forth looking for a place to set it down; finding no surface unoccupied, he was forced to take it back into the kitchen, and everyone took their mugs separately. They settled in the sitting room, trying to find places for their feet to rest among the debris. Oklade seated himself in a plush armchair facing the party and Yuma sat next to him on the armrest. They introduced each other and made small talk; Kyle tried a sip of his tea. It was somewhat like tea on Earth, but much more flavorful; it seemed to be made with fruit rather than leaves.

"So!" Yuma leaned forward, his hands clutching his drink, "what can we do for you?"

"They said they were interested in our studies!" Oklade cut in before any of them could answer.

"Really?" Yuma asked his colleague, then seeming to remember that there were others in the room turned to them, "really?"

"Yes," Nihs answered. "What you study is…relevant to our interests."

Yuma, like Oklade, was surprised. "You want to know about our studies in alternate dimensional theory? But you're adventurers, aren't you? Why would you be interested in that?"

"Most everyone else at this University isn't," Oklade said ruefully.

"Teshur! You've got that right. I told you we should have made that move to Eastia, Oke. But you said—"

"Don't bring that up again." Oklade seemed hurt. "You agreed with me in the end, remember what—"

Nihs coughed pointedly. "Anyway," he said, once the pair's attention had snapped back to him, "to answer your question, yes, we do want to find out about your theories. As it is, we know very little about how they work."

"You said they might be able to help you?" Yuma asked with surprising keenness. "Why would that be?"

"We can get to that later," Rogan said smoothly. He leaned forward, and soon all eyes were on him. Rogan could have a very commanding presence. He waited until the silence had reached its peak and then continued.

"For the time being," he said jovially, "would it be a bother for you two to give us an idea of how your theories work?"

Yuma frowned, looking to Oklade for support. "There's so much to go over," he said, "a lot of it wouldn't make sense if I just got into it. What exactly do you want to know about?"

"Alternate universes," Nihs said. "Most scholars deny they exist, but we want to hear your take on them. Are they real? How do they work?"

Both of the students' eyes glinted. They looked at each other again, and back to Nihs.

"Oh, *those*," Oklade said. "Hm, of course most scholars say they don't exist. But that's because they've never found proof."

"You've found proof?" Nihs asked excitedly.

"Well," Yuma said, bobbing his head, "not proof as such. But we've found things out. We're getting closer every day. We think we've almost discovered the—"

"Oh, you shouldn't tell them about that!" Oklade blurted.

"Hey," Lugh said, leaning forward as well. "It's okay, you can tell us. Trust me, we're not interested in letting other people know, we'll keep whatever it is secret if you want us to. Fact is, we need your help with something, and it sounds like you're the best ones to do it."

Oklade and Yuma looked at each other again. Kyle noticed that they did this very often. He imagined that they were not particularly strong or brave people—in fact, he realized, they were probably like the people Kyle had known back in college. The geniuses who got nervous whenever they had to talk to a real person, who hung out in labs drinking energy drinks at all hours of the morning coding computer programs.

"Well, in that case…we think we might be getting close to being able to summon otherworldly particles!" Yuma said excitedly.

"Really?" Nihs himself sounded genuinely fascinated. "That would prove that other universes exist, wouldn't it? But how does that work?"

"Oh, well," Yuma quickly seemed to be gaining confidence as he spoke, "the basic theory isn't really as out there as some people believe— the idea's been passed around in a lot of papers for a while. Do you know the Creationist theory?"

"Not really," Nihs admitted.

"Well, okay...it goes like this. The origins of the universe are unknown, correct? Because magic particles can't be created or destroyed, the fact that they exist at all seems to be a logical impossibility, yes?"

"Yes."

"Well, that gives birth to two schools of thought: one, that the universe's magic has always been here, from the beginning of time, and two, that the universe was in fact created at some point in the distant past by something that was powerful enough to bring magical particles into existence. That's the Creationist theory."

"Makes sense," Nihs said.

"Well, that's where the real crux of the whole theory lies, in the question of whether or not...oh, Oke, where did you leave the chalkboard?"

"It's in your room!" Oklade snipped.

"Oh, right...uh...one moment, please," and Yuma jumped down from the chair, scurrying into one of the back rooms.

"Sorry," Oklade apologized. "Anyway, the idea is, if there was such thing as a creator that made the Earth, then obviously whatever the creator was made out of would have to be some kind of matter that was...superior to magic, you understand? Because it's been proven that nothing magical can create magic. But it's *also* been proven that nothing non-magical can exist in our world...so if one accepts the idea that a creator exists, then one must also accept that the creator is from a different universe."

Kyle's heart was beating. He was taking in every word, just waiting for something to click and make sense, waiting for the truth to emerge. He was thinking of his own travel to Loria, and how his soul was made of different material than that of a Lorian's...it seemed to fit so well, he forgot that Yuma and Oklade were oddball students and started to believe everything that was being said.

Yuma arrived, pushing a dusty blackboard on wheels into the sitting room. Lugh had to jump out of his chair, push it aside, and then squish in beside Rogan and Kyle on the couch to make room.

"And that brings up the Creationist paradox," Yuma said, jumping onto the back of Lugh's chair and starting to draw on the blackboard. He drew a box first, and labeled it *Earth*.

"Imagine that this is the Earth," he said, "and so whatever it was that created it must have come from another universe, one *higher up*, as it were, than our world itself." He drew another box labeled *creator* above *Earth* and connected the two with a line.

"Now, because this universe itself exists, and is made of some kind of matter, then obviously *this* universe must have had a creator at some point, from an even higher universe, yes?" He drew a third box above the other two and another line.

"Do you see the paradox?" he said, turning to the others.

"Of course," Nihs said, "each creator lives inside a universe that must have been made by another creator. So there would have to be infinite universes and infinite creators."

"Exactly," Yuma said.

"But there's something else to that, as well," Oklade interjected. He got up, too, and took the chalk from Yuma. "Each universe isn't bare, is it? Containing nothing but a creator? Take the Earth, for example...there are billions of people living within it."

"But we're not creators," Nihs said at once, "we're just...normal creatures, living inside a universe."

"Ah." Oklade seemed pleased with himself and he threw the chalk up and down. "But consider what you're saying. If we are normal creatures, then what is a creator? Where do they live? Well, according to *our* theory, a creator is simply a creature of normal power who lives in a higher-tiered universe. All creatures have the power to create universes below their own."

"That can't be. How is it done, then, how come we haven't found out about this? Who's doing the creating?"

"Everyone," Oklade said, "all the time. Each of us—all of us—we create universes all the time. They are our thoughts."

There was a brief silence in the room. Even to Kyle, who had been trying to keep an open mind about the way that Loria worked, the theory sounded ridiculous. He knew what thoughts were—they were just electrical impulses being sent through the brain.

"How could an entire universe just be a thought?" he asked. "There's just not the power. Besides, we don't think of entire worlds most of the time. It's just things like words, or pictures."

"Not pictures," said Oklade, "scenes. Scenes from your past, or from your imagination...that involve beings, sometimes familiar, sometimes not...interacting with each other. Living for a flash of an instant in your mind's eye."

"But we've been taught about magic all these years that thoughts have as much strength as solid matter," Yuma interrupted.

Oklade turned on him angrily. "I was going to say that!"

"Sorry."

"*Anyway,* we've been taught all these years that thoughts have as much strength as solid matter. But maybe they have more than even that. Yuma and I have been studying this for a long time...we believe that the thought might in fact be the most powerful kind of particle there is. Enough to contain a tiny universe that to us is just a speck—but to its denizens, a home for possibly millions of years. After all, if you think us to be a universe infinitely more powerful than our sub-universes, then how much energy would it really take to lend one of these universes power?"

"And that is the hierarchy of creation," Yuma added. He was drawing multiple boxes shooting out of the box at the very top, creating a tree pattern. "Infinite universes expanding out from one main universe—a root universe—whose existence is a total mystery. From each universe is spawned a million more universes, and so on and so on...somewhere within all this is Loria. One creature created us, and we exist as a thought within their unfathomable brain...and a multitude of sub-universes have been created by us who live in Loria itself."

There was another pause as Lugh's party attempted to digest all this. Kyle didn't know what to think. Suddenly what the students were saying was making much less sense than before.

"I can see why most people resist the idea of the Creationist theory," Rogan said finally. "The thought that we exist as, well, just a thought...it's not very comforting. Doesn't that mean we could just wink out of existence at any moment?"

"Oh, no," Yuma said, turning to face him, "it doesn't work exactly that way. We've got a couple different theories as to how that's handled— the one we're working on now is that the thought that passes through a creator's brain might only appear to be a fraction of a world, but somewhere deeper in the mind the world is automatically fleshed out and becomes a full world complete with past and future. For instance, imagine that you visualize a scene that takes place inside a room. You might see only the room in your mind's eye, but what logically—subconsciously—has to exist outside the room in order for the scene to make sense?"

"The rest of the world," Nihs mused. "That works, in an odd way. So, allow me to jump forward for the sake of time. You said you thought you had found a way to summon otherworldly particles?"

Yuma, who had been swelling with confidence, appeared to sag. "Well," he admitted, "yes and no. It's very complicated. Overall I think our theory is sound enough, but there's one important component missing."

"Energy," Oklade said, as explanation. "Even summoning a single particle according to our calculations would take a vast amount of energy. We've tried using Ephicer energy, but we don't have access to any that are powerful enough."

"There's...another little concern, too," Yuma said in a voice that immediately indicated that 'little' was probably a gross understatement.

"And what's that?" Nihs asked.

Yuma looked extremely uncomfortable. "Well," he said, "we're not sure, but we're thinking that it's probably best we haven't succeeded yet. You see, we believe there's a small chance that bringing an otherworldly particle into our world might, er...tell them, Oke."

"Why do *I* have to tell them? The experiment was your idea anyway, I *told* you—"

"All right, *fine*, *I'll* tell them." They all waited for a moment as Yuma worked up the confidence to speak. He seemed unwilling to look any of Lugh's party in the eye.

"Well, the truth is, we think that summoning an otherworldly particle might, um, cause the universe to end."

There was a long pause, and then Kyle burst out laughing.

"What is it?" the others asked him, obviously surprised.

"Large Hadron Collider," Kyle said, still laughing. He was met with mystified looks from every direction.

"What...?"

"Never mind," he said, coughing awkwardly. He stopped laughing and tried to make himself look small.

Eventually the attention turned back to Yuma, who winced as he felt the stares on him.

"So, it might cause the universe to end," Nihs said in a neutral voice. "Why would that be?"

"We…think that otherworldly particles might react to those of our universe in a…volatile way," Oklade said. "After all, they would be charged with a kind of energy never before seen here on Earth…it's possible that they would contain enough power to ignite all of the magic in the world."

"So we've stopped trying for now," Yuma said quickly. "We don't have enough energy anyway. We're thinking of ways that we could create an artificial soul to contain the particle. That would make it safe to bring one over. But we've kind of hit a standstill right now."

"Which is why the University is pestering us to come up with something useful," Oklade said.

"Tish! We would have been able to if they were willing to give us more money, but no, they said, our research isn't worth it—"

"So instead, they spend it on that guy's project for the—"

"I mean, sure, it was certainly more concrete than what we have, but—"

"Excuse me!" Nihs said loudly. He waited for the others' grumblings to die down, and said slowly and deliberately, "Look. What you're doing here makes sense, it really does. And I think that you two are probably right about what you think. You see, the truth is, we came to you because we think we might have made an important discovery about the theory of alternate universes."

Yuma and Oklade had fallen silent. They were hanging on Nihs' every word.

"Well?" Yuma asked, "what is it?"

Nihs nodded to Kyle. "I think you'd better start at the beginning," he said, "with the boat."

The students' gaze snapped to Kyle as though he were a magnet.

"Well," Kyle said, "see, I was on this boat…"

He finished his story. The room had gone completely silent. Then Yuma and Oklade started talking both at once, very loudly, to everyone and each other.

"I don't believe it! I didn't think it was possible!"

"Do you realize what this means, Oke? That sounds like legitimate quasi-vertical cross universal travel!"

"I know, I know! You don't need to tell me! But that goes with everything that we've been saying, we were right about it all! Did you hear what he said about the magic and the soul sword?"

"Obviously! The soul sword...a cluster of otherworldly particles lodged inside a being otherwise populated with magic...it must be anchored to him because of his origins in Terra! The fact that he's able to contain and even control it is astounding. That must be the key to what we were trying to do—if only we could replicate the way that Kyle's soul works!"

"Okay—" said Nihs, but the two ignored him.

"We should get someone who can sense auras! Someone very skilled at it; they might be able to give us insight on the dynamics of it."

"And what about the magic reacting to his soul? It makes perfect sense with what we said before! The nuclear particles are of greater strength than our magic particles, but—"

"*Hey!*" said Nihs, and he finally found a tiny silence to speak into. "So how does it work?" he asked. "Why did Kyle come here, and what caused it? Where is he from? And can we get him back?"

"An inter-dimensional portal," Yuma said promptly, "of the like that Oke and I were trying to create. It must have opened up underwater near the cruise ship that Kyle was on—as for why, I have no idea. But the whirlpool was just a secondary effect to what was really going on. A hole in space...a blank area in the universe that acted as a vacuum for particles. Kyle got sucked into it and ended up here."

"But *why?*" Nihs asked.

"You see," Yuma said, back to the chalkboard and drawing rapidly, "a portal is nothing more complicated than a hole in space, you understand?

Magical theory tells us that all space in the universe must be occupied by a particle of magic. If it were possible to create an area where no magic existed, that space according to the laws of the universe would have to be filled by *something*. Our theory was that it would act as a supermassive attractor until it retrieved a group of particles that could fill the space—and that if it couldn't retrieve any magical particles, it would take the path of the next lowest resistance, and steal energy from an adjacent universe. Our goal in trying to create a portal was to open up a space in our world's atmosphere just a particle wide—so that we could attract a single otherworldly particle into the space."

"So a hole opened up in Loria and I fell into it to patch it," Kyle summed up.

"Essentially," Oklade said.

"But it is a little more complicated than that," Yuma hastened to add.

"So where is Kyle from, then?" Nihs asked. "If the particles that make up his soul are more powerful than magic particles, that must mean he's from the world that the Earth's creator is from, right?"

"Uhh, no, haha," Yuma said with a small laugh. "Not exactly. Or at least, not according to what Oke and I believe. You see, it's impossible for a being to enter the world populated by another being's creations—just as it would be impossible for me to live inside your thoughts. That means that no creature from our creator's world could come here. What would happen instead is…ah, how to explain…a *clone* of the creator's world would be made within their mind, and then something—in this case Kyle—would travel from *that* world to here. You see, the effects of a so-called *vertical* shift in the universe take place, but the shift itself is actually more *horizontal* in nature. That's why we call it quasi-vertical universal travel."

It took everyone a moment to wrap their heads around this. Kyle, who had been looking at Yuma's illustration on the wall, said, "So my world looks like the world that Loria's creator is from, but it's not actually that world? It's just a copy that exists in their mind?"

"Exactly," Yuma said, pleased.

"But it's made to be as close to their world as possible…so when I got *here*, it was as though I had really come from that world. That's why my soul is different from a Lorian's—why I have my soul sword."

"Precisely."

"Speaking of which," Oklade cut in, "could we see your soul sword for a moment? It might tell us something!"

Kyle shrugged, looking at his companions. "Sure," he said, putting his hands together, "why not. Don't touch it, though, that...doesn't work."

He drew the sword, and both Yuma and Oklade 'oohed'. Yuma approached it, bringing his hands close as though he wished to touch it, his face bathed in its blue glow.

"Amazing," he said, "it looks somewhat like a regular soularm, but it appeared inside your soul with no notice and reacts violently to anything it touches."

"My theory was that Kyle's nuclear soul was trapped inside of him by our world's atmosphere," Nihs volunteered.

"Mm," Yuma said, still hypnotized by the sword. "That's an interesting theory. What do you think, Oke?"

Oklade had started making frantic sketches on the blackboard once the soul sword had been drawn. "It makes sense," he said, tapping his beak with the chalk and observing his drawings. "Our science tells us that nothing non-magical can exist in our universe, correct? But this law was obviously broken when Kyle came through the portal. The universe had to improvise. Bereft of a way to send his soul back to where it belonged, it molded it into a form that makes sense for something of our universe, a soularm. Kyle experienced a period of near-death where his nuclear soul had been compressed but his magical soul had not yet formed."

Kyle leaned back. He wasn't sure of what he thought about Yuma and Oklade's theories, but he was sure that he wanted to believe they were right. If that were the case, then everything could make sense again. He was starting to feel grounded, something that he hadn't felt since he had landed in this world. If they were right about everything up until now, then maybe they would be right about one more thing...

"So," Nihs said, "that just leaves one question. How can we get him home?"

Oklade made them some more tea, and he and Yuma entered a quick, hushed conversation. It was only a couple minutes before they turned back to the group.

"We're sorry," Yuma said soberly. "We don't know."

Kyle's heart sank to the floor. The exultation he had felt on hearing the students' theories quickly dissipated. If they didn't know, who would?

"You don't have any ideas at all?" Nihs asked them intently.

Yuma shook his head sadly. "We have theories as to how an otherworldly particle could be brought *here*," he said, "but we haven't yet explored the idea of sending a particle from our world somewhere else. As far as we know, the type of portal that we were trying to create and that Kyle fell into only works one way; they represent an empty hole in the world's makeup. Our only guess is that in order to get Kyle home, you would have to reach into his world somehow and create a hole that he could then enter. But we would have no idea how to create such a hole, or how to control where in our world it opens up or what it consumes. I'm sorry."

They all sensed that this was the end of what Yuma and Oklade could tell them. Kyle felt miserable. It sounded as though the technology required to take him home didn't exist in Loria, and wouldn't for a long time—not before he was long dead, in any case. A possibility that he had never really taken seriously before became inevitable in his mind: he would be spending the rest of his life in this world. He didn't know why the concept bothered him so, as he was much happier here than he had been during almost every other time in his life. But when he thought of home...of Earth, of Cleveland, of computers and cars and TV, something tugged at him, and he felt a desperate urge to return there.

He tuned back to the real world to hear what Yuma was saying.

"...it's possible the elders of Proks, who are much more conservative than us scholars here in Reno, know far more than they let on. If you can win them over, then they might be able to help you further. Even if they don't know of how to get him back, they might have access to lore that speaks of similar incidents. It's amazing what you can find out if you dig deeply enough. But I feel it's only fair to warn you...even if a method exists to open a portal between worlds, my guess would be that accomplishing such a feat would take massive amounts of magical energy. We couldn't scrounge up enough energy for our portal, and we were only trying to summon one particle. The amount of energy required to send a person between worlds might frankly not be achievable."

"Thank you for all of your advice," Nihs said, standing up. "We have to try, one way or another."

Lugh and Rogan rose as well, and Kyle took the hint that it was time to leave. He stood as the others thanked Yuma and Oklade in turn. They headed out the door, the two scholars following behind them.

"Oh," Lugh said, as he left, turning in the doorway, "I'm sure I don't need to tell you this, but it would be best if no one else found out about Kyle, right?"

"Oh, that's no problem," Yuma said cheerily, "no one would believe us anyway."

They walked in silence as they left the University's campus, each lost in their own thoughts. Occasionally Nihs, who was full of some kind of nervous energy, would attempt to engage one of the others into talking about universal theory. His efforts, however, were in vain.

"So Yuma thinks it's a good idea to visit Proks next," Lugh said to Kyle, talking over Nihs. "He says the elders there might know something about whether this happened before."

"He's got a good idea," Nihs replied, changing track, "the elders of the Kol have extensive knowledge about almost everything. The magic in the caves tells them secrets about the world, many of which never make it out of the caves themselves. It's possible that they know about cross-universal travel, but tell no one about it because the subject is so controversial."

"But will they tell us?" Rogan asked pointedly.

Nihs sagged. "Well…" he left it hanging.

Lugh had been watching the expression on Kyle's face while they talked. At this, he said, "Hey, no worries, we can cross that bridge when we come to it. I'm sure they'll talk to us if we can prove that Kyle here is actually from another world."

Nihs, however, did not catch on. "Hm," he said dubiously, "maybe."

"Hey," Lugh said in a low voice to Kyle, "don't worry about it, all right? We'll get you home, one way or another."

"Right," Kyle said sullenly.

Lugh gave him a calculating look, and decided to drop it.

They crossed the main road and headed into the sea of buildings on the other side. The ground they were walking on sloped upwards for a few minutes before Kyle realized what was going on—they were heading up one of the raised roadways that soared over the city. It was only once they had gotten a ways up and Kyle looked back, that he realized the main road *itself* was raised. As it climbed up the hill going inland, it lifted from the ground, and Kyle could see other roads and lights underneath.

The road they were on curved to the right, arching over the northern side of the city. They walked for a while, and ended up quite high up. It was yet another face of Reno with which Kyle was unfamiliar; up here, the roads curved and bent around and through buildings that reached up to touch them, runners drove to and fro, and everything was bright and open. From their vantage point, Kyle's vision extended over some of the rooftops, and he could see the numerous aircraft that hovered over the city. The Buorish police ships were medium-sized, a quarter as large as the *Ayger,* and painted black and red. Other ships of different shapes, sizes and colors cluttered the sky.

As Kyle watched, a huge shape high up in the sky approached the city from in front and to the left of them. It looked like a massive floating island or an alien saucer, and moved with a ponderous slowness. Kyle could see its shadow start to fall over the city as it flew closer.

"What the heck is that thing?" he asked, awed by its enormousness.

Lugh laughed. "That's Mo.ji.ro," he said, "the world's first floating island. It's actually a huge ship that belongs to the city. It does a big circuit around the area every month or so."

"You *built* that?" Kyle was dumbfounded. His mouth hung open as the massive ship cruised along in the sky, rotating slowly as though it was merely drifting through water. "What's the point of it?" he asked.

It was Nihs' turn to laugh. "Reno is a rich city," he said, "they just wanted an excuse to build something insanely expensive and gratuitous. It's a tourist attraction. There are hotels, restaurants, resorts, fighting arenas…the main attraction are the Kol clubs, though. The biggest dancing clubs in the world are on Mo.ji.ro. That's where all of the most popular and famous Ly musicians show off their music."

"Seriously?" Kyle's tone was injected somewhat with cynicism. "So it's just one big party up there, is that what you're saying?"

"Basically. I've never been there myself."

"I have," Lugh said brightly. "I got invited once. I have to say, some of it is pretty awesome. The music gets on your nerves after a while—they *blast* it up there—but it's definitely worth seeing. We'll have to check it out someday if you stay here, Kyle!"

Kyle continued to stare at Mo.ji.ro as it passed overhead, unable to believe that it existed; the underside of the ship looked almost like real earth, except for six massive jets that shone blindingly with Ephicer light. The sky became dark as its shadow fell over them, then bright once more as it slowly drifted on its way.

They walked on, the road weaving between buildings and straightening out and dipping downwards. It touched back down onto the ground. This area of town was smaller and more condensed. Unlike the touristy dockside area and the serious, older government district, these streets seemed not to follow any kind of theme, and gave the impression of having grown and changed much over time.

"Here we go," Lugh said, nodding his head towards an older-looking building on their left. "That's our hideout."

The hideout's interior was newer-looking than the one in Donno, but still maintained the semi-dark, rustic look that adventurers were apparently fond of. The master, standing behind a counter ahead of them, was Orcish; Kyle had yet to see an Orc up-close, so he could not guess at their age or tell whether they were male or female. A quarter-spiral staircase to the counter's left led up to a second floor whose hallway was also the counter's roof. The right side of the room, only one floor high, was filled with tables. The hideout was moderately busy, with an assortment of adventurers lounging about and the bar quite full.

The master, who was talking to another Orc, acknowledged them with a brief nod as they approached the counter. They sat and waited, while Rogan, who was far too large to use the bar stools, stood behind.

Finally, the master turned to them. "Hello, friend," he said, his deep voice giving him away being male, "what can I do for you today?"

"We're looking for a job," Nihs answered for them, "one that will take us in the direction of Eastia, up to level forty if necessary, but we'd prefer non-fighting. Do you have anything like that?"

"Hmm," the master said, turning to a wall of files behind him. "Eastia, eh? Okay...I feel like I got something like that in recently...let me see..." He flicked through a couple of files and then turned to a stack of oddly shaped papers on the counter. After flipping through a few of them he pulled a sheet out.

"Knew it," he said. "You're in luck. I just got this one in earlier today. Two adventurers requesting an escort by airship to Rhian—it's a town in the west of Eastia. Pays nine hundred nells." He handed the paper to Lugh, who held it up so that he, Nihs and Rogan could cluster around it. The paper was yellow, and its border and back were navy blue; details were written on it in different styles and colors, and its shape was not rectangular but somewhat erratic, as though it were a puzzle piece made to fit against other pieces of paper.

"Wow," Lugh said, "that works out, doesn't it? That sounds perfect! I wonder why they're asking for an escort through the adventurer's guild, I'm sure someone here in Reno could do the run for a lot less."

"I suppose some adventurers prefer to trust only other adventurers," Rogan said, taking the paper from Lugh and scanning it. "But that really doesn't concern us. They haven't mentioned that they need protection from anything, so there's no reason why we shouldn't take it on."

"Sounds good to me," Lugh said. "Nihs?"

"Might as well. It'll only be about a day's flight to Proks from this Rhian place."

"Great." Lugh handed the paper back to the master. "We'll take it. That's Lugh, Nihs, Rogan and Kyle. Where are these people we need to escort?"

"Excellent." The master wrote their names on the sheet, and then pored over it with his finger. "Hmm...their names are Meya and Phundasa...they're staying here. I seem to remember them saying that they would be back later."

"Great," Lugh said, as the master rolled up the paper, sealed it, and handed it back. "We've got time to kill. How much for the info?"

"Sixty nells, thank you. Excuse me," the master had been looking at Rogan, "is your name Rogan Harhoof?"

"It is," Rogan said.

"I've got a dispatch for you," the master said, turning back to his file and drawing out another scroll, this one also sealed in deep red. He handed it to Rogan, saying, "It came in about a half-month ago. It's from Bargnor Greyarm."

"Greyarm?" Rogan took the scroll, his hefty brow knotted. His face was troubled as he broke the seal and skimmed over the paper.

"Just a moment, Lughenor," he nodded to Lugh, who nodded back as Rogan strode away from the group, poring over the scroll.

"Huh," Lugh said, "I wonder what that's about. Did Rogan ever mention a Greyarm to you, Nihs?"

"Not that I remember. I would imagine that he's one of the Minotaur Rogan knew from the plains."

"Hm. Oh, I just remembered!" Lugh turned to Kyle. "We forgot to pick up your armor from General Arms. Why don't we run over there while we're waiting for these folks to show up?"

"Good idea," Nihs said. "Rogan and I will stay here. Don't dawdle, Lugh!"

"Yes, *mom*. Sheesh. Let's run, Kyle."

The walk back to the market complex was uneventful. Lugh talked little, and Kyle took the opportunity to familiarize himself further with the city. No matter how long he looked, something always managed to surprise him: the appearance or actions of the city folk, or the stunning architecture that Reno possessed in endless quantity. Soaring roads, huge gardens, and buildings that bent the imagination were around every corner; Kyle couldn't begin to imagine how much effort had gone into constructing the city, let alone how much it had all cost.

At one point, the pair passed in front of an outdoor café, and Kyle was shocked to see three Buors—non-policemen, to go by the color of the sashes they wore—sitting outside together, sharing what instantly reminded Kyle of a hookah pipe. Their helmets contained special slots near the chin for accommodating the metal end of the pipe, which they were passing around the circle politely.

"Are those Buors *smoking*?" he asked Lugh, already shocked from what he knew about the race.

Lugh chuckled. "Hah, no, I can't even imagine a Buor smoking. That's how they eat. I don't really know how it works, but it's like, they evolved so that they could filter food out of volcanic ash. They pack their food into these cake things called *rouk* and then light them on fire and inhale the smoke. It's pretty weird, I know, but apparently that's how they do it. They don't have to eat often, because they're always inhaling food while they breathe, right?"

Kyle just shook his head in amazement. A race that ate through its lungs—now he had seen it all.

They stopped by General Arms and picked up the armor. The puncture the goblin's dagger had left in it had been mended, and the armor had been reinforced and painted a dark blue. They thanked the shopkeeper and left, starting the trek back to the hideout.

Though he was doing his best to memorize them as quickly as possible, Kyle was still not familiar with Reno's streets. As such, he did not immediately notice when Lugh improvised their route back. He did notice when they ended up going down a road sandwiched between two tall buildings, and Lugh started looking around with a pained expression.

"Hmm," he said. "Damn, I always get mixed up in this part of town. I think we're supposed to be up on that skyway there—" and he pointed at one of the roads above them.

Kyle craned his neck to see. "Okay," he said, "so do we go back?"

Lugh glanced to their left. "I think we can cut through here," he said.

The street was little more than an alleyway. Because of the close proximity of the buildings overhead, no road extended over the one they were on. Their footsteps echoed as they walked. There was no one nearby, but Kyle could see people growing in the distance ahead of them.

"Okay, don't stop or look freaked out or anything," Lugh said suddenly, his eyes locked forward, "but those guys up there look like they're looking for a fight. Typical back-alley Reno thugs, probably. They probably won't pick a fight with us if we look too threatening, so back straight, take big strides and make sure they see your sword."

Kyle's nerves tensed at Lugh's statement, and his heart started beating faster, but his mind, which remained cool and analytical always, stopped him from twitching his neck in Lugh's direction. Instead, his body followed, as if by clockwork, Lugh's instructions: he squared his shoulders and turned his eyes forward, pulling his left arm back to reveal the sword at his hip. He wished he had been wearing his coat; he had left it behind as it was quite warm in the city.

He shook as they approached the men ahead of them. They were human, and there were four of them that Kyle could see. They had been standing in a ring at the side of the road as the two approached, but they fanned out to block it when Lugh drew close to them.

"'Scuse me," Lugh said. Kyle immediately appreciated the masterful inflection that Lugh injected into the words—it was polite, confident, and challenging all at once. It was the kind of "scuse me' that instantly identified the speaker as someone who knew exactly what was going on.

Kyle eyed the leader of the group warily. He was a seedy-looking man, only a bit taller than Kyle but much bulkier, with a rough face and eyes that twinkled in a cold, frightening way. He grinned widely at Lugh as he spoke, his eyes shifting between him and Kyle.

"'Scuse you yourself," he said. "Fine day to be out for a walk, eh? In a hurry to get where you're going?"

He's screwing with us, Kyle thought, and to his surprise found that this irritated him more than anything else. He wanted to open his mouth and insult the man, but he was wise enough to leave the talking to Lugh. It was still possible that the Selk would be able to head off any fighting—though the prospect looked grim.

Lugh passed a hand over his forehead. "Listen," he said, "this is stupid of you, okay? Look at us. We're adventurers. Do you really think the four of you are a match for us? Why don't you just step aside and wait for an easier target to come by?"

The man grinned even wider and turned to his chuckling companions.

"Hear that, boys? We might be taking on more than we can handle with these two. What do you think?" He pretended to think for a moment, then shook his head. "Nah, I think we're good. As a matter of fact, our employer asked for you specifically. Why don't you just come along real quiet? He wants a little chat with you, that's all."

If Lugh was surprised by this, he didn't show it. "Well, you'll have to say sorry to him for us." He drew his sword. "We're not going anywhere with you. Move aside."

Kyle drew his own sword as well, though as he did, he noticed something out of the corner of his eye. He wheeled around, so that he was back-to-back with Lugh, and his heart leapt into his throat. Four more men had appeared behind them, so that they were boxed in and outnumbered four-to-one.

"Should've just come quiet," the man was saying behind him. A moment later, Kyle heard a rush of footsteps.

The fight never really had the chance to begin. Kyle swung his sword at the man on the right, who parried his strike with his own; one of the other men then gouged him in the ribs and he felt his sword wrenched from his grasp as he doubled over in pain. Another blow caught him on the head and he blacked out instantly, knowing nothing of Lugh's fate.

When Kyle came to, it was to the feeling of someone healing his head through magic. He recognized the sensation instantly. He regained feeling in his body unusually fast and his clouded vision cleared almost at once. When the healing light faded, Kyle took in his surroundings.

The one who had healed him sat across from him. He was a human man, in his sixties. His face was stern and lined, and his hair, meticulously combed back, was gray. He wore a faded black suit that looked very expensive, and a pair of very odd gloves—the left was perfectly white, while the right was perfectly black.

When he saw Kyle had woken up, he grabbed his chin with one gloved hand. He forced Kyle to look at the other, which he held up with four fingers raised.

"How many fingers am I holding up?" His voice was as stern as his look suggested.

Kyle squinted at him balefully. "Who the hell are you?" he asked.

The man slapped him on the face lightly. "Fingers, wretch," he repeated, his voice severe.

"Four," Kyle said with bad humor.

"Good." The man reached forward and peeled back an eyelid.

"Don't squirm. You will be fine. The master will wish to speak with you shortly." Getting up, he walked to a door at the far end of the room.

Kyle found his voice as the man was on the threshold. "Where's Lugh?" he called after him. The man paused.

"Your...friend...is being held elsewhere. You needn't worry, not if you are civil and cooperative."

He left, and a moment later another man replaced him. It was the same steely-eyed man who had led the ambush in the street. He grinned at Kyle as he entered, and then took up a position near the door. Kyle glared at him, but did not say anything. He didn't want to antagonize anyone before he knew what was going on.

He took in the room around him. He realized that he had been tied to a chair in the center of it, bound ankle and wrist. The room itself was gray and featureless. It looked like a back room for custodial staff, bare and concrete. There was a table to Kyle's left; apart from that, he noticed nothing of interest.

Okay, he told himself, *think. Someone hired a bunch of thugs on the street to ambush us and bring us here, wherever it is. Why bring us here and not just mug us? And they bothered to heal me, which means that whatever they want from me I need to be conscious to give them.*

His mind instantly jumped to the fact that he was from Earth. *That must be it.* Why else would anyone be interested in him? But who apart from Lugh and the others knew that he wasn't Lorian? He tried to rack his brains to think of where or when one of them could have slipped up. Was it when they went to the Iden office? But the Buors were supposed to be honorable and secretive, weren't they? The only other people who knew about Kyle were Yuma and Oklade. They didn't seem like they would be very reliable people, but who could they have talked to? In any case, that wasn't really his main concern at the moment. His mind was dominated by one thought—escape. Whoever these people were or whatever they wanted, they were willing to attack him and Lugh to get it, and that meant that they weren't friends.

Kyle glanced again at the man who was guarding him. He really didn't look particularly tough. He wore no armor, though he did have a sword belted to his waist. He carried no other weapon that Kyle could see. The man noticed Kyle watching him, and smirked, but still said nothing.

Of course they had taken Kyle's sword and dagger. But that did not mean he was unarmed. He still had the one weapon left, the weapon that no-one could take from him. Did these men know about his soul sword? It was more than possible. Kyle didn't know if he would be able to draw it with his hands held apart. He wondered if it was a coincidence that he had been strapped to the chair in such a manner.

He looked around the room again. It was unfurnished, but modern; it was inside one of Reno's newer buildings. If he managed to incapacitate his captor and escape the room, what next? He would have to locate Lugh, and ideally his weapon, then the two of them would have to escape the building together. It seemed like a long shot, but what else did he have?

He thought about Nihs and Rogan, waiting for them at the hideout. They wouldn't come for them—even once they realized that Kyle and Lugh were missing, they wouldn't be able to find the two of them in the huge city. So it was up to them...more specifically Kyle, as he had no idea where Lugh was or what situation he was in.

Kyle's ruminations were interrupted when the door to the room swung open again. Two men entered: one was the same elderly man as before, and the other was a tall, slight man with blonde hair and glassy blue eyes. He wore a suit of dusty gray that reeked of money, and moved with the measured pace of one brimming with confidence and style.

"Why, hello there," he said pleasantly to Kyle, his voice clear and light, "and how are we doing today?"

I hate you already, Kyle thought. "Pretty shitty," he said.

The man pulled up the same chair his servant had occupied before and sat down facing him. "I'm sorry to hear that," he said, "but I'm sure you can understand that it's necessary. I can't have you running off, I'm afraid, not when it's been so difficult to track you down."

"What do you want?" Kyle asked flatly.

"Oh, not much, not much. Just a bit of a chat." The man held out his hand behind him and the older man stepped forward, handing him a clipboard and a pen. He set it on his leg in front of him and faced Kyle like a news reporter in an interview.

"Really," Kyle said. "You were that desperate for company that you had to knock me out and drag me here?"

The man grinned at this as though he and Kyle were sharing a private joke, though when he spoke again, it was as though Kyle never had.

"What's your name?" he asked.

Okay, Kyle thought. *If they know my real name, then I might be able to make them think they've got the wrong person by lying. Worth a shot.*

"John," he said, trying to make it sound natural. He thought that this failed entirely, but his questioner seemed not to notice, or care that it was John and not Kyle.

"John," the man repeated as though it were that most fascinating name in existence. "Do you have a last name, John?"

"Not usually. I'm an adventurer."

"What is it when you *do* have a last name?"

"What's it to you?" Kyle said this partially out of spite and partially because he was trying to come up with one without the name 'Arbuckle' creeping into his conscience.

The man smiled. "Why, I'd just like to get to know more about you, of course." His voice was brimming with innocence, but Kyle could detect the irony behind it.

"Bullshit. Why would you care about me?"

The smile flickered. "We'll get to that. Your last name, please. I won't ask again."

It was a very delicate threat, but Kyle was keenly aware of the situation he was in.

"Ward," he said, choosing, out of convenience, his mother's maiden name.

"Ward," the man repeated again, writing the name down. His next question flicked out like a snake.

"Where are you from, John Ward?"

"Centralia," Kyle said at once.

"Where in Centralia?"

"You know. Around. I'm an adventurer, I don't stay in one place for long."

"Where were you born, then?"

Crap, crap, what was the name of that place near Reno? It sounded like Kenya. Oh, right. "Kena," he said.

The man gave him a piercing stare, and then sighed, handing his clipboard back to his servant. He leaned forward, his hands woven over his knee.

"John," he said, "I'll be frank. I know that that isn't your real name, and that you're not from Kena. As a matter of fact, I'm almost positive that you're not from Loria at all. So it would save time if you would just tell me the truth, and stop lying on some obscure principle. I'll give you another chance before I have my manservant read your memories."

Kyle matched him glare for glare, though his heart was beating hard. *How do you know?* "Go ahead. You won't find anything."

"Have it your way, then," the man sighed. His servant came close and placed his hands on Kyle's temple, and the gray suited man took hold of his servant's wrist. Kyle's eyes shut.

He did not know how to resist someone prying into his memories, or even if it was possible. He could do nothing but watch the images flicker in front of his mind's eye, and hope desperately that the search would prove no more useful to this man than it had to Ezki at the Iden office.

Soon the search was over, and Kyle's eyes reopened. His heart sank; the older man's expression hadn't changed, but the gray suited man was smiling in a self-satisfied way. He leaned forward in his chair, his eyes never leaving Kyle.

"Ah…so you *are* the one." He waved his servants away. "That will do for now, thank you."

The older man bowed and left, and the steely-eyed man sauntered out after him. Gray suit readjusted himself on the chair.

"Well, Kyle," he said, "I'll be honest with you. I was approaching this meeting with a certain level of reservation. Of course the signs were there that someone had…*invaded* Loria from another plane, but we can never really believe these things until we've seen them for ourselves, can we?"

"What do you want from me?" Kyle repeated flatly. He felt violated that his memories had been read so thoroughly, and the fact that the man seemed to be enjoying himself immensely didn't help.

"Kyle, in the long history of our world you are the first confirmed case of an otherworldly being existing on Lorian soil. I'm sure you don't need to stretch your imagination to see why you could be of interest to a myriad of different people."

"So you want something from my world?" Kyle said—there didn't seem a point in lying anymore.

"Broadly speaking, yes. There are many things you could provide that would benefit the people of Loria, some of which you may not even be aware of. In a world where practically no one has performed research on the subject of alternate dimensions, your existence raises—and hopefully answers—a good number of questions. I'm sure you can see why we went to such lengths to find you before someone else did."

"Yeah, about that," Kyle said, his head giving him a throb. "Seems a little funny to me that someone who's so interested in science hires mercenaries to beat people up and kidnap them."

For the first time, the man's benevolent manner dropped. "I'm afraid I have to apologize for that," he said, and Kyle was shocked to hear the sincerity in his voice. "What I *instructed* them to do was to find you and *convince* you to come with them. I suppose 'convince' is a bit too loose a term to use when dealing with people of their intellectual caliber. I'll have to select my words—or my assistants—more carefully next time."

"What about Lugh?" Kyle snapped. "Where's he?"

"Your adventurer friend, while a good one I'm sure, is not suited for this conversation. He has nothing to add, apart from an opinion derived from a very limited view of the situation."

"And what the hell do you mean by—"

"You want to go home, don't you?"

The man might as well have slapped him in the face. His mouth hung open, and he stared at his inquisitor. The man came even closer to him.

"Kyle," he said, "your friends mean well, I'm sure they do. But they are only a bunch of adventurers. They know nothing of physics, or of advanced magical theory, or of Ephicer engineering. You are loyal to them, of course, because they are the ones who found you and guided you into this world. Loyalty is a wonderful thing—but it won't get you home. How do you know that staying in their company will ever lead you to something fruitful? The odds are, it never will, and you will be trapped in Loria forever because of your loyalty and their good intentions.

"*I*, on the other hand, am different. I have understanding, I have science, and I have money. What I'd like to propose to you is a simple tradeoff, and one that you will find very appealing, I'm sure. Stay here with me, and my team and I will conduct experiments on you. Perhaps you can tell us of...*Terra*'s technology, which we can then reverse engineer. And as we learn more about you, we'll grow closer to the point where we know enough about you to send you back. I can't guarantee that we will find a way—perhaps there isn't one—but your chances are infinitely better with me than with anyone else."

Kyle was at a loss for words. His immediate thought was to throw the man's offer in his face, and yet...he couldn't help but see the logic in the argument. He needed help, a second opinion. It was all too much for him to process.

"Lugh," he said firmly.

"I'm sorry?"

"Bring Lugh here. I want to see him, and I want him to hear what you have to say...whether he's *suited for this conversation* or not."

The smile disappeared. "I cannot do that."

Kyle glared as fiercely as he could. "Then I'm not helping you."

"That's a tad irrational, don't you think? Use your brain and *think* for a moment, Kyle. This is the best chance of leaving this world you will *ever* get, I guarantee it. Lugh and the others can't help you. I can. Would you really throw that away for the sake of sentimentality?"

It was amazing how easy the answer came. "I would," he said.

The man seemed irritated by this, though he kept himself under tight control. He stood up. "I do hope you realize that you really don't have a choice in this matter. I wanted to be your ally, Kyle, and I had hoped that you would be wise enough to see the situation my way. I don't want to, but I'll get what I need from you by force if I have to." He spun around and left. The thug reentered, and took up his post again.

Shit, Kyle thought. So these men knew all about him, now. The gray-suited man's case had been compelling, but there was something wrong about him. What kind of person kidnaps someone and then tries to convert them to his side?

He had said that Kyle had refused because he was *loyal* to his friends. *Well, I guess I am.* Maybe Lugh and the others were only a bunch of adventurers, but they had always shown nothing but kindness towards him, something he couldn't say for gray suit, or nearly anyone else for that matter. He'd rather stay stuck in Loria with them on his side than stuck doing research with that man.

As the thought struck him, he realized that he *had* to escape and rescue Lugh, or die trying. He'd been nothing but trouble for the others, and it was the least he could do.

Kyle stole a glance at his jailer. The man's interest in Kyle seemed to have faded, and he now stood with a bored expression on his face. It was probably the best Kyle was going to get, unless this man was in the habit of falling asleep standing up.

Better now than never, Kyle thought.

His plan was simple: draw his soul sword if possible, cut the cables binding him to the chair with it, incapacitate the guard somehow—Kyle was not ready to think about killing him—and then get out of the room. Find Lugh, escape. He imagined that if he couldn't find Lugh right away, he could run to the hideout and gather Nihs and Rogan to help him. He would just have to find his way to the hideout and back, which may be a difficult task. But he could improvise when the time came.

He waited for his jailer's attention to waver, then he tested drawing his soul sword with one hand—he tried to will the silver particles to flow down only one arm, and for the blade to spring from that palm uniquely. The build-up began, and Kyle's arm began to glow, but he aborted it for fear of drawing the thug's attention. He felt as though it would work. Now he just had to wait for the exact right moment. He would only get one chance, and it had to be perfect.

Draw the sword, cut the bindings, strike the guard. Don't worry about trying to knock him out or anything like that. You'll just screw up. Don't feel bad for him.

The perfect moment came. The man stretched and yawned, rubbing out a crick in the back of his neck.

The sword sprang from Kyle's arm instantly; he angled his wrist to the left and the ropes snapped apart as soon as the sword touched them. He freed his other arm as the guard yelled "Hey!"—there wouldn't be enough time to free his legs. He dove forward, pulling himself off-balance and striking horizontally with the sword. There was a *crack* and the man fell instantly, Kyle half on top of him, his feet still attached to the chair.

Kyle retched. His sword had taken a chunk the size of a soccer ball out of the man's side. He was very, very dead. The eyes that had twinkled maliciously only a minute ago were now gray and vacant, and the once-smiling mouth hung open.

Don't lose it now. Move.

He freed his ankles and stood up. His thought was that he should search the man for keys or something similar, but he didn't want to get any closer to the corpse than he had to. Quivering with disgust, he took the man's sword, though he hung it to his belt instead of using it. Now wasn't the time to practice with a mediocre weapon; he would be using his soul sword to get himself out of here.

He opened the door carefully, his hand tensed to strike. The hallway outside, however, was deserted. Kyle glanced left and right. It looked much like his prison room, stark and unfurnished, a hallway that obviously wasn't meant to be seen by anyone but workers. Along the left side of the hall were many doors, while the other side had none.

Kyle was now faced with a dilemma. Was it possible that Lugh was being held in one of the other rooms? Or was it foolish for Kyle to do anything but escape from the building as soon as possible, and go for help?

To hold off making the decision, he ran and checked the ends of the hallway. At one end was a solid black door that was locked by some sort of keypad; he could likely use his soul sword to cut his way through, but he doubted that it led in a direction he wanted to go. At the other end was an elevator door. So he was in a building that required an elevator...he was probably in the basement, by the looks of it.

Kyle suddenly heard the sound of a door behind him, and someone shouted "Hey!" He wheeled around to see a man, presumably one of the thugs, staring at him with a bug-eyed expression—he had come out of the room beside Kyle's.

The man drew his weapon. Kyle dashed upon him and the two swords met. The man's shattered instantly; he screamed and dropped the shards of his weapon, instinctively throwing his arms up in front of his face. Kyle now saw the solution to his problem. He bulled into the man, pinning him against the wall with his soul sword pointed at his throat.

Kyle had never been a bully. He had always been one of the smaller, quieter kids at school and preferred to stay away from direct confrontations whenever possible. As such, the experience of having the other man—who was larger and probably older than Kyle—writhe and whimper in his grip was completely alien to him. The man seemed terrified of Kyle's soularm, twisting his body against the wall as if trying to shrink as far away from it as possible.

For a moment, Kyle was unsure of how to proceed. He had seen plenty of people roughed up for information in the movies...how did it go again?

The man's twisting and whimpering was getting on his nerves, so he settled for slamming him against the wall again and yelling.

"Shut up and sit still! I said SHUT UP!" He stabbed the wall behind the goon with his soul sword. A chunk the size of a watermelon was instantly blasted out of it and the man fell completely silent.

So far so good, Kyle thought. "Okay, listen," he said, trying to make himself sound scary and feeling a right fool while doing it, "you've seen what my sword can do. I'm sure I don't need to paint a picture of what it'll do to you if you don't answer my questions. Understand?"

The man found his voice. "Son a bitch," he said, quavering, "what kind of weapon is that?"

"That's none of your business," Kyle said, slamming him against the wall again. "Now listen. Another man was with me when I got captured...a sea Selk with blonde hair. Where is he?"

"He's...he's alright! I...I don't know where he is."

"You don't know?" he brought his glowing sword closer to the man's neck.

"No! I'm sorry!" the man shrieked, trying to protect his face with his hands. "They left the elevator before we did, I didn't see where they took him."

"Really? You were that distracted? I'm sure you can remember *some*thing." He moved the sword even closer. The man's eyes swiveled as they tried to keep it in sight.

"Uh, uh, there's another maintenance floor below this one. You get to it by pressing the keys for floor thirty-nine and forty at the same time. That might be where he is!"

"Where are we?" Kyle asked, burning with the desire for answers.

The man hesitated. "S'worth more than my job to tell you that..."

"I'm not threatening you with your job, am I? TELL ME!" Sparks flashed as another section of the wall was carved away.

"Aah! Aah! Don't hurt me! W-we're in Sky Tower!"

For a moment, Kyle was struck speechless. "What?" he asked in a much quieter voice. "Sky Tower? Livaldi's place? Is he in on this?"

"I don't know. Please believe me."

"Why don't you know? Who do you work for?"

"Michael Radisson. We're mercenaries; he's our leader. I don't know who's paying him."

Kyle narrowed his eyes, trying to sense if the other man was lying. He thought not. After all, it made sense. If Radisson's band of mercenaries would follow him in ignorance, what would be the point of letting them in on all the details?

"Fine." he said. "One more thing. How do I get out of here?"

"The main floor, floor zero. There are doors everywhere."

Kyle allowed himself a moment to pause, intimidating the man further before he said, "All right." Kyle was now faced with another problem—what to do with his prisoner. He couldn't kill the man, but neither could he leave him free to alert others. Inspiration struck him. "Okay. We're going down the hall. Turn around and walk slowly. One wrong move and my sword takes a chunk out of your back."

The man whimpered slightly as he walked, arms raised in surrender. Kyle marched him into the room where he himself had been held prisoner and instructed the man to sit down. Kyle jerked his chin at the slashed bonds he had just recently escaped from.

"Tie your legs to the chair."

The man reluctantly complied under Kyle's watchful eye. Kyle tied his arms and left. He knew that his solution had been a short-term one, but that didn't concern him overmuch. He was the hunter now, armed with an unstoppable weapon, and was convinced that he would be able to find Lugh and escape.

He entered the elevator and looked with dismay at the number of floors to choose from: one hundred and eighty of them. Nowhere was it indicated which floor Kyle was on. He decided to trust his captive's tip, and pressed the keys for floors thirty-nine and forty at the same time. The elevator doors shut, and Kyle immediately became familiar with the sensation of rapid downward movement.

Okay, he thought, *I was above floor forty. By quite a few floors, by the feel of it.*

The elevator ride was odd—boring and yet tense at the same time. The elevator was highly polished and well-decorated, both sides of it mirrored. There was even a small plant mounted in one corner. Kyle observed himself in the endless reflections created by the mirrors; his face was pale and drawn-looking, and a couple splotches of blood had made their way onto his clothes. He gingerly felt his head where he had been struck. It was sore, but not bloody, thanks to the older man's magic.

He felt the elevator slow down and immediately tensed; he moved to one side, squishing himself against the wall so that he wouldn't be visible from the outside. His judgment proved correct—as soon as the doors opened, somebody shouted, "Drop your weapon and step out slowly! I have a gun!"

Another voice sounded, "Geez, calm down, could be one of us."

"No one else is supposed to be here, you idiot, and look, he's not coming out—HEY! GET THE HELL OUT OF THERE OR I START SHOOTING!"

Kyle made a split-second decision. He retracted his soul sword and stepped out slowly, his arms raised.

The man had been telling the truth. It was another maintenance floor, almost identical to the one Kyle had been imprisoned on. Standing in the stark hallway were two men; one of them had been leaning against the wall, but jumped to attention when he saw Kyle. The other was standing facing the elevator directly, in his arms a golden assault rifle—the Eagle.

Both men were shocked by Kyle's appearance. "You!" the gun-wielder said in disbelief. "You're the one they brought in! What the hell are you doing here?"

"Got lost?" Kyle said with a smile and a shrug, reasoning that if he was going to die he might as well screw with his enemies one last time.

The man's face was a mixture of anger and uncertainty.

"What do we do with him?" the wall-leaner asked him.

The other man thought for a moment, then said, "Better put him in the room with the other. Okay, listen, you. You're gonna march past us and get in that room back there, okay? And no funny business. You move wrong, I shoot. Keep your hands on your head. Move it!"

Kyle complied, moving slowly and deliberately up the hallway until he was in between the two men. When he was, he acted in a flash—his soul sword sprung into his arms, and he struck, first to the left, against the more alert of the two men, then to the right. Their screams immediately tore through the air as the sword did its gruesome work.

It was too much for Kyle. Their wails of pain struck him like physical blows, and he forced himself to avert his eyes from the damage his sword had inflicted. What was he to do? Should he kill them and end their suffering? Their screams were loud and long—surely they would alert someone else. Forcing himself to think over his own roiling emotions, Kyle wrested the man's rifle from him and shot—each man twice. Pellets of energy, bright blue like Ephicer light, flew from the barrel of the rifle and buried themselves in the two men. The screams ended. Though the Eagle was a foreign weapon, it seemed almost familiar in Kyle's arms. It was held the same way as a rifle back on Earth, and the trigger was in the normal position. Even in this moment of peril—or perhaps because of it—Kyle was able to reflect on the unbelievable similarities between Loria and Earth, even down to details such as these.

Kyle forced himself to think, trying to calm his frantically beating heart. *I just killed three men, I just killed three men, I just killed three men*—the thought filled his entire mind. The feeling of self-loathing he experienced now was far worse than it had ever been, but he had no time to ponder why. A door to the right opened, a third man stepped out, saying, "Hey, guys, what's going on, why were you—" and he ran directly into the barrel of an Eagle rifle leveled at his heart.

"Back up," said Kyle quietly, in a tone of absolute authority. "Into the room. Back up."

Something had snapped in Kyle's brain, but something else was still keeping him going, a deep, built-in coldness and cynicism that had propelled him through his entire life. Even though his world was spinning around him, a small part of him always knew what was going on and what had to be done about it.

But now another voice came from inside the room the man was backing into, a voice that eased Kyle's mind and reassured him—Lugh.

"Hey, who is that? Kyle, is that you? In here!"

Kyle bullied the man until they were both completely inside the room. His heart leapt. Lugh was tied to a chair in the same fashion he himself had been. Not only that, but their equipment—their two daggers, Lugh's retraweapon and Kyle's changearm and armor—were piled on a table next to him. A nasty lump marred Lugh's head, and blood had trickled through his hair and onto his face, but it lit up when he saw Kyle.

"Woah! How did you escape? All right! Get him to untie me!"

Kyle nodded, motioning the man over with his rifle. "You heard him," he said, "untie him."

The man freed Lugh, and then the two of them tied him up in turn. They grabbed their weapons and Kyle donned his armor for convenience's sake. The familiar weight of the changearm at his hip reassured him, and he felt much less vulnerable with his armor on.

They stepped into the hallway. Lugh sucked in a breath when he saw what Kyle had done to the men outside—he allowed Kyle to move on after quickly taking a pistol. He peppered Kyle with questions as they walked down the hallway.

"How did you get out? Weren't they guarding you?"

"My soul sword," Kyle said, feeling much better now that Lugh was with him. "They didn't know I had one. I managed to surprise them."

Lugh shook his head. "I swear, if you keep pulling off bits like this you're going to be teaching us how to adventure. Any idea where we are?"

Kyle briefly told him everything that he had gleaned from the thug he had interrogated.

"Sky Tower! That doesn't seem right…why would they bring us here? Anyway, step one is to get the hell out of here, right? The place should be mostly deserted—it's still under construction, after all."

They got on the elevator again and punched the button for the ground floor. Kyle was shaking uncontrollably with adrenaline and emotion.

Lugh tried to calm him down as the elevator descended. "Look, I know it's hard, you never want to kill anyone, even an enemy. But you did what you had to do to keep yourself safe. That's the most important thing, okay? You're not a murderer, you were just defending yourself. These men started it, not you, and quite frankly, if you're going to become the type of mercenary that kidnaps innocent people then you should be prepared for retribution. They were criminals. If they didn't hurt us they would have hurt someone else. You're not a horrible person."

Kyle was only slightly reassured, but he didn't have time to be emotional now. "I know," he told Lugh quietly. "Let's just get out of here."

The elevator once again slowed down. Kyle was starting to feel better. Soon they would be free of this nightmare, and he would be able to lock himself in his room and clean himself off and try to forget about the whole experience.

The door opened. A voice from the other side said, "Going somewhere?"

The elevator door had opened into a huge atrium, a bubble-shaped structure with a glass roof. Kyle was reminded instantly of the market complex. Though the massive space was empty and abandoned, it was obviously meant to accommodate multitudes of people and much activity. Kyle, however, only had eyes for the group of people in front of them.

Flanked by four soldiers, all armed with Eagles, were two men—a dark-haired and dark-eyed mercenary armed with a large composite broadsword and shield, and the man in the dusty gray suit. The latter was now armed: an elegant golden rapier was buckled to his waist, looking strangely out of place with his formal attire. He stepped forwards and addressed Lugh and Kyle, who had frozen, their weapons in their hands, at the entrance of the elevator.

"Come now," he said, a smile on his face, "that's no way to behave, is it? I spend so much effort tracking you down and capturing you, and the first thing you try and do is escape?" He tilted his head to one side, considering them. "Well, I hope you've satisfied your desire for drama. Your attempt wasn't too bad, considering. But this is where the fun ends. Drop your weapons. Now."

"And just who the hell do you think you are?" Lugh shouted across the intervening space. Kyle could see that Lugh's eyes were flickering in every which direction, seeking out possible routes of escape. Kyle could not see what use this would be. No matter how quickly they ran, they would not be able to outrun the shots from four rifles.

The man ignored him. "Drop them, and things will be easier for you. I will count down from ten. Ten. Nine. Eight…"

"What do we do?" Kyle hissed.

Lugh said nothing. His face was pained.

"Four. Three—" the man's arm was raised, prepared to give his soldiers the command to fire.

Suddenly there was a disturbance to Kyle and Lugh's right. Everyone's attention was compromised for an instant as what looked like a twister made of black and white light appeared inside the atrium, coalescing into the elderly magician from before. The spell-weaver was panting, and his face was taut with concern.

"Sir!" he shouted at once, addressing gray suit. "The police are coming! You have to flee, now!"

Gray suit's expression instantly turned to one of anger. "*No!* Kyle comes with us!"

"There's no time! We need to leave him!"

Gray suit looked furious. He turned to the mercenary beside him and snapped, "What are you waiting for? Get your men out of here! Come *on!*" he shot at the older man.

"Here, sir!" The magic user ran to gray suit and threw his arms around him. A moment later, the two melted into a twister of light that dissipated upwards into the sky. The mercenary chief shouted a couple orders to his men, who all sprinted off down a hallway to the left, out of sight.

Kyle's mind was whirling. "What just happened?" he asked Lugh, but the Selk had grabbed onto his arm and forced him to the right, out of the atrium.

"No time! Trust me, we don't want to be here when the police arrive! Just run!"

And they did just that, sprinting down a set of glass steps and exiting the atrium. The base of Sky Tower was mostly deserted—the construction that was going on was on the upper levels, and few people had reason to be near it while the building was not yet open. Kyle had no time to take in any of this. He focused on following Lugh, who ran slowly enough for him to keep up, but only just. Reno's streets were a blur. They ran down a flight of steps outside the tower and onto the main street, which Lugh quickly turned off of. They ran and ran, down increasingly smaller streets until they were in a relatively quieter part of town. Only then did Lugh slow to a walk, allowing Kyle, who was gasping for air, to catch up with him.

"Okay," Lugh said, barely out of breath, "we've gone as far as we should have to, to avoid the heat. Now we just need to lie low, okay? That armor of yours looks a little suspicious, but no one should look twice unless we draw attention to ourselves. Remember, the police were on their way, and news spreads like wildfire through the Buorish police force. I'd say we've got about ten more minutes before every policeman in Reno knows about this."

"What do we do?" Kyle wheezed.

"We head back to the hideout and lay low. If those people we're escorting have shown up already, we'll try to get them to leave with us right away. If not, we spend the night and skip town first thing in the morning."

"Why didn't we want to be there when the police showed up?"

"Think about it. We don't want to get caught up with the law right now. The case would last ages, and it would definitely end with the Buors finding out about what you are. It would be bad news all around, trust me."

Kyle forced his racing heart to calm as they walked at an excruciatingly slow pace towards the hideout.

After a couple minutes, Lugh said, "Hey...how are you doing?"

"Okay."

Lugh sighed. "All right, then. Don't worry. Just a little bit longer, then we'll be done with this."

Kyle never would have admitted it, but Lugh had said just the right thing. That's all he wanted at the moment...for this to be over.

As they walked, Lugh got Kyle to recount in detail what he had gone through.

He shook his head when Kyle had finished. "Listen," he said seriously, "I'm not one to dish out praise for no reason, so believe me when I say you did an amazing job. I'll admit, I thought we were pretty done for back there...I had no idea how I was going to get out. But not only did you pull it off, you got me out of there too. So thanks."

Kyle was still not in the mood to talk, but he recognized the sincerity in Lugh's voice and nodded his acknowledgement of the statement.

Lugh went on, "Hoo...what a crazy thing, though, huh? I wonder what it was all about...and why were they keeping us in Sky Tower? They didn't seem to care about me at all, they just asked me a bunch of questions about you and then left when I wouldn't tell them anything...but I guess they know about you now, huh? That's not good...but if we can escape to Eastia quickly enough, they won't be able to follow us. But we can talk more about everything when we're with Nihs and Rogan again."

For as tense as Kyle felt throughout their walk, it was quite uneventful. At one point, they passed by a Buorish guard headed in the opposite direction. It was probably Kyle's imagination, however, that added the extra urgency to his step and set his destination to Sky Tower.

They arrived back at the hideout and entered to find that it had filled up significantly for the night. Due to Loria's short days, it was already approaching evening. They fought their way to the bar among the numerous adventurers and asked the master as to the whereabouts of the others.

"Ah, right," the barman nodded at Lugh's description. "Of course. They're around the corner, at a table in the back."

They found Nihs and Rogan seated at a table with two strangers. One was a young woman a little older than Kyle, who was wearing a white outfit that identified her as a spellcaster; both her eyes and hair were dark red, colors that shocked Kyle with their strangeness. The other was a large Orcish man whose black hair was tied in a knot behind his head. His features were blocky and he was heavily muscled. Kyle imagined that he must be a fighter of some kind, perhaps a warrior like Rogan.

Rogan was sitting across from the two, talking to them quietly. Nihs, seated on the table, was accessing the overhead, his tentacled head waving like seaweed in the ocean. Rogan turned and started as they approached.

"There you two are!" he said, as they sat down. "We were starting to worry about you. What took you so long? Did you have to tan the leather for Kyle's armor yourself?"

"It's a long story, I'm afraid," Lugh said quietly, "and one that might have to wait." He turned to the two strangers. "I don't think we've been introduced. Are you the ones who need the airship escort?"

The woman seemed slightly taken aback by Lugh's abrupt appearance, but she spoke politely nonetheless. "Yes, that's us. I'm Meya, and this is my travelling companion, Phundasa. We're on our way to Eastia."

Lugh shook their hands. "Pleased to meet you. I'm Lugh, and this is Kyle. Sorry we were late. We had an interesting time getting here."

"I'll say," Phundasa's accent was thick, making Kyle think of a Russian man. He gestured to his forehead with one huge finger, nodding to Lugh significantly.

Only then did Rogan and Meya notice the wound on Lugh's head. Meya gave a small gasp while Rogan asked again with more urgency, "what happened to you two?"

"It's a long story," Lugh repeated. He addressed the two newcomers, "I'm sorry about this, but would it be all right if we left Reno like, now? I'll explain later, but basically I don't think it's a great idea for us to be staying in town at the moment."

Meya and Phundasa seemed unsure of what to say.

Rogan, however, shook his head. "I'm afraid we can't, Lughenor. The honeycombs closed early tonight, and besides, we have things that need to be taken care of. For one, you need to get that head healed."

"What! They closed the honeycombs? Damn. Okay, fine, but we need to leave first thing in the morning, all right?"

"Lughenor," Rogan said in a tone of authority, "slow down. Let's hear your story first and get you healed, and then we can sort things out. We got a couple rooms for tonight. Let's move up there and we can hear the tale."

Lugh touched his forehead. "Fine. What's Nihs doing?"

"Looking for you. But he's been at it for a while now; he should be coming back any moment."

They waited at the table for a few minutes for Nihs to wake up. Apparently, Kol were not supposed to be moved while using the overhead. While they waited, Lugh and Kyle made small talk with Meya and Phundasa, and Meya rose to examine Lugh's head. She was a healer by profession and Phundasa was a brawler, a type of Orcish fistfighter. They had been travelling together for a number of years, and a recent contract was bringing them back to their homeland of Eastia.

"So," Lugh said, while Meya attempted to move his mane of hair aside, "Meya, huh? No offence, but I kind of expected you to be a bit smaller and greener with a name like that."

Meya laughed lightly. "Both Das and I have spent a long time among the Kol. Meya was the name of one of my tutors. I decided to adopt it once I became an adventurer."

"Fair enough," Lugh said. He turned to Phundasa. "How about you, Boombasta? How does an Orcish brawler end up being from Eastia?"

"There are more Orc in Eastia than people think," Phundasa said. "I came from a small village in the mountains…there are probably ten Orc for every Kol there, and many of us practice *thortnir*, what you call wrestling. It helps keep the cold of the winter away."

"I'll bet it does," Lugh said.

At that moment, Nihs surfaced from his meditation. "Nothing at all," he said immediately once he was awake, "no Kol in Reno has seen—hey! When did you get back? What happened to your head?"

Lugh sighed. "It's a long story."

They met in the large room that Rogan had rented for the four of them. Meya, who was clearly very skilled at her profession, had healed Lugh's head in a trice, and he was now telling everyone a somewhat censored version of what had happened to the two of them. It involved the replacement of Sky Tower with some unknown warehouse and the omission of the name of Michael Radisson, as well as the censorship of Lugh and Kyle's interrogations.

"...And then we just ran for it and made our way back to the hideout," Lugh finished. "That pretty much sums it up."

Meya looked troubled. "And you never got to find out what they wanted? It seems odd that they went to all the trouble to capture you just to ask you such simple questions."

Lugh shrugged. "My only thought is that they were going for a kidnapping and somehow got the wrong people."

"That's certainly a possibility," Nihs agreed. "They could even have seen your equipment and decided to 'accidentally' kidnap the wrong target in order to take it for themselves."

"That's very true," Meya said quietly. "Listen," she said to Lugh, "we believe that you were just innocent bystanders, but please forgive me if I ask why you don't want to stay and help the police with their inquiries."

Lugh shrugged. "Fair enough. There are a couple reasons, but the simplest one is that we just don't want to be held up here in Reno. We have a lot of work to do, and I don't care so much for justice that I'm willing to let the police latch onto us for half a month. Chances are the investigation wouldn't get us any closer to finding those men, and in the meantime we'd be stuck in the city."

Meya nodded. "All right." She stood up, and Phundasa rose with her.

"We can leave in the morning tomorrow. Good-night to all of you. *Adamia.*"

"Good-night," Lugh said. "Thanks for the healing."

Meya smiled. "It's my job."

Once they had left, Kyle asked, "What does *adamia* mean?"

"It's a blessing of the church of Saint Iila," Rogan rumbled, "it means 'peace'. Now…what *actually* happened to you two?"

Kyle and Lugh had just finished the original and uncut version of their story, and needless to say, the reaction was much more pronounced.

"Tesh*ur*," Nihs said quietly. "What does all this mean? How did they know about Kyle? And who has the power to gain access to Sky Tower like that?"

"Just for the record," Kyle said, "the man in the gray suit wasn't Livaldi?"

Lugh shook his head. "Livaldi's hair and eyes are purple, and he's slimmer and shorter than the man you described."

"Wait a minute." Kyle's curiosity overcame his desire to delve further into the story. "*Purple?* And Meya's hair and eyes are red. How can that be?"

The look he received told him yet again that he had much to learn of Loria. "Oh. So I guess that's normal here?"

"It is rarer than normal tones," Nihs said, "but not unheard of. You see, the color of one's eyes and hair has to do with the balance of different types of magic within the person's soul. Eyes are especially effected, as they're the part of the body most closely linked with the soul. In any case, in most people the dominant force is either the element of water or earth, hence blue and brown eyes. Less common is green eyes for wind, and less common than that is all of the other colors. Livaldi's coloring is very rare, it's one of the features that people say identify him as a genius."

"*Anyway*," Lugh said, "I don't think we can rule out Livaldi as the mastermind behind all this—it's his tower, after all. And that older man looked a lot like Saul, Livaldi's personal magician, from what I know about him."

"That's pretty conclusive, then, isn't it?" Kyle asked.

"Not as much as you would think. Remember, he called that blonde guy 'sir'. It's possible that *he's* the head of all this, and that he's undermining Livaldi's power."

"Would Livaldi be ignorant enough to allow that to happen?" Rogan asked. "He is supposed to be a genius, after all. And you said all of those men were armed with Maida weaponry—*recent* Maida weaponry. The Eagle hasn't even been released to the public yet."

"That's a good point," Lugh admitted. "And what about this Michael Radisson fellow? Do we know anything about him?"

Rogan shook his head.

Nihs said, "I'll ask the overhead about him. And while I'm at it, I'll ask about Livaldi; see if there are any new interesting things to hear."

"Sounds good," Lugh agreed. "Well, is that it? Are we done here?"

Rogan nodded. "I would say so. All we really know is that someone knows about Kyle and is out to get him. All we can do is fly to Eastia and keep our guard up. Only one last thing. What do we tell Meya and Phundasa?"

"Nothing," Lugh said at once. "The fewer people that know about Kyle, the better. If they ask, we stick to the same story that we did at the Iden office, agreed?"

They all did.

Then Rogan did something unexpected. He sighed, gathering all of their attention again. "There is…one more thing, Lughenor. When you leave for Eastia tomorrow, I'm not coming with you."

Both Kyle and Lugh exclaimed at the same time, "*What!*"

"Hey, what gives?" Lugh said. "Why not?"

Rogan shook his shaggy head and drew from his tunic the dispatch that the master had given him before. "This is an urgent message for me from the plains," he said. "Bargnor Greyarm sent it to me…he's an old friend of mine. He wrote to tell me that my father, Ravigan Harhoof, has died."

"Damn…I'm sorry, Rogan."

Rogan shrugged massively. His expression was impassive and unreadable. "It is all right. Minotaur are young and strong one day; the next, they grow old and die. Such is the way of life, and his was long and full. But there *is* a problem…my father was the chieftain of our clan, and there is trouble brewing among my people because of his death."

Lugh's mouth was hanging open. "What does that mean?"

Rogan sighed again. "I am the son of the clan chieftain. It is my duty to return to the plains and set right the problems that have arisen. Lughenor, I have to do this. If I do not return and intervene, a clan war may break out. I intend to find a ship tomorrow that will take me to the Ar'ac."

Lugh looked utterly downcast. "Hey, not cool," he said sadly, "you can't leave now; things were just getting good."

"It *has* been good, Lughenor," Rogan said pointedly. "But this is my duty. I'm sorry as well that this has happened, but happened it has, and my responsibilities are clear."

"We could come with you!" Lugh protested. "We could lend you a hand. We'd just be putting off the trip to Eastia for a little while, and Kyle could see the Ar'ac!"

"No, Lughenor," Rogan said firmly. "This is my duty, and mine alone. And you're forgetting that someone out there knows about Kyle. It's not safe for him to just wander around anymore—you need to get to the bottom of his story as soon as possible."

Lugh sagged. "What about my ship?" he asked desperately.

"I've spoken to Phundasa about the maintenance of the *Ayger*. He has sailed before, he'll be able to handle everything. Don't worry, he's trustworthy—both he and Meya are. You'll be in good hands."

Lugh sighed, defeated. "All right, then," he said sadly, "I guess there's nothing more for it...I'll be sad to see you go, friend."

"As will I, Lughenor, as will I." Rogan nodded sadly to his fellow adventurers and lumbered off to his bed.

Kyle was shocked and saddened by the news. Although he had only known Rogan a short time, he had already come to rely on the Minotaur's unwavering and reassuring presence. It seemed as though his life was losing all of its anchors, one at a time. Although Nihs had said nothing during the revelation, and was entering the overhead with a neutral expression on his face, Kyle sensed that he too was hurt by Rogan's imminent departure.

He tried to force himself not to think about it as they prepared for bed and killed time while waiting for Nihs to get back from the overhead. It was almost a full hour before the Kol returned, and they were all exhausted.

"Some interesting news," he said, "and some good news."

"Save best for last," Lugh said from his bed.

"Well, first, about Michael Radisson. Seems like he's just your run-of-the-mill mercenary chief, a hero by profession and the leader of a fairly large band of thugs. He's well-known in Reno for causing trouble, and his men are consistently arrested, though the police haven't managed to catch him yet. As for Livaldi, he was apparently at a business conference in mid-eastern Ren'r all day."

"Interesting," Lugh agreed. "So either he left to give himself an alibi or gray suit man took advantage of him being out of town."

"Exactly what I thought. The good news, though, is that the police are looking into the disturbance at Sky Tower...and Livaldi is under inquiry because of it!"

Lugh whooped silently. "Hah!" he said. "So he's in hot water, even if he *is* innocent. Ah, that makes me feel better about the whole thing."

"Agreed," Nihs said with a smirk. "Well, I suppose that's all for tonight. We'll be up bright and early tomorrow, ready to leave for Eastia!"

Lugh nodded. "And then we'll get the bottom of all this—one way or another."

Nihs curled up in his den and Lugh rolled over. Kyle attempted to follow suit, his thoughts churning inside his head. As shaken up as he was from the day's events, he was more resolved than ever to find a way back to Earth. He refused to believe that he would be stuck in this world forever—just as Lugh had said, he promised to himself that he would find a way home one way or another, no matter who or what might be after him.

Epilogue

At the age of ten, James Livaldi Jr. had been told by his father that if he did not make his first million by the age of eighteen, he would be considered a failure and an unworthy successor to the Livaldi name.

It was not, his father had continued, an unreasonable expectation. He himself had been worth eight figures by the time he reached twenty, and that had been as a result of personal enterprise—not even considering the worth of the family company, Maida, one of the biggest in Centralia.

It was a harsh requirement, but young James took it seriously, as he did everything his father said—it did not do to ignore James Livaldi Sr. Of course, he was not to go into the battle unarmed. As a family situated at the very top of Reno's upper class, the Livaldis had access to the finest means of education in the world, and Livaldi Sr. would not settle for anything less for his progeny.

The entirety of young James' childhood had been packed full of lessons of every sort; he attended a private school from the age of four, and was personally tutored by some of the brightest minds in the city. He received education in every field possible, and he excelled in every one, from mathematics to engineering to swordplay to magicianship. Growing up, everyone who taught young James had been blown away by his ability to grasp in minutes what other students struggled to learn in weeks.

That is, everyone but Livaldi Sr. He just scowled and said, "Brains mean nothing, boy, if you don't know how to put them to use. How much do you think your education is worth?"

"Two hundred thousand nells a year?" James had said.

Livaldi slammed his hand down on his desk, making his son jump. "*Wrong*, you little imbecile, *wrong!* That's how much your schooling is *costing* me! If you want it to be *worth* something, guess what? You had better make *back* all that it's costing me now, and then make enough money to cover the *time* it spent for you to get it. You think you're going to get all that time back, boy? And all that money? It's gone for good, and because of it you're in debt and you will be for the *rest of your damn life* if you don't make it back."

Like everything else his father said, James took this speech to heart, and when he redoubled his studying efforts they did not falter for a single day until he was admitted into university at age twelve. He graduated at fourteen, and immediately went to work on both his doctorate and a couple of personal, entrepreneurial projects. These would end up being successes, as would the several others that James took on while he wasn't studying.

Over the next two years James accomplished with his life what would have taken many people a decade. Still his father scowled and lectured and insulted, pushing his son to go faster, reach higher, become richer. It soon became clear to James that his father was literally impossible to impress. Just as no number could ever reach infinity, any height reached in the presence of Livaldi Sr. would only bring his attention to the next level above.

He had been a tall, big man, in many ways larger than life; he had certainly always dominated James' existence, his shadow constantly over his son's shoulder as he bent his mind to his work. He had possessed the same rare coloring that James did: his purple hair was a long, straight mane and his great beard over a foot long. He had been rough, and loud, and rude to anyone who wronged him—but, as the media would say, these were the qualities that made him the ideal representative of the Livaldi name, and had allowed him to expand their already tremendous empire. When he was younger, James had seen his father as some kind of wrathful god. Always in anger, always dangerous, immortal.

But Livaldi Sr. was no immortal, and just around the time young James was completing his second doctorate at sixteen, he died. The doctors had attributed his early death to chronic stress, a lifetime of intense work and unhealthy habits that had taken their toll on his body. When Livaldi—now that his father was dead, there would be no confusing their names—attended the funeral, he lingered for several minutes near the open casket. He was taking in the gray features of the man who, just hours before, had been so big, so imposing, so powerful. Someone had closed his father's eyes and crossed his hands over his breast. His face, relaxed, looked nothing like it had in life, when his scowl had been maintained by the constant efforts of his muscles. To Livaldi, seeing his father without a scowl on his face was, well, not seeing his father at all.

Of course, there was an issue—the inheritance. Maida was an enormous company that employed thousands of people, and it came as no surprise to anyone when the shareholders expressed their concern that a sixteen-year-old boy might soon hold the controlling stock in the company. But when Livaldi Sr.'s will was read, to all was revealed something that James already knew—the only thought that would have disgusted Livaldi Sr. more than that of leaving the company to his imbecile of a son, was leaving it to anyone else. He had left everything to James. He ended up inheriting even his father's old manservant, Saul, who among others had been offered an incentive to remain in service to the Livaldi family.

Naturally, this process would not prove so easy. The shareholders banded together to hire lawyer upon lawyer to try and seize the controlling stock, but Livaldi had money of his own, and from the beginning had proven himself at least as cunning and as resourceful as his late father.

The legal battle lasted for almost two years, by the end of which Livaldi found himself the sole beneficiary of his father's will, the inheritor of the Livaldis' legacy, and the owner of a massive corporation.

This had been just a few months before Livaldi's eighteenth birthday. He had found this to be quite humorous and ironic.

His first act as president and CEO of the company had been to call for a meeting of the board of directors. They had assembled with no small amount of trepidation; after all, none of them knew Livaldi on a personal level, and their only interaction with him had been to try and seize from him the controlling stock.

They filed into the boardroom and sat down. Livaldi greeted them, all smiles, with Saul standing guard behind as he always had for Livaldi Sr. He thanked them all for coming and prematurely forgave them for their attempt to rob him of his inheritance. After all, he had only been sixteen at the time, and what did he know?

He spoke for a while about nothing much, charming, complimenting, forgiving, understanding. Of *course* they were concerned about the company's future. Who wouldn't be? And yes, the public was getting antsy as well—it was all to be expected. The more he talked, the more reassured they all grew, and some of them truly thought they were better off with him than with his father.

He told them that he would like to introduce them all to his own plan for the company. This was when the shareholders stole glances at one another. Even charmed as they were, they had little confidence in whatever ideas for the company Livaldi had.

The plan was revealed; a rebranding of the company and a re-focusing of its resources. The newly christened Maida Weapons would be solely a weapon manufacturer. More specifically, one which made firearms.

"After all," Livaldi had said, buffing his nails on his shirt and holding them up to his face, "Maida is already a leader in Ephicer technology, and the firearm market is one that remains virtually untapped by almost any other company. It is my belief that three years of focused research and development could see Maida Weapons as *the* world leader in this area— unchallenged and unmatched, and one of the largest and most successful companies in human history."

There had been questions, there had been concerns. What about Adenwheyr? What about the dominance of traditional weapons in the world's adventuring community? What about the prohibitively high cost of gun parts and fuel cells?

Livaldi smiled and answered and reassured. He told them he would take their concerns into consideration, although of course he didn't have to because it was his company. He promised that he himself would lead the company's research and development efforts.

Three years later, Livaldi was proven right. At twenty-one, with two doctorates under his belt, he officially became the owner of the single most profitable company in the history of the world.

He announced that he intended to build a new headquarters for Maida Weapons as celebration. Sky Tower would set the record for the tallest building in the world, a suitable sister achievement to the company's.

James Livaldi Sr. had nothing to say about this.

D r. James Livaldi, Jr., president and CEO of Maida Weapons, Inc., was not having a good day. He had returned from an out-of-town business conference only to find his new tower swarming with policemen, who smothered him with questions the second he got in the door. They were polite and considerate, as all Buorish policemen were, but Livaldi found them infuriating nonetheless.

The conference had gone badly enough. James, who was almost always flawless in his public speaking skills, had delivered an abnormally poor speech to his business partners abroad—they had not been impressed. He was irritated, but it didn't bother him overmuch; next time, he was sure, he would be at the top of his game. He forced himself to keep smiling all through the policemen's questions, and resisted grating his teeth when they told him that he was officially under inquiry. He politely told them that he had nothing to do with what might have happened while he was away. The policemen told him that they believed him. He asked why, then, must he be subjected to this. They told him that as the disturbance had taken place on his property, he was a prime candidate to aid the police with their inquiries. He told them yes, this may be the case, but he was an exceptionally busy fellow and simply could not sacrifice the time away from his work. They apologized, and promised him that they would make the process as painless as possible.

"I am sorry," the chief of police repeated, bowing, "but I am sure that you see why it is necessary for us to take these measures." They were standing in Livaldi's office, which was currently on floor one-forty-four of Sky Tower, the highest finished floor. The view from the picture window behind Livaldi's desk was dizzying. Saul the magician sat off to one corner, tapping his fingers against the armrest of his chair, his expression severely impassable. Next to him sat a man with blonde hair wearing a gray suit.

Livaldi's smile was frozen in both flexibility and warmth. "Of course," he said. "Well, captain, I will be happy to provide you with the schematics of my tower and anything else you might need. As you said, the process must go smoothly."

The captain bowed again. "We thank you," he said. "If I may, we will now continue with our investigation. We will contact you again if your assistance is needed. Good day," and he and his two wingmen turned to leave. Livaldi's smile remained affixed to his face until the elevator doors had shut behind the three men.

There was a moment of silence. The clock in Livaldi's office ticked.

"Well," he said, seemingly to himself, "that could have gone much better, wouldn't you say?" His voice, even in private, was as clear as a bell and carried with professional ease into the corners of the room. Livaldi was a born public speaker, much like he was a born engineer, mathematician, magician, swordsman, salesman, and politician.

There was another moment of silence. Saul did not move, though the other man fidgeted nervously, as if he was a child waiting to be lectured by the principal of his school.

Livaldi folded his hands behind his back. He wore an exquisite suit of purple touched with gold that complimented his natural coloring. It had always been his favorite color. In the interest of diplomacy, he had temporarily discarded the golden rapier that he usually wore at his side.

Livaldi took a deep breath, his shoulders heaving up and down.

"Where is Radisson?" he asked into the silence.

"He's coming," gray suit said nervously, looking at the floor.

Livaldi said nothing. His eyes were closed and his arms were crossed. He seemed to be meditating.

A few moments later, the door to Livaldi's office opened, and in stepped Michael Radisson. The hero's expression was dark and murderous, and his bulky, rough frame was extremely out of place in the plush office.

"Ah, Radisson," Livaldi said brightly, "how nice of you to join us."

"Oh, excuse *me*," Radisson retorted rudely. He pointed an accusatory finger at Livaldi. "I've been hiding out for the last hour, thank you very much, after losing three of my men to that freak. How nice of *you* not to let us know that that little bastard had a sword that could cut through effin' *rock!*"

Livaldi remained completely uncowed. "'Effin' rock or not, the fact remains that it was one little sword, held by one little man, against your whole band of *rough, tough* mercenaries. What use *are* you, Radisson? Do you know how much it's costing me to keep you out of jail? For all the good your men did I might as well have tried to capture Kyle *myself.*"

Radisson growled and made to move for Livaldi, but Saul instantly disappeared from his seat in a flash of magic and reappeared between them. His hands were folded behind his back and he stood stock-still. His venomous gaze bored into Radisson's and the mercenary ended up balking.

"You know what?" he spat at Livaldi instead, "I don't give a *damn* how much you pay me—this job's been nothing but bullshit from the start!"

"That's enough, Saul," Livaldi said quietly, steering his manservant out of the way. "Oh, really?" he added to Radisson. "You seem to be forgetting that I'm the only one who stands between you and the Buorish police. How long do you think you'll last without my protection?"

"Did it before, I'll do it again," Radisson sneered, "and you won't snitch because the police will get on *your* case, too."

"Fine," Livaldi said breezily, "I'll kill you right now and hand in your corpse to the police. I don't really need the reward money, but it can't hurt, can it?"

Radisson jutted his jaw out in derision and put his hand on the handle of his composite weapon. "I'd like to see you try."

The tableau held for a few seconds, then Livaldi laughed lightly. He strode forward and patted Radisson on the shoulder. "Now, now…there's no need for us to fight, really. We can still be of service to each other. In fact, there's something you can do for me right now."

"Yeah?" Radisson grunted, his expression dangerous.

Livaldi's smile dropped. "You can go and fetch Lian and Lacaster, and then strap on an apron and clean up the mess your men left in the maintenance floors before the police find it. Apparently that's all you're good for here." He turned his back on Radisson and started to walk back to his desk.

"*You little shit*—"

Radisson lunged at Livaldi's retreating back, his sword drawn, but Saul stepped forward at once, intense magic flowing from his hands. He caught the blow with a web of white light that poured from his left hand, then thrust his arm forward, riposting. The light burned Radisson's arm and made his weapon glow red-hot. He yelled in pain, dropping the sword and clutching his smoking side.

Livaldi turned back. "Temper," he said. "If you know what's good for you, you'll learn to control yours *very* quickly."

Radisson looked almost insane with anger, but Saul was still standing over him, sparks flowing from his outstretched hand. Seething and cursing, he rose to his feet, turned, and left.

Saul lowered his arm once the door had shut. Meticulously, he pulled his sleeves back into position.

"Your judgment of others and ability to gauge danger remain as impeccable as always, sir," he said to Livaldi.

"Thank you, Saul, I appreciate that." Livaldi regained his position behind his desk, not sitting down but sighing and leaning his weight on it. His attention flickered to the right, where the gray suited man still sat, shocked into terrified silence by the recent events.

"What are *you* still doing here?" Livaldi asked him.

The man winced. "I...I did my part!" he said defensively. "None of this was my fault! Right?"

Livaldi passed a hand over his forehead. "First of all, it would be an act of greatest charity to call that horrendous, hacked, stuttering, *pathetic* thing you called a presentation *doing* your part to satisfaction. But, try as I might, I just can't force myself to care about that right now. You are dismissed, and consider yourself fired. You may keep the advance I gave you."

The man, stammering thanks, did just that.

"You should have had me do away with him, sir," Saul said mildly. "A man as spineless as he would certainly reveal information to the police were they to find him."

Livaldi waved away the statement, saying, "But they won't. There's nothing that points to his involvement, and he's too terrified of us to make a sound. He'll scurry back to his little life and be no bother to anyone."

Saul nodded. He knew enough not to say anything further.

Livaldi, meanwhile, had gone over to a small table near his desk. On it sat an expensive coffee machine, a favorite of his—he let no one else operate or even touch it. He poured himself a cup into a silver mug and turned to face the magician.

"We had him, Saul," he said, and his voice had changed somewhat. It had become less sardonic, more wistful, almost dreamy. "We had him *here*, in the tower. We *read* his *memories*. But he got away because of Radisson's damnable incompetence." His expression grew sour as he spoke the word. Livaldi hated dealing with incompetence. People called him a genius, but sometimes, secretly, he thought that everyone else was merely an idiot. If they would just *focus*, and *think*, then perhaps they wouldn't struggle to complete the simplest of tasks.

"It wasn't a complete loss, sir," Saul pointed out. "We know his name, and what he looks like, and the kind of company that he keeps. We won't let the soul sword surprise us again."

"It shouldn't have been an issue this time around. He's one man with no fighting experience. How could he have gotten so lucky as to escape? And now we've got the entire Buorish police on our doorstep."

"Do you think we should try to intercept them again before they leave Reno?" Saul asked, changing the subject.

Livaldi gave a small laugh, sipping his coffee. "Don't be ridiculous. They're doing our work for us right now as it is. The farther they get from Reno, the easier it will be to capture them. The police are nowhere near as fanatic anywhere else in the world as they are here."

"Where do you think they will go next?"

Livaldi paused before answering the question. He took another sip and closed his eyes, as though the steam from his mug was granting him prophetic vision.

"Eastia," he said at last. "They're travelling with a Kol, and the first thing any Kol does when confronted with something they don't understand is to ask their elders about it."

"Ask their elders about what?"

Both Livaldi and Saul turned. The doors to the office had opened, and two men stepped into the room.

Lian and Lacaster were former adventurers whom Livaldi had recruited for his personal use. They were twins, and apart from the equipment they wore were nearly indistinguishable from one another. Both had flaxen hair and eerie, piercing blue eyes. No one, not even Livaldi, knew much about them—one could tell that they were human by their rounded ears, but they looked and acted like few normal humans did. They did everything together. They had spent so much time travelling and fighting as a team that they even moved as one unit, standing very close and taking up only as much space as a single person.

Lian was a sage, a master of farsight. He held no weapon, but his entire being felt of magic and his eyes danced with malicious power. He wore a soft magic-user's suit of pastel blues and yellows. His brother, Lacaster, was a sniper. A ring bow was slung onto his back; a quiver full of blue arrows was attached to one hip and two swords, both thin, light and sharp as razors sat on the other. Once, Livaldi had had the opportunity to see what they could do when fighting together. He had been impressed, and Livaldi was not impressed easily. It was the twins' unique brand of fighting skills that he needed now.

"Ah," Livaldi said, smiling, "just the people I wanted to see."

Lian and Lacaster grinned widely at this. Lian leaned over and whispered something to his brother, who giggled.

"We won't fail like Radisson did," Lacaster said impishly. "Where do you need us to go?"

Livaldi's expression was distant. He was enjoying a vision in his mind's eye that only he could see—somewhere in Reno city, a ship containing a man from another world lifting off, its destination Eastia.

Kyle Campbell, Livaldi thought. Somehow, he had gotten out of Livaldi's grasp once. It wouldn't happen again. He allowed himself a smile as he drained the last of his coffee.

"You two," he said, "are going to Eastia."